Believing in Never

Believing in Never

katherine turner

Copyright © 2023 by Katherine Turner
www.kturnerwrites.com

First edition: December 2023

Editing by Kayli Baker
Cover design by Murphy Rae
Print formatting by Shanna Hammerbacher
E-book formatting by Jo Harrison

Library of Congress Control Number: 2023910288
Library of Congress Cataloging-in-Publication Data available upon request.

ISBN 978-1-955735-14-8 (ebook)
ISBN 978-1-955735-15-5 (paperback)

Josha Publishing, LLC
Independent Publisher
www.joshapublishing.com
Haymarket, VA

Printed in the United States of America

This story is for everyone out

there searching for their never...

Notes for the Reader

Content

This novel contains references to and some description of physical and sexual violence. While not intended to be unnecessarily graphic, the content may be triggering for some.

Music

Music plays an important role in this novel. For an enhanced reading experience if you enjoy listening to music, refer to the playlist on page 363 for a recommended soundtrack while reading.

Chapter One

Tasha

I bounced on my toes, my eyes already scanning the crowd, though I knew Drew probably wasn't even off his plane yet—it had just landed ten minutes earlier. But I couldn't help it—to say I was excited to see him would be an egregious understatement. It had been *years* since we'd laid eyes on each other, but my best friend was, at long last, coming to town and would be staying with me for nine days. Duncan, my boyfriend, was less excited about it—in fact, he was pissed—but he'd have to get over it; Drew and I were only friends, after all. And there was no way I was turning down a long-overdue visit from my favorite person since childhood, anyway.

Finally, *finally,* I thought I could make out Drew's form. He was tall—just a hair over six feet—and trim, with broad shoulders that tapered to his waist. The man in question ran a hand through his dirty-blonde hair and scanned the area ahead of him. His gray-blue eyes locked onto mine and it was confirmed—it was my Drew. The somewhat tense and tired expression he wore disappeared as if a switch had been flipped, his face lighting up as he grinned. I took off running toward him, giggling.

When I reached him, I jumped up, flinging my arms around his neck and wrapping my legs around his waist, and squeezed as hard as I could. I couldn't believe he was there. He stopped, taking his hand off his carry-on handle, and smashed my body into his with a giant bear hug.

"Nats!" he shouted his favorite of many nicknames for me, though it was muffled by my shoulder.

I laughed and squeezed harder. "You're finally fucking here," I replied, loosening my hold. "Took you long enough to come visit."

His arms tightened for a second, then he let me go and I slid back down to my feet. I couldn't stop grinning. My eyes scanned him from head to toe as his did the same to me.

"You seem taller," I said, craning my neck to look up at him from my five-foot-three-inch stature.

"You seem shorter," he replied.

I pushed his shoulder. "You're softer, too. Did you forget how to get to the gym?"

He snorted. "Did you forget to cut your hair?"

I shook out my wavy, light brown hair. I'd been growing it out, so it was now halfway down my back. It had barely reached my shoulders the last time I saw him. "You know you like it." I tugged on some hair on his chin. "Did you lose your razor?"

His hand ran over the growth on his face, and I could see his chest shaking as he tried not to laugh. "You don't like it?"

I cocked my head, considering his facial hair. He'd always kept clean-shaven, but it looked like he hadn't seen a razor in quite some time. "Haven't decided yet." I reached up onto my tippy toes and tousled his hair. "I *do* like this." His hair was maybe three or four inches long, but it was the first I'd ever seen him grow it longer than an inch. It was long enough now to slide your fingers into it and pinch the hair between them.

He pulled his head back. "I do, too. But I *don't* like that shit," he said, waving a hand in an ill-defined circle in front of my face.

"You don't like my face?" I balked playfully. "I can't do a damn thing about that."

He rolled his eyes. "I *do* like your face—that's the problem. I can't see it behind all that shit you've got on there."

"I don't put shit on my face—that's gross. This is called makeup. Can you say makeup?"

He wrapped an arm around my shoulders, then slid it up to put me in a headlock. "Still a smart-ass."

I dug my fingers into his armpit, and he jumped back after releasing a high-pitched squeal. Smirking and triumphant, I said, "And you still screech like a little girl when I tickle you."

"You're a pain in the ass," he grumbled.

I grinned. "Aw, you missed me, Dandy Andy."

He shook his head, rolling his eyes again. With an arm around my shoulder—without the headlock this time—we started walking. "Yes, I missed you, Bratty Natty."

Back in my apartment, Drew took his time looking around, taking everything in. His smile had faded when we pulled into the parking garage and his brow was still furrowed. It was making me feel self-conscious, not something I was used to around him. In fact, he was the only person I'd ever been able to count on *not* making me feel that way.

"Home sweet home," I said, gesturing around me.

He nodded absently, then slid his hand over his chin. "How long have you lived here?"

"I dunno... a few years. Why?"

He turned to me but didn't reply. His eyes were like storm clouds.

"What?" I snapped, not liking that it felt like he was judging me. This wasn't how I'd expected things to go once he arrived. "You *can* stay in a hotel if you want."

He rolled his eyes. "I didn't say anything, Nats. Calm down." He looked around again. "Where am I sleeping?"

I pointed to the alcove to his right. It was supposed to be a miniature dining room, but I just ate at the tiny island in the kitchen instead, or a tv tray at my sofa when I was home. I'd converted the little dining area into a miniature library and that's where I wrote, though I'd cleared the area out as much as I could so there'd be space for an air mattress for Drew, so my desk was now wedged between my sofa and the sliding doors to my miniscule balcony. It wouldn't provide much inspiration for my novels there, but it was temporary anyway. Besides, I didn't plan on getting much writing—or anything else, for that matter—done while Drew was in town.

He pushed his carry-on into the space I'd indicated, then stretched. "Got anything to drink?"

I rolled my lips under and nodded. I not only had something to drink, but I'd splurged and bought the nicest bottle of rye whiskey I could find in honor of his visit. It used to be pretty much all we drank when we were together, and I never drank it by myself, so didn't keep it in the apartment. This, however, was a special occasion.

"So," I said, plopping onto the sofa right next to Drew and handing him one of the two glasses of whiskey I'd carried over. "We're having dinner with Duncan in two hours, and there's your awards ceremony in a few days, but otherwise, our schedule is wide open, and we can do any and all of the things you want. Well, within reason." I *did* have limited funds.

Drew was a physical therapist and was receiving two national awards: one for public service and one for societal impact due to his research and pioneering of programs for trauma-informed physical therapy, specifically for survivors of domestic and sexual abuse. In my opinion, he was the best physical therapist and human on the planet and deserved more than just those two awards, but they hadn't asked me.

He ran a finger around the rim of his glass after taking a mouthful, then turned his stormy eyes on me. "About the awards ceremony—"

"Not a word," I said, bumping my shoulder into him. "I know I was acting like a brat about it, but it's totally fine, I swear. I know you can only bring one person, and it makes sense that it would be Becka because—"

"She's not coming, Nats."

My words came to a screeching halt, and I turned to face him. "What?"

He twisted his head side to side, staring toward my blank television screen. "Nope," he said, overenunciating the word.

"But—"

"So if you still want to come, I want you to."

I stared at him, and he turned, looking at me over the rim of his glass as he took a sip and shrugged.

"I wanted you to go to begin with, honestly, but Becka lost it when I told her that."

"Sooooo... why isn't she coming, then?"

My eyes flicked between his. I got the sense there was something major he wasn't telling me. And after the tension between us about the awards ceremony because I'd been upset with him for inviting Becka rather than me, this was a strange turn of events.

He sighed, his face looking tired and tense again the way it had before his eyes found me at the airport.

"Dude, talk to me," I said, bumping him even harder with my shoulder. "I'm your best friend. You can't keep shit from me. That's not allowed."

His hand ran over his chin again and he let out another sigh.

"A bit dramatic, aren't we?" I teased.

"I forgot how big an asshole you can be," he said with a reluctant chuckle.

I wriggled my eyebrows.

With a third sigh, he spoke. "I think we're over."

"Psh," I replied. "You've said that like... what? A dozen times before?"

He dropped his chin and stared at me.

"Two dozen?"

A small smile tugged at his lips. "Not helpful, Nats."

"Okay, fine. So what's *Becky's* problem now?" I asked with an impish grin, intentionally screwing up her name.

He shook his head and the smile widened as he chuckled. "You are about the most obnoxious person I've ever met."

"I'm a bit disappointed I'm not definitively *the* most."

I winked and he shoulder checked me like I'd done to him.

"For real this time. I think I'm going to go home to all my shit already in bags by the front door."

"What happened?" I asked, dropping the teasing. That was serious—he'd been dating Becka for years. And while I couldn't stand her, which was why I called her Becky when that wasn't her name, I knew Drew cared about her.

He shrugged. "Really? The same shit, different day."

"Meaning?"

He studied me, undecided, and I narrowed my eyes. What had he been keeping from me?

"I don't want to talk about Becka," he said at length. "I'm just saying I might be living in a hotel in a week."

"If it's really over, you can move out here and stay with me. There'd be nothing to keep you in Chandler anymore. You want to leave your practice anyway." I raised and dropped a shoulder. "Come out here like you promised years ago."

We'd always planned to move to Brinkley together after college, and I had, expecting Drew to join me when he finished his doctorate, but then he'd remained in Chandler with Becka. She'd refused to move to Brinkley with him, and he'd decided to stay with her halfway across the country. I'd understood, but I hadn't been happy about it. And the last few years were exactly what I'd been afraid of: never getting to see the only person in the world I considered family. I went through a string of bad boyfriends for a while—okay, for years— without Drew there to scare everyone off like he always did. Time had yet to tell about Duncan, who I'd been dating a little less than a year, the longest I'd *ever* dated someone, but he didn't have the most toxic traits my exes had. He wasn't perfect, but who was? And he seemed to actually care about me, unlike my previous boyfriends.

I didn't really have friends other than Drew, and Duncan, if I could count him. I had acquaintances I'd met through Duncan or my exes and considered friends in some respect, I supposed, but not like Drew was. Except the friends of Duncan's, I didn't even talk to the others more than a few times a year at most. I'd always been a bit of a loner, and now that I was a full-time author, I got out even less, and it was hard to make friends when you lived like a hermit, had a tight budget, and didn't like people.

Drew swallowed the rest of the whiskey in his glass, then stared through the bottom of it for a minute. "Are dogs allowed?" he asked, glancing at me.

I grinned, knowing that question meant he was considering what I'd said. "Yes, they are. And now you *have* to move out here because I miss Watson."

"He misses you, too," Drew said.

Watson was Drew's eighty-plus-pound yellow lab he'd rescued as a puppy the summer before our senior year of college—though we both knew Watson thought he was actually *my* dog.

"So, when're you moving in?" I asked, trying not to laugh.

Drew rolled his eyes and put me in another headlock. "I didn't say I was."

"You will," I said with a laugh. "You won't be able to live without me after this week."

Chapter Two

Drew

I stood under the shower water, done with my quick wash-up before we left to meet up with Duncan, running through the last few weeks in my mind. I'd told Tasha that I thought Becka and I might be over, but I *knew* we were. I'd said things I could never take back. Not that they weren't true, but I never should have said them, and in Becka's mind it just confirmed what she'd been determined about already.

It had begun long before this trip for the awards ceremony. In fact, it had begun years earlier—pretty much as soon as we started dating. Becka had never really liked the idea that my best friend was a woman, but it had gotten even worse after she met Tasha. She'd been a total bitch to her, and Tasha had dished it right back out. It hadn't helped that I'd laughed at Tasha's antics, but I couldn't help it—Tasha was funny, and Becka deserved it after the way she'd treated her for no damn reason. But ever since, Tasha had been a sore point in our relationship. Becka and I fought every time Tasha and I talked, even though I'd stopped doing video calls with her not long after she moved as an olive branch. Becka had even had the nerve to get mad at me early in our relationship when I moved in with Tasha for a few weeks to nurse her back to health after she had surgery for ovarian cancer.

Then there was the damn awards ceremony... I could bring one person with me, and I knew at once that person would be Tasha. She *deserved* to be there because *I* wouldn't have been going if it weren't for her. *She* was the reason for everything. I'd never have even applied to college if it hadn't been for her convincing me that I was smart enough and sitting next to me to make sure I filled out the applications and mailed them in. I'd never have declared the major I did or applied for my doctorate if it hadn't been for her convincing me that I could be whatever I wanted, including a physical therapist. And I'd never have gotten these awards without her, either. The trauma work I did was for her, because of what she'd grown up in.

I'd been neglected and emotionally abused, sometimes physically as well, but when Tasha and I met when we were fourteen, she was not only those things, but watched her parents physically abuse each other, was severely physically abused herself, and sexually abused by her stepfather. And because of that, she was sensitive in ways other people weren't about the way she was touched even for medical care. When she was in physical therapy for a hip injury after her mother lost her temper about a dirty spoon in the sink, she'd freaked out on her therapist. That was when I resolved to become what she had needed: someone who could help her heal physically while being sensitive to everything else she'd been exposed to.

Becka didn't know all of our shared history, but I'd told her before that I had Tasha to thank for my success. I hadn't expected her to get upset about me choosing to take Tasha to the ceremony, especially because Becka didn't take any kind of interest in my career as long as I was able to pay for our life together, but I'd been wrong. Just as I'd been wrong about her accepting—however unwillingly—that I was going to make a vacation of the trip so I could spend some time with Tasha before coming back home. Instead, she was furious. She started blaming Tasha for everything wrong in our relationship, even claiming Tasha was the reason I hadn't proposed yet.

That's when I opened my mouth rather than keeping it shut and said things without thinking that, however true, I never should have said. I told her she was right because I'd never marry someone who couldn't accept that Tasha would always be the most important person in my life. Tasha and I were family—the only family we recognized, anyway. We always would be. And family would *always* come first.

Then Becka told me I had to choose: her or Tasha. She said if I got on that plane to fly out to Brinkley even a day earlier than the awards ceremony and stayed anywhere other than a hotel, she and I were over for good. This was two days earlier. I'd sat on the sofa in our living room, my head in my hands for a long time, Watson's head on my lap, trying to figure out what to do.

"What do you think, Watson?" I asked. "She wants me to turn my back on Tasha."

At the mention of Tasha's name, Watson let out a small whine and thumped his tail on the floor. He adored her. Unlike Becka, who he was fairly lukewarm toward.

I sighed.

I wasn't willing to give up my friendship with Tasha, but I'd also invested the better part of a decade into this relationship with Becka. And choosing was so stupid anyway because Tasha was my *friend*. It had been going on an hour of mental debate when my phone pinged from the coffee table in front of me. I flipped it over to find a message from Tasha. It was a gif of a man who looked a little bit like me, I supposed, but with a beer gut, wearing stained and stretched out tighty-whities while dancing on a stripper pole and a message below it.

Please tell me your stripper name is Droopy Drew...

Despite the situation with Becka, I laughed, revolted. And before I had a chance to ask her what the hell was wrong with her, she sent a bundle of images—all screenshots of different things going on the week I was going to be spending with her. Everything from book fairs to live music to pottery classes—a little of everything the two of us liked to do. I texted her back suggesting we do them all, then found Becka and told her I'd pack my stuff and move out when I got back from my trip.

I let out a sigh, cranking the hot water a little higher. My neck and shoulders were killing me—I always got stiff when I was stressed out. The whole situation with Becka sucked, but what the hell was I supposed to do? What had she expected? I'd known Tasha over half my life now.

I wanted to vent about it with Tasha, but I couldn't. As much as she hated Becka, I knew she'd feel guilty about what happened as if it was her fault when she'd had nothing to do with it. It was between Becka and me. But because of her asshole parents, underneath that self-assured exterior she showed the world, Tasha struggled with insecurity. I knew she would feel like she wasn't worth the end of my relationship with Becka if she knew. But the thing was that Becka was the reason it ended... and Tasha was absolutely worth it, anyway.

"Don't get out," Tasha's voice interrupted my thoughts as cold air swept into the bathroom.

"What the hell are you doing?" I asked, peeking around the shower curtain. "I'm in the shower, Tasha."

"I said stay put," she chastised. "Get back behind the curtain. I've had to pee for like an hour, and you seem determined to find out if it's possible to use all the hot water in the complex."

"It hasn't been an hour," I retorted, letting the curtain fall back into place. "Hurry up—I was getting ready to get out."

"Right—you've been wasting water for how long and now you want *me* to hurry up?"

The toilet flushed.

"Holy shit that was fast," I laughed.

"Unlike how you shower," she responded while washing her hands. "I'll send you my water bill," she added, then the door shut.

Chuckling, I turned off the shower and made a mental note to send her some cash for all the extra utilities I was going to use up. She had a contract for two books and had been paid a nice advance for them, but that money had to stretch until she was able to get more contracts and have royalties start coming in, so she lived on a tight budget. She was joking about the water bill, but I would send her money for it anyway. One perk of being Dr. Richards was that I made more than enough to live well on.

And maybe I'd take her up on her offer to live with her for a while if I moved to Brinkley. We'd lived together before, and we got along well sharing a living space. If I did, I could keep an eye on her—her building was in a questionable neighborhood, and it made me anxious to think about her living someplace like this alone. Besides, I wouldn't mind the extra time with her after not seeing her for so many years. And if I did that, I'd take on half of the expenses, and that would free up some money for her. I could just give it to her— and I'd thought about it before since I owed it all to her anyway for helping me get where I was—but she'd never accept it that way. She would, however, if I was living with her.

✦

"I think you're really going to like Duncan," Tasha said for the fourth time since we'd left her apartment. We were nearly to the brewery where we were meeting up with him for dinner.

I stifled a snort. I'd never liked any of the guys she always gravitated toward. They were all assholes, and I didn't really expect this one to be any different. But I'd promised Tasha I'd give him a chance before making up my mind about him, so it was odd she was so nervous about it already.

"You know you've said that four times in the last thirty minutes?"

"Just making sure you heard me—at your age, hearing is one of the first things to go."

I chuckled. "I'm a few months older than you."

"What? I can't hear you," she replied, laughing. "So, what do you wanna do tomorrow?"

Shrugging, I said, "Whatever you want. I don't remember when all those things you sent me are. I said we should do them all."

"I can afford like two. Maybe three or four if you're lucky. Depends on which ones you pick."

12

"I'll pay—my treat."

"No."

"Yes."

She frowned. "Uh-uh."

I slipped my arm over and put her in a partial headlock as we walked. "I'm the one saying I want to do them, I'll pay. Capiche?"

"Fine, Mr. Moneybags," she said, sliding out from under my arm and giving me a sideways shove.

"Better than Droopy Drew." I barely got the words out before we were both laughing. "Where the hell did you find that gif?"

"I was going to search for parrots for one that was repeating 'are you ready' and it autofilled pole dancer after I typed the 'p.' I had to bite and see what came up. It was gold."

"It scarred my retinas. I'll be blind by the time I'm thirty-five."

"Perfect timing. Then you won't be able to see how soft and wrinkly you're becoming."

My chest shook as I laughed, a comeback escaping me.

"Okay, we're here," she said, sobering. Her shoulders rose up and she turned to me with her eyes wide, her mouth in a thin line.

I wrapped an arm around her shoulders and pulled her into my side, planting a quick kiss on the top of her head. "I promise to be open-minded, Nats," I said. "Don't be nervous." I gave her shoulder a squeeze and let go. "I'll definitely be nicer than you were the day you met Becka."

She rolled her lips under, trying not to laugh. "I'm sorry—I should have been nicer to Becky."

My eyes scanned the crowd as we walked in, trying to see if I could figure out which guy was her boyfriend before she told me. She had a type she tended to go for: douchey and self-absorbed. She lifted a hand and I searched, finding someone with their hand raised at a table on the far side of the expansive room. As we walked over, I looked at him, trying to get a read on him, but his expression was closed off as he eyed me back.

Well, I didn't know exactly what he was thinking, but the way he was looking at *me* more than his girlfriend told me he was jealous and felt threatened by me. I sighed and reminded myself that I'd promised Tasha I'd give him a chance.

"Duncan, this is my best friend, Drew," Tasha said as we shook hands. "And Drew, this is Duncan."

"Her boyfriend," he added.

Yep—jealous. I almost laughed, but I didn't want to make things worse for Tasha, so I held it in. He'd either get over it—unlikely—or their relationship was entering its final countdown—much more likely. I was okay with that. I didn't like the idea of her dating him, anyway. I didn't like the idea of her dating at all. There wasn't anyone out there good enough for her, but her standards weren't high enough, so she ended up with these jackasses who didn't respect or appreciate her.

Duncan patted the table next to him and Tasha shifted from sliding into the chair across from him to walk around and sit next to him.

I don't like this guy.

I sat across from Tasha and watched her eyes dart between Duncan and me. She was trying to figure out what we thought of each other. I winked at her, and she smiled gratefully.

"You've got to try their IPA," Duncan said as I looked over the menu. "It's the best in the state."

I inclined my head to acknowledge I heard him and kept looking over the menu.

"And the flatbread is good, too."

Again, I acknowledged with a nod and finished reading through. Duncan would obviously be getting the IPA and the flatbread. I looked at Tasha. "What're you getting, Tash?"

"Uh," Duncan said, looking at me.

"What?"

"Uh. Tash-uh. Tasha. Her name is Tasha. Not Tash."

It took every ounce of self-control I had not to laugh at this guy. "Actually, her name is *Natasha*. Tasha, like Tash and Nats and Nattie and pretty much anything else you could do with her name are nicknames." His jaw tightened and I turned to Tasha, who looked like she was simultaneously about to laugh and cry. "What're you getting, *Tash*?"

She began to laugh, then tried to cover it with a throat clear.

"She's getting IPA and the strawberry salad," Duncan said.

"Tash?" I asked, looking at her and ignoring Duncan. I *really* didn't like this guy.

She shrugged, her eyes shifting between Duncan and me.

"You don't like IPA," I said, drawing back. "Or salads."

"Yeah, she does," Duncan replied for her again. "You don't know her that well anymore, I guess."

I stared back at Tasha, waiting for her to correct him. She avoided my gaze and said nothing. "I guess I don't," I said, willing her to look at me.

She didn't.

We ordered, then I made an effort to ease the tension for Tasha's sake. "So, what do you do, Duncan?" Tasha had already told me he was a project manager at some tech firm, but he didn't know that. And the question worked—he was happy to talk about himself.

The next hour and a half couldn't have passed more slowly. Duncan was about as interesting as wet paint and Tasha barely spoke. Not only that, but his determination to answer questions for her was grating on my nerves more with every passing minute. I was relieved when we stood to leave and I had managed to stay polite. *That's* what I really deserved an award for.

Chapter Three

Tasha

Even though he hadn't said anything outright rude, Drew meeting Duncan hadn't gone well. And then Duncan and I were arguing while Drew was in the bathroom just before we left—the same argument we'd had several times already leading up to Drew's visit. Duncan wanted me to spend the entire nine days with him in lieu of my own apartment. He was even more vehement about it after meeting Drew, and I could feel his anger surrounding me as he clutched the back of my chair so hard I was surprised he didn't break it. But I wasn't going to insist Drew stay with me only to disappear. It wasn't fair to Drew or to me—I'd been looking forward to this visit since he first told me about the awards ceremony happening in Brinkley.

Duncan was reiterating, forcefully, that his girlfriend wasn't going to sleep in the same apartment as any man other than him when my eyes shot up to see that Drew had returned from the bathroom and was watching us with narrowed eyes. Luckily, he didn't say anything, and Duncan stopped as soon as he realized he had an audience. It wasn't the end of the argument, I knew, but for the time being, it would have to wait.

We left, heading into the cool early spring air.

"There's another brewery less than half a mile away," Duncan said, a hand grasping the back of my neck as we stood outside the building.

Drew's eyes lingered on Duncan's hand and his jaw tensed. "I think I'm breweried-out," he said, looking at me instead of Duncan.

"Me, too." I'd been breweried-out before we even got there. I didn't really like beer at all, especially IPA, but Duncan loved it, so just about everything we did involved a brewery. What I wanted was a seedy, hole-in-the-wall bar where I could fade into the décor with really good whiskey. But Duncan didn't like whiskey or places like that—if it wasn't a brewery, it had to be upscale.

Duncan got a little handsy when he kissed me before leaving, something he'd only ever done if there were other guys around, and I internally rolled my eyes, grabbing his hands to stop him. It made me uncomfortable for him to be touching me like that when I knew it was because he was trying to prove something, especially in front of Drew. He slipped one hand around the back of my neck again, holding me still while he kissed me for an obscenely long time. When he finally stopped, he looked at Drew.

"I love you," he said, his eyes only flicking to me briefly.

"You, too," I rushed out, turning out of his grasp on my neck and heading toward my car. "I'll call you tomorrow."

As soon as I saw Duncan start in the other direction, I slammed my shoulder into Drew. "Thanks a lot, asshole," I laughed. "Could you have emasculated him any more than you did?"

"I didn't do shit and you know it," Drew retorted with a chuckle. "He already felt that way."

"The name comment?"

Drew threw his hands up in front him. "He started it by trying to correct me for calling you Tash as if I can't do that or something."

I rolled my eyes. "Yeah, he can get a little..."

"Possessive," Drew said, all trace of good humor gone. "He's possessive. And I don't like it, Nats."

"So are you," I teased.

Drew didn't laugh. "There's a big difference. He's…" He inhaled and exhaled loudly, shaking his head as if he was deciding against something. "Just be careful with him, okay? I don't trust him."

"He's harmless, Drew. He's really a nice guy, you just threw him off tonight."

"And since when do you let someone talk for you, Nats? And order for you—especially shit you don't even like. What the hell was all that about?"

I shrugged, my face heating. "He likes to do it and it doesn't hurt anything."

"But that's not you. None of that"—he gestured back toward the brewery—"was you."

I looked fleetingly back toward the restaurant, uncomfortable with the conversation. And a little aggravated. Maybe Duncan wasn't perfect, but no one was. And Drew had dated Becka, who was way worse in my opinion, for years.

"So when's the last time you played your guitar?" I asked, raising my eyebrows. "Hm? Oh wait, that's right—you can't. Because Becky convinced you to get rid of it."

"Touché, a-hole," he said. "And her name's Becka."

"Close enough," I said with a shrug. "You know, Duncan plays the guitar," I added airily with a smirk.

"Does he?" Drew asked, his voice tight.

"Mm-hm," I replied. "And he's not bad, either. He's probably better than you now." It wasn't true—Duncan wasn't very good at all, and Drew at least used to be—but I knew it would get to him if I said that.

We'd reached my car and he hung a hand on the top of it, not opening his door, glaring at me. "I know what you're doing right now, and you're a brat."

"That's why you call me Bratty Natty." I cheesed. "There's a music shop with a great guitar selection not far from here. They're open 'til nine. Wanna go?"

"What the hell do you think?" he grumbled, climbing into my car.

I grinned to myself as I walked around to the driver's side. Dinner had been a nightmare, but the rest of the night was going to be a blast—I'd get to sip whiskey and listen to Drew sing and play guitar. It had been too many years since we'd spent an evening like that, and I couldn't wait.

Drew had been in deep conversation with the salesperson in the music shop for at least thirty minutes about the guitars they had for sale. Apparently, the salesperson was a guitar connoisseur. I wandered around and looked at everything—which was no insignificant feat considering the small shop was packed with everything you could think of related to instruments and music—then walked outside to sit on the bench in front of the shop for some fresh air.

My phone had been vibrating in my pocket every few minutes, and I finally pulled it out to take a look. Message after message from Duncan, which I'd expected. He'd obviously seen Drew as competition even though I'd assured him that Drew and I were just friends. We *had* kissed once, years earlier, when we were teens, but we had agreed it was weird, like kissing a sibling, so it had never happened again. But I wouldn't dare tell Duncan that. He'd be even more pissed that Drew was staying in my apartment with me if he knew.

He wanted to know what we were doing and where we were, wanted to know when we were going home, and exactly what we had planned the next day. Just reading all his questions was exhausting and I sighed. I knew he was only asking because he cared—and it was sweet, really, that he cared enough to get jealous—but it was aggravating. I just wanted to focus on spending time with Drew while he was in town—who knew how long it would be before I saw him again if he and Becka stayed together.

But, to placate Duncan, I told him I'd let him know as soon as Drew and I decided what we were doing the next day and that he could join us; it was the weekend, so he wouldn't be working. Then, when Drew eventually walked out with a new guitar, I even texted to let him know that we were heading back to my apartment, though I didn't usually keep him apprised of my every move.

Back in the car, Drew was running down all the features and stats for his new guitar, and I listened intently despite having no idea what he was talking about. I didn't have to, though—it was fun listening to him so animated about it. He hadn't sounded that animated about something other than work in years.

"I'm getting changed and then I'll get us some whiskey," I said as I locked the apartment door behind me.

He nodded, and I disappeared into my bedroom after swiping his sweatpants I'd seen sitting on the top of his pile of clothes in his suitcase earlier. His were always more comfortable than mine, and I'd stolen several pairs when we lived together before, but they'd all worn out and I needed more, so I was glad he'd brought a few with him. I'd take the rest of them before he left.

I changed into Drew's sweats and a t-shirt of mine, pulled my hair back, and washed my face. I felt like myself again and was ready to spend my evening listening to Drew's deep singing voice and soothing chords with some whiskey. He was well into tuning when I walked back out, and he looked up. His eyes started to fall again to his guitar, then shot back up.

"Are those my sweatpants?"

"Duh. Why do you seem so shocked?"

"I've been here for like six hours."

"And? You have the best sweats."

He rolled his eyes. "I want those back—they're my favorite."

"Finders keepers, Andy Roo."

"You didn't 'find' them, you stole them."

I shrugged, pouring our whiskey. "To-may-to, to-mah-to." I walked over and set his glass on the coffee table before settling onto the sofa next to him. "What are you gonna play?"

"I was thinking a little Johnny Cash, a little Metallica, Sam Tinnesz of course... What do you wanna hear?"

I closed my eyes and sighed, sinking into the sofa cushions, the whiskey warming my throat as it made its way down. "I want 'Be

Here for You,' 'Never Leave Your Side'... all our songs. Then other stuff."

"Okay," he said.

He strummed a few chords, then began singing in his bass voice so deep I could feel the vibrations through the cushions. Those vibrations used to soothe me when we were teens, as if they were vibrating away whatever I'd just run away from at home. Tonight, however, it was vibrating emotions and memories back to the surface. Things I hadn't thought about in so long now moved through my chest, making it tighten and squeeze, making my eyes water so tears slipped between my closed lids and tracked down my cheeks. It was bittersweet because, in many ways, those first few years we knew each other were some of the worst in my life, but they were also the years when we were closest, when we were practically inseparable. Those long nights we spent together as fresh bruises formed or blood dried were the first times in my life I'd ever felt loved. Cared about. Important to someone. Maybe even as important as that someone was to me.

I dropped my head sideways onto his shoulder like I used to and, just as he used to, he leaned down to kiss my crown between verses. I knew he was thinking about the past just like I was. And we didn't have to talk about it—this was enough.

He took a break after several songs, flexing his fingers out. I thought briefly about making a snarky comment about him being out of shape for playing guitar, but decided against it. Instead, I said, "I missed you, Drew."

With his voice still deep from singing, he replied, "I missed you, too, Nats."

"I can't believe we went so many years without seeing each other."

I could hear him swallow and he slipped an arm around my shoulders, squeezing me into his side. "That's my fault," he said with remorse. "I won't let that happen again."

"It's mine, too," I said, not wanting him to feel guilty. "I could get a real job so I wouldn't be so broke."

"What you're doing *is* real," he snapped. "Who the hell told you that writing isn't a real job?"

I ignored his question; it was too many to count. "Seriously, though. If I had something that paid me a regular paycheck, maybe I could have come to visit you. I'm sure Becky would have loved that."

He gave me another squeeze, pulling his arm from my shoulders and setting up on his guitar again. "*Becka* would have had a conniption. And you don't need a job with a regular paycheck, Nats. You're a writer—a *brilliant* writer. That's what you should be doing. And in time it'll bring in more money than you'll even want. It's not on you that we didn't see each other. It's on me. But we'll do this more often from now on."

"Promise?"

"Promise."

"How often? Like every week?" I giggled.

"I don't make *that* much money," he chuckled. "How about twice a year?"

"Not good enough," I snickered.

"Well, more than that and I can't come for more than the weekend if I'm going to keep any clients."

"That's fine. Two weekends and two weeks, split up over four trips. I think I can handle that."

"You think Dunky can?"

I tried desperately not to, but burst out laughing anyway. "*Dunky*?"

"Yeah—your boytoy."

I positively cackled at that description for Duncan. If he heard it, he'd be furious, but it was par for the course for Drew to make insulting comments like that about whoever I was dating. "I can't believe you."

Drew shrugged, his chest still shaking as he strummed the first chords to another song. "I like him about as much as you like Becka. Maybe even less."

"Well, that sucks, because he wants to come with us tomorrow."

Drew flattened his hand against his strings, effectively silencing his guitar, and narrowed his eyes at me. "Does he have to?"

I sighed. "Yes. I told him he could already."

"What are we doing tomorrow?"

"Up to you. There's a pottery class and a farmer's market and a book fair in the morning, and four or five different places with live music you'd like in the afternoon."

"What's Duncan least likely to want to do?"

I laughed. "He hates all of it—the stuff in the morning, anyway. He never does these kinds of things with me. He only wants to go because of you."

He drew his head back. "He never does stuff like this with you?"

I averted my eyes. "No. He likes to go out for brunch, followed by breweries on the weekends. He does like live music, but usually they have some at the breweries."

"What do you guys do that *you* like?"

My fingers smoothed out the bottom of my t-shirt. "I have more time than he does, so I do stuff I like on my own when I feel like going out by myself." Which was rare; not only because of the cost, but because constantly meeting new people was exhausting and I was always anxious about what people thought about me. Besides, doing stuff like that alone just made me feel even more lonely than I already did all the time.

Drew started strumming chords again. "You decide what we're doing tomorrow," he said, then began to sing.

Chapter Four

Drew

Ta-sha," I called in a sing-song voice as I knocked on her bedroom door with a constant tapping using the knuckle of my index finger; I knew it would annoy her. "Oh, Ta-sha. It's wakey, wakey time."

Something thumped against the back of the door, and I chuckled. I was sure she was hungover after how much whiskey she'd had the night before, but I didn't care. She needed to get her ass out of bed.

"Come on, up, we have shit to do. I've got water, aspirin, and coffee with your name on them."

"Go away," she called out, her voice muffled, before something else thumped against the door.

I turned the knob and pushed the door open. Tasha was hidden except for some tangled hair peeking out from under her comforter. I walked over and opened the blinds, letting in the bright spring sunshine.

"Come on, get out of bed," I said, grabbing the comforter and whipping it back off her.

"Hey, I was using that," she grumbled, curling into a ball.

I chuckled and grabbed her hand, giving it a tug. "Seriously, get up. I have coffee and meds for you. I swear your headache will be gone in an hour."

"How the hell are you so perky?" she asked as she dragged herself into a sitting position, yawning and scrubbing her hands over her face.

"I get up early every day. It's how I get in my workout before work. Come on, Nats, out of bed already. Put on something you can sweat in—we're going to the gym."

She groaned as she slid off her bed to her feet, but I had no sympathy for her. I'd told her not to have the last glass of whiskey, but she was bullheaded and did it anyway.

"Go away. I need privacy," she yawned.

"Five minutes," I said, walking out and pulling the door behind me. "If you're not out in five minutes, I'll be back." I heard the click of the door locking. "And I can pop that lock, you know."

I waited in the kitchen, sipping a glass of water. I was already dressed for the gym in athletic shorts, tank, and tennis shoes. She'd said her building had a really nice gym, and we were going to find out if she'd been telling the truth. She and I used to work out together— it was one of the hardest things to get used to when she moved to a different city and I had to work out alone—and I wanted to do it again while I was in town. I missed it. She made working out fun, and we both knew just how to push each other to be our best.

Despite what I'd said, I was giving her ten minutes before I would harass her again, and she shuffled out after nine, her shirt still in her hand. I suppressed a laugh at her disheveled appearance and tipped my head toward the counter. "Coffee, water, and meds, as promised." My eyes strayed down her sports-bra-clad torso as she pulled on her shirt and stopped on the scars just above the waistband of her shorts from her surgery when she had cancer. I lifted my gaze and she glanced down at her scars before giving me a small smile. We were both glad that was in the past.

She stepped up to the counter, tossed back the aspirin with the entire glass of water, then picked up her coffee mug and moaned obscenely. "This smells amazing."

I shifted, uncomfortable with the way my heart had picked up speed when she was moaning, and waited while she drank her coffee. I'd already had mine—I'd been awake for hours. I'd played and sang until late, and Tasha had fallen asleep with her head on me. When I'd called it quits, I'd carried Tasha to her bedroom and tucked her in, kissing her forehead. But then I'd woken a few hours after laying down, thinking about her and about Becka and about what the hell I was gonna do when I got back to Chandler.

At last, we made it to the first-floor gym, and Tasha had been partially right in her assessment. To call it a nice gym was a bit of a stretch, but it was definitely much nicer than I expected for such a shoddy complex, and it had everything we'd want to use, which was perfect. We jogged next to each other on the treadmill as a warm-up, then spotted each other as we took turns lifting weights and doing bodyweight exercises, ending with a return to the treadmills for a sprint. By the time we were heading back up to her apartment an hour and a half later, we were both breathing heavily and drenched in sweat, carrying our soaked shirts.

"Not bad," I said as we waited for the elevator. "I didn't expect you to be that strong."

She winked, the red of her exertion-flushed face deepening. "Likewise. But if you really want to test us, I have some ideas."

I quirked an eyebrow. "Yeah? Like what?" I'd thought we'd already tested ourselves, doing burpees and push-ups and pull-ups and crunches to failure.

She grinned. "I'll show you when we get back. I need my phone. Your lame ass isn't on social media, but it's a big thing on there. Fitness challenge videos. They look like so much fun, but Duncan isn't interested in even trying with me."

I shrugged and cleared my throat to cover my irritation. The more I learned about this guy, the less I liked him. Could he be any more self-centered? "I'm up for a challenge. You know I'll try just about anything."

"Yup," she agreed. "One of my favorite things about you."

"Your many favorite things, right?" I smirked.

She rolled her eyes, laughing, and shoulder-checked me. "By the way," she said, changing the subject. "When the hell did you get that tattoo? And why the hell didn't you tell me?"

The tattoo in question was on the left side of my chest. And I hadn't told her because I hadn't wanted to tell her what it was. I lifted my hand and rubbed over it, sighing out a deep breath. The tattoo was a name logo style of Tasha's name, and I'd gotten it when she reached five years cancer free. I'd wanted to be there with her when she went to her appointment and to celebrate with her afterwards, but I'd caved to Becka's insistence that I stay put in Chandler. Because of that, I'd had her name tattooed over my heart in a way Becka would never know what it was. She thought it was just some weird design.

"You cuss a lot," I said.

She shrugged. "Sometimes. Stop deflecting. What's up with the tattoo?"

"None of your damn business," I said. "I don't have to explain myself to you if I want to get a tattoo."

She drew back like I'd said something bizarre. "Yes, you do. That's how I make sure you don't do some stupid shit like what you did there."

My hand covered my tattoo again. "It's not stupid, Tasha," I said, stepping off the elevator ahead of her. She had no idea how much I'd cried that day because I was so relieved she'd reached the mark that meant it was unlikely the cancer would ever come back. She had no idea how much worry I'd carried for her during the years leading up to that day after she first got the diagnosis. She had no idea how many nights I laid awake, terrified I was going to get a call that she was sick again, but that this time surgery wouldn't fix it. And she had no idea how much regret I had for my decision to stay in Chandler when I should have been with her for her appointment.

I waited at her door, and she caught up a few seconds later, grabbing my hand. "I'm sorry, Drew. It's not stupid."

My eyes flicked down to hers.

"Well, maybe a little," she said, tilting her head to the side with an impish grin.

I shook my head and gave her a grudging smile. "You are such an asshole sometimes."

"You know, Drew," she said, unlocking her door and pushing it open. "You cuss a lot."

It was mostly silent at first, but within a moment, I was laughing out loud. She was, bar none, the most obnoxious person I'd ever met. Her laughter joined mine as she grabbed her phone, but it tapered off almost immediately and she frowned at the screen.

"What is it?"

She gave a sharp headshake, sighing. "Duncan. Give me a sec, then I'll show you the challenges." She typed furiously into her phone for a minute, then walked over and showed me several videos of a man and a woman doing these joint fitness challenges.

"They don't look that hard to me," I murmured, sliding her phone from her fingers and backing up about fifteen seconds on the current video to watch again. They looked pretty straightforward.

"That's what I thought when I saw them, too. Wanna try one of them?"

"Yeah—pick one."

An hour later, we were working on our fourth challenge, but things were deteriorating. We were both exhausted and weak and kept collapsing in laughter when we inevitably failed. It was a miracle we'd managed to nail the first three after a series of attempts, but this fourth one just wasn't going to happen. After failing—again—we stayed on the floor in her living room. We were both on our backs, our heads next to each other and our feet pointing in opposite directions. Tasha's cheek kept brushing mine as she giggled almost hysterically. My laughter abated as I worked to catch my breath, then sighed. Tasha let out a sigh of her own.

"It feels good to laugh," she said. It sounded almost like she'd forgotten I was there, she'd spoken so quietly.

I turned to face her. "You don't laugh anymore?" I asked, barely any louder.

She turned toward me. Our noses bumped. That same speeding in my heart that had happened earlier happened again. It used to happen all the time, but it hadn't in a while. I wished it wouldn't happen at all. I ignored it, closing my eyes.

"Not really. You?"

I moved my head a fraction side to side, then mirrored her words. "No. Not really."

I could feel her breath breaking across my forehead, could still smell the faint mintiness from her toothpaste on it.

"Do you ever wonder if we're just not meant to be happy like other people?"

"Tasha—" I started, her words worrying me because she'd said them to me before, years ago, when she was in the depths of depression and was suicidal.

"No, I just mean like maybe what we went through broke something needed to fit in and find your place and be happy. Or maybe not *we*, but *I* feel that way a lot. Like maybe my expectations are too high and I'm wanting something it's not possible for me to have. You know?"

"Neither of us is broken, Nats," I replied, speaking in a soft voice. "That shit tried to break us, but we were too strong for it. And if our ability to fit in and be happy was broken, then how do you explain how you and I fit together? How do you explain that we're happy when we're together? Obviously, we're *not* broken. We just... fit with fewer people, I guess."

A minute or two passed in silence and our breathing began to match in cadence, though my heart was still doing that skippy thing every time I felt her exhale wash over my skin.

"I don't want to be alone for the rest of my life," she whispered. "I'm so afraid of that."

"I know." I swallowed. "It's why you're in another one-sided relationship."

She sighed. "Duncan really is nice. He's so much nicer and more stable than anyone else I've ever dated. He's got a career; he knows what he likes and doesn't like. He's interested in me."

"Hmph." He wasn't interested in anything other than himself.

"Well, he is more than anyone else I've dated. And he buys me flowers and jewelry and tells me he loves me."

"You don't like flowers and jewelry."

"I don't know... I mean, it's sweet, right? He's thinking of me, and that's what matters."

He didn't really even know her, that was obvious, but I kept that to myself. I didn't want to argue with her right then. I'd try to get her to see it before I left, but it wasn't going to happen right now, anyway. "I guess."

"You'll give him another chance? For me? I might end up with this one—I'm not getting any younger and need to... accept reality and stop hoping for a fairy tale, I guess. And if I do, I really want you guys to get along."

I bit back what I really wanted to say—that it didn't matter how many chances I gave him, I was always going to hate the guy because he wasn't anywhere near good enough for her—and instead agreed. "For you—anything." Then I shifted and pressed my lips into her forehead.

I'd kissed her forehead before—many times. But this time, it took several long seconds before I could make my lips leave her skin. I was having a hard time breathing, and it felt like I was having a heart attack or something.

"Thank you," she murmured, then kissed my forehead the same way I'd just kissed hers.

Now I couldn't breathe at all. Things—inappropriate things—were flashing through my mind. Images of holding Tasha's head to me and kissing the hell out of her. Images of kissing her jaw. Her neck. Images of her kissing *my* neck. Molding her lips into mine. I cleared my throat and sat up.

"We should probably get cleaned up. You stink."

"Not as bad as you do," she retorted.

"Figure out where we're going. And tell your *boyfriend* before he sends any more messages." I snagged her phone and tossed it at her as I stood, annoyed that I couldn't keep the disgust out of my voice. "I'll shower first while you talk to him."

"Leave me some hot water," she called after me.

I smiled and rubbed my hand over the tattoo on my chest.

Chapter Five

Tasha

D rew seemed to take my request seriously and was—dare I say nice?—to Duncan when he showed up to spend the day with us. I'd decided on the farmer's market because I went to the quarterly book fair almost every time it came to town, and there was another pottery class later in the week that Drew and I could do, and it would be more fun if it was just the two of us. That was probably the activity Duncan would have hated the most, and he would have been so unhappy, it wouldn't have been enjoyable for anyone else there.

Even with all the forethought on his behalf and Drew's efforts to be friendly, Duncan appeared to be determined to be miserable. Within minutes of arriving at the farmer's market—the largest one around—he was antsy to leave.

"It's all the same crap after you've seen one of these things," he said over my head to Drew as we left the fresh produce booths for the handmade goods, his arm draped over my shoulders. "I don't understand why anyone would want to see them all."

I opened my mouth to tell him we could go, feeling guiltier by the second for dragging him around doing things I knew he didn't like, but before I could speak, Drew did.

"It's not all the same. And it's not crap—it's handcrafted. It takes a lot of time and dedication to make all this stuff to sell. It's pretty incredible when you think about it. I know *I* couldn't make any of it."

"You actually want to look at this crap?" Duncan asked in disbelief.

"It doesn't matter if I do or not," Drew snapped. "It's not about me."

"It's okay, guys," I spoke up. "I can come back another time on my own. We can go."

"What? No. We're—"

"Drew," I interrupted, imploring him with my eyes. "It's okay. Really."

"Tasha," he said, his voice tense but low enough Duncan couldn't hear him from where he'd stepped over to throw out his empty cup. "We didn't drive all the way out here to leave after seeing two booths. We're not going anywhere until you've looked through everything you want to see. He'll get over it."

"It's not fun like this," I whispered back. "I don't even want to look anymore." And I didn't. Knowing Duncan was irritated and impatient ruined my ability to take my time and enjoy myself. I just wanted to get out of there and to somewhere Duncan actually wanted to be.

Drew's jaw tensed and he let out a frustrated huff, but he didn't say anything else. Duncan's mood improved considerably once we arrived at a brewery that served brunch—his two favorite things in one place. Luckily, he'd missed Drew rolling his eyes about it. I'd mouthed 'please' at Drew, and he'd rolled his eyes again, but he did dial back his visible aggravation with Duncan.

We'd been at the brewery for most of the day, joined after a while by a group of Duncan's friends, and Drew and I sat, listening to them talk about software development and lifecycle management as if we weren't even there. I'd tried interrupting a few times to suggest we move on—I really wanted to take Drew to one of the performances I'd found—but Duncan blew me off each time, saying there was plenty of time and for me to just relax already. I could see Drew becoming more and more tense every time it happened, and I felt like I couldn't win. No matter what I did, I was pissing someone off.

"This sucks," I muttered at one point.

"Finally something I agree with you about," Drew retorted.

I bit my cheeks, trying not to laugh. It wasn't even funny—Drew was *really* mad. But for some reason, the normalcy of him expressing his irritation with me that way struck me as laugh-worthy. My eyes darted up and caught Drew's. He glared at me, exasperated. He was *not* amused. He was giving me the kind of look that was meant to chastise me. It was so severe and just utterly ridiculous. It only made me want to poke at him.

"Oh, come on, Drewy..." I said, altering my voice at the end to mimic Becka, who called him that despite his repeated requests for her not to.

His eyes widened and his jaw clenched harder. "Don't, Tasha."

"Baby," I finished, now giggling.

He looked like he wanted to hit something for a second, but then his clenched jaw turned to sucking in his cheeks as he tried not to laugh. I waggled my eyebrows and his deep laugh filled the air between us. My giggles morphed until I was hunched over from laughing so hard.

"You are such a brat," he muttered between chuckles.

I winked. "You bring out the best in me, *Drewy Baby*."

We broke into a fresh round of laughter and now garnered the attention of Duncan and his four friends, who mostly looked bewildered, with a dash of distrust from Duncan. I opened my mouth to explain but ended up giggling when Drew caught my eye. He was still chuckling, albeit less noticeably.

"What's so funny?" Duncan asked, looking between the two of us.

I shook my head, unable to speak yet, and slid my sleeves up. It had been warming up steadily, but after that laughing fit and the embarrassment of being questioned by Duncan, I was too warm.

"Tasha said something stupid, that's all," Drew offered.

"What was it?"

I shook my head again, still laughing. "It won't make sense to you. It's..."

"An inside joke," Drew finished for me when I couldn't think of what to say. "Basically." Drew pushed his own sleeves up his arms as he finished speaking.

"Is that the same tattoo Tasha has?" Duncan asked, incredulous.

At the same time, Drew and I both rolled our forearms up—Drew his right and me my left. Because he was sitting to my left, that meant our arms were right next to each other. We did in fact have the same tattoo—we'd gotten it together right after we turned eighteen. We'd both—at different times—struggled with being suicidal after we became friends and helped each other make it through those bouts alive. The second we were able to, we'd gotten a semicolon tattoo to remind ourselves that, no matter what was happening, there was more to life to come. It was what we'd told each other when in our darkest moments... moments in which we'd nearly succeeded in ending our life stories. We'd spent countless hours connected by those two hands to keep the other from doing something that couldn't be undone, so it had made sense to put our tattoos there. If we held hands now, the tattoos touched. And whenever I was feeling down or lonely, I looked at and touched my tattoo and could hear Drew's voice telling me not to give up.

Drew shifted to rest his arm over mine, confirming that his thoughts were in the same place mine were.

"Yes," he replied to Duncan's question, offering no further explanation.

"I thought you were a physical therapist, not a writer," Duncan said.

"I am."

Duncan's brow furrowed as he turned to me, pointing at my wrist. "But I thought that was some kind of literary tattoo."

Maybe he had, but it was an assumption he'd made—I'd never actually told him what it meant, and he'd never asked.

"A semicolon is punctuation, but that's not why I have the tattoo," I said with a shrug.

My eyes shifted to Drew's and his face softened. I was sure mine did, too. Even with Duncan's questions, my mind was in the past, thinking about everything Drew and I had been through leading up to getting our matching tattoo together.

"You got any more?" one of Duncan's friends asked, looking at Drew. He had several tattoos on his forearms and was always interested in those on other people.

The mild screech and muffled thump of microphone feedback cut in before Drew could answer; a band had finished getting set up not far from us, and everyone's attention turned to them.

Well, almost everyone's.

Drew bumped my forearm with his and I looked over. His stormy eyes were intense and there was a flutter in my belly, exactly like the one I'd felt that morning when we were lying face to face on the floor of my living room.

"Love you, Nats," he said, quiet and serious.

"I know," I replied softly. "Love you, too."

The band ended up being pretty good, and Drew seemingly enjoyed himself, which allowed me to relax enough to appreciate the music. By the time we were heading back to the car, he and Duncan were even holding a conversation about guitarists. While Duncan couldn't play nearly as well as Drew, he loved talking about anything related to guitars almost as much as he loved talking about beer. It was a relief to see them getting along, even if only briefly. It gave me hope that maybe they could accept each other's presence in my life in the long-term, which would certainly make my life easier.

When we reached my car, however, Duncan and Drew both headed for the driver's side.

"I'll drive," Drew said.

"No, *I'll* drive," Duncan said. "It's *my* girlfriend's car."

"I don't give a shit whose car it is—you shouldn't be driving with how much you had to drink."

Duncan opened his mouth to argue, but Drew cut him off before he had a chance to speak.

"If you try to drive, Tasha and I will find another way home."

He'd spoken with an air of finality. And while I agreed that Duncan was too intoxicated to be behind the wheel, I didn't want them to end up fighting. But I wasn't sure how to solve this problem because I wasn't comfortable driving, either.

"Duncan," I said, sliding an arm around his waist. "Drew only had two beers all day. Just let him drive. You and I had too much to drink."

"I'm not drunk, Tasha," Duncan bit out.

"I didn't say you were," I soothed. "But you don't have to be drunk to be over the legal limit, and we've both had enough to drink that we are. Drew isn't."

Duncan finally agreed, grudgingly, and I climbed into the back seat knowing it would help ease things a bit if I wasn't sitting next to Drew. And sure enough, by the time we were halfway to Duncan's apartment, he was talking about guitars again, which he did all the way until he shut the car door after getting out without even giving Drew a chance to say a single word.

"Move up front, Tasha," Drew bit out before pulling away from the curb. "It's ridiculous you're in the back seat in your own damn car."

I switched seats hastily and buckled, then Drew started driving. There was a tense silence in the car until he broke it, bursting out in frustration. "Why the hell do you do shit like that? If it was me, you'd have told me to kiss your ass before sitting in the back seat, but you just let this guy walk all over you and you treat him like he's the only thing that matters. You matter, too, Tasha, and you need to start acting like it."

"Got it, Daddy Drew," I snarked. I was only half-kidding; I didn't like getting chewed out the way I was, so I'd said something I knew would piss him off.

"Damn it, Tasha—I'm being serious. Can't you do the same for once? Not everything is a goddamn joke."

Anger flared through my chest. He had no idea what it was like for me trying to make sure they got along, trying to keep Duncan from getting too pissed off or jealous. He'd be leaving in a week and wouldn't have to deal with the fallout if I didn't keep Duncan pacified.

I would.

"You want serious? If I hadn't done that, he wouldn't have gotten in the damn car, Drew."

"I didn't care if he got in the car or not! The only thing I cared about was that he wasn't in the driver's seat of any car *you* were in. If he wanted to get himself home, that would have been *his* problem." He paused and shot a glare in my direction. "You go through all these guys who treat you like shit, but that's because you let them. You pick guys who don't respect you, and you accept it because you have no respect for yourself. If you did, you'd never put up with their bullshit, and this guy isn't any different. Maybe he *seems* nicer or whatever, but he's a jealous, self-absorbed asshat who doesn't really even know you, let alone give a shit about you except as it relates to him."

I sat, stunned, gaping at him from the other side of the car. My ability to process what he'd just said to me was slow, as if everything was on a delay.

He ran his hand through his hair, huffing out a frustrated breath. "One day it's really going to backfire on you, Tasha. If I wasn't here tonight, you'd have gotten into a car with a drunk driver! Jesus, Tash, think about that. I know that you knew from the start that he was in no shape to be driving, but you didn't say a single damn word—not one. All you cared about was placating him. Fuck placating him! What's that gonna matter when he crashes into a median and you end up dead? Is that what you want? After everything you survived as a kid, after beating fucking cancer—you want to die because you got into a car with some drunk asshole because you were too afraid of hurting his feelings to tell him he shouldn't be driving?"

He smacked the steering wheel and his jaw ticked. I couldn't do anything but continue to stare at him for a long time. My anger had grown into burning fury, but I couldn't tell who I was more furious with: myself because I knew deep down that everything he'd said was true, or him for pointing it all out the way he did.

I was also upset and ashamed. I was supposed to be this badass, take-no-shit woman—and maybe I truly was at one point, I didn't know—but now it just felt like I was constantly pretending to be something I wasn't. And after only twenty-four hours, Drew had not only seen it, but called me out on it. The problem, however, was that I didn't know any other way to be anymore.

Chapter Six

Drew

I'd sat awake most of the night as well as the last few hours before dawn, thinking about Tasha and how I'd yelled at her in the car. I'd been pissed off—I still was—but I felt bad for yelling at her. I knew, underneath her anger, I'd really hurt her. And yelling wasn't something she should be subjected to anyway—especially with the household she'd grown up in. I knew that more than anyone else and yet I'd raised my voice.

Nice job, asshole.

My hand scrubbed over my face, and I shifted on the air mattress, staring at the ceiling. I was worried about her—*really* worried about her. I should have known that things weren't as rosy as she'd made it seem over the phone, but I'd been so wrapped up in my research and trying to keep Becka happy that I'd missed it. I never should have been so far away from her, let alone go four years without seeing her. I wasn't sure if it was from being alone or the string of jackass boyfriends she'd had, but she seemed to have misplaced parts of herself. And how the hell was I supposed to help her find them from halfway across the country? Or when I was yelling at her?

Damn it.

I stared at Tasha's bedroom door; I wanted to go wake her up and tell her I was sorry. I wanted to hold her until her broken parts healed back together again. I wanted to tell her I'd never leave her again, that I would always be there for her.

That's it!

I had to go back to Chandler for at least some period of time, and I wasn't sure where I'd go after that. Tasha insisted I move to Brinkley with her like we'd planned on years earlier, but I wasn't sure I could do that anymore. I wasn't sure I could be so close to her where I'd have to see her all the time with a boyfriend. It didn't matter who it was—I didn't like even thinking about her dating someone; seeing it was torture. It would just add stress to her life because I was never going to like any boyfriend she had. But I'd always be there for her if she needed me. That would never change, and it didn't matter what else was going on in either of our lives. I'd never again go so long without seeing her. Or date someone else who tried to control my relationship with Tasha. But I needed a way to show Tasha that, and I knew just how to do it.

I jumped off my air mattress, my mood much improved now that I had a plan to repair things between us, and strode to her door, knocking loudly. "Wakey, wakey, eggs and bakey!" I called through the door.

"Fuck off!" she shouted back.

She was still mad at me. But that was okay. It wasn't the first time. And while I'd rather not spend the short time I was visiting with her pissed off at me, I knew it wouldn't last. It never did.

"Breakfast in twenty minutes," I called back through the door.

After a thorough inspection of her refrigerator and cabinets, I was happy to find that I had everything I needed for a pancake breakfast and set about making it, singing "Be Here for You" and "Never Leave Your Side" loud enough for her to hear. These were the songs that were going to help me out, because if there were any songs we'd call *our* songs, not just ones we'd listened to together or that I'd played for her, it was these two.

Sure enough, she was glaring, but shuffled into the kitchen while I was still cooking. I cheesed at her. "Good morning—aren't you just all smiles today?"

Her glare narrowed.

I started singing "A Beautiful Morning" by The Rascals.

She snorted, then began to laugh. "I'm still pissed off at you," she said a minute later.

"I know. And I'm still pissed off at you. But no reason we need to be grumpy about it, right?" I reached over and pulled her into a headlock.

She dug her fingers into my armpit, and I let her go before one of us ended up burned.

"You're an asshole," she said, angrily pulling her hair into a ponytail.

"And you're eloquent first thing in the morning," I replied. "You sure you're a writer?"

She laughed again. "Stop making me laugh when I'm mad at you."

I scrutinized her face for a moment, and she did the same to mine. I could see in her eyes that she was still mad, but she was letting it go. We were okay again. My chest relaxed. "I'm sorry I yelled at you last night."

"You should be," she bit out.

"I am. But I stand by everything I said. I just should have said it less yell-y."

"That's not a word."

I smirked, flipping the pancakes and bacon, and stirring the eggs.

"You're right, you know," she said, her voice much softer. "You didn't have to say it the way you did, but you're not wrong. At least about some of that stuff."

I looked over my shoulder at where she was now sitting cross-legged on top of her tiny table. She was staring through the floor, her fingers absently picking at the hem of her t-shirt. What I wanted to do was turn the stove off, take the few steps needed to close the distance between us, and pull her into her my arms. I wanted to hold her to me and tell her how she was worth so much more than she thought she was. And in the past, I would have. I *had* before. But now... that urge was mixed in with thoughts I shouldn't have been having. Thoughts about how her lips might feel against mine or what it would be like to wake up next to her in bed. So, I decided to leave her with her thoughts and turned back to the stove to finish breakfast.

"I love your pancakes," she muttered after taking her first bite.

I winked. "That's because they're the best damn pancakes on the planet. But now that I've cooked your favorite for you, when are you making me mac-n-cheese?"

She hmphed. "When you're not being a dick."

"I haven't been a dick all day today," I countered.

"The day is young, Dicky Drew."

That was a new one. She caught my eye and we both laughed.

"I'll make you mac-n-cheese for dinner," she said. "*If* you can manage to be nice today."

"No problem—I've *got* this. I'll be the nicest person you've ever met in your life. I'll get a Nobel Prize for this shit."

It became a game for the day. Tasha intentionally baited me repeatedly, this impish grin on her face as she waited to see if I could resist taking the bait. It was torture. So many good comebacks faded into nothing, and my tongue was sore from actually biting it to keep my mouth shut. But it had also been one of the most fun days I'd ever had with her, and it was full of genuine laughter, in spite of Duncan's near-constant messages and phone calls.

Tasha and I had gone out—*without* Duncan this time—to the farmer's market we'd left so abruptly the day before and spent almost the entire day there. We walked around and talked to the people running the booths about what they were selling, how those things were made or acquired. We learned about jewelry-making and soap-making, about handmade lotions and lip balms, about working with resin and knitting and pottery and farming and more. And all the while, Tasha had taken notes in the little notebook she carried with her everywhere to record tidbits she wanted to remember to maybe use in a novel one day. We'd eaten lunch there from a local BBQ place with a booth set up, its smokers making the entire neighborhood smell enticing, before continuing through. By the time we'd seen the last booth, it was late afternoon, everyone was packing up, and I carried several bags, having bought a little something from most of the shops for Tasha. At first, she'd protested, but I'd assured her that I was doing it because I really wanted to, ready to counter any argument she raised. To my surprise, she'd blushed and agreed without any fuss.

When she'd blushed, my heart had done that skippy-speed-up thing again, and I'd had an urge to reach down and hold her hand. Instead, I'd pulled her in and kissed the top of her head.

Now, back in her apartment, I was playing my new guitar while she flitted around the kitchen preparing mac-n-cheese for dinner. And not just any mac-n-cheese, because she was a master at making it. She was making different varieties: one that was herb-forward, another with veggies, one with crab meat, and one that was her classic mac-n-cheese. All the additives we'd picked up fresh from the farmer's market.

As I strummed the opening chords for "Be Here for You," I thought about how much fun I'd had with her. Duncan had asked me the day before if I really wanted to go to a farmer's market, and the truth was that I likely wouldn't have stopped at one if I was out by myself, but I couldn't think of a better way to have spent a Sunday than wandering around with Tasha, talking to artisans and farmers, learning things I'd never have learned otherwise.

And now, sitting there on Tasha's sofa, playing my guitar and singing while she made dinner after spending the day out with her—a day that commenced with me making her breakfast—I felt content in a way I hadn't before. I was content with my career—I loved being a physical therapist and helping people heal and strengthen, and I loved making an impact on the profession in a way that would help survivors of different kinds who were in need of the type of medical care I could provide—but I'd never felt content otherwise.

Until right then.

I could see myself spending my weekends—no, *all* my free time—with Tasha for the rest of my life, I realized. Not only could see it... but I wanted it.

My chest ached under my tattoo. I took that ache and channeled it into my voice as I sang our songs to Tasha again.

"I'm not mad at you anymore, you know," she said, her back to me as she mixed her ingredients together in the various baking dishes. "I already wasn't. You don't have to keep playing our songs."

I grinned. "I know." Then I sang "Never Leave Your Side" anyway, just because I could and I wanted to.

"You're gonna make me get all emotional," she said, plopping onto the sofa next to me after setting a timer on the mac-n-cheese.

I was already feeling that way. "You know, I still mean every word of these songs when I sing them to you."

"I know," she sighed out, resting her head on my shoulder, her body feeling heavy where it leaned against me. "I do, too."

"I know," I said, turning and kissing the top of her head. "So, I was thinking, we could maybe use a reminder of that." This was the idea I'd had that morning.

"A reminder?"

"Yeah. Something we can look at to remember we always have each other, no matter what. No matter how many years pass, no matter how many miles are between us, I'll always be here for you, and you'll always be here for me. But it can be easy to forget sometimes."

"Yeah. It hasn't really felt that way in a long time," she said faintly.

A knife lodged itself somewhere inside my chest. "I know. And we're not going to go this long between visits again. But for the times between, maybe it's time for another tattoo."

She sat up and looked me directly in the eye. "Really?"

"Yeah," I said with a small nod. "Another *matching* tattoo."

Her eyes brightened and she pulled her bottom lip sideways between her teeth. She was thinking. "What did you have in mind?"

"I don't know, maybe a claddagh? Or an infinity symbol? Or pair of golden fish?"

She laughed. "Fish?"

I smiled back at her. "Yeah. I learned a lot about Japanese symbols from the artist who did my chest. Two golden fish represent trust between two people for taking on the challenges of life together."

"Hm." She chewed on her lip, her eyes darting aimlessly around the living room. "What about putting the fish curved and nose to tail so they form a circle and putting a verse from one of the songs inside them?"

We debated for a while, but we couldn't agree on which verses to use. Then I had an idea. "What if we tattoo different verses, but we pick them for each other? So, I'll pick the words I want you to remember for you to get tattooed and you'll pick the words I get tattooed on me?"

"Ooo, I love that idea."

"Where do you want it?"

"Thigh," she said without hesitation. "My right and your left. Then we would have something together on each side."

"Perfect."

"When do you wanna do it?"

I turned toward her and had another urge to kiss her. The urges were getting stronger and more frequent. I cleared my throat and turned to face away from her. "I was thinking this week while I'm here. After Tuesday, though, because of the awards ceremony. That would suck to have to wear a tux with a fresh tattoo."

"It sucks to wear *anything* with a fresh tattoo," she laughed. "But we can see what we can find. I'm not sure anyone that's any good will have an opening on such short notice."

"Don't worry about that," I said, bending over to start playing again. "I'll call my guy—he's got connections. It might cost extra, but that's fine."

"I don't know if I can afford extra," she said with a nervous titter. "I don't know if I can afford a tattoo this size at all, as much as I want it."

"My idea, my treat," I said, then started playing and singing before she could protest. As much as it was my money, I'd always felt like it was hers, too, because of the role she'd played in me getting where I was.

Chapter Seven

Tasha

Why the hell was I so nervous about going to this awards ceremony with Drew? It wasn't like I hadn't been his "date" for things before—not romantically, of course, but as friends. We'd gone to homecomings and proms with each other in high school and things like this awards ceremony in college. But it felt like I had a flock of birds in my stomach and chest cavity, and I was shaking. Shaking so badly I got mascara on my face.

Again.

"Damn it," I muttered loudly. This was the fourth time I was going to have to start over on my makeup.

Drew appeared behind me in the mirror. "Seems to me your face is trying to tell you something."

I rolled my eyes. "Oh yeah? And what's that?"

He grabbed the mascara tube off the counter and flipped it back and forth between his thumb and forefinger, holding my gaze in the mirror. "That it doesn't want this shit on it."

"It's not shit, it's makeup."

"And since when do you wear makeup, anyway? You never wore this crap before."

I shrugged, using a makeup remover cloth to wipe my face back to a clean slate. "I started wearing it a few years ago when I decided to seriously date. Guys like it when you get all dolled up for them."

"Not this guy," he said. He pointed at me in the mirror. "That's your real face right now, and that's what *I* like seeing. Wear that crap if you really want to, but you look much better without it."

I huffed out a frustrated breath as he walked away, staring at myself in the mirror. He was right—I'd never been into wearing makeup before. It began with the second guy I dated after I moved to Brinkley. On our first date, the jerk had asked me why I didn't wear makeup to look prettier like other women—was I allergic to it? *Ugh.* That guy was a real winner. And yet, I'd bought makeup the next day and ended up dating him for several weeks. I picked up the mascara tube Drew had set back down on the counter and looked at it. I *hated* mascara. *Hated* it. The only thing I hated more was foundation. I grabbed my trash can from beside my toilet, held it up to the edge of the counter, and swept all my makeup into it.

Enough trying to be something else for other people.

Besides, the person whose opinion mattered most to me in the world didn't think I needed it.

After my dramatic statement in the form of tossing over a hundred dollars' worth of makeup into the garbage, I went to my room to get dressed, shouting out to let Drew know the bathroom was free for him to do the same. I fingered the satiny material of the gown—this was a classy evening affair. It was the nicest dress I'd ever owned. It was a deep reddish-coppery color that Drew said accentuated the caramel undertones of my eyes. It had a fitted bodice with a sweetheart neckline and open back, and a full floor-length skirt with a slit on one side where the material crossed, giving peeks of my leg all the way up my thigh when I was walking. I'd lucked out and found it on clearance at a bridal shop. I felt like I belonged on the pages of a fairy tale with it on; it was heady to feel that beautiful and sexy.

I walked out of my room to tell Drew I was ready to go, but he was still in the bathroom, so I waited, looking around. His stuff was neatly stacked and folded, his blankets neatly made over the air mattress. His neatness and my messiness were the biggest reason we'd butted heads when we lived together. I smirked; nothing had changed for either of us in that department. I reached over and grabbed the t-shirt he'd been wearing Sunday—it was gray and blue and made his eyes practically glow, not to mention that it fit perfectly to highlight his muscular physique. I decided I was keeping that shirt as a reminder of the amazing day we'd had together. The last two days had been fun, too, but Sunday had been different. We'd had fun, but we'd also grown a lot closer. It was as if something that had appeared between us like an invisible barrier over the last several years had come down. I wanted as many mementos of that as possible, which was why I'd agreed without much fuss to let him get things I liked from the different vendors.

Well, part of the reason. The other part was that the way he'd said he was doing it because he really wanted to get those things for me had made something flutter in my chest and I actually *wanted* to let him. The first time I'd ever wanted to let anyone—especially a guy—spend money on me.

I stuffed his t-shirt under my pillow and scurried back out to the living room just as he emerged from the bathroom.

"Holy shit," I said, the words falling out without thinking. I was rooted to the spot as I looked him over from head to toe and back up.

He drew in a sharp breath. "That's an understatement."

"Humble much?" I said, though I was still taking in his appearance. He was wearing a tuxedo, and while I'd seen him in one before, none of them had fit him the way this one did. I'd always known he was attractive—how could I not?—but right now, my body was electric as I looked at him. It felt wrong, but I couldn't tear my eyes away, either. My heart sped up.

"I was talking about *you*," he replied.

I dragged my eyes from his body to his face. He was watching me intently. If I wasn't mistaken, he was a little out of breath, too, and he was definitely flushed. I thought about making a smart-ass comment about that, but I couldn't get the words to form while he was looking at me that way. I'd never in my thirty years on the planet been looked at the way he was looking at me right then. As if I was the sun and the moon and the earth and the sky, as if I was the air he breathed—the reason he chose to breathe at all. As if he couldn't believe I was standing there before him.

I swallowed—with difficulty because my throat didn't want to cooperate—and wondered if my thermostat had been cranked up to over a hundred degrees somehow. I was pretty sure I could walk barefoot—no, naked—in Antarctica right then and still be too hot.

"Well," I said, but nothing followed. I couldn't think straight, my thoughts jumbled because the feelings in my body were taking over.

"Well," he echoed in the same deep voice he used for singing.

My skin broke out in goosebumps.

"Are you cold?" he asked.

My face leapt into flames that he was paying such close attention to my skin. I eventually tore my eyes away and sucked in my first deep breath in a while. "You ready to go?" I asked, ignoring his question.

"To the thing I'm dragging you to?"

"You're not dragging me," I said soberly. "This is a big deal, Drew. I'm really proud of you. I'm excited to go."

"I know," he replied, slipping an arm around my shoulders and squeezing me into his side. "And that means a lot to me."

"Of course, it will probably be boring as hell," I added. "I may end up sleeping through the whole thing."

He chuckled. "You're lucky we need to leave and don't have time for you to fix your hair if it gets messed up—otherwise, you'd be in a headlock right now."

After an hour of texting on my phone almost constantly with Duncan, I decided I was done. I wanted to be present with Drew, and I'd seen his furtive glances with cloudy eyes several times. What was the point in going if I wasn't paying attention because I was too busy texting my overly-jealous boyfriend? I shot off a message to Duncan that my phone battery was dying and I'd text him once I was home later, then turned my phone off and handed it to Drew. I didn't carry purses in general; I only owned one and had never even used it. I preferred pockets, but this dress didn't have any—my only complaint about it.

He gave me a small half-smile as he accepted my phone and slid it into one of his pockets to join my ID and insurance cards. "Everything okay?" he asked quietly, so we wouldn't disrupt the other people at our table listening to the presentation.

I grunted. "Like you really care."

"I do, actually," he said, sliding a hand along the back of my chair and leaning closer. "I care if everything's okay with *you*. It's him I don't give a shit about."

"It'll be fine," I said.

I wasn't sure about that. Duncan was really worked up. It was Tuesday evening and I hadn't seen him since Saturday night, and while that wasn't unusual under normal circumstances because he often worked long days, he was not handling it well with Drew here. Duncan had demanded a picture of what I was wearing, so I'd had Drew take one before we left and sent it to him. I was aggravated and didn't want to do it, but I was trying to keep the peace, so I did it anyway. It might have been better if I hadn't, though. He called the instant I sent it, but I didn't answer because we were heading down to get a cab, and that began the constant texting. He was fuming about my dress and wanted me to change. Into what, I had no idea— the dress was the only thing I had that was appropriate for this kind of thing. When I explained that to him, he said it *wasn't* actually appropriate when I was out with a friend. When I asked what he meant by that, he said it would only be appropriate if I was with *him*.

And on and on it went, his jealousy ramping up by the second until he was demanding I leave immediately and spend the rest of the week with him in his apartment. I told Drew none of this, though I found him reading over my shoulder, his jaw tensed, more than once. I'd reached my limits, however, of arguing with Duncan when I was supposed to be out supporting Drew, and I'd deal with the fallout later.

I gave Drew a smile, took and released a deep breath, then turned my attention to the front of the room, my shoulder tingling where Drew's fingertips rested against me.

The rest of the presentation, followed by dinner, flew by; the final part of the evening would be the actual awards ceremony. Drew's leg bounced under the table when the host took to the microphone, and I leaned over.

"You're nervous," I whispered.

He nodded, but didn't say anything or look away from the front of the room.

"Why?" I persisted.

He shrugged. "I don't know. I feel like I'm going to walk up there and they're going to say it was a big mix-up and I didn't earn the awards after all. I feel like a fraud."

Anger roared to life in my chest, my hands, my entire body. Anger like I hadn't felt in a long time: anger toward Drew's parents. As confident as he often was, he was also still the little boy his parents had told was worthless and too stupid to do anything with his life. He'd never felt like he deserved any good thing that happened to him because of the damage his parents had done to him when he was a kid, and this was no different.

I grabbed his hand and laced our fingers, squeezing tight, our semicolon tattoos pressed firmly together, then leaned over so my mouth was right next to his ear.

"You are the most genuine, real person there is. You are not a fraud—you couldn't be if you tried. You're going to walk up there and they're going to give you these awards because you earned them. Because you deserve them. Because you're an exceptional physical therapist and have done work to improve healthcare for so many people who've been largely ignored. People like us. You're amazing and are making a real impact on people's lives. That's incredible. You deserve so much more than just these awards."

His eyes were still trained ahead, but I could see they were glassy, and his hand was crushing mine. It hurt, but I didn't say anything—it wasn't painful enough for me to take that connection away from him right then.

"I love you, Drew," I added. "And I'm so proud of you." Then, on impulse, I kissed his cheek.

His jaw clenched and I could see his breath stuttering in and out. He was dealing with a torrent of emotion, and I focused on trying to squeeze his hand as hard as he was squeezing mine to let him know I was there, and that I was with him for all of it. Hell or high water, as the saying went, I was always gonna be there for him.

And then they called his name. I reached into his pocket and retrieved my phone as he rose to his feet and walked toward the front of the room through thunderous applause. Powering it on, I stood and used my phone to record every second of this important event in his life. He shook hands with the national board members, and the applause picked up again as he headed back toward our table. Once it quieted down, the host, like she had for every other award recipient, launched into a long list of Drew's career highlights, focusing on the aspects that had influenced the board's selection.

Drew set the two glass awards down on the table in front of him and turned to me, his eyes as glassy as they had been, but he was beaming this time. He lifted his index finger into the air.

"It's like they're talking about someone else," he said. "I know it's me, but it feels weird to hear it like this."

"Sounds like someone pretty epically awesome, right?" I lifted and lowered my eyebrows playfully.

He huffed out a breath. "I guess. Yeah. It does."

I leaned in. "I'll tell you a secret. You listening?"

"Yeah."

"That guy they're talking about right now? I know him."

"Oh, do you?" he asked with a chuckle.

"Mm-hm. Shocker, I know."

"And?"

"Well, don't tell anyone, but... he moonlights as a stripper named Droopy Drew."

I barely got the words out before I was laughing so hard I had tears in my eyes, and, despite scathing glares from our tablemates for being too loud, Drew was laughing just as hard.

Chapter Eight

Tasha

I woke up the morning after the awards ceremony in a much better mood than I expected after spending half the night on the phone, fighting with Duncan. Drew had opened my bedroom door several times and signaled at me to hang up, his jaw clenched, his eyes shooting fire, but I waved him away and stayed on the phone anyway. I knew he didn't like hearing me arguing—he'd never tolerated people upsetting me very well—but hanging up on Duncan would just make things worse.

Today, though, was tattoo day. We had to be there by ten, and I was already awake at six, my excitement refusing to allow me to sleep any later. I was also feeling inspired to sit down and write. I'd stuck to my plan to take the week off while Drew was visiting, but I was itching to work this morning. I slipped out of bed and dragged my comforter and a fresh notebook and pen to my little balcony. I'd have liked a cup of coffee, but I didn't want to wake Drew by moving around in the kitchen, so decided to wait on it.

"What're you working on?" Drew asked, stepping onto the balcony with two steaming mugs of coffee about an hour later. "One of your books?"

He set the cups down on the little table in front of me, then stretched, his shirt pulling up and his sweats sliding down to reveal a strip of muscly abs and curly hairs below his belly button. I swallowed and looked back at my notebook.

"No," I replied. "Well, I mean, yes, but no."

He laughed, sitting in the only other chair and picking up his coffee mug.

"What I mean is that it's going to be a book, yes, but it's not one of the manuscripts my editor is waiting on. I'm feeling inspired to work on something else this morning, so I am."

"Tell me about it?"

I shrugged, feeling a little self-conscious. "It's autofiction."

"Auto what?"

"Autofiction. It means fiction, but based on my own real life."

"Got it. So, you're going to write a story about a woman whose best friend is a brilliant and sexy beast?"

I laughed.

"How are you describing me? Can I read it?"

"I haven't yet. So, you better be nice to me or I'll write you as cross-eyed and muscle-less with a limp, a mullet, and pustules covering your body."

"What covering my body?" he asked, laughing.

"Pustules. Think pimples, but larger and grosser, usually associated with some incurable disease."

"Jesus."

"Yeah. And I'll give you a name like Derpy Derpkins and have you fall in love with a rabid racoon or something and spend the rest of your days lamenting that the object of your affection doesn't return it. A horrifying tale of unrequited love."

Drew's chest was shaking, and he was laughing so hard, there wasn't even any sound. I grinned, taking a sip of my coffee.

"That's brutal, Tash," he said once he caught his breath, wiping tears of mirth from his cheeks.

"Don't piss off a writer," I said, giggling.

We sat in silence as the world around us continued to wake.

"Seriously, can I read it?" Drew asked after a while.

I studied his face. "Yeah. But not yet. I've taken some notes and just started drafting it. You don't want to read a first draft anyway. First drafts suck."

"First draft or fiftieth—doesn't matter to me. If you wrote it, I want to read it. I've told you that before. Hell, I'd happily read every draft. Especially if it's about us."

I took another sip of coffee. "It is. Or it will be, once it's written. And okay. Once I have something to read, I'll let you read it."

Drew and Robert, the primary tattoo artist, chatted briefly about their mutual acquaintance, Drew's artist from back in Chandler, before we talked about our designs. Drew had already sent over information for Robert, and he'd mocked up a design for what we wanted and showed us. We had him make a few adjustments to the koi he'd drawn for our golden fish, then it was time to begin.

Drew settled into a chair and hiked up the leg of his athletic shorts to bare his muscular, freshly shaved thigh. Seeing his leg almost to his hip made my heart race, and I looked away as I slid off my sweatpants. Underneath, I wore the shortest bike shorts I owned and slid up the material on the leg getting tattooed before taking a seat in the chair next to Drew. Ken, another artist, and Robert transferred our designs onto our legs and kicked off with inking the fish.

After the needle first touched my skin, I felt something prodding my arm. I looked over and Drew was pushing on me with his hand. His eyes were closed as he laid back in the chair, but he was trying to get my attention. I unclasped my hands from my lap.

"What?" I shouted over the noise of the tattoo guns.

He opened his eyes and looked over. After a split-second pause, he grabbed my hand, then closed his eyes again. And that's how we sat—eyes closed, hands clasped between us—until the tattoos were finished. As soon as Ken and Robert told us to take a look, I sat forward and looked down eagerly. Drew and I had decided to let the words we picked for each other be a surprise, and I was dying to know what he'd had me tattoo on my body—what words he wanted to be sure I never forgot. For him, I'd chosen lines from a few different stanzas in "Be Here for You" and tweaked a tad: "I can't drown the flame / Take away the pain / But I promise I'll be here for you / Under the ashes you'll find gold / You're stronger than you even know / And I promise I'll always be here for you."

His hand squeezed mine hard as I took my time to read the words on my own thigh that he'd pulled from "Never Leave Your Side": "When the world is broken / When you don't feel safe / I'll never leave your side / Catch your breath, I'll hold the line / Together's keeping us alive / I'll never leave your side."

I squeezed back and sniffled as tears rolled down my cheeks.

"It's perfect," I whispered. "Thank you."

"So's mine. Thank *you*, Nats," he whispered back.

In spite of the pain, I was on cloud nine. I couldn't stop looking at our thighs, reading and re-reading and re-reading the words. I knew them by heart and still I read over them, giggling like a crazy person to see them permanently on our bodies.

"I *love* our new tattoos," I said for about the millionth time after we'd gotten back to my apartment for the evening.

"I do, too," he said, getting his guitar situated. We'd eaten leftover mac-n-cheese for dinner and were now sipping on whiskey, and he wanted to play for a while before we watched a movie.

All-in-all, it couldn't have been a more perfect day.

Chapter Nine

Drew

I barely slept my last night with Tasha. I didn't want the morning to come, because morning meant only hours left with her before I had to fly back to my life halfway across the country. The week with her had been the best week I could remember ever having, and I wasn't ready for it to end. We'd laughed and cried and fought and made up, and all of it was perfect because it was *us*. I wanted so much more of it. I wanted to spend every day with her to make up for years of not seeing her.

Her relationship with Duncan was bothering me, too—a shitload. I didn't like her dating *anyone*—never had—but I especially didn't like Duncan. Despite all the things Tasha told me about him being nicer and more stable than any other boyfriend, something about this guy didn't sit right with me. He was so jealous and possessive over her, and I didn't trust him. He wasn't just self-absorbed, and possibly narcissistic, but with that level of jealousy... I was afraid he was dangerous. I could still see the way he held the back of Tasha's neck when we walked out of the brewery that first night—it was an action designed to establish and exert dominance, one I was familiar with because my dad had done it to me when I was a kid. I'd wanted to punch Duncan when he did it to Tasha and tell him not to fucking touch her ever again. I still wanted to and was beginning to wish I hadn't had the restraint I did.

Tasha began to stir in her bedroom, and I sighed. The new day had arrived regardless of my best efforts to put it off. But I was going to make the most of my last few hours with her, starting with making her coffee and breakfast, so I pushed up and padded the few feet from my mattress into the kitchen.

Before long, we sat down to eat breakfast, but the air was filled with more silence than normal between us and a distinct lack of teasing or obnoxious comments. We kept glancing at each other, and she appeared to be as bothered by my impending departure as I was. We'd planned to take the pottery class we hadn't done yet, but neither of us brought it up. Rather than going, after breakfast, we inspected our legs for signs of infection, then moisturized our tattoos before settling next to each other on the sofa. Our last hours together were spent playing and singing all our favorite songs.

Then, much too soon, we were driving to the airport. The air in the car became tense and anxious, and I could see her thumb beating against the steering wheel as quickly as my leg was bouncing. For some reason, seeing that we were both feeling the same way and keeping it to ourselves made me laugh.

"I'm going to miss you, too, you know," I said, giving her knee a quick squeeze, careful to avoid her fresh tattoo.

"You better." Her eye caught mine, and she grinned before turning back to the road. "And you better show up here in three months like you promised."

"Three months *or less*," I clarified.

She nodded, then navigated to the curb at the arrival gate. All I had was my carry-on and my guitar and I didn't need help with it, but she climbed out of the car anyway and walked around to where I was setting my luggage on the walkway. I wrapped her in my arms and she wrapped me in hers, and we both squeezed tight. She pushed her tattooed leg into mine and I winced—it hurt like hell—then pushed back. This parting was painful; it made sense to feel it where we'd marked our bodies for each other.

"I love you, you know," I said into her ear, feeling a deep sadness already settling inside me.

She nodded into my chest "I do. And I love you, too."

"I know you do," I murmured. Then added, "I wish you didn't have a boyfriend."

I could feel the catch in her chest and mine ached. I'd meant the words, even if I hadn't intended to utter them out loud. Drawing back marginally, I turned and held my lips against the corner of her mouth for a long moment, trying to communicate everything I felt for her—things I couldn't even name right then. Over the years, I'd kissed the top or side of her head somewhat often, sometimes kissed her cheek, but other than the one time when we were teens and tried kissing each other, I'd never touched her lips with mine.

Until now.

My body hummed as if the blood moving through my veins was suddenly vibrating. My heart did that skip-then-speed-up thing again, except it knocked the breath out of me this time. With a final squeeze of my arms and pressing of my lips, I stepped back and turned to face the building. Pulling away instead of going back for more hurt. *A lot.* It was so unexpected that I teared up. I cleared my throat and grabbed my suitcase, not wanting her to see that I was about to cry.

"I'll text once I land," I said, still not facing her.

"Okay," she said, her voice faint and breathy in a way I'd never heard it before.

I turned because of that new tone of voice and found a tortured expression in those caramel eyes I'd always found gorgeous since the night we met, her fingers resting over the spot my lips had just been touching. Her eyes were also about to spill over.

I cleared my throat again. "Bye, Nats."

"Bye, Drew," she said in the same faint tone.

And then I walked away from her, back to the life I didn't want because it didn't include her.

The first thing I saw when I landed and turned my cell phone back on was a message from Tasha that she hoped my flight had been as boring and uneventful as it gets. It made that ache under the tattoo on my chest worsen at the same time it made me smile. While I was typing a response, she sent another message.

You need new sweats, by the way. I forgot
to tell you.

I chuckled. Of course she'd stolen some of my sweatpants. She'd done the same thing when we lived together. What she didn't know was that I'd packed a few extra, just for her.

How many?

All of them.

Anything else, brat?

Maybe a t-shirt.

Just one?

Maybe two.

I snorted, wondering which shirts she'd kept and if it really was only two or if she'd swiped more than that. She asked again about my flight, and I texted her back, regaling her with an exaggerated version of my seatmates, and we were still texting when I hopped out of the cab in front of the apartment I shared with Becka, my suitcase in hand and my new guitar slung over my shoulder.

My body felt like it had just gained about a hundred pounds, and it was hard to make my legs carry me inside. I might not have even succeeded if it weren't for knowing that Watson was waiting inside for me. I'd been so wrapped up in Tasha while I was gone, I hadn't had time to miss him, but now that I was back, I realized how much I actually did.

I could hear Watson whining with excitement on the other side of the door before I'd even unlocked it and grinned. He knew my gait, so already knew I was home. And sure enough, when I opened the door, all eighty-couple pounds of yellow lab barreled into my arms as if he were a tiny lap dog. I fell backward and just laid on the ground inside the door while Watson walked all over me, alternately whining and licking my face as I petted him and assured him that I was back home and had missed him. Once he had calmed somewhat, I snapped a picture of him lying on my chest on the floor and sent it to Tasha, then sat up, moving him to my not-tattooed leg.

"I missed you, too, boy," I said again, kissing his head and scratching behind his ears some more.

He licked my face again and I laughed, then leaned over and dragged my carry-on closer before laying it down and unzipping it.

"I have a surprise for you, boy, from your favorite person."

He whined and thumped a paw down on my lap, his ears perking up.

"That's right—Nats sent something for you."

He whined again, thumping my lap repeatedly with his paws, licked my face again, then jumped up to his feet, his eyes looking at the door behind me.

"No, she's not here, but she sent something for you."

Once my small suitcase was opened, Watson buried his nose in it, sniffing around almost frantically as he whined. It was sweet and a little sad—I knew he could smell Tasha and was looking for her. If ever a dog adored a human, it was Watson with Tasha.

"I know," I laughed, rummaging around through my clothes. "I miss her, too."

I pulled out the handmade chew-toy Tasha had picked out for Watson at the farmer's market from the bottom of the case and held it out for him. Taking it with care, he settled next to me on the floor, gnawing happily on his new toy. I snapped a picture of that as well and sent it to Tasha before standing and zipping my suitcase closed. Once I was on my feet, I turned to head deeper into the apartment and found Becka standing noiselessly, watching me. I hadn't noticed her appear and didn't know how long she'd been there.

My smile faded.

"Hi," I said. "I'm back."

She gave a small nod and sniffled, turning away. That was when I noticed how red her eyes were—she'd been crying. Guilt shot through my chest.

"I haven't found a place yet, but I can pack up some more clothes and get a hotel until I do." I glanced at Watson. "Can he stay until I get a new place?"

She nodded again. "You can stay, too," she said quietly.

"You told me if I went to visit Tasha, that we were over, and I went. I knew what it meant when I left."

"I know. But I've been doing a lot of thinking while you were gone, and I maybe shouldn't have said that. I was really angry and was trying to force you to do what I wanted you to, and I shouldn't have done that."

I sighed, not sure what to think or feel. I was fairly certain I should have felt hopeful and excited by what Becka had just said, but I didn't. I wanted to tell her it was too late, that she couldn't change her mind. That she'd forced me to make a decision, and that I had, and that I had no regrets about choosing Tasha over her.

She sniffled loudly and wiped her cheeks, still staring at the floor. More guilt began to pile up. I didn't want to hurt her.

"This was the worst week of my life," she whimpered, her jaw trembling.

Now the guilt was choking me, and I tried to swallow it down. I wasn't going to lie to her—the worst week of *her* life had been the best week of *mine*. I remained silent.

"I don't understand your relationship with that woman—"

"Her name is Tasha," I said, my voice hardening.

"Whatever her name is, I don't understand how you have *any* kind of relationship with someone like her, but—"

I picked up my suitcase and walked past her. I'd let her talk about Tasha like that in the past, but I was done—I wouldn't listen to it anymore. I silently asked Tasha to forgive me for ever having put up with Becka badmouthing her.

"Where are you going, Drew? I'm trying to talk to you," Becka said, following me.

"I'm not going to listen to you talk shit about Tasha anymore."

"I'm not trying to!" Becka shouted. "Would you just listen?"

I stopped inside our bedroom and turned to face her.

"This is what I'm talking about—you throw up these walls when it comes to her, and I can't even have a conversation with you."

"I'm done talking about Tasha with you."

"Drew—"

"No."

"Please. I want to fix things between us. We've been together for *years*. We can't just throw that away. There's a reason we've been together this long, Drew. We have something worth saving."

She stepped closer and grabbed my hands. I flinched, but let her.

"What I was trying to say is that I don't understand your relationship with *Tasha*, but I'm trying. And to help me with understanding you and you with understanding me and why I have a problem with... her... I found us a therapist who specializes in working with couples and booked the first session for next week."

"What?" I balked.

"Couples therapy," she said. "Lots of people do it. It saved Constance's marriage and my parents' marriage—they've done it several times, actually. It can save our relationship, too."

"Save *what*?" I growled out, pulling my hands from hers and feeling angrier than I thought I should be. "How do you view this relationship we have, Becka? Huh? Because from my side, it consists of catering to whatever you want in order to avoid pissing you off. It means giving up things I enjoy doing and turning my back on people I love."

"Don't say that," she said, crying.

"This was the worst week of your life because you didn't have someone here to do whatever you asked and agree with everything you said. But me? I remembered what it's like to feel alive and enjoy my life again, to spend time doing things that make me happy and do so with the people who make me happy."

"What *people*, Drew?" she shouted. "You don't mean people—you mean *her!*"

"You're right, Becka. That's exactly what I mean. Tasha. Because being with Tasha makes me happy. This was the best week of my life. *My life.* The worst part of it was having to come back here."

"You're an asshole," she bit out.

I turned and strode into the bathroom, pulling the door closed behind me using every ounce of self-control I could find to keep from slamming it. I sank onto the toilet and dropped my head into my hands. What the hell was I doing? Why had I said that to her? It was true, but the only purpose of saying it had been to hurt her, which I'd only wanted to do because I was so pissed off about the way she talked about Tasha. Why did it even matter anyway? I was supposed to be moving out.

There was a scratching on the other side of the door, followed by a whine. I opened it and Watson trotted in, resting his head on my lap. I scratched behind his ears absently and let out a heavy breath.

Becka was trying. She wasn't perfect, but neither was I. No one was. And I was testy because I missed Tasha already, but that wasn't Becka's fault.

My eyes stared unseeing through the bathroom door as I thought back to my last minutes with Tasha, standing next to her car at the airport. I could smell her again—a mixture of strawberries and flowers—and feel her skin under my lips, her body in my arms. I could see her smiles—all of them, because she had several. There was her sad smile when she was feeling nostalgic or something bittersweet was happening, like when I played those first songs for her after buying my guitar. There was her excited grin, like when she saw me and came running toward me at the airport when I arrived. There was her devilish grin when she was saying something to intentionally aggravate me, the curving of her lips with brightening eyes when I surprised her like I had with the idea of getting the tattoos, the slight rolling of her lips as they pulled up at the corners when she blushed like when I complimented the way she looked for the awards ceremony, and her so-much-love-it-hurts smile like the one she gave me after reading the words tattooed on her thigh the first time.

The thought of not seeing any of those smiles again for months hurt like something was prying my chest apart. The thought of someone *else* getting all those smiles made my hands ball into fists. The thought of that someone being Duncan made me want to hop on a plane back to Brinkley and do something to make sure they never spoke again.

Realistically, I could do it. I didn't need to stay in Chandler if Becka and I were splitting up. I could go anywhere. And I knew where I wanted to be, but I couldn't be there with Tasha while she was dating. I'd go out of my mind seeing her with Duncan or whoever else was lucky enough to be considered her boyfriend for some period of time. No, her life was there, and mine was here. With a woman who was at least *trying* to salvage our relationship. I needed to stop expecting perfection and accept what was right in front of me.

I bent over and gave Watson a kiss on the head. His tail wagged as he looked up at me and I gave him a lopsided smile.

"I guess we're gonna give this thing another go, boy."

Chapter Ten

Tasha

Another text message arrived from Duncan, and a quick scan told me he was driving over. Seeing him, let alone going out somewhere like he wanted, was the last thing I wanted to do while still reeling from Drew's departure. But I wouldn't tell him that—I wouldn't dare. Things had been tense enough between us since Drew had arrived, and now that Drew was gone, I couldn't keep avoiding him. I already had the day before, telling him I thought I was coming down with something. But now it was Sunday, a week since we'd last seen each other, and he wasn't going to take no for an answer.

My head tipped back up toward the ceiling, resting against the back of the sofa. I wasn't seeing my ceiling, though. I was seeing Drew. Well, feeling him would be more accurate. The corner of my mouth still buzzed from where he'd kissed me outside the airport. I touched the area with my fingertips and sucked in a breath—it was as if he were there doing it all over again.

But why had he done it? Had he meant for his mouth to touch mine? Or had he meant to kiss my cheek and just didn't realize he'd missed his mark? We were friends. We'd always been friends—*just friends*. At the same time, there had been moments while he was visiting that things between us felt like something... *more*. Moments when my body reacted to him in ways it shouldn't. And then there was the kiss at the airport. I'd wanted so badly to yank him back to me and full-on kiss him, despite how things had gone the only time we'd ever kissed that way.

My fingers moved over my phone screen, and I looked down. I'd almost texted him at least a dozen times a minute since he'd left to ask him if he'd meant to do what he had or if it had been an accident, but I didn't know how to ask him without giving away how badly I wanted to know the answer... how badly I wanted the answer to be that it was on purpose.

I think.

Though that would complicate things in a way I didn't need in my life. My life sucked enough as it was. And yet, I couldn't stop thinking about that kiss. Maybe it wouldn't hurt to find out because things were already complicated thanks to having feelings I didn't want to be having for my best friend.

Not-friend feelings.

If Duncan knew, he'd lose his mind. He was already losing his mind because Drew had stayed with me all week when he'd told me no. Besides, Drew was trying to fix his relationship with Becka, so what did it matter whether or not that kiss had been intentional? He was determined to make things work with her—he said he was even going to do couples therapy with her. And as much as I hated her— way more than the other girlfriends Drew had in college—it was maybe better this way. For Drew, anyway. I wanted him to be happy, and if that was with bitchy Becky, then I could deal with it.

Bitchy Becky... it was catchy. I hadn't thought of that one before. Just for fun, I texted it to Drew. I told him their wedding invitations should invite people to the union of Bitchy Becky and Droopy Drew. Then I laughed, because I knew he'd roll his eyes, equally annoyed and amused when he read it.

Duncan and I went out to brunch, followed by a brewery, just as we did every Sunday, and he was noticeably less argumentative with Drew gone. His possessiveness, however, was as severe as it had been with Drew around. While he'd never done it before, he was asking me about every male who even said "excuse me" in passing and his eyes never left me, even when I got up to use the bathroom. I was feeling a bit smothered and annoyed, but reminded myself that he just loved me, and this was how he was expressing it. Even if it was annoying, it was harmless. Besides, I felt bad being aggravated with him when I was sitting next to him and thinking about Drew rather than paying attention to what he was saying.

"Tasha," Duncan said, waving a hand in front of my face.

I startled and focused my eyes on him as images of Drew holding me at the airport faded. "Yes?"

"What the hell are you thinking about? You haven't been paying attention all afternoon."

"I'm just tired." At least that was true—I *was* tired because I hadn't slept much the night before. "What were you saying?"

He launched into a monologue of the merits of the IPA he was drinking compared to the IPA from his other favorite brewery—a monologue I'd heard many times before. I sighed and tried to be interested, but I didn't like beer to begin with, and he went through this at least twice a month. I was sick of it. I wanted to do something different.

"Let's go somewhere next weekend," I said, interrupting him.

He scowled. "What?"

I shrugged. "Let's go somewhere. We never go anywhere—let's do something different."

"Like where?"

I shrugged again. "Anywhere. Just somewhere that's not here."

He stared at me for a minute. "What's wrong with being here?"

"Nothing," I said, struggling to hide my irritation. "But I want to do other things, too. I want to go other places. I actually like traveling and trying new things. You know, a little variety."

"Variety? Is that what Drew was—variety?"

My heart stopped. "What?"

He tossed back his beer. "I saw the way you guys looked at each other, and I'm not stupid, Tasha."

"Drew is my *friend*," I bit out. "He has been my *friend* since I was fourteen."

"Friend you fuck?"

His face was hard, his hand in a white-knuckled grip on his beer glass. I couldn't believe he'd accuse me of cheating on him or being fuck buddies with Drew. I moved to stand, but Duncan clamped his hand over my forearm, pinning it to the table. I lowered back into my chair, my heart now racing and my breathing shallow.

"Answer me, Tasha," he ordered in a low, menacing voice.

"I've never *fucked* Drew," I said through clenched teeth. "He's my best friend and that's all. I told you that, and I'm *not* a liar." My eyes flicked down to my arm that was hurting under the increasing pressure of his hand. "Let go of my arm, Duncan."

As soon as he lifted his hand, I jerked my arm to my body, caressing over the sore spot I now had. I couldn't believe what he'd done—he'd never done something like that before. I looked back up at him.

His eyes fell to my arm, then filled with remorse. "I'm sorry, Tasha. I'm so sorry." He reached over and touched my upper arm gently. "I didn't mean to, I swear. I got... it doesn't matter. I shouldn't have done that—I'm so sorry. Is your arm okay?"

Technically, my arm *was* okay, though it did end up bruising. And every time I looked at that bruise or accidentally touched something with it, I felt this strange mix of shame and anger and nausea. Duncan had been extremely apologetic, going out of his way to be more thoughtful than normal, sending me flowers every day all week long, and surprising me with takeout for dinner twice. It seemed to have been a fluke occurrence, especially when Thursday night came and, over take-out, he told me he had a surprise for me: a trip to Vegas. He'd been listening to me.

"Not this weekend, but next," he said. "For a long weekend. We'll go Thursday and come back on Sunday. I would have taken you this weekend, but I couldn't get time off from work this week. Is next weekend okay?"

Who was this guy? Where had he been? He'd never surprised me with anything more than flowers or jewelry or an occasional fancy dinner out, but he'd been doing things all week, and now he was surprising me with the trip I'd asked him for. To Vegas. I didn't especially want to go there, but I didn't *not* want to go there, either. It wasn't high on my list of places to see, but it was on it.

"Next weekend is great," I said, smiling.

He kissed me and it felt like the incident at the brewery was from a different lifetime. If it weren't for the bruise that was still visible and tender, and my heart that had been racing ever since it happened, I'd have been inclined to think I'd imagined the whole thing. I felt like I was crazy for feeling so anxious about him. It was a mistake and that was all—he hadn't meant to hurt me, and he wouldn't do it again.

After Duncan left, I opened my phone to text Drew, but my fingers hesitated over the keys. I wasn't sure what to say. I was going to tell him that Duncan was taking me to Vegas and have him be excited for me, but I was worried he wouldn't be. He hadn't been himself since he'd left. I knew it was because of all the tension with Becka, but it still hurt that he was so short in his responses and didn't text me if I hadn't texted him first.

I let out a sigh and pulled up the picture of him pinned down by Watson when he'd gotten back. I loved that picture. He was laughing, his gray-blue eyes glowing and crinkled at the corners. He loved that dog.

Watson. The dog *he'd* gotten, but we'd named together. We'd chosen Watson after the Sherlock Holmes sidekick. When we were teens and we snuck out together at night, around him playing guitar, we'd take turns reading Sherlock Holmes stories to each other. It was calming to focus on something else, and I, at least, really enjoyed trying to piece together the clues before Holmes revealed his logic.

We'd worn my book out to the point the spine was beginning to fail by the time we left for college. When Drew rescued Watson, he'd been attached to our hips—especially mine. He always seemed to know when one of us was feeling down in the dumps, and he would shove his head under our hands and climb onto our laps and rest his face on our shoulders, keeping us from descending too far down into the darkness of our minds. Like Watson had done for Holmes. So, two weeks after getting him, we'd changed his name from Boomer, the name he'd come with, to Watson.

I missed Watson. I missed his dog-smell and his wet, cold nose that made me yelp when he came up behind me and sniffed my leg when I didn't know he was there. I missed the way he loved me so unconditionally and never tired of snuggling with me when I was upset, how he didn't care how much I cried on him. How he mushed himself into my side in public when someone who unsettled me came near, and how he slept curled around my feet when I was writing. I loved that dog at least as much as I loved his owner.

I closed the photo and typed a text to Drew.

Bring your better half when you visit next.

I smirked, watching the three little dots appear almost instantaneously, and waited while he texted. This was the fastest he'd responded in days.

Better half? I AM the better half.

I snorted, then giggled.

Compared to who?

Anyone.

Not Watson.

I can't actually argue with that.

So you'll bring him for your next visit?

Maybe. I was thinking about coming out
next weekend, just for the weekend, but I'd
have to fly and I can't bring him if I do that.

My heart skipped. He was coming back out already? He hadn't been responding to me, but he was thinking about coming to visit? Maybe I was expecting too much. He was back to work on top of everything with Becka, and his job wasn't like mine—he couldn't just text whenever he felt like it. But just as my chest filled, it deflated. I wasn't going to be home.

You can't come next weekend. :(

Why not?

I'm going to Vegas.

I'll meet you there, then. I haven't been to
Vegas before. It'll be fun.

With Duncan.

The three little dots indicating he was typing appeared for a long time, then disappeared without a new text coming in.

Chapter Eleven

Drew

I waved to my final patient for the day as she left. She was in her early seventies and had recently had a hip and knee replacement. She was sweet and I enjoyed listening to her talk about her grandchildren for the three hours a week we worked together. This was a patient I would miss.

Earlier that day, I'd talked to the partners who owned the practice I worked for about leaving. I didn't know yet where I was going, but this wasn't the right fit for me anymore. I'd devoted years to research and starting programs for trauma-informed physical therapy, and I wanted to be somewhere I could work with patients with trauma. This practice was full and had a long waitlist of patients who could work with anyone there. Not to mention the increasing pressure to take on more and more patients. I was grateful for the years I'd spent there, but it was time to move on somewhere else.

The partners had been understanding and requested that I stay until they'd recruited someone to take my place—they were already running over capacity and couldn't afford to distribute my patients among the remaining therapists. And since I didn't already have something lined up, I agreed, which meant I could remain there for weeks or months, depending on how long it took them to find a replacement with equivalent experience.

I drove home to let Watson out before couples therapy, my thoughts bouncing between where I might want to practice and thinking about Tasha on her way to Vegas with the boyfriend I didn't trust. My knuckles turned white where they were wrapped around the steering wheel just thinking about it. When she'd told me she was going with him, all but saying that meant I couldn't go, I'd wanted to book a flight out there anyway, to just show up and surprise her there so I could keep an eye on Duncan. But I knew that would create problems between them if I did, and I really wasn't trying to make her life any harder than it already was.

I fiddled with a fidget toy, only half-listening to Becka and Grace, our therapist. We were seeing Grace twice a week and this was our fourth session. While I'd tried to approach therapy with an open mind and give fixing my relationship with Becka my full effort, my heart just wasn't in it—especially today. All I could think about was the fact that Tasha and Duncan would be checking into their hotel room in Vegas right about then. She hadn't texted to tell me their plane landed safely like I'd asked, but she *had* told me in advance what flight she'd be on, and I'd kept an eye on it, so I knew it had.

"Drew? Are you listening?" Becka asked, placing a hand on my thigh.

We were sitting on the same sofa opposite of Grace, about two feet between us. I turned from where I'd been staring through the wall to my right and sighed.

"Sorry, I missed that."

"This is what I mean," Becka said to Grace. "He's so distracted lately."

"I've got a lot on my mind," I said, aware I sounded defensive. "Cut me some slack, Becka."

"Okay," Grace said. "Have you tried talking to Becka about what's on your mind?"

I grunted and shook my head. It wasn't funny at all, but I had an urge to laugh at the ridiculousness of that question. I could never talk to Becka about what was on my mind—none of it. It either had to do with Tasha, which was most of it, work, which Becka said got boring to listen to me talking about, or my past, which Becka didn't really know that much about. No one did except Tasha.

"You can talk to me, Drew," Becka said, facing me. Her eyes were imploring me, but I wasn't sure why. She didn't really want to hear it. "What's on your mind?"

"Okay, Drew," Grace said, "Becka has expressed that she wants to listen. Now you can open up to her. Pretend like I'm not here."

I stared back at Becka blankly. "For starters, I'm worried about my best friend," I said, intentionally not using Tasha's name to give Becka a chance to react with something other than anger.

She didn't; she rolled her eyes and lifted her hand from my thigh. "Tasha. Again. Tasha's always getting between us."

"She's not getting between anyone, Becka. You said you wanted to know, and I told you. And instead of asking why to try to actually understand, you got pissed off. And that's why I don't talk about this stuff."

"Because it's *her*, Drew!"

"Alright," Grace intervened. "Let's take a minute or two to collect ourselves, take a few deep breaths." She paused for about a minute. "Okay, when we're calm and ready with an open mind, we can talk about what just happened here and figure out what we can do differently."

"What we can do differently is get that woman out of our lives," Becka muttered.

Instant rage engulfed me. I was furious. "You lied," I seethed. "You promised me if I did couples therapy with you, you would stop badmouthing Tasha and make an effort to understand my relationship with her. Is this what you call understanding? Because nothing's changed, Becka! You're saying the same shit about her you always have."

Suddenly, Becka was shouting and crying, and Grace was trying to rein things back in. I turned away from her and stared through the wall again. I didn't want to be there. I didn't have enough energy for this shit. Becka was never going to accept Tasha's presence in my life.

Why was I even fighting for that? I couldn't have Tasha in my life in any greater capacity than I already did while she was dating someone else. Like the asshole she was in Vegas with.

My jaw clenched tighter. I couldn't stand the thought of them on a trip together. I knew, realistically, they must have been sleeping together—they'd been dating for quite a while—but it had been easy to pretend they weren't until now. I knew they were sharing a room and that meant I couldn't pretend anymore. And the thought made me feel sick, like I might actually throw up. I wanted to fly to Vegas and physically prevent it from happening.

"Drew," Grace said, pulling me from my thoughts of Tasha and her boyfriend. "You said 'for starters' earlier... would you like to share what else is on your mind?"

No.

"Please," Becka pleaded, her voice nasally like it always was after she'd been crying. "I want to listen."

"I told Jim and Edgar today that I'm leaving the practice."

"What?" Becka practically shouted. "When did that happen?"

"Today."

"B-but why now, I mean?"

I stared at her for a long minute. "I told you *a year ago* that I wanted to leave the practice at some point. It's time."

"You said eventually, I didn't think you meant anytime soon."

"What does timing matter?"

"I don't want to move, Drew," she said.

I clenched my jaw. "Your only concern is whether or not we're moving. You don't care about the reason I want to make a professional change at all."

"Of course I do."

"Since when? You've never once asked me why I'd want to leave. Even now, you didn't ask."

She had the decency to look embarrassed and perused her lap. "Why?"

I let out a short laugh. "I want to work with different kinds of patients."

She shook her head, clearly not understanding.

"I spent the last few years doing research and pioneering programs for trauma-informed therapy, particularly related to domestic abuse and sexual assault survivors, Becka. But you probably don't remember me telling you that."

"Of course, I do," she rushed out, still looking down.

"What did I travel to Brinkley for?"

She narrowed her eyes. "To see *her*."

"That's why I spent a week there, yes, but the trip originated because of the awards I was receiving. Do you know what those awards were for?"

"Drew—"

"Tell me, Becka. What awards did I receive?"

She inhaled sharply, unable to meet my eye.

"You should remember," I continued, my body hot with anger, "since when I told you, you said you were proud of me but that it didn't sound like that big a deal and you didn't understand why I wanted to be there in person so badly or why it mattered to me who was there with me."

She was still silent and that made me angrier.

"Public service and societal impact, Becka. For my work on trauma-informed therapy. And for the record, the reason it mattered so much to me who went is because Tasha not only knows exactly what my awards were, but she understands exactly why I'm passionate about this and why receiving these awards was such a big deal to me. She knows, and she remembers, and she cares. Unlike you."

Becka started crying again and Grace stepped in, saying something about taking a breather to calm ourselves, but that we did a good job, and I tuned out the rest, back to staring at the wall. Becka had a lot of nerve to be so upset when she was the one who'd blown off something so important to me. I'd been used to it and become almost immune to it over the years we'd been together, but after spending a week with someone who truly cared, Becka's self-centered indifference was infuriating. In some ways, she reminded me of my parents, though I'd never seen it before just now.

The end of therapy was unproductive as Becka never stopped crying. And I felt like an asshole, but I didn't care this time. I didn't relish being the reason any person cried, and I did care about Becka, but I just didn't care today. I was sick of her crying and then me caving. Grace said she'd see us Tuesday and to work on communicating our thoughts in the meantime, but I wasn't sure I was going back. I wasn't sure I cared to try to fix things with Becka anymore. I couldn't even look at her without feeling angry.

That night as I headed to bed early, Tasha called, but I was so pissed off knowing she was calling while she was in Vegas with Duncan that I turned my phone off. But then I laid awake, listening to Becka sleeping on the other side of the bed, until the sun rose the next morning, unable to stop thinking about Tasha anyway.

With my millionth heavy sigh in the last few weeks, I powered my phone on and hopped in the shower after taking Watson for a long walk at sunrise—a walk that became even longer when I realized his waste bag dispenser had fallen off his leash again. It was happening more and more often, but I refused to replace it—it was the one Tasha had picked out for him when I first got him. When I was almost done washing my hair, Becka walked in and there was a loud *thunk* on the counter.

"Your phone is blowing up with text messages from *her*," she bit out. "It won't shut up." She slammed the door on her way out with the last word.

I finished rinsing and got out, snatching my phone from the counter after the quickest dry-off in my life. Why the hell had I been so petty that I turned off my phone the night before? Something might have happened with the asshole Tasha was with, and she hadn't been able to reach me.

Please let her be okay.

I got my screen unlocked and opened my text conversation with Tasha. My eyes scanned through line after line of texts, my stomach twisting tighter the more I read. When I reached the end, I threw my phone onto the counter, unsure what I wanted to do most: throw up or hit something or cry.

"Damn it!" I shouted, grasping the edge of the countertop, wishing I could turn back time and answer my phone rather than having turned it off. "Fuck!"

Chapter Twelve

Tasha

My nose was compressed against the tiny glass window like the little kids on our flight as our plane neared Las Vegas. It was the largest city I'd ever seen, much larger than Brinkley or the city where I'd gone to college, let alone the mid-sized town where I'd grown up. Excitement and trepidation raced down my spine. I was excited to explore a new place, but it also made me nervous. It would be significantly more crowded and had a much higher crime rate than Brinkley, and while Duncan cared about me, I would have been more comfortable with Drew by my side for this trip.

My eyes flicked over to Duncan, who was flipping through one of the magazines from the seat back in front of him, the screens set into the seat backs having been turned off since we were so close to landing. More of that guilt I'd been feeling so much of ever since Drew told me he was coming to town and Duncan and I began arguing all the time settled on my shoulders. Why did I feel safer with Drew than with Duncan? If there was some sort of threat, Duncan would surely do everything he could to protect me. I shoved away my irrational concern and turned back to the window.

In what felt like the blink of an eye, we were walking into our hotel. I hadn't stayed in many hotels in my life, but this one appeared to be pretty nice, and I wondered briefly how much this trip was costing Duncan. He was comfortable financially, but this was surely a big expense, and I hoped he'd found a bunch of deals or something—the idea of him spending a lot of money on me didn't sit well.

Inside the room, I stopped rolling my carry-on suitcase and stared out the giant window with a view of the city. It was beautiful and mind-boggling and humbling.

Duncan wrapped his arms around me from behind and kissed the side of my neck. "Nice view, huh?"

"Yeah. It's incredible."

"I paid extra to get this view for you," he said. "I'm glad you like it."

I turned and gave him a tight smile, wishing he hadn't done that. "Thank you."

"You know what I want to do?" Duncan asked, sliding his hands up the sides of my shirt. "I want to fuck you in front of the window."

I let out a small laugh and stepped away. "What?"

He followed, his hands now pulling my shirt off. "I want to fuck you in front of that window," he said again. "Right up against the glass." He started on my jeans, his mouth just below my neck.

I pushed against his chest and turned out of his grasp, trying to rebutton my jeans, but I was trembling and having a hard time getting anything to cooperate. "People could see us, Duncan," I said with a nervous titter. I wasn't interested in having sex where people could watch—that thought made me exceedingly uncomfortable. I didn't even like having sex with the lights on. And I didn't want to have sex at all right then. I'd been avoiding it since Drew's visit, in fact. And as excited as I was about seeing a new place, I also felt really overwhelmed. The why eluded me—I liked new experiences and was usually more excited than anything else. But instead of excitement, I felt trepidation and desperately wanted to be back home, alone in my apartment. I probably just needed to get out more.

Duncan followed me again and kept walking, backing me up toward the window as he reached behind me and unhooked my bra while I was still struggling to rebutton my jeans. Shock ran through me as my bare shoulders connected with the cool glass. He grabbed my wrists, holding them in one hand behind me, then used his other hand to undo the button I'd finally managed to push through the buttonhole and lower the zipper on my jeans. He slipped a hand in the front of my panties, and I wanted to tell him to stop, but I couldn't. He'd never been quite so aggressive about sex before, and he'd never pinned my arms so I couldn't move. I felt paralyzed, both physically and mentally—I didn't even know how to speak.

"That's the point," he said against my cheek. "Everyone can see who's fucking you, who you belong to."

I was so stunned that even once he let go of my wrists to use both hands to pull down my jeans and panties, I didn't move. And then my entire naked backside was smashed against the glass in broad daylight.

"What's this?" Duncan asked, his fingertips running over the new tattoo on my thigh.

I swallowed, panic exploding in my chest because I wasn't sure how to best answer that question. Especially after what he'd just said about me belonging to him. "It's new."

"I know it's new, Tasha," he snapped, "but you didn't tell me you were planning to get any more tattoos, let alone that you *had*. When did you do this? It wasn't there a month ago."

"A few weeks ago," I replied, evasive, hoping he would lose interest in it before he read the words.

He squinted down and I knew he was going to read the lyrics on my leg. The panic inside me grew—no matter what I said, he'd know they had to do with Drew, and he'd lose his mind. I should have thought about that before I'd had the words tattooed on me, but now it was too late and I didn't know how he'd react—I just knew it wouldn't be good. I reached out and grabbed the hem of his shirt and pulled upward to distract him.

It worked, his attention shifting away from my tattoo as he seemingly remembered what he'd been planning to do and forgot about what had distracted him. Then he got what he wanted: fucking me up against a window where any number of people could see us.

I'd wanted to shower alone after Duncan had put my naked body on public display against my wishes as a bizarre way of staking his claim on me. It had left me feeling gross and slimy and upset about the whole experience, but Duncan didn't stray more than a few feet from my side. Even when I said I wanted privacy so I could get ready for dinner with him, he'd kissed my neck, his hands on my ass, and told me he wanted to watch me get ready. The only time he'd left me alone at all was when someone knocked on the door and he walked back into the bathroom carrying a vase of red roses.

"For you, baby," he said.

"Good god, Duncan," I said with an uncomfortable laugh. "You didn't need to get flowers."

He kissed my neck again, his new favorite spot to kiss, it seemed. "I know. But I thought you'd like them."

"It was very thoughtful of you," I said.

And it was. But I also was thinking about how much money those had cost on top of the trip. Duncan was spending a lot more money than he was usually comfortable with, and that made me anxious. I felt an immense amount of pressure to make sure this trip lived up to whatever his expectations were because of how much he was shelling out for it.

It was an hour and a half later when we sat down for dinner. My fingers had been itching to text Drew for a while now to get out everything I was feeling so maybe I could be more present with Duncan, but if I did, it would piss Duncan off. He was testy about all things Drew and it was better to just pretend Drew didn't exist around him. I hadn't even been able to let Drew know we'd landed safely like I'd promised to do because Duncan was looking over my shoulder when I powered my phone back on as we waited for the plane to taxi to a gate.

Dinner was fancy and delicious, though I felt rather out of place at the restaurant—it was the nicest establishment I'd ever been to, and while Duncan gave the impression of being comfortable and fitting in with the suit he wore, the sundress I'd packed wasn't appropriate attire, really. When Duncan had told me to pack something nice to wear, I hadn't realized he meant nicer than I wore when we went out to dinner in Brinkley.

We ordered dessert after our dinner dishes were cleared away. I wasn't hungry—I hadn't even been able to finish my dinner as tasty as it was, my stomach roiling uncomfortably—but Duncan had ordered dessert and a second bottle of wine for us anyway. By the time we left, I was likely to be rather drunk; I'd consumed probably two-thirds of the first bottle of wine myself. Maybe even more of it. Duncan had also had two IPAs before he moved on to the wine with me, so he was possibly going to be even more intoxicated than I was.

Duncan talked the entire time about what we were going to do each day, which he'd already picked out after finding several microbreweries in town. He debated with himself the apparent merits of each based on what he'd read online all the way through placing the order for dessert. Then, as the waiter walked away, he leaned forward, his eyes intense.

"I love you, Tasha Williams."

"I lo—"

"And you love me," he continued, cutting me off. "I think it's time for us to make this official. What do you think?"

"Official?" I echoed, cocking my head as I looked at him. Was that some kind of proposal? It couldn't be. We weren't that serious quite yet—we'd been dating less than a year. We hadn't even spent a night together yet.

He stared at me with no trace of humor. "Yes. Let's get married. We don't even have to wait—we can do it while we're here."

My breath stalled in my lungs. He wanted to get married and he wanted to do it right away. I hadn't expected that—*none* of it.

"Come on, baby, say yes."

I looked away, then coughed to buy some time. That wasn't what I wanted right then. I hadn't really thought seriously about marriage at all, let alone with Duncan—I hadn't even wanted to live together when he asked me to move in two months earlier. But he didn't just want to get married one day in the future, he wanted to do it right away. And while I didn't really care about having a big wedding, I wanted more than a few hours to get used to the idea of being someone's wife.

On the other hand, someone cared about me enough to want to marry me. I'd gone through how many guys before finding one who cared that much about me? It wasn't likely I'd find another man willing to marry someone damaged like me. If I didn't want to grow old alone, I needed to seize the opportunity before Duncan changed his mind. I *did* love him... at least I thought I did. Though I wasn't really sure what love was supposed to feel like. I cared about him, for sure, and more so than any of the other guys I'd dated. That was love, wasn't it?

Although, it was nothing like how I felt about Drew. Drew made me feel like every cell in my body was alive. No matter how upset or angry I was, when Drew was there, I was also happy—even if he was the reason I was upset or angry. And that's how I wanted to feel all the time. But that was asking too much—my expectations were too high. I felt that way with Drew because he knew and understood me in a way no one else possibly could because no one else had been there through everything he had.

Oh my god. I gasped. *I think I'm in love with Drew.* I raised my hand up and my fingertips rested gently over the corner of my mouth where he'd kissed me outside the airport. My chest hurt with the memory, and I couldn't breathe, the same way I hadn't been able to when it happened.

I shook my head. *No.* This couldn't be happening. Drew was my best friend.

"Tasha?" Duncan's voice broke into my spiraling thoughts. "What do you think? You'll marry me, right?"

"Y-yes," I stammered out, my thoughts scattered, jumping between Drew's lips touching mine with a warm, gentle, emotional kiss, and the impersonal claiming Duncan had done in the hotel. "B-but we should wait."

"Why? We want to marry each other, what's the point in waiting? And we're already here—we can get married tonight and the rest of this trip would be our honeymoon. We can have a party at home to tell friends and family and celebrate sometime after you've moved in and we've gotten settled."

"I..."

"Take a minute to think about it," he said. "I know it's a lot of excitement and happiness all at once. I've gotta take a leak and you can think about it while I'm gone." He stood and kissed the side of my neck. "I'll be back in a few, baby."

For the first minute he was gone, I stared blankly through the tabletop, trying to process what had just happened, what he clearly expected from me. I knew if I didn't agree, he would be devastated—he'd clearly expected me to be as on board with the idea as he was. When the waiter returned and set down our desserts, I realized I had a small window of time before Duncan returned and pulled my phone from the pocket in my dress.

My fingers flew across the screen to unlock it and press my speed dial for Drew. My thumb tapped rapidly against the phone as I waited for him to answer. I was sure he would. He'd only ever missed a call from me when he was with a patient and his phone wasn't on him, and I knew he didn't have patients that late in the day. He'd even stopped in the middle of sex with Becka before when I'd called, though I'd wished then that he hadn't because the last thing I'd wanted to do was think about him having sex with her.

Drew didn't answer. I hung up and dialed again, but it went straight to voicemail the second time—his phone was off.

I stared at the screen. He'd turned his phone off when I called?

My head moved side to side with sluggish slowness. That couldn't be. He wouldn't have done that. There must be some issue with cell signal wherever he was. Drew would never ignore me that way. He just wouldn't. Even if he was mad at me, which he seemed to have been for the last week, he wouldn't intentionally ignore me.

My eyes darted around, but I didn't see Duncan returning yet. I opened my text messages with Drew and began typing furiously,

hoping to get everything out and a response from him before Duncan returned.

I need you to call me. It's an emergency.

I'm here, in Vegas, with Duncan, and he asked me to marry him. Like tonight. And I don't know what to do.

He's nice, and I may never meet another nice guy who wants to marry me, so I should do it, right?

Except I don't think I want to be married.

I also don't want to be alone. I don't handle being alone very well—you know that. And I love him. At least I think I do. I just don't know about marriage.

But that's better than being alone, isn't it?

I need you.

Please pick up your phone and read these and call me. I need to talk to you. I'm scared and can't think straight right now. And I've had too much to drink.

I need you to help me figure this out because it's a big deal, and I don't have a lot of time. Duncan will be back soon, and I can't text you in front of him or he'll get really angry and he wants an answer and he's expecting me to say yes and I don't know what he'll do if I say no.

My fingers froze, hovering over the screen as something dawned on me. Duncan had planned the whole thing out. I'd thought he'd chosen Vegas because I'd mentioned once that I thought Vegas would be a cool place to visit, but he'd planned to come here because of being able to get married without waiting. That's why he was spending so much money—he'd expected me to say yes the whole time. This wasn't a spur of the moment thing for him like I'd thought. And for some reason, that bothered me. Spur of the moment was that kiss from Drew—the one I couldn't seem to stop thinking about.

> When you left, at the airport—did you kiss me on purpose? I mean where you did? Did you realize your lips were touching mine? Or was that an accident? I can't stop thinking about it and I need to know. Did you mean to kiss me, Drew? Did you actually want to? If you did, that… that changes things. Because I can still feel it.

Shit. I'd typed all that to him, then realized I was saying way too much and meant to delete it and start over but had hit the arrow to send the message in my rush. *Shit, shit, shit.* I was out of time. Duncan was returning from the bathroom. I shoved my phone back into my pocket, my stomach in knots.

"Are you ready to be my wife?" Duncan asked as he lowered himself into his chair across from me, wasting no time in getting to the point.

My mouth flapped a few times, no sound coming out.

"Tasha, baby?"

"I… this is really fast, Duncan…" I looked down toward my lap and tried to slide my phone out of my pocket without him noticing to see if Drew had responded yet. He hadn't.

"We've been together for about a year—that's a really long time."

Was it? I thought of my sixteen-year friendship with Drew as a long time. Was a year really all that long?

"You do love me, don't you?"

"Yes, of course I do."

"Then what's holding you back? We love each other, Tasha. Why *not* get married?"

"It's just so fast," I said again. I was trying to figure out what to say, but my already fuzzy thoughts were racing too rapidly. "I'm not sure I'm ready to be married yet. I don't... I like living by myself."

"I know, but you have to make sacrifices for relationships, right? We can sacrifice our independence. I know it's a big step, but we're ready for it, Tasha. We're good together, and I love you, and you're already mine—this just makes it official."

His words rubbed me the wrong way and I bristled. It felt like another way for him to stake his claim on me, much like what he'd done in the hotel. I lifted my wine glass and downed everything the waiter had poured when he dropped off the desserts. Duncan immediately refilled my glass.

"Drink up," he said. "It'll take the edge off your nerves. That's all this is, baby. It's just nerves. I know you want this as much as I do."

Do you? Because I don't think that's true.

I snuck another peek toward my lap where I'd left my phone after sneaking it out. Still nothing from Drew. *Shit!*

"Think about it, Tasha. We'll never spend another night alone because we'll always have each other. We'll never have to do anything alone ever again."

That sounded as reassuring as it did claustrophobic. I didn't want to be alone in general, but I also needed time for myself. He made it sound like there'd be no such thing as time by myself if we got married. My mind flashed to the hotel when I'd asked for privacy and instead he'd showered with me, then sat a few feet away, watching me dress and do my hair and makeup. Was that how it would be all the time if I agreed?

"There's a chapel not too far from here. I called them, and we can go there straight from dinner. We can be married in less than two hours, Tasha. You'd be my wife and I'd be your husband. A little over an hour, really. No waiting and worrying something might happen because it's already done. We'd have someone to spend the rest of our lives with—and not just someone, but the person we love most in the world."

The person *I* loved most in the world was in Chandler... and he was ignoring me.

"Come on, Tasha," Duncan continued. "You like to be spontaneous—well, this is spontaneous."

Except it wasn't, because he'd planned it from the start. And I had never said I liked to be spontaneous—I'd said I liked to try new things and have different experiences. I took another hefty swig of wine, my head already spinning from how much I'd had.

"Let's just go. You don't have to decide yet, but let's just go there and you can make a decision then. You'll be able to see it all, and pick a ring, and I know you'll realize you want this like I do."

A little less than two hours later, from the ladies' room at the chapel, I swayed even though I was sitting on the toilet; it felt like the room was moving around me. It had been years since I'd been that drunk, but Duncan had been shoveling alcohol at me, and I'd been sucking it down to get through the evening. After several failed attempts to unlock my phone, I ultimately succeeded and navigated to my text messages with Drew. My chest was filled with anger and sadness and regret, though convention dictated I should be ecstatic. Below my other—still unanswered—messages, I typed:

> The words on my leg are a lie.

> I needed you. And you ignored me.

> And now I'm a wife.

> I hate you.

Chapter Thirteen

Drew

Becka eyed me when I barreled into the kitchen twenty minutes or so after she'd brought my phone into the bathroom. I knew she'd heard me shouting and cussing, but I offered no explanation, deciding to ignore her and head straight to the coffee pot. There was already a pot brewing, so I stood there staring at it as I waited. Watson sat on the floor next to my feet, leaning heavily into my leg. I glanced at him, then back to the coffee pot. My leg was bouncing violently with a will of its own as I leaned onto my hands on the counter, and my knuckles were white where I grasped the edge.

Tasha was married.

To Duncan.

And I could have stopped it.

It was clear from her messages that she'd wanted me to tell her not to do it, clear that she didn't want to marry him but felt like she had no choice. I wanted to hunt Duncan down and hurt him for getting her drunk and pressuring her into getting married.

Even more, though, I wanted to beat the hell out of myself for being so damned self-pitying that I'd turned my phone off when she was trying to reach me.

"You okay?" Becka asked.

"Like you care," I muttered.

"I do, actually, Drew," she snapped. "Did something happen? To... you know, *her*?"

"Wouldn't you like it if something did," I bit back, my hands squeezing the counter even harder.

"Jeez, Drew—how could you say something like that? I don't want bad things to happen to her any more than I want them to happen to anyone else. I'm being sincere. You seem really, really upset right now after seeing your phone. I know I was pissed off you were getting texts from her, but it hadn't occurred to me that something might have happened to her."

I turned my head, my hands still on the edge of the countertop, and studied Becka. She had circles under her eyes, her shiny blonde hair in a messy ponytail. Her brow was furrowed and I could see genuine worry in her eyes. Mine filled with tears as some of my anger gave way to a searing pain in my chest. I turned back to face the coffee pot, clearing my throat.

"What happened, Drew?" she asked.

Screw coffee this morning. I couldn't stay in this apartment any longer, couldn't be still, couldn't listen to another word from Becka. I turned to head back to the bedroom to pack a duffel bag. It was supposed to be a rest day, but I was going to go into work early and hit the gym before my first client.

"I don't want to talk about it," I said as I passed Becka. "I'm going to work."

I pushed myself dangerously hard in the gym, especially since there was no one there to spot me if I failed on a set, but I needed to do something to release the toxic energy building up inside me. I was hurt and so damn pissed off I didn't know what to do with it. The last time I'd felt that level of pain and anger mixed together, I'd just turned seventeen. It was the first time Tasha told me about what exactly her stepfather did to her when she'd snuck out and met up with me afterwards one night. I'd barely been able to hear everything she said because my ears rang with all the emotion pulsing through me at the thought of him doing those things to her.

The next day, I'd walked outside and waited on the sidewalk in front of Tasha's house like I did every day before we walked to school together. That morning, her stepfather walked outside at the same time she did. Tasha must have seen the rage that consumed me because she widened her eyes and gave me a small headshake. It had taken everything in me to stay where I was. But then he touched her, his hand on her lower back, almost her ass, and kissed her cheek. I could see the panicky revulsion in her eyes, the stiffness in her body.

I lost it; I dropped my backpack and went after him. I got in a few good hits to his face before he beat me to the ground. He might have killed me, but Tasha threw her body over top of mine. He picked her up and flung her off, but then I passed out. I spent a month in juvenile detention after being cuffed to the bed in the hospital. The only regret I ever had was that I had no way of even talking to Tasha for that month, let alone to be there for her at night when she was escaping the hell she lived in.

I was told he was pressing charges and that I would be tried as an adult and it would go on my permanent record. I hadn't cared—even if I'd never been able to go to college or get a job, it would have been worth it. But for some reason I still didn't know, he'd dropped the charges before the court date and the arrest was expunged from my record when I turned eighteen. I always suspected he realized that if I was in a courtroom, I'd have spilled all his dirty secrets.

And now I felt that same consuming fury and hurt, but I didn't know what to do with it. Duncan was on the other side of the country, and, really, I was angriest with myself, anyway. I was the one who'd let her down. I'd promised her I'd always be there no matter what. That no matter where I was physically, I would never actually leave her side. And then I'd intentionally ignored her when she needed me.

I hadn't known she needed me, but that didn't really matter. I never should have ignored her to begin with.

Drained and drenched, I rinsed off in the locker room shower, threw on my clothes for work, and made it into the main therapy room just on time for my first patient. I wondered as I went through the motions, struggling to focus, if I should just cancel the rest of my patients for the day. But when I realized I had no idea what I'd do with myself if I *did*, I decided against it.

For the midday hour I had no patients, I stared at my phone, debating calling Tasha. I desperately wanted to, but I was also afraid. I didn't know what to say. I could make up some story about not getting her call and messages, but I wouldn't. I wasn't willing to lie to her. So I was back at square one with no idea what to say to her. I was sorry—more sorry than I'd ever been about something in my life—but those words weren't enough. So I didn't call. I decided I'd call in the evening, after I had time to figure it out.

Except that evening came, and I was no closer to figuring it out. Alone in the apartment, I sat on the floor in the kitchen, leaning back against the cabinets, and told Watson everything as he alternately whined, shoved his nose under my hand, licked my face, and laid on my leg. But after going through everything with him, I was no closer to figuring out what to say to Tasha if I called and she answered.

I wiped my face with the back of my hand and leaned my head against the cabinet behind me, staring up at the ceiling. My life had become a total clusterfuck. And not just since I found out about the awards ceremony. It already was before that in some ways.

The most important ways.

Professionally, I was doing well. But outside of that... I'd forgotten who I was. Forgotten what things made me *me*. Forgotten what I even liked. The week I spent with Tasha had brought all that back. I liked trying new things and playing guitar. I liked making jokes and snarky humor and laughing until I cried. I liked working out with someone who pushed me to work harder as much as they made me laugh, and having friendly competition with fitness. I liked being around someone who would speak their mind no matter what, and would not only tell me when I was being a dumb ass, but was also my biggest cheerleader. All of those things had been missing in my life for so long, I'd forgotten what they were like and how important they were to me.

But now I remembered, and I could see how incongruent my life was with what I wanted from it. All because of Tasha. She was my homebase, my north star. Together, we didn't know how else to be other than ourselves.

It was over with Becka; I knew it without a doubt. What I wanted from life was incompatible with what she wanted from life. And who I truly was wasn't who she loved. She loved the version of me she'd molded me into—an illusion. And I wasn't sure I'd ever actually loved her in return. I'd cared about her; I'd been spending my life with her. But when I thought about how differently I felt about her and Tasha... I didn't see that I'd ever loved anyone other than Tasha. If that meant I ended up alone, then I'd end up alone. I'd rather that than live as someone I wasn't anymore.

I sighed, scratching behind Watson's ears. I'd tell Becka that weekend and find a long-term hotel to stay in—hopefully one that would allow me to bring Watson with me. I didn't want to leave him there with her. The lease on the apartment was up in a few months, and I'd pay it up for Becka so she'd only need to worry about utilities and finding a place she could afford on her own. Then I was going to start my search for a new practice in Brinkley. I didn't know how long it would take, but I was going to find a way to show Tasha how sorry I was and that I was ready to do anything to be a part of her life, whatever that would mean now.

Chapter Fourteen

Tasha

Duncan and I argued for the entirety of the plane trip back from Vegas about where I was going to live. Now that we were married, he expected me to move in with him immediately. But I didn't *want* to live with him. The only person I'd ever lived with since I'd left home when I was seventeen was Drew, and I had no desire to change that. I liked my independence and my ability to be completely alone when I wanted to be. Not to mention that I still had the better part of a year left on my lease. And because I'd been drunk the entirety of our trip, I was now hungover and argumentative.

We were still arguing as we headed toward ground transportation, and I suggested we get separate rides.

"No," Duncan said with finality, his hand clamping around my forearm. "You're my wife now, Tasha. We are not riding separately. And we are not living separately."

He was hurting my arm, but rather than making a scene with how busy it was around us, I agreed. "Okay."

His grip loosened and I pulled my arm away. He spoke animatedly about the party he wanted to throw to announce and celebrate our marriage, and about how surprised all our friends would be—though he really meant *his* friends because I didn't have any now that Drew had turned his back on me. I half-listened and tried, without success, to come up with some way to convince him to let me stay in my apartment at least until my lease was up.

We went to my apartment first so I could pack up a large suitcase of my things to take over to Duncan's. When we arrived, though, my aversion to moving in with him grew, and I suggested I stay alone in my apartment for the night, giving the explanation that I could get a lot packed up that way and be able to move in sooner. He studied my face for a minute, then shook his head.

"No. As much as I want all your stuff out of this shithole as soon as possible, we just got married, baby, and I don't want to be apart from you. You can pack your stuff while I'm working tomorrow."

"I can do *some* packing tomorrow, but I have to work, too." It was true; I hadn't worked on either of the books my editor was expecting from me since Drew had come to visit. Every time I sat down at my desk, all I could think about was the story I was drafting based on mine and Drew's history together. I needed to get refocused on the books that I was under contract to deliver, though I might *have* to get out the new story first.

"Work?" he asked, in the most condescending tone.

"Yes, work. I have to work on my books. I have deadlines."

Duncan huffed dismissively. "That's not real work, Tasha. I have an actual job that pays me that I have to do. You don't, so you can work on packing."

I clenched my jaw. "My writing is a real job, Duncan," I ground out. "And I do get paid—I was paid an advance for my books, and I'll get royalties after they're published. Assuming I meet my contract deadlines. So, no, I can't blow off working."

He rolled his eyes but didn't say anything.

That infuriated me. Drew had ignored me as if I couldn't have something serious I needed him for, as if he hadn't promised to always be there for me, and now Duncan was blowing off my life's passion and work.

"Get out, Duncan," I seethed. "This is my apartment, and I don't want you here right now."

His jaw clenched, and his eyes narrowed.

"I'm staying here tonight. *Alone*. Because I want to and it's *my* decision where I sleep at night."

"Not when you're a married woman, it isn't," he hissed out.

"Married or not, I'm still my own person, Duncan."

Duncan strode toward me, and I instinctively backed up until my back slammed into the living room wall. His body and face were less than an inch from mine. I could smell the alcohol on his breath from what he'd been drinking on the plane, and it turned my stomach, reminding me of my mom and stepdad when they'd get angry after drinking and corner me just like this. Fear paralyzed me.

"The only person you are now," he started, speaking with a deliberate slowness, "is mine, Tasha. *Mine*. You're my wife now, which means I'm the one who decides how you spend your time, who you spend it with, and where you do it."

His palm slammed the wall next to my face and I jumped. He hadn't even touched me, and yet it was the most afraid of him I'd ever been. It was the most afraid I'd felt of someone since I'd left home the week after high school graduation. Drew had found a place for us to stay in the city where we were both going to college. It was the first time in my life I'd felt safe when I went to bed, and it was when I promised myself I'd never go to bed feeling unsafe again.

I'd kept that promise to myself... until now. I'd never spent an entire night with anyone before except Drew—not even Duncan. Until Vegas. And now, backed against the wall, aware his hand could have hit me, I was more afraid of what Duncan would do if I refused to go with him again than I was of what might happen later that night.

I nodded quickly. "O-okay," I stuttered out.

He glared at me, then stepped back, his hand sliding unhurriedly from the wall next to me.

I scurried from the room and was grateful he remained behind as I pulled out my full-sized suitcase, tears skating down my cheeks. I swiped them repeatedly with my palms as I tried to settle my mind enough to think through what I should prioritize packing, but I couldn't; it was racing, trying to figure out how I'd gotten myself into this situation.

Drew had tried to warn me. He'd told me he didn't like Duncan. I'd figured he just said that because he didn't like any guy I dated. But I should have listened to him. Instead, I was so determined that anything was better than being alone, so determined that Duncan was really a nice guy and that I wasn't ever going to do any better than him.

And then I'd fucking married him? What the hell was I thinking?

I was thinking I was desperate not to be alone. That Duncan wasn't giving me much of a choice. And I was drunk—no shape to be making a decision like that. If I'd been completely sober, there's no way I'd have gone through with it. I would have found a way to convince Duncan to have a long engagement or something. At least I thought I would have. I wouldn't have sent all those panicked texts to Drew only to have Drew ignore me. I wouldn't now be stuck married to a man who it turned out wasn't as nice as I'd thought he was.

I should have known better, really. If nothing else, I should have realized what Duncan might be capable of after he'd bruised my arm at the brewery, but he'd never done something like that before and had been so apologetic that I'd believed it was a fluke and wouldn't happen again. Now, I knew he would if I disagreed with him—he'd done it in the airport. And he might do worse if I continued to piss him off. I couldn't help but feel that him hitting the wall so close to my face had been a kind of warning.

I slipped my phone out of my pocket and stared at the screen. I wasn't sure what I was expecting; Drew had never gone so long without responding. Ever. Even when he'd lost his phone once and needed a new one, he'd called me from a payphone to let me know. This was different. I didn't understand why, but I knew it was. He was shutting me out of his life for some reason. It had taken longer, but in the end he'd proven himself to be as impermanent as everyone else in my life had always been. And while that wasn't so different— having people disappear on me—I'd never thought Drew would be one of them, and that hurt more than anything else in my life ever had.

I wanted to call him. I wanted to lock my bedroom door, call Drew, apologize to him for whatever I'd done to make him want nothing to do with me, beg him to be my friend again, and implore him to come help me get out of this situation I'd gotten myself into because I had no idea how I was going to extricate myself. And I would have done it if I'd thought he would answer, but I was sure he wouldn't—he hadn't even responded to my text messages. Why would he answer if I called again? Besides, even if he did, he was halfway across the country—there was nothing he could do about Duncan being in the next room.

The next morning, I pretended to be asleep when Duncan got up for work and kissed me goodbye. I didn't move until I was positive he'd left and wouldn't come back, then I jumped out of bed, showered, and threw on my clothes. Duncan had insisted I give him the key to my apartment the night before, and I was hoping he'd left it lying around somewhere. If I could find it, I'd be able to go back to my apartment and lock myself in. If I couldn't, that wouldn't be an option.

I was still searching frantically when there was a knock on the door. I froze, staring at it for a minute, confused about why someone might be knocking. Tiptoeing, I peered through the peephole. It was a flower delivery guy. I unlocked the door and opened it.

There were two dozen roses from Duncan, with a card that read: *For my beautiful wife on the first of many mornings together in our new life.* It was sweet, but it just made me feel sick. Though I then felt guilty for my reaction. Duncan had done something really thoughtful and written a romantic message. Maybe the remnants of a severe hangover the day before had screwed with my head and made things seem worse with him than they actually were. It was hard to believe a man who'd do something like send flowers with a sweet note could be the monster he'd become in my mind.

I walked the roses into the kitchen and found there another note held to the refrigerator with a magnet. "Good morning, my beautiful wife. I hope you have a wonderful day. I love you." I touched the note with my fingertips, feeling my anger toward him begin melting away. Maybe I was being unfair and bratty. Drew *had* told me on several occasions that I never outgrew being a brat. Duncan obviously loved me. And I'd married a man who did thoughtful things like leave me notes and send me flowers. I could have done a lot worse.

Really, I was lucky.

Chapter Fifteen

Tasha

My middle finger on my right hand tapped over the "k" on my keyboard as I contemplated the last word I'd typed. The word wasn't quite right for what the main character in my novel was feeling, but I was drawing a blank. I yawned and arched my back to give it a stretch. I hadn't slept well the night before. And while I never did the last few nights leading up to a gyno checkup, which I had in a few hours, I hadn't slept well since I'd moved in with Duncan two months earlier.

I ran through the alphabet for inspiration and found it when I got to N. Nostalgic. That was the word I was looking for. Why the hell had it been so hard for me to remember that word? I shook my head. Time for a break. *Always* time for a break, it seemed. My thoughts were constantly wandering to the story I *didn't* have a contract for rather than the two I *did*. The pull to write the new one was even stronger since the estrangement between Drew and me. I'd planned to just get it out, but Duncan had begun reading over my shoulder, taking an unusual interest in what I was writing after he'd caught a glance of the screen and voiced his suspicion that I was writing about

Drew. That had happened not long after we'd had a fight about Drew. It was the only big fight we'd had since the one in my apartment the day we got back from Vegas.

Duncan had asked me for the passcode to my phone so he could look at the pictures I took in Vegas. When I offered to unlock it for him instead, he'd instantly become suspicious that I didn't want him to know my passcode, and I'd had to give it to him before he'd believe I wasn't trying to hide something. He hadn't just looked at our pictures from Vegas, however. He'd scrolled back through my photos from when Drew was visiting, including the pictures I'd taken when we got our thighs tattooed together.

I'd watched the rage building in Duncan as he scrolled and frozen, trying to make myself small and unobtrusive. I had no idea what to expect. It was the angriest I'd ever seen him—even more than in my apartment the day he hit the wall next to my face. He'd turned the phone around and shoved it into my face, demanding I explain. I'd stuttered out that Drew and I had gotten tattoos while he was visiting. I'd intentionally avoided telling Duncan exactly when I'd gotten the tattoo and that Drew had not only been with me, but had gotten a matching one.

"What the fuck is this, Tasha?"

I swallowed and stepped back as he stepped closer. "It's a picture. From when I got my tattoo."

"That's not just *your* leg," he ground out, his voice low and menacing.

"D-drew got a tattoo, too."

"I can see that. You guys got matching tattoos."

"Yeah."

"I thought those were just lyrics you liked—did you get them for him?"

I opened my mouth, but couldn't think of how to answer his question fast enough. He flipped the phone back around and scrolled through a few photos until I knew he'd reached the close-ups I'd taken of each of our tattoos. His eyes moved over the screen; he was reading what was on our legs. My stomach dropped and I had an urge to run from the apartment. But I knew that if I did something like that, it would make things worse, so I remained still.

He shifted to glare at me—he looked mad enough to burn the building down around us. He let out a noise that began as a low growl and grew in volume.

"Duncan—" I started, desperate to calm him before things spiraled out of control.

He shoved me, two hands against my chest. I flew backward, tripping and landing on his glass coffee table. The glass broke and cut into my legs. The fury in his eyes disappeared to be replaced by panic. Apologies flew out of his mouth over and over as he rushed me to the hospital to have the glass removed and the gashes stitched up.

When they asked what happened, he told them I'd been looking at my phone while walking through the living room and had tripped over the coffee table as a result. He looked at me with pleading, remorseful eyes and I didn't have the heart to contradict him. I nodded in agreement with his blatant lie.

Duncan had been almost nothing but loving since then, sending me flowers almost daily, texting me to check on me throughout the day, and he'd given me a diamond necklace that he insisted I wear every day. I only wore jewelry when going out, but made an exception when he became suspicious of me not wearing it around the clock. He was remorseful about what he'd done, and I knew it had been an accident, and he hadn't done anything like that since. I had some hope he never would again.

My phone rang, startling me out of my thoughts, and I answered it. The call was from my doctor's office, telling me my appointment for later that day needed to be shifted up—I now had to be there in thirty minutes, and it would take me nearly that long just to get there.

I flew into the bedroom and changed out of my sweats, then threw on some deodorant—there was no time left for showering—brushed my teeth, and tossed my hair into a sloppy ponytail. With any luck, I'd still make it on time—we'd see how long the metro took today. Heart pounding with dread about my appointment, I texted Duncan on my way out the door to let him know I was going to be at the doctor earlier than he was expecting so he wouldn't come home to surprise me for lunch like he sometimes did and find me gone.

I found a seat on the metro car, which I plopped into gratefully; my legs were already getting shaky. I went through this every six months. It used to be every four months, so this was an improvement. With any luck, it would soon become an annual thing. And while they'd found nothing since my surgery for ovarian cancer years earlier, I still got just as nervous before every exam as I had for the first one.

As the metro train hurtled over the rails, I couldn't help but think about Drew. It was Drew who'd held me when I found out at twenty-two that I had cancer, who'd gone with me to talk to the doctor about my treatment options. It was Drew who'd gone to the hospital with me for my surgery and come home with me afterwards to take care of me while I recovered. He'd even come to every checkup for the first year so I wouldn't have to go alone. I debated texting him for some reassurance, my finger hovering over my phone. He had viewing rights to my personal calendar and had kept track of my appointments ever since the diagnosis. He always called or texted within an hour of the appointment ending to find out how it had gone. But would he do that this time? Was he still paying attention to when my appointments were? I slipped my phone back into my pocket without sending a message.

My jaw clenched as I perused the ceiling tiles from my prone position on the exam table. I hated these exams. I was so sick of being poked between my legs and having fingers and metal instruments shoved inside me. The exams were necessary—I knew that—but instead of getting easier over time, each one was harder to stomach.

"Scoot closer to the end of the table and spread your knees a little wider," Dr. Luca said, a hand on my knee.

I scooted and forced my legs to widen, though they were tense.

"Relax a little, please," she said, inserting two fingers.

I tried, but I sucked at relaxing my pelvic floor. We'd talked about it a thousand times. She'd even suggested I see a pelvic floor physical therapist, but the thought of having more people messing with me down there was a hard no, so I hadn't done it.

"Arg!" I exclaimed, a sudden sharp pain near the inside of my right hip joint.

"Hm," Dr. Luca said. She pushed her fingers harder inside me and pressed down over that spot again.

"Ow, that hurts."

She moved to the other side. "What about over here?"

I shook my head. "Nothing."

Dr. Luca withdrew her hand and pulled her gloves off, rolling her chair over to her laptop. She tapped for a while, then turned back to me. "I think you've got a cyst," she said.

My heart refused to beat.

She gave me an encouraging smile. "Don't worry yet. You know ovarian cysts aren't all that uncommon."

"For me, they are," I muttered.

"That doesn't mean this is anything other than a benign cyst. It could also be something muscular. I want you to make an appointment to get an ultrasound, though, just to be on the safe side." She scribbled onto a piece of paper and pulled it off, handing it to me. It was a referral. "This week, if you can. And I'll call you as soon as I get the results."

I dressed and left the office in a daze, calling the same imaging center I'd used before to make an appointment. They had an opening shortly, so I hopped back into the elevator and rode up to their office.

An hour later, I walked out with confirmation that I had a cyst on my remaining ovary—a *large* cyst. But was it benign? Or was it cancer again?

Chapter Sixteen

Drew

Wiping sweat from my brow, I squinted at the clock on the wall in the gym in my new apartment building in Brinkley. My old practice had brought on a replacement a few weeks after I'd let them know I was going to leave, and I'd moved from the hotel I was living in with Watson in Chandler to one in Brinkley until I moved into the apartment I was now living in two weeks earlier. I'd found a new practice that was looking to become the first practice in the region that specialized in working with trauma survivors and requiring all practitioners to undergo the related training. It was exactly what I'd hoped to find somewhere. I also worked with them to implement a rotational program at Brinkley General Hospital, so I'd work a few days a week with patients who required physical therapy before they could be discharged. I'd never worked in a hospital setting before and looked forward to the new experience and being able to put my knowledge of trauma to use more often. In just over a month, I'd be seeing patients again as a full partner at my new practice.

Right now, however, I was just trying to keep myself busy to pass the time until Tasha's appointment was over. I'd never ended up calling her or responding to all the messages she'd sent me from Vegas because I'd never been able to come up with a sufficient way to apologize to her. Part of me was also afraid of finding out she was happy with Duncan. I was no longer wrestling with what exactly my feelings were for Tasha. She was my best friend *and* I loved her... in a way I'd never loved Becka. It was why I'd moved to Brinkley—because it's where she was. I just hadn't figured out how to tell her I was sorry or risk apologizing and having her still hate me for what I'd done. But the only thing that mattered right now was that she got a clean bill of health.

My eyes sought out the clock again. She might still be in her appointment, but I couldn't wait any longer. I had to know she was okay. And maybe breaking this silence between us to ask about her appointment would lead to us repairing our relationship—a repair that was needed because of me.

Sometimes I wondered if maybe my parents had been right about me being worthless after all. The one person who'd never believed it was the person I'd turned my back on when she needed me.

Worthless or not, though, I *had* to know if she was okay.

I grabbed my phone and unlocked it, my eyes scanning through all the last messages Tasha had sent me again. I didn't need to read them—I'd read them so many times I could recite them from memory—but I couldn't help it. I read all of them several times a day when I opened my texts with her and wondered how to fix what had happened between us. I typed and deleted a message several times, trying to figure out how to start. Did I apologize first? Or should I preface my question with something like, "I know we haven't talked in a while"? Ultimately, I decided to just get to the point and base my next message off her response.

Are you still in your appointment?

I moved around the fitness center, continuing to work out, carrying my phone with it open on my messages so I'd know the instant she responded. After thirty minutes, she replied.

My appointment was changed.

I waited, but she didn't send anything else. I opened up her calendar on my phone, but it was still showing the original appointment.

I don't see a new one on your calendar.

She didn't respond to my message. Her calendar didn't update either.

Fuck.

After several sleepless nights, I tried again, sending another text asking her what the doctor had said. Three little dots to indicate she was typing appeared, but then she must have decided not to send whatever she'd typed because no message ever came through. It gave me hope, though, my heart beating hard and fast in my chest. I didn't want to talk about my feelings for her over text, but she'd said in one of her last messages that she couldn't stop thinking about me kissing her at the airport. Maybe if I told her it was the same for me, she'd stop shutting me out.

I can't stop thinking about kissing you, either.

I spent the next several days with my time split between walking and jogging with Watson and lifting in the fitness center in my building. When I was too physically exhausted to do any more, I showered, then played my guitar, even though it meant thinking about Tasha. I'd never once played without thinking about her and the hours and hours I'd played and sang to her throughout our lives. I'd been so sure my last message would bring a response—*anything*—but it hadn't. And now I didn't know what to do. I'd confessed something significant, and it hadn't been enough. I had no idea what else might get her to talk to me. I considered telling her more, elaborating on what I'd already sent, but I didn't want to tell her how I felt about her in a text message; that was a conversation I needed to have with her in person.

A week after the last message I'd sent to Tasha, I'd just gotten back from a run and was downing a glass of water in my kitchen, Watson lapping up water from his bowl, when my phone pinged with an incoming text. I stared at it for a moment, the number vaguely familiar, though I couldn't place *why* it was until I opened it. I read the words on the screen twice before they registered and I understood why I'd recognized the number; I'd only stared at it anxiously for hours on end, waiting for updates to come through when Tasha had surgery to remove her cancerous ovary. My hands shook and my heart raced, just like they had back then, because I'd received a notification text from the hospital providing a status update on Tasha's surgery.

Tasha was having surgery. The cancer must have come back.

I spun around and took two steps toward the door, shook my head, then set off toward my bedroom. I made it halfway there when I pivoted back toward the door. My thoughts were racing and scattered simultaneously, and I couldn't figure out what to do first. Did I leave immediately? Did I at least put on dry, clean clothes first? Did I shower?

Damn it! Think, Drew!

The message said she was in pre-op, which meant she hadn't gone back for surgery yet. The last time this happened, they'd let me go back with her after the pre-op procedures were done while she was waiting to be rolled back to the operating room. If I hurried, I might make it in time to see her before the surgery started.

I grabbed my keys and wallet from the bowl on the counter and seconds later was on my way to Brinkley General Hospital.

Chapter Seventeen

Tasha

Even with my eyes closed, I could still see the ceiling I'd been staring at for over an hour. I knew there were nine rectangular tiles across and thirteen lengthwise in the room. I'd finished my pre-op procedures, and now I was just waiting to be rolled back. Despite the fact that this was a more minor surgery intended only to remove the cyst and have it biopsied, all I could think about was the last time I'd been in a room like this—knowing part of my reproductive system was riddled with cancer. What if it was again? Would surgery fix it this time if it was? Would it matter? Was there any reason to fight to stay alive this time? I'd had Drew before, but now we might as well be strangers. Would Duncan even let me tell Drew if it was cancer again? What was it going to be like recovering from surgery with Duncan instead of Drew?

Duncan had brought me in, and he'd wanted to stay with me, his eyes moist with worry, but I'd convinced him to leave and go to work after he dropped me off. I hadn't told him they'd have allowed him to come back with me because I needed a break from him. Ever since

I'd told him about the need for a biopsy, up until it was time to leave for the hospital, he'd been optimistic it wasn't cancer.

Too optimistic.

It was infuriating. The way he dismissed my worry made me want to scream at him. I knew he meant well, that he thought telling me I was worried for no reason would help me worry less, but he didn't know what it was like to have been through this before only to find out I *did* have cancer. And I didn't like the conflicting emotions I had when he looked at me with so much love and worry in his eyes after what he'd done a week earlier.

He'd been closer to my phone than I was when Drew had texted me that he couldn't stop thinking about kissing me. The entire message had shown on the preview on my lock screen. It was like watching Bruce Banner turn into the Hulk. Duncan's body gave the impression of growing in size, his skin reddening, and the air around him charged with anger and violence. He'd demanded to know what Drew was talking about.

I told him about when Drew and I had kissed when we were teens, and he swore he'd always known there was something between us. I'd told him there wasn't, that we'd agreed then that it was like kissing a sibling. Duncan had narrowed his eyes at me and unlocked my phone, then scrolled through my messages with Drew. He didn't have to go far to see the message I'd sent to Drew that first night in Vegas talking about the kiss at the airport.

That's when Duncan exploded. I remembered the look on his face, in his eyes, the look that said he wanted to hurt me, and then the back of his arm caught me in the face, sending me flying off the stool where I'd been sitting at his bar-height table. I'd lost consciousness briefly and came to with Duncan cradling me in his arms, apologizing over and over as he rocked me. There'd been a gash on my cheek, my nose had bled for a long time, and I'd ended up with a black eye from catching the corner of the table as I'd gone down. When we'd arrived at the hospital an hour and a half earlier for my surgery, the bruising and healing gash had been explained away as clumsiness. I'd supposedly leaned too far over when trying to reach for my purse and fallen out of my chair.

But I couldn't really even think about Duncan's extreme jealousy or violent outbursts right then—not when I was about to undergo surgery because I might have cancer again. In my mind's eye, I counted the ceiling tiles again, my thumbs beating against one another where my hands were clasped over my midsection as I laid back on the hospital bed. They'd told me after my pre-op procedures that the operating room was running a little behind, so it might be a while before I was taken back. I understood; I knew how it went. Every second was torture, but it wasn't anyone's fault. I'd texted Duncan to let him know, so he wouldn't worry that he wasn't getting notified of me being in recovery anytime soon, then told him they were taking my cell phone so I wouldn't have to keep texting him.

There was a soft swish like the privacy curtain at my feet was moving, but no one said anything, so I assumed it was for someone next to me. But then my skin broke out in goosebumps. The air had changed, and, somehow, I knew that Drew was there. It wasn't possible, but I could feel his presence nonetheless. I squeezed my eyes shut harder, clasped my fingers more tightly together, not wanting the bizarre sense of his presence to disappear. I wished it was real, that he was actually there with me. He was the only person I wanted right then, as much as Duncan would go off the deep end if he knew that. Or if Drew ever came near me again. Though, right then, I wouldn't even care what Duncan might do to me afterwards if I could just have Drew there long enough to get me through the surgery.

Something warm touched my hand and my eyes flew open, my heart skipping a beat. I hadn't been imagining anything—Drew was there. He was actually standing right next to my hospital bed, his palm now resting over my hands.

"I'm so scared," I whispered, starting to cry. In that instant, I knew there'd be a reason to fight to live just as there had been last time: the man looking down at me.

Drew perched on the edge of the bed next to my hip and pulled me into his arms. He cradled my head against his chest and held me tight as I cried out all my fear and worry over what Dr. Luca might find when she opened me up. Once I'd drained most of it out, I pulled back, wiping my face with my hands. Drew looked around and found a box of tissues, bringing it over for both of us to use.

"How bad is it?" he asked, his hand gripping mine tightly.

I shook my head, staring through him. "I... I don't know. It might not be anything. I have a cyst. Dr. Luca found it at my appointment the other week. It's big, but they can't tell if it's cancerous. Today they're going to cut it off and do a biopsy to find out. I won't know for a few days or so if it's cancer or not." I looked up at him, my breath shallow. "But I'm so afraid it is, Drew."

"I am, too," he said gravely, squeezing my hand even harder.

I squeezed him back.

"But if it is, you'll get through it. You've done it once and you can—and will—do it again if you need to. And I'll be right here—you weren't alone before and you won't be this time, either. I promise."

I nodded vigorously, feeling so much remorse crashing over my head for the last few months. For having been so stupid that I succumbed to Duncan's pressure to get married, for the things I'd said to Drew via text, for having ignored him when he texted me recently. "I'm sorry."

"Oh, god, Nats," he said, his voice breaking. He wiped under his eyes as they stared into mine with a breathtaking intensity. "I'm the one who's sorry. So fucking sorry. I didn't..." He paused, his jaw trembling. "I didn't know how to tell you how much... I'm so goddamn sorry."

"Me, too," I whispered, giving him a watery smile.

Everything in my life was screwed up, and there was a possibility I had cancer again, but at least Drew was there right then. We studied each other for a long time, as if it had been years—not the months it actually had been—since we'd last seen each other. Drew's eyes kept getting stuck on my cheek and eye, and I knew what he was seeing. I didn't want him to ask me about it. I swallowed and turned to face the other wall so he couldn't see my face anymore.

"You smell like shit, you know," I said. It was a bit of an exaggeration, though not much. He smelled like Drew—vetiver and orange—and sweat, with a little bit of body odor like his deodorant had recently reached its capacity for odor control. But it didn't actually bother me—I'd once been used to that smell when we lived closer and worked out together. I found it comforting more than anything else. I just wanted to distract him from my face.

He let out a small chuckle. "I'd just gotten back from running with Watson when I got the notification, and I came straight here."

"What notification?"

"That you were in pre-op."

I flipped my head back to look at him. "You got a notification about that?"

He lowered his chin, his brow furrowed.

"Oh my god," I muttered, suddenly realizing I'd forgotten to update my emergency contacts with the hospital system. "Duncan..." He wasn't going to get the notification I'd told him he would after the surgery, and he was going to be furious about that. I could never tell him he didn't get the notifications because they had gone to Drew—that would send him over the edge.

Drew's face hardened. "I can see the fear in your eyes, Tasha," he said. "And I can see..." His voice trailed off and he touched my face gently with his fingertips. "Marks I never thought I'd see on you again."

"It's not what it looks like," I said hastily, turning away again and choking down my shame. I'd never flat-out lied to Drew before, and I was sure he'd be able to see right through me.

"Really?" he asked sarcastically.

I winced. "It's not like that," I said quietly, thinking of my mom and stepdad. They were mean and enjoyed hurting me just for the sake of doing it. And they did it all the time. Duncan wasn't like them. He was mostly a nice enough guy who just lost his temper sometimes. And it wouldn't have been a problem at all if I hadn't done things to make him that angry to begin with. "I was trying to reach for my purse and reached too far and fell out of my chair and hit the table on the way down," I said, repeating what Duncan had told the nurses.

As soon as the words were out, I knew I'd said the wrong thing. Why the hell had I said that to Drew? He knew I didn't use a purse and wouldn't have been reaching for one.

"I know you're lying to me, Tasha," Drew said after a long moment of silence. He gathered my hands in his, his jaw working back and forth for a while. "It doesn't matter how many lies you tell me, though. I'm always going to be here when you're ready to tell me the truth. And I'm not going to be mad at you. Okay? I'm here. I'll always be here. I'll never leave you."

His words irritated me—if they were true, we wouldn't have been talking about bruises on my face because I wouldn't have married Duncan. Not even Drew meant it when he said "never." No one ever did—never was too long a time. "Except when you do," I snapped, pulling my hands back and crossing my arms over my chest.

He sucked in a sharp breath, hurt settling into his features. "I deserved that," he said. "I made a mistake. A huge one. But it's one I'll never make again."

"Never. Right," I muttered. "Because never lasted such a long time before."

"I fucked up, Tasha. But I won't fuck up like that again. I promise you that. I'm always going to be here from now on."

My gaze flitted over him, then away. He *was* there when I needed him this time—maybe even more than I had in Vegas. But how?

"How did you get here so fast?" I asked. "Chandler is a few hours away by plane, but you made it here less than an hour after they called me back from the waiting room."

Drew swallowed and let out a sigh. "Becka and I split up the day after you married Duncan, and I'd already started the process to leave my practice in Chandler. As soon as they had a replacement for me, I moved to Brinkley. I live in an apartment less than a mile from here."

He was local? "What?"

He nodded solemnly. "That week I spent here with you opened my eyes, Tasha. It took me a little bit after I got back to fully realize everything and do something about it, but after that week here, I couldn't go back to the life I had before. If I'm being honest, deep down, I already knew before I even left that I was going to come here to be near you like I promised you I would years ago."

My thoughts bounced around in my head like a pinball machine. He was there, in the same town as me again. Not only that, but he'd come because of me.

Duncan could never find out.

"And I'm not going anywhere unless you do," Drew added.

He leaned forward and pressed a kiss to my forehead. My eyelids lowered as my shoulders dropped from my ears. Then he kissed the corner of my mouth again, just like he had at the airport. He stayed there for a long time, his breath washing over my face, his sweaty, musky scent filling my nostrils. I should have told him to stop, or pushed him back, but I didn't. I didn't even turn away from the kiss. Because the longer he was there, the calmer I became. The more I felt that somehow things would work out and I'd be okay, and I could barely remember the last time I'd felt that way.

The first thing I saw when the nurses rolled me from recovery into a regular room was Drew. I was still a bit foggy from the anesthesia and felt rather out of it, but seeing Drew set me at ease. He was wearing different clothes than he had been earlier—sweats and a t-shirt rather than sweaty athletic shorts and tank—and his hair looked clean. He must have gone home and showered. He looked tense—his whole body did—but he relaxed a little when we made eye contact and even gave me a small smile. As soon as the nurses had me situated and said Dr. Luca would be in shortly to talk to us and left, Drew dragged a chair to my side and pulled up one of my hands, kissing the back of it.

"How're you feeling?" he asked, his eyes searching mine.

I looked around at the ceiling. "I don't know. A little loopy."

His smile broadened. "That's normal. The update said everything went well, though it doesn't give any details. We'll get more information from Dr. Luca when she gets in here."

I gave a nod and closed my eyes; I was tired. Drew brushed a hand over my forehead, moving my matted hair off my skin, and began to hum the song the lyrics on my leg had come from. It was relaxing and I was nearly asleep when Dr. Luca swept into the room.

As always, Dr. Luca was bubbly and upbeat as well as direct and to the point. She went through the surgery, but I wasn't really following—she was speaking too fast for me to keep up right then. Had I been alone or with Duncan, I would have worried about missing something, but Drew was there. He was nodding, his eyes focused intently on her, asking questions here and there; he was handling things and could fill me in later when I was more focused. The only thing I gathered from the whole exchange was that she'd had a bit more difficulty with getting the cyst removed than she'd expected because part of it was growing into the wall of my ovary, and for some reason that meant she wanted me to spend the night in the hospital before going home.

My eyes drooped as they continued to talk. I didn't mind staying for a while before going home... I wouldn't have minded staying for a long time. I felt relaxed and content there, resting with Drew close by. Besides, home wasn't somewhere I liked to be all that much. It often felt more like a prison than anything else because it was so easy to set off Duncan's jealousy and I couldn't leave without his permission.

Duncan. *Shit!* My eyes flew open wide, and I stared at Drew. Duncan never would have gotten a notification for the end of the surgery. I needed to text him before he showed up and found Drew in the room with me.

"Drew," I rushed out as soon as Dr. Luca left the room. "You have to leave. I need my phone and you have to leave. Where's my phone?"

I tried to sit up, crying out in pain, and Drew pushed me back, gentle yet firm, his eyebrows in a deep v. "Nats, don't do that. You can split something open. If you need your phone right now, I can get it for you. Don't try to get up."

"You don't understand," I said with urgency. "You have to leave, Drew, you can't be here."

He dug through my bag of belongings and pulled out my phone, powering it on before handing it to me. "I'm not leaving you alone in the hospital, Tasha."

My fingers flew over the screen, texting Duncan to tell him I was out of surgery now and that there'd been an issue with their notification system. I told him everything had gone well but they were keeping me overnight, and not to rush over because I was tired and going to sleep anyway.

"Drew," I said again, my eyes filling with tears. "You have to. You can't stay here. You can't... when Duncan... You have to leave before he gets here."

My phone buzzed as I finished speaking and I looked down. Duncan said he'd been freaking out and had driven over to demand an update. That he was parking and would be inside in a few minutes.

"Drew, please," I pleaded, my tears slipping out. "He's already here. Please go before he sees you."

Drew's jaw clenched and unclenched, his eyes glassy, alternating between tortured and furious. He ran a hand over his hair, then the side of his face as he stared at me.

"Please," I whispered, my panic rising with every second he was still there when Duncan was getting closer. "He... you..." I shook my head slightly, at a loss for words for how to explain that Duncan lost his mind when it came to him.

"Okay," Drew said at last, giving the room a cursory glance and checking his pockets. "Okay, I'll go. But I'm coming back to check on you."

"Please don't," I said, panicking more. "I'll text you."

"Tasha—"

"Drew, I'm begging you. Please don't come back."

He sniffled loudly, then moved his head in agreement. He leaned down and compressed our cheeks together, his hand cradling the other side of my face. "Please text me."

And then he was gone, less than a full minute before Duncan rushed in.

Chapter Eighteen

Tasha

I kept my word, sneaking texts to Drew when Duncan used the bathroom or went to get food or coffee; I was afraid if I didn't, Drew would return to check on me, and that would be disastrous. As it was, I was hoping Dr. Luca would come back when Duncan was out getting food because I was sure she'd mention Drew. Drew had gone to appointments with me before and been there in the hospital for my first biopsy as well as my surgery to remove my cancerous ovary, so they were familiar with each other. She even asked after him from time to time at my checkup appointments. After talking to him post-surgery, I had no doubt she'd ask about him when she came back to check in on me.

My anxiety about Duncan finding out Drew had been there was so prominent that I didn't really even notice much of the pain I was in or have time to worry about what the biopsy results might indicate. Every time I started to think about one of those things, my thoughts strayed back to Drew—what Drew would think or do if I had cancer again, what he'd done after my last surgeries to help me manage the pain and recover, and so on.

Of course, after a while, I felt like maybe I was crazy and exaggerating my worry, that maybe it had all been ill-founded. Though I still had bruises from the last time Drew's name had been mentioned with Duncan, he was such a different person most of the time. Self-absorbed, as Drew had said, yes, but sometimes thoughtful and sweet. And now, with me in a hospital gown and a hospital bed, he was solicitous and caring, obviously worried about me and uncomfortable with seeing me in pain.

"What can I get for you, baby?" he asked for the thousandth time.

I shook my head, grimacing because my painkillers were wearing off. "Nothing. I just have to wait until I can take some more Tylenol."

He stroked my arm. "I want to do something. I don't like seeing you like this."

"I know. But there's nothing you *can* do."

"There has to be," he replied. "There has to be *something*. Do you want your computer? Your notebook? I can go home and bring them back for you. More flowers? Or I can put something on the television?"

All I really wanted was for him to stop talking so I could rest. His anxiety was making mine worse. I needed him to be more calm... more like Drew was in situations like this.

And so it was until I was discharged the next day. I'd lucked out and seen Dr. Luca when Duncan was home showering. She had asked about Drew, commenting that she was surprised he wasn't there because she remembered he'd refused to leave the hospital grounds until *I* did the last two times I'd been there for a surgery. I smiled softly without responding. We'd gone through my recovery expectations, medication and movement requirements, things to look out for, and all the other things I'd heard several times before, though it was good to get a refresher since it had been seven years. She'd reiterated that she'd call me as soon as she had the biopsy results and that I should try not to stress in the meantime, then it was just waiting for another hour for everything to be processed so Duncan could take me home.

Once home, Duncan worried over me nonstop, wanting to make sure I was comfortable. It was sweet, but a bit smothering. I could do some things myself. And some things I was supposed to be doing myself even though they hurt, but Duncan didn't want me to do anything that caused me discomfort, no matter how many times I explained what Dr. Luca had said. By the time we'd been home for two hours, I couldn't wait for him to go back to work the next day.

As soon as Duncan was out the door to work the next morning, I texted Drew. I'd been careful to only text when Duncan was occupied, making sure to delete the messages since he was prone to checking my text history, along with my emails and phone calls, without warning, but he hadn't been occupied for more than a minute at a time since we'd left the hospital. I knew Drew was waiting for an update.

I'm home and settled.

How do the incisions look?

Fine, I think. One is a little red compared to the others.

Is it tender?

They all are.

Send me a picture.

I rolled my eyes, but I was actually grateful he was willing to look. Duncan had been no help before he left, too bothered by the stitches in my skin to focus on helping me figure out if one appeared to be infected compared to the others. While he wasn't a surgeon, at least Drew had a medical background and wasn't so squeamish. Not to mention he'd monitored these incisions for me before, so he knew what to look for. After snapping a single pic of my entire abdomen and a close up of each of the four incisions, I sent him all the photos and waited.

That one looks irritated, but not infected. Like something's rubbing on it. Are you wearing pants?

Yes.

Take them off. The waistband must be rubbing. Don't wear pants until the stitches come out. Or just wear the sweats you stole from me.

I gave him a thumbs-up on his message and, with a whiny groan, worked to remove my sweatpants. The last two times I'd had this surgery, I'd lived in Drew's sweats until the stitches came out because they were comfortable and loose enough they didn't rub anywhere, but if I put them on, Duncan would go crazy. He didn't even know I had some of Drew's sweatpants hidden in my dresser back at my apartment. I'd just have to live in a t-shirt for a few days.

Can I come see you?

No. You can't even keep texting me.

After a second or so, a picture arrived of a hopeful looking Watson. Drew was probably holding a treat off-camera, but it looked as if he was pleading into the lens. I laughed, tearing up as I ran my thumb over Watson's fur on the screen. I missed that dog so damn much.

Watson says pleeeeeeease?

I'm betting he's saying please give me the
treat you're holding behind the phone.

Maybe, but this isn't because of a treat:

I waited again, and over a minute later, a video popped up. I clicked to open it and there was Watson. Drew said, "Hey, boy, guess who I'm sending this to? Tasha."

Watson whined.

"Yeah, Tasha. You wanna see Tasha?"

Watson pawed at the ground, whining some more before letting out a bark.

"Tell Tasha how much you love her."

Watson whined and barked again, his tail slamming repeatedly into the floor from how hard he was wagging it. He looked around then stood, like he was expecting something.

"No, she's not here, boy. But maybe we can go see her."

Drew's hand petted the top of Watson's head, and Watson turned to lick him with another whine, then the video ended.

I played it again right away. Watson and I had a special connection. It didn't matter that he was a canine and I was a human, that dog and I were soulmates, and I hadn't seen him in almost five years. I saved the video and the last picture Drew had sent to my phone so I could look at them after I deleted all the messages before Duncan came home. I didn't think he monitored my photos anymore since I never took any. Then I responded to Drew.

I wish I could see you guys, but I can't.

Because of Duncan.

He's my husband now, Drew.

Husband. Not keeper. Not owner.

I started to type that Duncan didn't act like those things, but realized that wasn't actually true and deleted my message.

How about a phone call? You can tell me
how you're doing and I'll put you on
speaker so Watson can at least hear your
voice. He misses you, you know.

I know. But I can't do that.

Is Duncan at work?

You can't call me. And I can't see you
again. Give Watson a hug and a giant kiss
from me. That's the best I can do.

And I can't keep texting you. I'll send you a
message when I'm able after I get the
biopsy results, but no other messages. I
mean it.

Thank you for being there. At the hospital. I
needed you and you were there this time. It
means a lot to me.

Drew continued to text me, trying to talk me into keeping in regular contact, and I wanted to—god, I wanted to, more than I'd ever wanted *anything* before—but I was afraid. I knew Duncan would never be okay with me having any sort of relationship with Drew. He already hadn't been, then the tattoo and the text message about Drew kissing me had made things even worse. And while I hated the way Duncan was so jealous, that he sometimes lost his temper and became violent, I knew what set it off and I could prevent it from happening by avoiding anything related to Drew. I'd married Duncan—I couldn't take that back, as much as I would if I could—so I needed to make the best of it. Surely with time we'd settle into our marriage, and I'd learn to accept the things that bothered me. Relationships required sacrifice as Duncan had said, and I was in this relationship whether I wanted to be or not. At least it meant I wasn't alone.

Though I did sometimes wonder, when I was looking at bruises I'd obtained at Duncan's hands, if maybe I'd have been happier and better off alone. If maybe I'd been wrong all along and being alone wasn't the worst thing, but being in a relationship like the one I had with Duncan was.

Once Drew stopped texting me, I carefully deleted every message after the one he'd sent telling me he couldn't stop thinking about kissing me—the last message on there Duncan had read. As I'd told Drew, the only message *I* sent after that was to relay my biopsy results: that the cyst had been benign and I was still cancer-free. He'd replied with an emotional video of himself and Watson telling me how relieved they were, how worried they'd been waiting to hear from me, and how much they missed me. I'd cried—sobbed, really— watched it two more times, then deleted it from my phone, along with my message to him.

Chapter Nineteen

Tasha

I heard the door to the apartment open and grinned; Duncan was home, so I could share the good news with someone. After my surgery six weeks earlier, I'd finally been able to seriously focus on the first of my novels that was due to my editor and get it into a relatively polished state so I could send it in. While waiting to hear from her, I'd let myself return to my autofiction, working on it only when Duncan was at the office. I wrapped up my first edit on that draft only minutes before getting an email from my editor; she'd finished the novel I'd submitted and said she'd be sending back her minor edits and comments soon, but that I'd done a great job with it. I was thrilled and wanted someone to be excited with.

I'd almost texted Drew, but we'd had no communication since the day I'd gotten my biopsy results, so I didn't. He'd probably moved on with his life without me, and that was for the best anyway—for *both of us*. It was hard because I knew how happy he'd be for me and that he'd understand everything this moment meant to me more than anyone else ever could. Perhaps even more than I could understand myself. However, I didn't want to open that can of worms again. Things had thankfully settled down with Duncan, and while my life was far from what I'd ever imagined it would be and I'd given up a lot, we got along well enough, and he still did sweet things like randomly sending me flowers or bringing home a gift for me. We still spent our weekends at breweries with his friends, but that was okay, really. It wasn't very exciting, or what I wanted to be doing, but it made Duncan happy, and that was good enough for me.

"Duncan!" I shouted excitedly, bounding out of my desk chair and heading toward the door.

"Yes, baby?" he called back, amused.

"Clara loved it!"

"Clara?"

"My editor—she loved my book! She just emailed me back a little bit ago."

I flung my arms around his neck, and he lifted me off my feet and spun me around in a circle, kissing me.

"Congratulations, baby! That's great!"

"I know," I said, blushing. "I'm so excited."

"We should celebrate."

I grinned. "Yes. Please."

"What would you like to do?" he asked, slipping his hands around to hang on the back of my neck.

"I don't even care, just something. Anything."

"Wanna go out for dinner? We can go somewhere nice. There's a new restaurant on Granger. I can call to see if we can get a reservation. It's mid-week, so maybe."

"That sounds perfect."

He kissed me again, returning my grin. "Get ready and I'll call."

I flew into the bathroom and got cleaned up as quickly as I could, arranging my hair and makeup the way I knew Duncan liked best, then put on the nicest dress I had that was appropriate for dinner. Duncan's eyes darkened as he eyed me up and down when I emerged into the living area in my flirty dress.

"How many weeks left before we're allowed to have sex again?" he asked.

I laughed, rolling my eyes. He asked me that almost every day. It normally bothered me, but right then I was in too good a mood to let it get to me. "Six more weeks."

Dr. Luca had said six to twelve weeks, but with my medical history, I always followed the conservative end of the range, and that included abstaining from sex for three months post-surgery. Duncan had a very strong libido that got even worse when we got married, however, and as he liked to tell me, this no-sex thing was torture for him. He'd pushed me into performing oral sex just about daily for the last five weeks. The thing was, I had an aversion to oral sex because of the memories it brought up of my stepfather. Duncan didn't know that, of course. I'd tried to tell him once, but hadn't been able to get the words out, and he had let it go, saying it must not have been that important if I didn't tell him.

That couldn't have been further from the truth—it was *because* it was so important that I couldn't tell him. I still hadn't developed the kind of trust with Duncan that I needed to talk about my past. And my stepfather was the only other person on the planet who knew everything he'd done to me; not even Drew knew because much of it had happened after he went to juvenile detention. It had been my agreement with the asshole my mother married so he'd drop the charges against Drew. I couldn't stomach Drew's future being ruined because he'd tried to protect me. But he'd have lost it on Wayne all over again if he'd known what was happening, so I'd never told him.

"You know," Duncan said, kissing the side of my neck, "we have a little time before we have to leave." Another kiss. "Just enough time." He pulled my hands to the waistband of his pants.

Of course... he wanted another blow job.

"Not if we hit any traffic," I said, pulling my hands back and stepping away, laughing to cover my discomfort.

He looped an arm around my waist and pulled me back to him, grabbing my hand and manipulating my fingers to unbutton and unzip his pants. "We won't. And I can be quick." Then, with a hand on my shoulder, he pushed me down to my knees.

Duncan was in an exceptionally good mood during dinner, no doubt courtesy of the blow job he'd literally pushed me to give him, but it meant he was actually listening to me. And it was such a nice change to be able to chatter on about my writing, something I loved to talk about as much as Duncan hated to listen to it, that the resentment I had for what he'd done before we left mostly faded away during dinner. Was it really such a big price to pay to be able to spend my evening feeling almost like myself because I had a rare opportunity to talk about things that mattered to me?

We ate with a bottle of wine, then Duncan ordered another bottle with dessert. I was happy to have more, but was starting to worry about him driving us home. While he routinely drove after several beers or glasses of wine, this would be an entire bottle or more that he'd consumed himself. I drank mine faster so I could get more of the second bottle into *my* glass than his, hoping that would be enough.

As always when I drank, my bladder filled to the point of pain almost instantly. While we waited for dessert to arrive, I excused myself for the third time to use the restroom. Earlier when I'd gone, I was so preoccupied with the purpose of our celebration that I hadn't paid much attention to my surroundings, but now I had leisure to study the area near the bathroom hall since there was a line for the ladies' room. The walls were rustic wood with iron decorations, some of which looked like actual tools from the turn of the twentieth century, while others looked like they were made for display only. The light fixtures all looked like old lanterns and there was a sexy, sophisticated low glow throughout the restaurant. It had been open for a couple of months, but this was the first we'd been there. And while it was pricey enough that we wouldn't go often, I thought we'd likely be back when we had something to celebrate. The food had been delicious and I liked the atmosphere. It was a really nice restaurant, but it wasn't stuffy like most of the nicer places Duncan liked to go to. I felt more comfortable here. The line moved forward and I stepped along with it, then leaned against the wall and scanned the dining area.

The table closest to me had an older couple, maybe in their sixties. The woman, with her white hair pulled back into a bun and a few tendrils falling down, was adorable and animated as she talked to her male companion, laughing often, using her hands and utensils to gesture. The man, who I presumed to be her husband, was listening, nodding along between bites. He didn't seem to speak much, but it was clear he was engaged with whatever his wife was talking about. I wondered how long they'd been together, how they'd met, if they were retired or still worked. I wondered if they had children and how many, where they'd grown up, if they had other family alive. I wondered how they'd ended up in Brinkley and coming to this restaurant on this night so that I was watching them interact while waiting to use the bathroom. I analyzed their features and mannerisms, thinking I'd like to write a novel about this couple, about the rich life they'd led that culminated in them being in this place at this time.

My eyes traveled to the next table where there was another couple, but younger. Maybe a few years older than me, ten at most. This woman was also talking, but her hands were in her lap even though there was a plate full of food in front of her, her arms tight against her body. Her face was flushed and she was obviously upset or angry. Her eyes were fixed on the man sitting across from her, who was avoiding eye contact with her and glaring at his food as he shoveled it into his mouth between gulps of a mixed drink of some sort. Interrupting her, he said something, his lips moving while hers still were, then banged the table with his fist. The woman jumped and looked down at her plate, her skin reddening even more, and the man shoveled another angry bite into his mouth.

Again, I wondered what the story was behind this couple, but I stopped my thoughts in their tracks; it was too uncomfortably familiar. I realized they reminded me of Duncan and me when Duncan was angry. Quickly, I shifted my eyes to the next table, not wanting my thoughts to go there. Not today when I had so much to be excited about. Besides, it had been a long time since I'd done something to make him that kind of angry.

My heart lurched to a stop. There, three tables from where I waited in line, was Drew. He was sitting at a large table with six other men and women. If I'd had to guess, they were all physical therapists like he was. I knew in his old practice, they all went out together once or twice a month, something he'd pioneered to foster better working relationships, so I wouldn't have been surprised if he was doing the same thing again.

I couldn't tear my eyes from him, even as I moved forward another few steps in line. He appeared relaxed and animated, and like he was comfortable with the other people at the table, all of them talking and laughing. He looked good. He looked happy. I wondered if one of the women at the table was also a romantic interest and tried to figure out which one, but I couldn't see if the women wore wedding rings. That didn't mean he didn't have a girlfriend, though. I couldn't imagine he didn't have one by now. Women were drawn to him—always had been since about halfway through our undergrad. I just hoped, whoever she was, she didn't turn out to be like Becka. She had sucked the life from him, and he deserved better than that. But I hoped that Watson didn't like her too much... I liked being Watson's favorite person in the world.

At length, I dragged my eyes away and steadfastly avoided looking in his direction again. I wanted to talk to him, to hug him, to feel his lips touch mine again, and none of those things could happen. I shouldn't have even been having thoughts like that. If Duncan knew... At least Drew's table was in a completely different area of the restaurant than ours, and Duncan wasn't likely to notice him unless he suddenly became more observant than he'd ever been before. My heart beat hard against my ribcage knowing Drew was so close by, and it took everything I had not to look up toward him again before I went into the bathroom.

"Everything okay?" Duncan asked when I returned to the table.

I smiled, trying to act the same way I had been before I'd left the table. "Yeah, there was just a long line."

We ate dessert without incident, and I sucked down more wine. I wasn't sure about Duncan, but I was definitely bordering on drunk by the time we rose from the table. On the way to the exit, however, Duncan stumbled. He promptly recovered, but not before I'd noticed. And Duncan didn't typically stumble.

"Maybe we should get a cab or uber or something," I suggested. "I think we both had a little too much to drink."

"I'm fine, baby," he said, sliding his arm over my shoulders and kissing the side of my neck. "I've had more than this and been just fine to drive before."

"Duncan... I know, but we should be safe. Let's just get a cab. We can get your car in the morning."

"I said I'm fine, Tasha. I know my limits. And I'm not leaving my car here so someone can break into it overnight."

I flashed back to when Drew was staying with me and he'd stopped Duncan from driving, about how he'd yelled at me after Duncan was out of the car about how stupid I was for being so willing to get into a car with Duncan when he'd been drinking so I wouldn't hurt his feelings. He'd been right. And I was about to do it again. But I wasn't just afraid of hurting his feelings this time... I didn't want to set him off.

But I hadn't set him off in a long time. Maybe the times he'd lost his temper on me had been flukes and it would never happen again. I slipped my arm around his waist and squeezed him into my side.

"I'd really rather get a cab," I said. "I'd rather be safe than sorry. Please?"

"Tasha—"

"Please, Duncan. As a favor for me, okay? Just this once?"

He clenched his jaw and narrowed his eyes. "Fine," he said with a frustrated huff. "But only because I said I'd give you anything you wanted today."

"Thank you," I said, giving him another squeeze.

When we made it home, safely thanks to keeping Duncan from getting behind the wheel, he hopped in the shower. While I preferred showering in the morning, he preferred showering at night and just rinsing off in the mornings, if anything. I was relieved to get a few minutes to myself and sat under the blankets in bed with my phone, Drew on my mind after seeing him. I wished I hadn't deleted the last video he'd sent me of him and Watson, but I had, so I opened the only other video I had on my phone with him in it: his awards ceremony.

I was on my second time through the video when Duncan walked into the bedroom. My heart slammed into my throat and my ears rang. I'd been so focused on the video that I had missed when he turned off the water. I hit the button on the side of my phone to lock the screen without even closing the video and slipped it onto the nightstand, hoping he hadn't noticed.

"What were you doing?" Duncan asked, suspicion creeping into his voice.

I shook my head and yawned. "Just screwing around while I was waiting for you." I forced a smile. "Thank you for tonight."

He returned my smile, slipping under the blankets and leaning over to kiss me. "You're welcome, baby."

Duncan twisted back to his nightstand and turned his light off, plunging the room into darkness. I slid down further under the blankets, trying to control my breathing, but with how erratically my heart was beating, it was nearly impossible. But Duncan didn't say anything else about my phone or about my breathing, and after a while, it evened out. I'd been careless, no doubt because I was tipsy, but it seemed that it was only close and nothing more. Duncan's jealousy hadn't been aroused.

Chapter Twenty

Drew

The leaves were just beginning to change on the trees along the street as I walked over to the hospital for my shift, though I barely noticed as I moved along. Like everyone in my new practice, I had shifts at the hospital to work with in-patients, with priority given to patients who were survivors of the types of trauma I specialized in. It was the most emotionally draining, as well as rewarding, part of my career. While I worked exclusively with trauma survivors in my new practice and conducted trainings for other physical therapists throughout the region who wished to become trauma-informed, it was working with hospital patients that was most fulfilling. These were the patients who were likely in the hospital because of violence, meaning the trauma was fresh. They were at their most fearful and vulnerable, and I had an opportunity to help put them at ease, to help them feel safe, even if only for the thirty or sixty minutes of our sessions together. It was an honor and something I took very seriously, to be able to provide that to people who were reeling from whatever had happened and the resulting injuries they were now dealing with.

And because it had been several days since I was last on shift, it was likely only one or two patients at most were patients I'd already worked with. The others would have been discharged by now. Sometimes they used our practice, but sometimes they didn't—it usually came down to insurance, though my practice was working on being able to accept any and all insurance policies so that would never be a barrier for someone who needed the kind of specialized care we provided. I also hoped to implement need-based pricing and payment plans for the uninsured.

This morning, though, my thoughts weren't entirely on work. No, this morning, as I walked through the brisk, cool fall air, I was thinking about Tasha. I'd seen her two nights earlier when I was out for my practice's monthly dinner and hadn't been able to stop thinking about her ever since. She'd been with Duncan, so I hadn't talked to her, as much as I wanted to, but I'd seen her. I'd stood and watched her for a while, though she had no idea I was there. She was excited about something—I could see the sparkle in her eyes and the genuine curl to the corners of her mouth even as she was speaking. I'd guess she had good news related to her writing. Maybe a new book contract or something. I hoped so—she deserved it. She was a really talented writer.

I wondered if it might even have been related to the autofiction she'd started writing when I was staying with her in the spring. I still wanted to read that story, but I'd have to wait until it was published one day. I knew I couldn't text her to ask to read it sooner. She hadn't said it explicitly, but I'd understood that the reason we couldn't talk was that it wasn't safe because of Duncan. My fists clenched and I took a deep breath, releasing them. The thought of him hurting her... I could still see the bruising and cut on her face when she was in the hospital for her surgery. She'd lied to me about what happened—I knew Duncan had done it to her.

I walked into the building, greeting the nurses and doctors I passed, trying to push Tasha from my mind. By now, most of the faces and names were familiar, and I asked them about their kids or pets, and they asked after Watson and my trainings. Like most of Brinkley, the hospital staff were friendly, and it was a positive, upbeat environment to work in.

After receiving my schedule for the day, I always got a quick rundown of injuries and any declared or suspected trauma for each patient so I'd know how to best work with them before meeting them. A domestic violence survivor who'd had an arm broken would need to be handled a bit differently than a rape survivor, for instance. The background on their trauma helped me be better prepared to set them at ease right away rather than figuring it out through trial and error while I was working with them. Even if unintentional, triggering someone to put their guard up could mean it never came back down, and the more relaxed they were with me, the more effective our time together would be for helping them heal physically. I wanted to think it also helped them emotionally.

I listened, looking at patient charts, as I got the rundown for each. When we reached my third patient for the day, I winced at the first x-ray. It was one of the worst breaks I'd ever seen—maybe *the* worst. The patient's femur had been broken completely in two, with one side jutting upward all the way through the muscle and almost through the skin.

"Jesus," I muttered, my hand running over my chin. I'd never been squeamish, but that x-ray tested my limits. The second x-ray showed a metal rod that had been inserted from hip to knee to stabilize the break. "I missed what you said," I said, looking up at the nurse, apologetic. "That x-ray caught me off guard."

"It's a bad one," Marge agreed sympathetically. "Patient had surgery last night—we had to call someone in from Harper General— but she arrived yesterday morning by ambulance."

"How did she end up with a break like this?" I asked, looking at the first x-ray again.

"Stairs, we think."

I looked up at Marge. "Think?"

Her lips spread into a thin line. "Patient said she tripped over a shoe and hit the arm of her couch on the way down."

"Let me guess—that's not what actually happened?" My heart ached for whatever this woman had been through, for the fear that was driving her to cover up for whoever was responsible.

"No," Marge replied, shaking her head. "What she described... it would be almost impossible for this kind of break. We usually see this kind of thing with auto accidents. And she was found in a stairwell by the paramedics. She claimed that was after she fell, that she was trying to get to her car to drive to urgent care. And none of it makes sense with the second and third degree burns on her legs for which no explanation was provided." She gestured over the x-ray image to indicate where the burns were; I'd need to take them into consideration when working with the patient.

I sucked in a sharp breath.

"Anyway, she's been adamant that her husband isn't responsible, but she also asked that he not be allowed to see her once they were separated after she arrived. He's been here a number of times already. Upset, then explosively angry when he isn't allowed back. Appears to be genuinely worried for her, but who knows—that doesn't necessarily mean he isn't the one responsible. Bottom line is she doesn't want him near her, so we won't let him back while she's here."

I nodded. It wasn't the first time something like this had happened. Sadly, many ended up back with their abusive spouse when they were discharged because they had nowhere else to go.

"How long is this one in here?"

"At least a few more days. Surgeon wants her to have at least six PT sessions before she's discharged."

I tucked that information away, then we moved on to the next patient.

A couple of hours later, I'd finished with two of my morning patients. I'd be working with one more—the one with the broken femur—then taking lunch before seeing the rest of my patients for the day. I pulled out the clipboard with the patient's info. I always looked through again to refresh my memory, though I didn't need to—I'd been seeing that x-ray in my mind all morning. My eyes scanned over the top page, looking for the patient's name. I usually did that when going through with Marge, but I'd been distracted by the x-ray image.

I came to an abrupt halt in the hallway two rooms down from my destination, my eyes stuck on the paper on my clipboard. The rest of the page dissolved into nothingness around the name.

Natasha Williams Avery.

It had to be her. She was Natasha Lynn Williams, but Duncan's last name was Avery. The woman with the worst femur break I'd ever seen was Tasha.

My Tasha.

I flipped around and headed to the nearest staff break room, tossing the clipboard onto a table. I paced back and forth, my hands over my mouth, trying to keep my jaw from trembling. I'd just seen her two days earlier. Less than two full days. And now she was in the hospital with her leg snapped in half.

Turning, I rushed into the staff bathroom and threw up. When I was emptied out, I stood and splashed icy water on my face. I snatched from the cabinet a disposable toothbrush and mini toothpaste and brushed my teeth, a difficult feat with fingers trembling, then splashed more water on my face. I couldn't imagine walking into that room and seeing Tasha that way. My chest was tight, and my heart was having trouble beating as if I was having a heart attack. The professional course of action would be to notify Marge that I had a personal connection to Tasha and that they needed to transfer her to another doctor. I was in no state to treat Tasha anyway, throwing up and crying and having a panic attack in the bathroom. I grasped the sides of the sink and looked at my reflection.

You can do this, Drew. This is what you do. Tasha, right now, is just another patient. You need to walk in there and work with her like you would if she was someone else. There is no one who is better at this than you are, no one who understands every bit of trauma she has like you do. You are more qualified than anyone else to help her right now—don't let her down. Go in there and do your damn job.

I thought I might throw up again, but I choked it down. With a final splash of cold water on my face, I walked out, relieved no one else was in the breakroom right then, grabbed my clipboard, and headed back toward Tasha's room.

Her eyes were closed when I walked in, and I stood there without a sound, taking her in. Her left leg was bandaged and in a stabilizing brace, her hands clasped tightly over her abdomen. Her mouth was turned down in a deep frown, her face swollen with cuts on her lip and bruising on her cheek. I clenched my jaw against the emotion crashing over me, forcing back the tears that were trying to find their way out. Then I swallowed, took a deep breath, and rapped the side of her open door with my knuckles to announce my presence.

I typically called out a greeting when I knocked, but I didn't this time. I couldn't. My voice was stuck somewhere below my vocal cords.

Tasha's eyes flew open, and her head snapped toward me. I could see that same fear in her eyes I'd noted the last time I was this close to her, before she registered that it was me and not Duncan. The fear slipped, allowing pain to show through, then she turned away, tears running down her cheeks, her face reddening.

I walked over and stood awkwardly next to the bed. I wanted to sit and wrap her in my arms the best I could without hurting her. I wanted to kiss the bruises and swollen skin on her face and tell her I'd never let him hurt her again. But I didn't know how she would react. And I was in my scrubs, wearing my nametag, because I was on duty with the hospital.

I cleared my throat. "I'm your physical therapist for the next few days."

Her chin dropped an inch in acknowledgement. "I didn't know you worked at the hospital."

"I do a few days a week. Everyone in my new practice takes shifts here."

"You get to wear scrubs."

I laughed in surprise. I'd told her in college that the only thing that sucked about being a physical therapist was not getting to wear scrubs every day. "Yeah."

She turned, giving me a small smile even as she sniffled. "Are they everything you ever hoped for?"

My heart ached as I smiled back at her. Here she was in the hospital, bruised, cut, her leg broken almost beyond repair, undoubtedly in a lot of pain, thinking about me and teasing. "I'll tell you what. I'll get you some and you can tell me what *you* think." She didn't reply and I sighed, my face falling. "I saw the x-rays. That's one hell of a break, Tash." I watched her carefully and asked, "How did it happen?"

She looked away, silent.

"I know you didn't trip over a shoe. You're not a klutz."

Her shoulders began to shake and guilt slammed through my chest. I shouldn't have been pushing her to talk about it right then. Or ever, really. As her physical therapist, that was inappropriate.

"I'm sorry," I said. "It's none of my business. I shouldn't have said that."

Her jaw shifted and she continued to face away from me. "I don't want to talk about it."

I took a deep breath and released it, then forced myself into professional mode. We spent the next thirty minutes working on keeping some mobility in her hip and knee without bending her leg too far; she wouldn't be able to fully bend it or even weight her leg for at least six weeks while the torn muscle was healing. Even if healing went well and she did all of her physical therapy, she likely wouldn't be walking unassisted for months.

After the last exercise, she dropped her head back onto her hospital bed, breathing heavily. "That was fucking hard," she grumbled. "And exhausting." She narrowed her eyes at me. "I had no idea that, as a doctor, you were a hard-ass."

I laughed and shrugged. "Or maybe you're just a lazy patient."

She snorted, then smiled. I smiled back at her, but her smile faded and she began to examine the ceiling.

"You have another patient, I'm sure."

I stepped closer to the bed. "I do, but not for a while. It's my lunch break now."

She gave a small nod. "I hope your food sucks as much as mine does."

I chuckled. "It doesn't. I bring my own lunch. Do you wanna share?"

"What is it?"

"Pasta. Blackened chicken with spring veggies."

"Oh my god, yes," she rushed out with a short laugh. "I'm pretty sure I just drooled all over myself."

I returned a few minutes later with my pasta, heated up, and a vending machine sandwich. I pulled over the bedside tray table and helped Tasha sit her bed up a little higher, then put my pasta and fork down in front of her.

"Enjoy," I said, pulling the cellophane from the sandwich and taking a large bite as I sat down in a chair next to her.

"You sure? This is your last chance to get your pasta back because it'll be gone in about five minutes. I'm starving."

"I'm sure."

We ate in silence. I wanted to talk to her, but I didn't know what to say. I didn't want to push her to talk about things she didn't want to talk about yet or piss her off and not be able to come back and see her again. When we were finished, I grabbed the dishes from her and told her I'd be right back. I put my container and fork with my stuff in my locker and stopped by the vending machine again to grab a brownie. When I got back into the room, I split it, giving her two-thirds of it. Brownies had been her second love in the world ever since we were kids—second only to pancakes. I used to make batches of brownies just to have some for her when we snuck out together at night.

She closed her eyes as she chewed. "This brownie sucks," she said, taking another bite.

I chuckled. "Yeah. It does. But it's the best I could do on short notice."

"It's better than none."

She let out a sigh, lowering the rest of the brownie and setting it on the tray table. She stared through the table for a while without taking another bite. I watched, my heart still beating painfully in my chest, wishing I didn't have to leave soon to work with other patients. Finally, Tasha turned and held my gaze. Neither of us spoke for a long time, just taking each other in.

"Thank you," she said in a small voice.

"It's my job," I said, my lips pulling up on one side.

"Not for that."

I nodded and reached over, touching the back of her hand tentatively. She flipped it over and slid her fingers between mine, squeezing hard. I curled my fingers over and held on tight. Her eyes closed and her shoulders shook as she cried. Using my other hand, I smoothed along her arm, up and down, even after she'd fallen asleep. But then I had to leave—I was going to be late for my next patient.

I stood, pulling my hand from hers, and bent over, kissing her forehead. She stirred, her eyes fluttering open. I smoothed her hair back and smiled at her.

"I have to go—I have more patients to see. But I'll be back after."

Her eyes probed mine. "Please."

Chapter Twenty-One

Tasha

My head was still spinning after Drew walked out of my hospital room to see his other patients. I wasn't quite sure I could believe that he'd been there, that it hadn't been a dream. It was surreal. But he smelled the same, plus the bite of hospital sanitizer. Sounded the same. Looked the same. He appeared to be a little bigger and more muscly, but that was probably just me because of the fear coursing strong through my veins nonstop. I'd always felt safest with Drew out of anyone else in my life—even safer with him than I felt when I was alone—but there'd been a hum of fear even with him. I wasn't sure I'd ever truly feel safe again with *anyone.*

I was glad he said he was coming back. I hadn't wanted him to leave. Even with the undercurrent of fear, I knew there was no way Duncan could hurt me again if Drew was there. It didn't matter that we hadn't talked in months—Drew wouldn't let him. I'd told the nurses when I was rolled into the Emergency Room from the ambulance that I didn't want Duncan near me, and they'd kept him away, but I was afraid he'd manage to get back to me anyway.

It was unlikely he'd do anything else to me. His remorse and horror had been immediate, his tears and anguish and worry all very real. But just the thought of him being anywhere near me made me feel panicky. I couldn't keep him away from me forever, but at least while I was in the hospital, I could have the space I needed. And maybe they'd decide to keep me longer than they thought. Though I had no idea how I would ever pay for any of the medical care I was receiving; I was without health insurance. I'd cancelled mine because Duncan was going to put me on his, but then something had been misfiled, and so I was without insurance until it was resolved. But that was something I could worry about later. My first priority was to keep Duncan away from me.

I never should have believed he wouldn't hurt me again. It was stupid—I should have known better. I was so desperate to feel loved, to feel like I would never be alone, I'd ignored what my gut was telling me, what Drew tried to tell me—that Duncan wasn't safe. I'd made excuses for every time he'd hurt me, blamed myself even. But I couldn't do that anymore. Not after *this*.

My eyes shifted to the clock. It had only been forty minutes since Drew left. How many patients did he have before he'd be back? How many hours would that be? What if he didn't come back? I reached over for the remote and turned on the television, restless. I wouldn't be able to focus on anything—not that I liked watching tv anyway— but maybe it would help the time pass.

"Knock, knock," Drew's voice rang out throughout the room. It was six-thirty in the evening and I'd just had a hospital dinner delivered to the room, having given up on him returning before my next therapy session in the morning.

"Hi," I said, feeling emotional at seeing him again, noting that he'd changed and appeared to have showered as well. My heart flipped over and my eyes teared up. I blinked hard to make the moisture go away.

He lifted my food tray, grimacing at the contents, then moved it over to the sink. "I brought dinner with me. I would have been here a while ago, but I wanted to get cleaned up and grab some food for us, and I needed to let Watson out. He sends his love and asked me to give you some kisses for him, but I doubt you want me to lick your face, so I figured I'd just pass on the message."

I snorted and grinned. "I appreciate that." I tipped my head toward the bags in his hands. "What did you bring?"

He waggled his eyebrows, grinning. "All kinds of good shit." He set the bags down in the reclining chair and reached into the first one to start pulling things out. "I went with Italian. Tomorrow, maybe Thai? Just let me know what you're in the mood for. For tonight, chicken marsala for you, eggplant parmesan for me, and bruschetta."

"No tiramisu? What the hell kind of Italian dinner is this?" I teased.

Drew laughed, pulling another container from the bag. "Tiramisu."

I groaned, blushing a little because he had already thought of it.

He winked at me. "I know you, Tasha. I know better than to forget tiramisu when we have Italian. I did that once, remember?"

I laughed, nodding. I remembered. A long time ago, he'd forgotten that vital part of my order and told me, if I wanted it that badly, I could take my lazy ass back out to get it myself because he'd already done a food run and he was starving. I'd agreed to go, but when I'd left, I'd taken all the food with me so he wouldn't be able to eat until I got back.

"I was such an obnoxious asshole," I said, still laughing.

"Yeah, you were," Drew agreed.

We ate, sharing our dishes with each other, and reminisced about fun parts of our past, laughing often. I could almost forget that I was married and we were sitting in a hospital room because my husband had lost his temper and burned me and broken my leg, and that I hadn't spoken to Drew in months before today.

When I reached my tiramisu, I picked at it, not wanting to be finished because I didn't want Drew to leave. He was telling me about his new practice and the other therapists he worked with. He sounded really content with where he was, and I was happy for him. When he started cleaning up what was left from our dessert, I knew our time together had come to an end. But then, rather than leaving, he sat back down and reached into a tote bag he'd brought in with him.

He held up a worn book, twisting it in the air. "You up for a few?"

I recognized the book immediately: *The Collected Works of Sherlock Holmes*. The exact same copy we'd read to each other as teens. I'd thought I'd lost it, but I must have left it at Drew's before I moved. No matter what else was happening in our lives back then, we'd had each other and that book—I was glad he had it. I nodded, teary. "Yes."

We took turns reading for the first few just like we used to, but I grew too tired to read any more of them and let Drew take over. It was relaxing to listen to him, his voice and the stories both so familiar. The fear even dulled and nearly disappeared, and my body relaxed in a way it hadn't in a very long time. I reached over and grabbed Drew's hand, squeezing it in gratitude.

He squeezed it back, glancing over at me, then returning to the story, still holding onto my hand.

I was drifting in and out of sleep when I realized Drew was no longer reading. I blinked my eyes open and looked in his direction. The book was closed on his lap, his head resting against his hand as he studied me. I'd caught him in an unguarded moment, and I could see the depth of the pain in his eyes... the sadness. My hand was still in his, and I gave it a small squeeze.

"Don't worry about me. I'll be alright," I said, my voice soft. "I always am."

He lifted my hand and held his lips against the back of it for several seconds. It was so gentle and tender and loving... the opposite of what Duncan had done to me. The opposite of Duncan all the time, really—he'd never been gentle or tender in any way. I tried to swallow the lump in my throat, but some tears slipped out anyway. Drew reached over and I flinched when his thumb touched my skin. He drew back.

"I'm sorry," I rushed out. "I didn't mean to."

"Don't apologize," he whispered.

"You can touch me," I added. Even though I'd flinched, I wanted him to. I wanted to feel being touched in a way that wasn't threatening.

He reached back over, more slowly this time, and used his thumb to wipe away the tears on my cheeks, his touch no stronger than his words had been.

"I'm here for whatever you need," he said, his voice low, his blue-gray eyes intently focused on me. "For whatever you'll let me be here for."

I started sobbing. Like a dam breaking, everything came pouring out of me, starting with the first time Duncan had ever physically hurt me when he clamped down on my arm at the brewery after Drew's visit. Lastly, I told him how Duncan had been up before me the morning before, as usual, but I found him standing in the kitchen with my phone, the coffee behind him almost done brewing.

I'd sensed danger in the air and wished I was in more than a t-shirt, but ignored it, trying to prepare for whatever he was about to say so I could try to calm his jealousy. He'd watched me walk in, his face hard and eyes raging, then gestured for me to come closer when I stopped on the other side of the room. I took two steps, and he gestured me closer again.

"Come. Here. Tasha."

I stepped still closer, though everything in my body was screaming at me to run. He grabbed my wrist and yanked, spinning me so my back was against the refrigerator, and planted a hand near my collarbone to keep me there. Using his other hand, he did something on the screen of my phone and turned it around. The video from Drew's awards ceremony was playing. My eyes darted from the video to Duncan's glare.

"What is this, Tasha?"

"D-Drew's awards ceremony," I stuttered out. "It's from months ago."

He gave a cold nod as he looked at the screen again. "You were watching this last night."

I didn't bother to deny it—he'd obviously unlocked my screen, and it would have opened on the video since I hadn't closed it before he'd walked in from the bathroom.

"Want to tell me why?"

I didn't say anything.

"That's okay." He raised his arm and threw the phone across the room.

I jumped when it slammed into the wall. My heart was beating so fast I thought I might pass out. The edges of my vision were already black.

"I decided to see what other videos you had on there, since I hadn't realized you kept videos of Drew on there to begin with, and saw a recent one with a dog. I didn't think much about that one at first, except that voice talking to the dog was familiar. It was Drew again. But I didn't see anything in your text messages, which means you must be deleting your messages."

He sighed and shook his head. "Just in case I was wrong, I scrolled back through all your old messages with him, but I never found one where he sent the video of the dog. But you know what else I didn't find? Where he sent you the video of him at the awards ceremony. But that was a long time ago—you wouldn't have deleted that one. Which means you took the video yourself."

He stared at me, waiting for something, so I nodded. I *had* taken it.

"That's what I thought. But you know what the problem is with that, Tasha? You told me your battery was dying." His jaw clenched. "Tell me how you managed to take an almost ten-minute video with a dead battery, Tasha."

I stared at him, frozen. There was nothing I could say or do to calm him down at this point. All I could do was try not to make it any worse.

"You lied to me!" he roared, his face only inches from mine. "And he's still a problem."

He took his hand off the base of my neck and reached over to grab the coffeepot like he was going to pour a cup of coffee.

"He has no place in our relationship," Duncan continued.

I could see in his eyes that he was far beyond reason, and fear ran down my spine, unsure what he was about to do. At first, he did nothing but stare at me with more rage than I'd ever seen before. Then, without warning, he rammed the bottom of the pot onto my thigh over my tattoo. I screamed in pain and shoved him back, hot coffee spilling from the pot down my legs. He was much bigger than I was, but adrenaline must have been on my side because he stumbled backward.

As he tried to catch his footing, I bolted to the door. In the time it took me to unlock it and fling it open, he caught up to me and grabbed my arm, backhanding me when I spun around. I lost my balance, tripping backward over my feet until I hit the wall on the other side of the hall at the top of the cement stairs.

"You want him so badly, then fucking go!" he shouted with a hard shove.

Everything after I started tumbling was hazy. I was falling, then I wasn't, but I couldn't move my leg. Nothing really hurt, but I was out of it. Duncan was there, cradling my torso and crying into my hair, apologizing over and over and over. There were sirens in the distance, though I wasn't sure who'd called for the ambulance that arrived. And then I was on a stretcher and being slid into the back of the ambulance alone. The doors were shutting, and Duncan was shouting that he was right behind me. The paramedics were asking me questions, and I made up a lie about what had happened, like I'd grown accustomed to. I repeated the lie over and over during the next hours, though as soon as they rolled me into the hospital, I had begged them to keep Duncan away from me.

My breath was shuddering out of me when I finished talking and looked over at Drew. He was staring at the wall, his cheeks wet, the vein in his temple ticking. He opened his mouth, his jaw trembling violently, then closed it without saying anything. He swallowed, wiped his face, then tried again, but nothing came out this time, either. In the end, he broke down and cried with his head down, my hand cradled in both of his.

Chapter Twenty-Two

Drew

I hated that I broke down with Tasha after she told me about everything Duncan had done to her throughout their relationship, but I couldn't stop it from happening. I'd been unprepared for everything she told me, unprepared for how matter of fact she was about it because she'd become so accustomed to it. What she needed was for someone to be a rock for her, which I resolved to do as soon as I was able to rein in my emotions. I could let them all loose again when I got home and it was just Watson and me.

"What can I do?" I asked once I'd composed myself, rubbing the back of her hand with my palm, pausing to kiss it. "I'll do anything you need."

She shook her head and sighed. "I don't know." Her eyes searched the far wall aimlessly in the dim light now that it was dark outside her window. "I have my apartment still, but he's got a key. And most of my stuff is at his place, anyway. But he'll never let me leave, so it doesn't really matter."

"He doesn't have a choice," I bit out.

"You don't understand, Drew—he'll never accept it."

"He doesn't have to. You're not doing this alone, and I won't let him come anywhere near you again."

Tasha began to cry again, though I could tell by the way she was trying desperately to keep her mouth from turning down that she didn't want to. I reached up and brushed a hand over her hair, my thumb smoothing over her forehead.

"I can get your locks changed out for you so he can't get in. Or you can just stay with me. I'd rather you did that because I could keep you safer and he wouldn't know where to find you. You're also going to need help around the clock for a while, and it would be easier at my place."

She shook her head. "I can't do that to you. You have your own life, Drew. I can't just come storming back in when I'm at rock bottom and expect you to save me from my own stupid decisions."

"You didn't. And you're not."

"I can't let you—"

"You'd do it for me." I stared hard at her, daring her to deny it.

She didn't. She lowered her gaze. "Okay."

"Have you talked to the police yet?"

She shook her head vehemently. "I don't want to do that."

"You're not going to press charges?"

Again, she shook her head. "No, I don't... no. He could lose his job for something like this. I don't... I'm not trying to ruin his life."

"Like he's ruined yours?"

Her jaw trembled. "I don't want to do it, okay? I just want to get a divorce and never see him again."

I felt a little bit like an asshole for what I'd said. I was angry because of what he'd done to her, but I couldn't imagine what she was going through right then. Pressing charges would be a lot of time talking to lawyers and police officers and in court, reliving what Duncan had done to her over and over. After what she'd been through, could I really blame her for wanting to avoid all that?

We talked a little more and she told me Duncan's address. I had a couple of friends I'd ask to help me out with getting Tasha's stuff, in part to keep me from ripping him limb from limb. Hopefully he wouldn't fight us, but my guess was that he would. Once Tasha was asleep, I left her a note that I'd be back soon and headed out.

I made several calls on the way back to my apartment, where I took Watson out for his long-overdue evening walk around the neighborhood before packing a small bag and heading back over to the hospital. Security was pretty tight, but I wasn't willing to risk Tasha being alone if Duncan got through to her room. Except as required for Watson and my job, I wouldn't be leaving her side while she was in the hospital.

As expected, Duncan didn't cooperate with the friends I'd called when they went over to get Tasha's stuff. We'd agreed it would be less contentious if I didn't go with them, as much as I wanted to so I could give Duncan a taste of what he'd done to Tasha, so they'd gone while I was seeing patients at the hospital. I didn't tell Tasha about his lack of cooperation—she didn't need any more on her plate than she already had. But I needed to figure out what to do about it.

I'd run home to make pancakes that morning and brought them back for breakfast, and Tasha had perked up considerably since the night before. I got to see her three times during the day since she was scheduled for two PT sessions and I had lunch with her again, and while she was noticeably more tired during the second session, her spirits were much higher than they'd been the day before.

She had another two and a half days there for me to figure out how to get her stuff from Duncan's apartment, so I avoided talking about it at all and we spent another evening reading from Sherlock Holmes until she fell asleep. As I had the day before, I ran home to walk Watson and shower, then came back to spend the night next to her.

It was the following day that I had an idea for how to get into Duncan's apartment. It wasn't entirely honest, but at that point, I didn't really care. I spoke with one of the paramedics who I knew had a brother who was a police officer and explained the situation to him. He was one of the medics that had brought Tasha in and was more than happy to help in any way he could. He called his brother, and in no time it was set; the same two guys who'd gone over already would meet Officer Halston at Duncan's apartment the next day. With any luck, the uniform would scare Duncan into cooperating.

Early that morning, as I headed home to walk Watson and make breakfast to bring back for Tasha, I got a call from Officer Halston. I was surprised because he should have been on his way over to Duncan's soon; hopefully nothing was amiss.

"Before heading over there blind, I did a little digging on this guy," he said right off the bat after I answered. "The good news is, I think he won't give me any trouble."

That was a relief, but I was wary about the way he'd worded that. "And the bad news?"

There was a loud sigh over the line. "This guy has a history. He's been married and divorced already. When his ex divorced him, she brought charges against him and he did time. He stabbed her during an argument and she almost died."

"Jesus Christ," I muttered, feeling sick.

"Wasn't the first time, either. She'd filed and dropped charges for spousal abuse half a dozen times before that. Claimed he'd get jealous and go off the deep end."

Exactly what Tasha had said.

"Anyway, he won't give me trouble today because part of his deal to reduce his sentence was an agreement that if he ever had charges brought against him again, he'd serve his full sentence, and with his record, he wouldn't be able to plead it down. His name was Darien Hopkins, changed it and moved to Brinkley a couple of years ago, right after he finished serving his sentence. I'm gonna bet his employer didn't do a background check."

My mind raced with all this new information. Tasha had been in even greater danger than I'd realized. And I wasn't sure if I should tell her or not. On the one hand, I thought she should know because she should understand he wasn't a nice guy who made a mistake and that he'd never been what he projected to her. And it might change her mind about pressing charges to keep him from doing the same thing to someone else. But on the other hand, it would be devastating to her to find out how wrong she'd been about him, and I didn't want to do that to her. Her self-confidence was already shaky at best, and this might permanently shatter it.

"Anyway, wanted to let you know what I found out. Headed over there now and I'll call with an update once we're done."

"Thank you for doing this."

"Happy to help, especially with an asshole like this guy."

Chapter Twenty-Three

Tasha

It was Sunday—discharge day. Part of me was looking forward to leaving the hospital, maybe even figuring out how to have a real shower instead of a sponge bath, but mostly, I was nervous. *Really* nervous. I'd be going home with Drew for a while—until I could do at least basic things on my own and the locks had been changed out on my apartment door, however long that might take. Management at my complex wasn't the most responsive.

I was anxious about living with Drew, though.

I was also anxious about living on my own again somewhere Duncan would be able to find me once I left Drew's.

And I was anxious about running into Duncan as I was leaving the hospital.

Just anxious in general. About everything. As much as being in a hospital around the clock sucked, I'd also started to feel safe there, and I wasn't in a rush for that sense of safety to disappear.

I watched as my surgeon went through all my discharge instructions with Drew and they discussed the medical details of my break, using significantly more medical jargon than when either was speaking to me. I only half-listened, knowing Drew would remember every word and could tell me anything I needed to know later when I was better able to focus.

Drew and my surgeon shook hands, and before I knew it, Drew was helping me into a wheelchair, a nurse standing behind. It was embarrassing how much help I needed, but I was grateful Drew had insisted on being the one to help me so he was the one leaning against me to hook his arms under my armpits and maneuver me around until I could sit in the wheelchair. I wasn't up for being touched by anyone else.

"This is humiliating," I muttered, out of breath.

Drew's brow furrowed. "Your femur is broken, Tasha. You're gonna need help. But I promise we'll work on you being able to do more for yourself, okay?" He squeezed my hand. "You're strong and stubborn and determined, and you have your own personal physical therapist—you'll be moving yourself around in no time." He winked.

I sighed. My heart raced as my thoughts shifted to the possibility of running into Duncan after we left the room.

"I'll meet you guys at the entrance," Drew said.

My eyes flitted to his and I clutched his hand more tightly. "You're not walking out with me?"

He paused. "I need to bring my car up, and I don't want you to have to wait outside." His eyes flicked over my face, then he continued in a determinedly calm voice. "He's not even allowed inside the building—I made sure of it. And there'll be security at the doors, and I'll be there by the time you get there, too. If he's outside, he won't get anywhere near you—I won't let him. I promise."

Drew's confidence had been well-founded because leaving was uneventful aside from the difficulty of getting me into his SUV. Drew talked through the short drive to his apartment about how happy Watson was going to be, and I felt a modicum of excitement. I was also going to be happy to see *him*.

Once Drew had parked, he produced a wheelchair seemingly out of thin air.

"You keep a wheelchair in the back of your car? That's not weird or anything."

He chuckled. "I got this yesterday because you'll need one for a while, brat."

I grinned. "Whatever you say, Droobie Drew."

My grin faded away, forgotten, as Drew lifted me from the car and set me down in the wheelchair; any tensing in my broken leg was excruciating, not to mention that rubbing against Drew's body felt like the burns were happening all over again. I gritted my teeth against the pain, not wanting to complain because I understood it couldn't be helped.

"I'm sorry," Drew said with sympathy as he pushed me toward the building. "I was being as careful as I could."

"I know," I replied, my voice thin and teary.

"It'll get better."

I nodded and he gave my shoulder a light squeeze.

As we neared his door, I could hear Watson whining and barking and generally going crazy with anticipation. I was nervous about him jumping on me, but otherwise felt as excited as he sounded. At the door, Drew opened it a fraction, slipping inside to try to calm Watson down. After a minute, I supposed he must have given up because he opened the door, holding it with his foot so he could wrap his arms around his enormous lab to keep him from jumping onto my lap.

I cried at seeing him, and Watson was whining and frantic, his paws up over the armrest of the chair, alternately nuzzling me and licking my face. I laughed, tears streaming down my cheeks as I talked to him. He tripped over his own feet trying to keep his face touching me as Drew wheeled me inside. My heart felt like it was going to explode with love, and I couldn't stop grinning and talking to him.

Eventually, Watson calmed enough for Drew to wheel me around for a tour of his apartment. It was the nicest and largest apartment I'd ever been in, and I told him so. His cheeks turned pink, and he shrugged.

"I liked it and it's a good location—I can walk to the hospital and the office. It's still cheaper than the apartment I had in Chandler." He scratched behind Watson's ears. "And I wanted Watson to have plenty of space to roam, too."

We continued the tour, seeing the kitchen, dining room, living room, den or office space, and large bedroom.

"I already unpacked all your clothes—you've got the right side of the dresser and the closet." He opened the drawers and closet doors to show me. "You'll take the bed—I've got an air mattress that I'll put on the floor here for a while since I'm not sure I'd hear you in the den if you needed something. Once you're able to get yourself to and from the bathroom, I'll move to the den."

"Drew," I breathed out, feeling really emotional about how much my presence was disrupting his life. "I can't make you sleep on an air mattress in your own apartment."

He ran his fingers down my arm and clasped my hand. "I will never let you sleep on anything but the bed, I don't care whose apartment it is."

I eyed his king size bed. We'd shared a much smaller bed before—many times. "You can sleep on the bed, too," I offered quietly.

He gave my hand a squeeze. "We'll see." He pulled his hand from mine and wheeled me into the bathroom. "Luckily, I have a walk-in shower. As soon as you can stand for a while on one leg and use a walker to get around a bit without weighting your broken leg, you can shower."

"Can we try it now?" I asked. "I'm dying for a real shower."

"No," he said, his voice full of regret. "I won't have a walker for you until tomorrow. I can pick it up after noon. As soon as I get back with it, we can see if you're able to shower. But it also depends on how things look under the bandaging on your legs. Does that work?"

"Don't you have to work tomorrow?"

"No."

"You don't work on Mondays?"

He turned me around and we headed back into the bedroom. "I do, normally, but I took this week off. I figured you wouldn't want a home nurse coming in all day while I was gone, and I wasn't nuts about that idea, either. I'd rather be the one here helping you. Hopefully by next week, you can manage while I'm gone. I'll be able to come home at lunchtime every day, so it would only be a few hours at a time."

Again, I felt guilty. "I can deal with a nurse, Drew. I don't want you changing anything for me."

He'd stepped over to the dresser, but turned around and leaned back against it, his arms crossed over his chest as he considered me. I could see from the swirling in his eyes that he had a lot he wanted to say and was holding back.

"Tasha… I love you." His voice cracked and he ran his hand over his jaw, his eyes scanning the ceiling briefly. "What I'm doing is the only thing I *can* do when it's you. No amount of change to my life for you would be too much."

I felt his words like a hammer to my chest. I loved him, too—I loved him more than I'd ever loved anyone—but I didn't understand why he still cared about me. I was stupid and pathetic, having gotten myself into the situation I was in because I was too screwed up from my childhood to make sound decisions or listen when the only person who'd ever truly cared about me tried to warn me.

Drew knelt down near my feet at the first whimper to escape me, then draped himself over my upper body, wrapping his arms around me as I sobbed into his chest. I cried for what I'd been through in my life, as a child and as an adult. I cried for having been so needy that I'd married someone abusive. I cried for having been stupid enough to justify what Duncan had done to me and for staying with him as long as I did. I cried for how much I knew my decisions had already put Drew through, and what I knew they were putting him through right now. I cried for what might have been with Drew if I hadn't married Duncan.

And I cried because I wanted the love Drew was offering me, but it also hurt to accept it.

Chapter Twenty-Four

Drew

Tasha wore me down about a shower until I agreed on Wednesday to wrap her bandages with plastic even though I knew her surgeon would say no. I understood that dry shampoo and wiping yourself with a washcloth for a week was miserable, and I couldn't stand seeing her so unhappy any longer.

We'd gotten into a routine where I managed to help her change for bed and get dressed for the day while allowing her to maintain some of her privacy. I could tell how uncomfortable she was, and I didn't want to make that any worse. And as much as I'd thought about Tasha naked before, when she had no choice about it wasn't how I wanted to see her. So I'd very carefully avoided looking any higher on her thigh than necessary when wrapping it with plastic, just as I did every time I applied ointments to her burns.

For the shower, until the back-ordered shower bench came in, we'd agreed that I would hand her a soapy cloth and she'd wash what she could easily reach, and the walker would be there for her to use for support as needed to make sure she didn't weight her broken leg. I'd be in the bathroom the whole time just in case. If she tired out before she was done, I'd hand her a dress that she would pull on in the shower so I could lean in and wash her hair for her. Otherwise, her towel and wheelchair were right outside the shower, so when she was done, she could dry herself while sitting down. I was worried that something would go wrong—that she would lose her balance or be too stubborn to notice herself fatiguing and end up standing on her broken leg, shredding the muscle again. If she did that, she might never walk again.

"How're you doing?" I asked for at least the seventh or eighth time since she'd gotten in a few minutes earlier. It took everything in my power to keep from turning around to physically keep an eye on her.

"Still fine, worry wart," she replied with a laugh, though her voice sounded noticeably more strained than it had. "Working on my hair now."

I asked her four more times how she was doing before the water shut off.

"Can you pull the door open?" she asked.

I reached behind me, still facing away from the shower, and pulled the door open. "Are you sure you can get over that lip?"

I'd helped her into the shower, but she would be getting herself over the raised lip of the shower pan to get out since she was now naked.

There was a small grunt behind me. "Already past it," she said a second later. "I'm good. You can go. I'm about to sit down."

I walked past Watson, who was lying by the sink to wait for Tasha, into the bedroom and eyed the floor next to the bed as I went. My air mattress was there, as neatly made as the bed it was next to. I'd been sleeping there every night since bringing Tasha home with me, and I likely would for another night or two before I moved to the den. She woke up often at night, either in pain or having to use the bathroom or from a nightmare, and I was able to help her right away because I was so close. From the den, I might not even hear her, and I knew she wouldn't intentionally wake me up unless she felt she had no other choice. I also knew better than to suggest a baby monitor. As much as I told her I'd rather she wake me up unnecessarily than not wake me up at all, she continued to feel like a burden to me. As if anything to do with her could ever inconvenience me.

"I never thought a shower could be so tiring," Tasha said, out of breath as she wheeled herself into the living room a little while later.

I turned, taking her in. Her damp hair hung around her shoulders and her cheeks were flushed with exertion. I could smell her shampoo and body wash, and she looked more like herself. She was so damn beautiful. I'd always known it, but for some reason she was taking my breath away right then. My chest ached under my tattoo, but in a way I mostly liked. I rubbed a hand over it and grinned at her.

She returned my smile tentatively, her face turning a deeper shade of red.

"Do you want to lay down?" I asked, standing. "I can help you get into bed."

"What are my other options?" she asked with a smirk.

I frowned. I knew it was pretty boring for her. "We can go for a walk once your hair is dry."

She glanced down at the growing wet spots on her shirt. "I wanted to dry it, but I'm too tired."

"I can dry it for you," I offered, already heading toward the bathroom.

I returned with her hair dryer and brush, then situated her so she could look out the living room window while I dried her hair. I'd never done it before, and I hoped I didn't screw it up—I wanted to do something nice for her.

When I moved from the hair in the back to the hair on the side, I saw that her eyes were closed, a peaceful expression on her face. It made that ache intensify, and I wanted to bend over and touch my lips to hers. I didn't, because I couldn't. I knew that. But it didn't change that I wanted to.

"Thank you," she murmured, blinking her eyes open languidly. "That felt amazing. I might let you do that more often."

"I will happily be your personal hair dryer."

"Just like you're my personal physical therapist?"

"Yeah," I said, taking the dryer and brush back to the bathroom.

Tasha's demeanor was still relaxed, but there was a sadness to it when I walked back out. That happened a lot, but I knew that over time it would get better and tried to remind myself to be patient. My first instinct was to try to find a way to fix it, but some things just couldn't be fixed; they simply had to be allowed to exist.

"There are a lot of other people who need you, Drew," she said, just over a whisper. "It's selfish of me to have you to myself."

"I don't agree, but it wasn't your decision anyway—it was mine."

"They need you, Drew. You should be helping *them*. Not *me*."

I sighed. "Sofa?"

She nodded, staring through the floor. I helped her move from the wheelchair onto the sofa and get situated so her leg was propped up. After moving her wheelchair to the side, I sat next to her, sliding an arm around her shoulders and squeezing her into my side before placing a kiss on the top of her head.

"I never told you when I decided to become a physical therapist. Or why."

"I know why, Drew. You want to help people. And you really want to help people like us."

I kissed the top of her head again. "That's all true, but that's not it. Physical therapy never crossed my mind as something I might be interested in until I was a teen." I paused, taking a deep breath and allowing the emotion from my memories to pass so I could keep speaking in a calm, level voice. "The first time you saw a physical therapist, you were fifteen. We both were. Your mom had pushed you and it messed up your hip."

"I remember."

"That night, after physical therapy, we snuck over to the park, and you broke down telling me about it."

"Yeah. Dr. Baker. He pushed his fingertips into my ass and grabbed the inside of my thigh. He was just working on my leg at the end, but I freaked out."

"Yeah," I said, now running my fingers through her hair, seeing her that night. "I felt so helpless and angry. Not only were your parents abusing you, but someone who was supposed to help was making it worse because they didn't know any better. I thought if it had been me, I'd have known not to touch you in certain ways because of what was happening at home. That was the night I decided I wanted to be a physical therapist."

She sniffled and I realized she was crying. I reached over—slowly so I wouldn't startle her—and wiped the tears from her cheeks.

"You needed me as I am now back then, but of course I couldn't help you then. I can now, though. And being able to help you—*you*, Tash—is the whole reason I became a physical therapist. There isn't another person on this planet whose needs come before yours as far as I'm concerned. Not now, not ever."

Chapter Twenty-Five

Tasha

While it was awkward to have Drew by my side when going into a meeting about divorcing Duncan, I was more grateful than I knew how to express that he'd been willing not only to take me but to be there with me the entire time. Once inside, we only waited a minute or two before being ushered into the lawyer's office. He introduced himself as Roger, then asked me to tell him in my words why I was seeking a divorce and what I was looking to get out of it. We'd already talked briefly over the phone, and I'd sent him some information in advance, but he wanted to start from scratch while we were on the record.

My eyes darted to Drew nervously, but his hand was squeezing mine with reassurance.

"It's okay, Nats," he said soothingly.

I looked down at my lap. All of this was hard for him—I knew it was. And while he knew many of the things Duncan had done, having to listen to them again was another matter. With a deep breath, I gave the shortest summary I could, unable to maintain eye contact.

"Duncan has hurt me. Several times. And I want a divorce as quickly as possible. That's all I want."

"Can you be more specific about what you mean by hurt?"

My heart raced as if it was trying to escape a comet or something. It would be the first I'd confessed to anyone other than Drew the things Duncan had done to me... the things I'd *allowed* Duncan to do to me by staying with him. I cleared my throat. "Most recently... he pushed me down a flight of stairs. It's why I'm in a wheelchair right now."

Roger's eyes looked up from his notetaking, filled with sympathy. "And your injuries?"

"Broken femur."

"And second- and third-degree burns from holding a coffee pot to her skin and the contents spilling on her," Drew added. "And bruising and lacerations to her face."

"Is that correct, Ms. Avery?"

My stomach dropped. "Yes. But please don't call me that. Tasha or Ms. Williams—anything but Ms. Avery. That's *his* name."

Roger inclined his head in acknowledgement. "And were there other instances of violence?"

I nodded, inhaling tremulously, then told him about other times Duncan had hurt me. I wasn't sure I'd recited all of them, though; the longer we were there, the more anxious I was, and my thoughts were becoming scrambled.

"Any sexual violence?"

My stomach dropped again. I didn't know how to answer that question. He hadn't hit me or anything like that when it came to sex, but he'd been pushy and hadn't cared when I didn't want to have sex or give him a blow job. Did that count? Was it considered violence when he wasn't striking me? When I wasn't fighting back?

Drew's hand tightened on mine, and when I looked up, his jaw was clenched tight.

"I don't—I don't think so," I finally said, my face flaming. I felt so stupid that I wasn't even sure. It was so confusing because he hadn't been violent exactly, but the way he'd been starting in the hotel in Vegas when we arrived—the way he'd been so aggressive when I didn't want to have sex, and the way I'd felt the need to distract him by giving him what he wanted to keep him from blowing up about my tattoo was like my stepfather had been, and I knew that had been wrong. "I mean... not like the other stuff," I added, the faintness of my voice reflecting my uncertainty.

"But there are things he did?" Drew asked, his voice quiet and tight.

"He just... he got pushy when I didn't want to... really pushy. Not all the time, but when he really wanted to and I didn't."

Drew swallowed and it was loud in the silence following my words. He was turned to look away from me, but I could see the tension in his body. He was furious and barely containing it. I was sure if I could see his face, it would look like it did the day he attacked my stepfather.

"You've got police reports?" Roger asked.

I shook my head. "No. I never filed any charges against him."

"None?"

"None."

"And you guys have been married for less than a year?"

"Yes."

"And you got married in Las Vegas. Was it a planned elopement?"

I shook my head again. "No. He planned the trip as a getaway, and when we got there, he said he wanted to get married. I didn't, but I ended up doing it anyway. He was... pushy. And I was stupid."

"Were you coerced?"

"No? He was insistent, and I was drunk and scared and really stupid."

"Stop calling yourself stupid," Drew cut in.

"I was."

"No, you weren't."

"Yes, I was, Drew. Duncan wasn't taking no for an answer, and I was afraid, and I was really drunk by the time we got to the chapel—on purpose—because I saw it as inevitable. I didn't think I had any choice. But there was also a small part of me that thought going through with it would at least get back at you for ignoring me."

I heard Drew's sharp intake of breath, felt an increase in the tension in his body. "What?"

"I told you I was stupid," I muttered.

"For fuck's sake, Tasha, stop saying that," he bit out, sounding equally aggravated and upset. "You aren't stupid, and you never were. You were hurt. That's not the same thing."

Roger listened, watching us with faintly narrowed eyes until Drew and I finished our aside and I looked back toward him, flushed with embarrassment.

"Anything else?" Roger asked.

My head moved side to side. "No. I don't think so."

Roger sat up, scanning his notes. "So, the good news is that we live in a state that recognizes spousal abuse as grounds for divorce, and it doesn't require the standard one-year separation period first. You don't even need Duncan to agree to the divorce for you to get it, though it will slow things down if he doesn't, possibly several months. If he cooperates, you could be divorced in as little as six to eight weeks."

He set his pen down and clasped his hands on his desk. "The bad news is that you haven't filed any police reports, which provide needed evidence. You will need to file a police report at least for this most recent assault if you want to get a divorce on the grounds of spousal abuse. And while you didn't file for any previous assaults, any documentation can be helpful, including hospital records of any injuries you received treatment for. You do have on your side that he has already established a pattern of violence during his last marriage."

"His last marriage?" I asked, sure I heard wrong. Duncan had never mentioned being married before.

"Yes. He was married previously and divorced for spousal abuse then as well. His ex-wife pressed charges and he was incarcerated."

I felt ill—really ill. Like I might throw up and pass out, and my mind was spinning and my lungs not properly functioning. "I had no idea," I said faintly.

"I'm sorry, Ms. Williams."

"You're sure?"

Roger gave a short nod.

"He stabbed his ex-wife and she almost died," Drew added gently.

"You *knew*?"

"I just found out while you were in the hospital, I swear."

"And you didn't think you should tell me?" I shouted. It was like a rug had been pulled out from under my feet.

Drew's jaw worked back and forth. "If I had found out before I did, you'd have known within seconds. But while you were in the hospital, I didn't think I should tell you. You had already decided to stay as far from him as possible, and I didn't see that telling you would do anything but hurt you more. So no, I didn't tell you, because I didn't want to hurt you."

"You should have told me."

"I didn't want to hurt you, Tasha," he repeated emphatically. "You were already hurt enough."

Anger and guilt and gratitude and frustration and fear all warred for prominence, and I blinked rapidly to keep from crying. It was a miracle I hadn't yet, and I was hoping to make it at least to the car before I broke down.

Roger cleared his throat and continued. "Once you file a police report, we shouldn't run into much trouble with getting your divorce finalized, though as I mentioned, if he doesn't cooperate, it could drag out a little longer. I also advise that you request alimony if you aren't going to ultimately press charges against him and collect damages."

"I don't want anything from him," I said. "Except for this divorce."

"You should do it, Tasha," Drew said quietly. "You said you don't have health insurance. And he should be the one to pay for your medical bills—not you. And he should be paying your lawyer fees, too."

My head was spinning more than it was before. "I don't know. I just... I don't know." I couldn't even get my eyes to settle on a single focal point.

"I advise you do this, Ms. Williams," Roger said. "Off the record, I also advise that you press charges against him so he can't do this to another woman."

Those words sucked the air from my lungs. I hadn't thought about that... that he could do this to someone else. I was the second...

at least. How many more might there be if I didn't do something to keep it from happening again? I let out a sigh and swiped at a few errant tears slipping out.

"Okay. I'll do it. All of it."

Chapter Twenty-Six

Drew

I was worried about Tasha by the time we left the police station, which she'd insisted we go to straight after leaving the meeting with the lawyer. I'd suggested we go the next day to give her an emotional break, but she disagreed. She was pale and withdrawn, and barely indicated she even heard me when I spoke to her. When we got out of the car, I wasn't sure what to do. All I knew was that if we went inside the apartment, she would probably ask to go to bed, and that could make things worse.

"How about a walk?" I asked. It was early fall, and the weather was perfect—not too hot and not too cool—and today was sunny with a bright blue sky. We went for at least one walk almost every day already, though we always had Watson with us.

"Okay," she said, nearly inaudible.

I sent a silent apology to Watson that he was going to miss out and pushed Tasha's wheelchair toward a small urban park a few blocks away. It wasn't large, but it was pretty, with lots of trees and grass on its one-block footprint. I walked us around the perimeter, then along the little walkways until we'd covered all of them, the whole time in silence aside from the breeze rustling the leaves in the trees. Lastly, I pushed her wheelchair up to the end of a bench and locked the wheels, then sat down on that end of the bench, right next to her. After a while, I reached over and touched her hand gently with my fingertips, running them over the back and then toward her palm between her thumb and forefinger. She rolled her hand over and I continued down over her semicolon tattoo, then back up and across her palm, ultimately keeping our palms together as I slipped my fingers between hers.

She was still staring into the distance, but her jaw now trembled, and she squeezed my hand tight. My chest more than ached—it was splitting apart to see her in so much pain. I wanted to take it all from her—just lift it off her and rest it down on myself. I could handle anything as long as I could keep it from her. She'd already been through more than any person ever should before Duncan, and I wanted to rage against the world that she was going through this right now. It wasn't fair.

"It just... it hurts, you know?" she said, still staring into the distance. "Not because I loved him that much—I didn't, really. But I feel stupid and embarrassed that I allowed myself to get into this position, that I allowed myself to be duped like I was. I'm so ashamed of what I let him do to me—of what I justified and blamed myself for. That I lied so he wouldn't look bad. I kept telling myself if I just didn't talk to you, then it would be okay since you set him off, but... you were the worst, but you weren't the only one he was jealous of. He was starting to get jealous of anyone who spoke to me or looked at me. But I thought if I could just keep him happy, then he'd love me. And I wanted so badly to be loved."

She sniffled and wiped at her cheeks as I swiped at mine. I wanted to tell her that she *was* loved—desperately loved... by me. As loved as a person could be. I'd known for a while that I was desperately in love with her, and it was the reason I'd refused to share a bed with her. It hadn't felt right to do that when I had these kinds of feelings for her and she didn't know it. I wanted to tell her now, to confess everything. But it wasn't the right time—it wasn't what she needed right then—so I didn't.

"And, I know how stupid it sounds, but finding out he was married before... I'd thought I was special, you know? I mean, he hurt me, but I thought he loved me, that I was someone special to him. But he had done this whole thing with someone else before... How much of what he said to me was exactly what he'd said to his first wife? I know it's ridiculous."

I lifted her hand and kissed the back of it. "It's not ridiculous." I kissed her hand again. "And it's his loss, Tasha. You *are* special. Even if *he* didn't really see it, I do. I always have."

After our walk, we spent the evening in the apartment, and I was glad I'd taken the day off; I'd almost just taken the morning for meeting the lawyer. Now that I was back to work, I was gone most of the day with patients. And the next day I'd be starting my three shifts at the hospital again. While I was there, I was going to see what I could do about shifting around my patients and schedules so I could have weekends off again instead of working every Saturday; that way, I'd have two full days every week with Tasha. Now that we were in each other's lives again, I wanted to spend less time working; working six or seven days hadn't mattered that much to me before, but it did now.

After over an hour of playing my guitar and singing, as much for Tasha as for myself, I was feeling more relaxed and connected with her, and she seemed better than she had. I suggested she teach me to make her mac-n-cheese for dinner that night and she actually laughed.

"I can try to teach you all you want, but it'll never be as good as mine."

I smirked. "Challenge accepted."

She raised her eyebrows. "Good luck."

"You can't sabotage me, either."

She rolled her eyes. "I won't. That would be cheating. And I don't need to cheat to win. I can give you directions all day long, but you won't have that special touch."

Grateful to have a large kitchen, I managed to get Tasha situated comfortably and safely on the counter so she could actually see what I was doing, then per her instructions pulled out ingredients and set them on the counter. By the time we'd made it through the first step to prep the seasonings—which included such precise measurements as large handful, small handful, and different sized pinches—it was clear she'd been right. There was absolutely no way my mac-n-cheese was going to be anywhere near as good as hers because my hands were a different size, and I couldn't seem to get the handfuls and pinches to be the right size.

Not that I cared at all—I didn't care if it was completely inedible and I had to cook something new or order takeout. The air was filled with teasing and laughter, and I was thoroughly enjoying myself. Eventually, I got the mac-n-cheese into the oven, feeling somewhat triumphant that I'd made it that far with such vague measurements and instructions, and leaned a hip against the counter next to Tasha, watching her.

Her face was flushed from laughing and her eyes were sparkling and full of mischief. She looked absolutely beautiful, and I couldn't breathe.

She quirked an eyebrow. "You alright there, Drewby?"

I rubbed my hand over my chest and smiled. At the park hadn't been the right time, but was it now? Could I tell her right then how I felt about her? The words wanted to burst out of me.

"I think you need more cardio if making mac-n-cheese gets you out of breath," she said with an impish grin. "Maybe I should go down to the gym with you in the morning and give you some pointers."

I started to laugh, but then realized I actually loved the idea. She could get up and come down with me while I worked out, and between my sets, we could do her physical therapy. It would be like working out together. "I think you're going to be hard-pressed to find room for improvement in my routine, but you're definitely coming to the gym with me in the morning. And you're gonna be working, too."

She smirked. "We'll see who's working harder by the end."

I laughed and reached a hand over to tuck some hair that had fallen in front of her face behind her ear. My fingertips burned. The laughter fell from her eyes to be replaced with a fiery intensity that looked a lot like how I felt.

I swallowed.

She swallowed.

Looking intently into each other's eyes, I was trying to tell her how I felt without words and trying to read if it would be welcome news. Her cheeks were steadily turning pink.

"It wasn't..." I began before trailing off. She'd left the hospital less than two weeks earlier because her husband had pushed her down a flight of stairs. Even if how I felt was welcome, sharing how I felt about her right then would have been another weight on her shoulders.

"What wasn't what?" she asked.

I shook my head and gave her a small smile. "Ready to go to the living room until the mac-n-cheese is done?"

I lifted her from the counter and back into her wheelchair, then rolled her into the living room, where I got her settled comfortably with her phone before walking back into the kitchen to check on the food. When I returned to the living room, Tasha was looking at her phone screen, her eyes glassy and mouth pulled down.

"What's wrong?" I asked, afraid Duncan had found another way to reach her. His number had been blocked before she was even discharged from the hospital, but it was only a matter of time before he figured out he could reach her if he changed his number.

She gave a small headshake and a forced smile, setting her phone down.

I sat next to her, looping my arm around her back. "Talk to me, Nats."

"Do you think I could be walking by November?"

That was another two and a half months away. "Maybe. You'll definitely be on crutches, though, if you are. Why? What's in November?"

"The largest book fair and expo in the country. I go every year."

"That's the one you've told me about that you started going to after you moved out here?"

"Yeah, that's the one."

"We can go. Where is it this year?"

"Pittsburgh."

"You'll like it there," I said, thinking of the strip with its old buildings.

"You've been?" she asked.

"Yeah, for a medical conference once. There's a lot to see, though, and I didn't have a lot of free time. I'd love to go back. How long is the expo?"

"It runs for three days."

"Wanna go for a week so we can explore the city after the expo?"

Her eyes searched mine, clearly confused. "You actually *want* to go?"

I laughed before I remembered why she'd be asking me a question like that... because Duncan never wanted to do anything she did. I looked away for a minute so she wouldn't see how angry I was. "It doesn't matter because it's not about me, Tash. But yes, I *do* wanna go."

Chapter Twenty-Seven

Tasha

After getting dressed—with painstaking slowness—for exercising and hobbling into the bathroom to brush my teeth, I sighed, noticing mine and Drew's shared toothpaste tube was empty. I'd noticed the night before, but had been hoping he'd pull out a new one since it would be easier for him than for me to do so wherever he kept them. At two months post-surgery on my leg, I now moved around much better and had been on crutches for a couple of weeks, but getting into an under-sink cabinet to root around for another tube of toothpaste would be a challenge.

"Oh, Drewy Baby," I called, smirking because I knew how much he hated when I called him that. "Please tell me you have another tube of toothpaste in here and that it's easy to get to."

There was no response, but a few seconds later Drew walked into the bathroom. He peered over at the spent toothpaste tube as he grabbed his toothbrush.

"You've got plenty."

I squinted at the empty tube, then grabbed it to toss it into the trash can. "I'm calling bullshit. Where's the toothpaste?"

Drew snapped it out of my hand. "Don't waste my toothpaste, brat."

"If you're so convinced there's plenty in there, prove it. I bet you can't get any more out of there."

He set the tube down on the counter, then used the back of his toothbrush to smooth from the back to the front of the tube. It was obvious before he even took the cap off that there was more toothpaste sitting there to come out.

"See? At least a few more days' worth. Don't be so wasteful."

"I'm not wasteful."

He shrugged. "You were getting ready to waste all that toothpaste." He winked and squeezed some onto his toothbrush.

I narrowed my eyes at him. "I bet I can get more out of it than you can."

He hmphed. "Good luck."

"I don't need luck," I muttered, then began brushing my own teeth.

I looked up at Drew, still breathing hard from the grueling exercises he made me do, plus the work of getting to the elevator. "I hate crutches," I grumbled loudly. I was starting to walk without them, but only under Drew's watchful eye. But crutches were exhausting and uncomfortable and I couldn't wait to be done with them.

Drew chuckled, still catching his breath from his last sprint on the treadmill before we left the gym. We went down to the gym every morning together—we had for the last six weeks. It was possibly my favorite part of the day and definitely the best way to start my day. We'd established this routine together, and I liked it. I was starting to feel settled, though I was about to upend that sense of security because maintenance had *finally* changed out the locks on my apartment door. As long as I didn't do anything to hurt myself in the meantime, I would be moving back into my own place in a few days' time.

I hobbled onto the elevator ahead of Drew and pushed the button for his floor before using my forearm to wipe the sweat dripping down my forehead. Drew reached over with my shirt and wiped my temples and over my forehead again before using his shirt to wipe his own face. Not that I understood the point as I eyed the sweat dripping down his chest.

"It's like trying to save the Titanic with a one-gallon bucket, isn't it?"

Drew burst out laughing, glancing down at his chest, then shrugging. "Whatever. That sprint was hard."

Normally, I would have run with a comment like that, but my brain wasn't functioning; it was too distracted by Drew's naked torso. I was starting to get used to being brainless for a while, however, since this happened every morning. Forcing my eyes away, I looked down at my own torso, which was just as sweaty as his. It was gratifying that I could also see muscular definition—not as much as Drew had, but it was there. And I'd worked hard for it.

"When I'm out of these crutches, I'll show you what a hard sprint actually looks like."

"You have never and will never run faster than me."

I shook my head, tsking. "It's not all about speed, Drew. There's this little thing called endurance. You need to work on it." I winked, then grinned, adjusting my weight on the crutches.

He was still chuckling as his eyes roamed downward when I shifted, and his good humor faded. It happened from time to time when he saw my legs—scars from a long incision that had been closed with staples and burns marring my tattoo as well as much of my skin.

"It's okay," I soothed. I knew when this was happening, he was hurting for what I'd been through, feeling misplaced guilt for not having somehow protected me from my own stupidity.

He sniffed loudly, looking up at the floor indicator above the doors. "It'll never be okay," he said, his voice low and quiet.

"Maybe I should just start wearing pants." I'd thought about it to begin with, self-conscious about all my scars, but Drew had convinced me not to—he knew I overheated easily and hated working out in pants.

"No," he said with a small headshake. "I'm sorry. I don't mean to make you self-conscious."

"I know you don't. And I don't mean to make you feel bad about what happened."

The elevator doors slid open, and Drew waited for me to exit first, an arm ensuring the doors wouldn't close on me.

"You're not making me feel bad about anything, Tasha. How I feel is on me—not you."

We moved in silence the rest of the way to Drew's apartment, where he slipped inside ahead of me to keep Watson from jumping on me. It didn't matter how short a time I was absent, Watson went crazy with excitement every time I came back through the door. After dishing out plenty of love until Watson was content while Drew showered and got ready for work, I was ready to get myself cleaned up. I was sticky with dried sweat and didn't smell that great, either.

Drew walked out from the bedroom in scrubs; it was a hospital day for him. I smirked, looking him up and down. There was something about him in scrubs that I *really* liked. When I raised my eyes, Drew was watching me, his blue-gray eyes stormy; I'd been caught. My face heated and I looked away. I knew I shouldn't have been looking at my best friend the way I just was, but sometimes I couldn't help it. I was attracted to him. More so every day.

"I'm going to miss this," I murmured. I hadn't intended to think aloud, but I had and my skin went from warm to hot.

Drew leaned back against the counter, his hands holding the edge. "You don't have to move out, Nats," he said with a measured slowness. "You can stay here... with me."

My eyes scanned the floor restlessly. I wasn't looking forward to moving out—I really liked living there with Drew. But I couldn't stay. It was a one-bedroom apartment and Drew was still sleeping on an air mattress. Not to mention that being in such close proximity was making it ever more difficult to remember we were only friends.

"No, I need to go back to my apartment."

"You don't have to," he said again. "Watson and I like having you here."

I smiled, a warm glow spreading through my body. "I like being here with you guys. But I need my own space, and you need yours back, Drew. Just think—you'll be sleeping on a real bed again."

He grunted.

"And I won't have to deal with this retina-damaging view every day," I added, gesturing generally in his direction.

He chuckled.

"If I stayed much longer, I'd end up blind."

"Alright, brat, that's enough," he laughed, running a hand through his hair. "You think my hair is too long?" he asked.

"What?" I asked, drawing my brows in.

"Do you think my hair is too long? Should I cut it?"

"No," I replied, drawing the word out and making it sound almost like a question.

"My beard, then? You never did tell me if you liked my facial hair or not."

Then it hit me: he was feeling insecure. I was so used to him being self-assured that I forgot sometimes that he struggled with self-doubt just as I did. Not as much as he used to—and nowhere near as much as I still did—but it happened from time to time. Either something someone said or something he saw or had been thinking about triggered a memory and brought the feeling of worthlessness his parents instilled in him flooding back.

I hobbled over until I was standing directly in front of him and, very carefully, weighted my broken leg and leaned my crutches against the counter. Shuffling slowly as Drew watched me with concern, I got my feet situated so I had one on either side of his, then leaned my body into him, winding my arms around his neck, cradling the back of his head in my hands. He shifted and wrapped his arms tight around my waist, his face pressed into the crook of my neck.

"I was only joking," I said into his ear. "I think your hair looks great this length, and I love your beard. And you know you have a nice body and are funny and a gifted physical therapist." I sighed. "You're amazing, Drew—you're perfect. I love you exactly the way you are."

His arms tightened, crushing my ribs, and he let out a shuddering breath. "Why does it always feel like I'll never be good enough?" he asked, his voice muffled because he was talking directly into my neck.

"Because your dad was a complete asshole."

He snorted.

"And your mom was a raging bitch."

He snorted again.

"So was *bitchy Becky*, actually."

He left out a soft chuckle.

"They're the ones who'll never be good enough for *you*, Drew—not the other way around. You're more than good enough—you always have been, just by being you."

He nodded against me.

"Besides, there isn't a thing I'd change about you, and my opinion's the only one that really matters anyway."

His chest shook and rumbled under me as he laughed and I smiled, using my fingertips to lightly scratch the back of his head. His body shivered, his neck all of a sudden covered in goosebumps. I kissed the side of his head, breathing in the smell of his freshly shampooed hair.

"Love you, you know," I said.

He sighed, his body feeling heavier against me. "Love you, too."

Chapter Twenty-Eight

Tasha

verything of mine at Drew's was packed up, and it was time to move it back to my apartment only a week before our trip to Pittsburgh. I was pretty much useless in that endeavor—even if I could have done some of the actual moving of my stuff, which *I* thought I could, Drew was adamant that I wasn't strong enough yet and that I touch nothing. I surveyed the inside of his apartment from where my things were piled up near the door. I was *really* going to miss living there, and it was definitely going to require an adjustment to go from his upscale apartment in a nice neighborhood to my shoddy apartment in a sketchy neighborhood. I'd been accustomed to it before, but when Drew and I had gone by to get the new keys and make sure the old keys no longer worked a few days earlier, I realized for the first time just how rundown everything was. But it was what I could afford until I had money coming in more regularly from my books.

Which, with any luck, would start happening soon. With two books through editing and release dates over the next eighteen months, I had a small measure of hope. I was also hoping to be ready to submit my autofiction novel by the end of the year and was already crossing my fingers that I'd get a contract for it. I had more autofiction ideas, too—I might have found my writing groove.

"You sure about this, Nats?" Drew asked, his brow furrowed. He'd become more and more agitated and worried about me moving back to my apartment as the date neared. He scratched behind Watson's ears as Watson passed him on his way to my side. "You don't have to go."

"Yeah. I'm sure." And I was. As much as I wanted to stay, I *needed* to go. I needed to be on my own for a while. I'd realized recently that this stretch of time since Duncan had put me in the hospital, if I considered myself out of a relationship for that entire time, was the longest I'd gone without a boyfriend by about double... in years. *Years.* Since my freshman year of college in fact. It was embarrassing. And sad. Especially when considering some of them only lasted a few weeks.

I realized I didn't really know how to be alone. Ever since I'd met Drew when we were kids, I hadn't been—I'd always had him when we were growing up. Then, when we went to college and saw a lot less of each other, I was so scared of being alone that I dated any guy who looked twice at me. I needed to figure out how to be alone and be happy with myself. I needed to make some damn friends. Not that Drew wasn't the best friend any person could ever want, but he shouldn't be the only one I had, and he was. He was also a loner, yet even *he* had made friends in the few months he'd lived in Brinkley. I'd been there for years and didn't have a single real friend. Because I'd always thrown all my energy into my latest romantic interest. I supposed in a way that moving back to my apartment when it wasn't what either of us wanted was my way of testing myself. It also wasn't fair to Drew for me to stay. It wasn't fair for him to sleep on an air mattress any longer than he already had. And he needed a place to bring someone back to when he was ready to date again.

Bile rose into my throat at that thought. *Maybe I should stay so he can't date anymore.* I liked that idea a lot better than him finding a woman he wanted to bring home for the night. I shook my head sharply, trying to rid myself of those thoughts. I'd have to deal with it eventually when he found someone, but for now I could just pretend it wouldn't ever happen. There might have been a chance for us to be something more than we were once, but I'd trampled that chance into oblivion when I married Duncan.

Besides, I'd surely fuck it up somehow if we ever did date. Just like I fucked up everything in my life.

Watson pushed his head under my hand and looked up at me with the saddest eyes. I felt guilty about leaving him behind. "I know, boy," I said, rubbing his head. "I'm going to miss you so much, too. But your daddy's going to bring you to visit, right?"

I looked up at Drew and he nodded, though he was grimacing. Then my words hit me. I'd called him Watson's daddy, because he was in a sense, but I suddenly had a flash of Drew holding a baby in his arms, chasing a toddler around the park with Watson. He was so caring and organized and smart and kind and everything you'd want the father of your child to be.

Oh my god... am I really thinking about what it would be like to raise a child with Drew? What the hell is wrong with me?

I shook my head again, a bit more violently, and bent the best I could with my crutches to kiss the top of Watson's head. "Love you, Watson."

Watson whined and circled me restlessly.

"He knows you're leaving," Drew said.

I studied the best dog on the planet. "It'll be okay, buddy."

Watson voiced his disagreement—loudly. I laughed, and when I peeked at Drew, he was smiling, looking at Watson.

"Why don't you take Watson with you?" Drew asked, glancing at me as he stepped over to love on Watson, too.

"No, I can't do that," I said. "He's *your* dog, Drew. I can't take him from you."

"Just for a while, Tasha. We both know he loves you more, anyway. And I think now that you've been living here, it's going to break his heart to be away from you. Besides, I'm gone during the day working, but you'd be able to keep him company."

"But I can't even walk him right now."

"That's fine—I'll come over to walk him."

"Three or four times a day? Come on, Drew."

"Yes," he said, no trace of humor. "I'd come more than that if I needed to. It'll be better for you and better for him."

"But you'll be so lonely without him."

"I'll survive. I'll still see you guys every day. And I'll sleep better knowing you've got him there with you." He stalled. "He'd keep you safe, Tasha," he added, with his voice lowered and grave. "You know he would."

It got a little harder to breathe. "You think I won't be safe? You think he'll come for me after all this time?"

Drew straightened from petting Watson and stepped in front of me, running his hands up and down my arms. "The truth or reassurance?" His eyes were a stormy gray.

"Truth."

"I do. His silence bothers me."

I let out a shaky breath. "I mean, he hasn't been *completely* silent. He hasn't signed the divorce papers yet. He told Roger he thought things could be fixed between us." I paused, watching Drew's jaw tighten. "And he's cooperating with the police—he isn't denying that he hurt me."

"He's also not telling the truth."

I shook my head. "No. He's not."

"The fact he maintains that you guys can reconcile is what scares me the most. That and knowing he's got to be furious that he knows he's going to end up back in prison because of this. That's what makes me afraid he's going to show up one day."

"I hope you're wrong and he doesn't. I hope he realizes he's crazy and just signs the fucking papers and accepts the consequences for what he's done."

"I hope so, too, Tash. I hope so, too."

"Well, if you help me some, I'll make you mac-n-cheese," I said after Drew finished unpacking the last of my stuff and grocery shopping for me. I hated sitting around and just watching. I was itching to be helpful; making dinner for him was the least I could do, though I'd need his help.

"You sure you want me to touch it?" he laughed.

I smirked. His mac-n-cheese hadn't been bad, but it hadn't been very good, either. "I have to take my chances. I can't move bowls around and put the baking dishes in the oven."

He leaned against the back of my small sofa and crossed his ankles. "Why don't you make it tomorrow after we go to the farmer's market? Then you can make different kinds again. That was fucking delicious when you did that in the spring."

I bobbed my head side to side for a minute. "Okay. But I still want to feed you tonight for doing everything for me."

"Why don't we just order something and watch a movie?"

I bit my lip. "You sure? I feel like I owe you something homemade."

He pushed off the back of the sofa and headed around to the front of it. "You do. And you're going to make it tomorrow."

We ended up ordering Thai and watching both Sherlock Holmes movies, complete with a running commentary of what we liked and didn't like compared to the books. By the time we turned off the television, yawning widely, it was late. I was exhausted and I was sure Drew was, too.

"You won't fall asleep driving, will you?" I asked as Drew yawned again, then bent to scratch Watson's ears.

"No, I won't," he replied with a sleepy, lopsided smile that made my heart thump against my ribcage. "But I'm going to run Watson out one more time, first."

He left with Watson, and I went in to my bedroom to change into my pajamas. When I was finished, I headed back toward the living room, noting the differences in sound. It was much quieter at Drew's—better windows, most likely—and I rarely heard sirens there. Here, they were common, and I heard some even now. It would take some getting used to again. As I passed through the living room, taking in being in my apartment again, I looked to my right and froze.

In an instant, I was transported back in time. Backed up against the cold wall, Duncan's glare and anger freezing me in place. I could smell his alcohol-laden breath again, feel it on my face. Could feel the air displaced by his hand when he nearly hit me. Could hear his palm slamming into the wall.

My body flooded with fear, and when I pulled myself from the flashback, I was shaking violently. I tried to move away from that spot, but my good leg was so shaky that, when I weighted it to move my crutches forward, it collapsed and I fell. I half-shouted, half-screamed, in equal parts surprise and pain. God, I hoped I hadn't just damaged something. I tried to stand again, then decided against it. I wasn't sure I even *could* get myself up from the floor without fully weighting my broken leg, anyway, and there was a possibility I shouldn't even try if I'd just refractured my femur or something. So I laid there, my tears soaking my face, while I waited for Drew and Watson to return.

"Tasha?" Drew called a few minutes later as the door opened.

"I'm here," I called back, though my voice was a little thin from crying.

"Tash?" He stepped into view just as Watson bounded over to me. "What the hell?"

Drew was there in an instant, on his knees next to me.

"I, um… I fell," I said, my voice shuddering as I tried to stop crying. "I don't know if I hurt anything."

"Okay," Drew said, his eyes scanning over me a second time. "Tell me everywhere it hurts." His hand gently skimmed over my lip, which I'd busted with one of my crutches on the way down.

"My ass and back hurt because I went backward. And my leg hurts. My thigh. It's not excruciating, but it hurts."

"I'm going to pull your sweats down, okay? I need to see if there are any bulges in the muscle."

"Alright."

He lifted the waistband out and moved them down, making sure they didn't touch my left thigh, stopping at my knee. His hand felt over the top of my thigh as he inspected intently from the top and sides. Then he pushed gently with his fingertips in several areas.

"How's that feel?"

"Just a little more painful than normal," I replied. It was uncomfortable, but not much more so than when he was working on my leg for physical therapy.

He replaced my sweatpants in the same way he'd pulled them down then squeezed along my calf. "What about this? Anything hurting or numb?"

I shook my head. "No."

He took my foot and ankle in his hands like he did for PT and guided my leg until it was bent a little further than ninety degrees. "What about this? Any pain?"

Again, I shook my head. "No. A little tight, but it always is."

Drew manipulated my leg for several more minutes, then let out a big sigh. "I don't think you hurt anything, thank god."

He leaned down over my torso and slipped his arms under my back to pull me up to a sitting position. A hug felt like what I needed, though, so I wrapped my arms around him and pulled him toward me instead, more tears squeezing their way out. He hugged me back, tightly, his weight on top of me reassuring. After a while, my crying tapered off.

"Can we get off the floor now?" Drew asked with a chuckle that rumbled against my chest.

"You're so whiny," I said. "Yes, we can get off the floor now."

He pulled me up to a sitting position, then stood and reached down under my arms and lifted me to my feet.

"Can you hand me my crutches?"

"You don't need them," he replied, scooping me up to carry me to my bedroom, gently placing me in bed. He left and returned with my crutches, which he arranged within reach of where I was lying. Then he sat on the bed next to my hip and scrutinized me. "What happened?"

I inhaled deeply and shifted my eyes to the ceiling. "If you walk into the living room, on the right-hand side, there's a stretch of empty wall to the left of the television."

Drew nodded.

"The day we got back from Vegas, when he almost hit me—that's the spot he backed me into." I took a deep breath. Two. "When I was walking to the kitchen to wait for you and Watson, I looked over and it all came rushing back." I turned to face Drew, who was watching me intently. I shrugged. "It made me shaky, and I fell."

"I'm so sorry, Tasha."

I gave him a tight smile. "Me, too." I sighed. "I'm still feeling panicky. Would you mind..." My voice trailed off because I felt like what I was about to ask was really needy. I wasn't used to asking for things, but I'd promised Drew and myself that I was going to change that. Even so, the words stuck in my throat. Nothing had even happened—I needed to suck it up. "Never mind."

"You don't have to be so strong all the time, you know," Drew said, reaching up and tucking some of my hair back from my face.

I don't? For some reason, his words caught me off guard. It felt like a shock to hear them and my eyes filled up again.

"Take a break for a while, Tasha. Let me be strong for you."

My jaw trembled.

"Tell me how I can do that for you right now. Would you like me to stay?"

I let out a slow breath. "Please."

"Absolutely."

"And will you stay in here with me until I fall asleep?" I whispered. "I don't want to be alone right now." I nearly choked on the words because I was so embarrassed to be uttering them.

"Of course."

He leaned forward and kissed my forehead, then stood up. He pulled my air mattress and some blankets from my closet and snagged an extra pillow off my bed, then dumped it all in the living room. When he came back, he turned off my bedside lamp and climbed onto the other side of the bed.

I rolled toward him, carefully, and I was soon enveloped by his warmth and security, his arms snug around me, my face resting against the base of his neck as I sniffled back a few errant tears. His heartbeat was steady in my ears, vetiver and orange strong in my nostrils, and I felt safe and bone-weary. He began to softly sing our songs, and within minutes, I was sound asleep.

Chapter Twenty-Nine

Drew

Could the time take any longer to pass? It seemed every time I looked at the clock, only seconds had passed, though it felt like hours. I was between patients at the hospital and had one more before heading home for a quick shower, then to pick up Tasha for our trip. I'd been counting down the minutes for this trip since she moved back into her apartment the week before. I hated not having her around all the time, even with seeing her several times a day to walk Watson and work out together. It just wasn't the same. My apartment felt cold and sad and lonely with her gone. I missed her presence and energy.

I wondered if she'd ask me to sleep in bed next to her. When I booked the room, I got one with an extra bed so we could sleep separately, but that wasn't what I wanted. Especially after lying in her bed while she slept in my arms a week earlier. She'd fallen asleep in short order once I'd begun to sing to her, but I kept singing for a long time anyway, feeling her relaxed weight against me, smelling her, hearing her slow, deep breathing. It felt right and I didn't want to get up. And I didn't for a long time—I stayed there for hours, awake, soaking up every moment. When I grew tired enough I was afraid I'd fall asleep there, I carefully untangled myself from her and left her bedroom, but it had hurt to walk away in the same way it had hurt not to go back to kiss her more at the airport.

Maybe I could do that again on this trip. Maybe this trip would be the right time to tell her how I felt—that I wanted something much more than friendship with her. That I wanted to spend the rest of my life with her. There was no doubt that I loved her with every cell in my body. And now that I wasn't denying it, I could see I always had and simply lied to myself about it.

But I also didn't want to overwhelm her by telling her too soon after everything with Duncan. She wasn't even divorced yet, though Roger had told her the day before that things were moving again and might be finalized by the end of the year if there were no more snags. It couldn't happen soon enough. While it was really just a technicality at this point, it was one that was creating a lot of stress for Tasha—stress she didn't need.

I wished we could just leave already. Tasha and I had taken quite a few trips together when we were younger, and it had always been this way—the anticipation that nearly killed me before it was time to leave. Though nothing would ever compare to the mix of excitement and anxiety of the first time we'd ever gone somewhere together for longer than the day.

It had been a week since I'd seen her, just before leaving the night of our high school graduation, and two days since I'd last heard from her. I'd wanted to leave a week earlier as soon as my last exam was done, but Tasha had begged me to wait so we could graduate together, and like with most things she asked me for, I'd agreed.

We'd snuck through the crowd of graduates and their families and said our goodbyes at my truck, everything I owned packed into it so I could go straight from graduation. With our arms tight around each other, I'd promised I'd be back as soon as I could. It had been so hard to let her go and drive away; I wanted to say fuck our plans to save us some money and rent a trailer or something for her stuff so we could leave together. I didn't want to leave her behind for even a day. But she'd refused to leave yet, wanting to make sure we had enough money to get us through until we had jobs where we landed.

She'd also been insistent she pick up my diploma for me so I could have it. I hadn't given a shit about it when it meant leaving her there with the monsters who claimed to love her, but *she* had.

I'd regretted it within hours of leaving, knowing she'd be stuck at home all day with her parents for at least a week before I'd be able to make it back for her. It had been a grueling week of driving and finding somewhere cheap enough for us to live for the summer, as well as finding a job, but I'd done it. I'd even found a tiny apartment so we wouldn't have to live out of a motel like we'd planned. And it was cheap enough we could stay there rather than moving into the dorms in the fall as long as I kept working full-time through the school year. The only thing left to do was get Tasha. I'd been texting her updates and calling at night, but the last two days, she hadn't responded and her phone had gone straight to voicemail. Every second that passed without hearing from her brought with it wild scenarios of what might have happened to her because I hadn't been there for her.

I flew down the highway driving back to her and arrived early. I wanted to barge into her house and get her, but I couldn't; I knew that. She was still seventeen for another few months, and her parents would never just let her walk out with me. I didn't expect they'd try too hard to find her once we were gone, but they wouldn't just let her waltz out the front door, either—especially her stepdad. I needed to stick to the plan we had, but it was torture waiting for the hours to pass until there was little risk we'd get caught.

Finally, the time arrived, and I rolled foot by foot down the dark, quiet street with my headlights off, parking so it would be a straight shot from her bedroom to the truck with her stuff. I slipped down from the front seat after turning off the dome light and pushed my door gently until it was mostly closed. My heart was in my throat as I tried to figure out what I'd do if she wasn't there like we'd planned. I'd get a crowbar from my dad's garage and pry her window open if I had to, and I'd search the entire house until I found her if she wasn't in her room. I didn't care what it took, what the consequences to myself would be, I was getting her out of there.

It was apparent as I neared her window that, while her lights were on, her curtains were drawn, and my pulse kicked into overdrive, wondering if I should go ahead and grab the crowbar. I peered in through her curtains and could just make out her back on her bed. I tapped faintly on her closed window, but she didn't move. Rapping a little harder this time, I whispered her name loudly, though there was no way she could have heard my voice through the glass.

I could see she was moving on the other side of the curtain, and then she was there pulling it back. Her face was puffy and there was a pale bruise on her cheek, her eyes red and swollen from crying, and she looked almost surprised to see me. She froze for a second, then scrabbled to lift her window. Then her screen. Then my torso was inside and I had her in my arms. She was hurt, but she was okay.

She clung to me, her body trembling, and I held her as long as I thought we could safely get away with. We still needed to get her stuff into my truck and leave before anyone noticed. I pulled away, kissing the side of her head, then held our foreheads together for a few breaths before tucking her hair behind her ears.

"Are you ready?" I asked softly, my eyes searching her for a clue to what had happened in the last week.

She nodded, her eyes shifting nervously to her door.

"Your door is locked?"

She nodded again, then she turned. Bending, she pulled half-full garbage bags from under her bed, passing them through the window to me. Minutes later, all the belongings she wanted to take with her were outside, minus whatever she had in her backpack and overnight bag. She passed those to me, one at a time—both very heavy and likely filled with her favorite books—then flipped her middle finger at the back of her bedroom door and climbed through her window. We paused, listening and looking for any sign of movement along the street, then ran, taking two trips to get her things tossed into the back of my truck before we hit the road and never looked back.

It wasn't until thirty minutes later when we were on the highway that I relaxed enough to let out a deep breath and peek over at her to see how she was doing. We hadn't spoken a word since we'd left, and she was now sitting against the passenger door, her knees in her chest as she stared out the window.

"Nats," I said, leaning over and slipping an arm around her shoulders, pulling her toward me.

She undid her seatbelt and slid across the bench seat to the middle, then re-buckled there. With my eyes still on the road, I tilted my face just enough to kiss the side of her head and squeezed her into my side. I was so relieved to have her there with me. We drove in silence, aside from the sound of the wind whipping into the open window, until I had to stop for gas again.

I pulled into the gas station, yawning. Now that I had her with me, a lot of my anxiety had faded, and I could feel my exhaustion. But I didn't want to stop until we arrived where we were headed; I was afraid if we even slowed down this close to home that someone would find us and tear her away from me. I couldn't let that happen.

After I pumped, I grabbed some drinks and snacks from inside, including several that were highly-caffeinated to help me stay awake. My eyes were on the truck the whole time. Realistically, her parents would still be asleep since it was the middle of the night, but I had this irrational fear that if I looked away for too long then she'd be gone when I turned back. That they would have somehow found us already and would take her back and I wouldn't be able to get her out of there again.

When I got back to the truck, Tasha had her knees pulled up again and was staring blankly ahead. After closing my door, I turned, sliding a hand across her shoulders.

"You okay?"

She nodded. That was the only way she'd communicated to me since I'd shown up. I kissed her head again.

"This is still what you want?" I couldn't imagine her preferring to stay behind, but I hadn't expected her to be this way when we left.

She shivered. "Jesus Christ, yes," she replied.

My shoulders sagged in relief, and I wrapped my arms around her again, my hand molding to the back of her head as I held her to me. A flash of all the fear and worry I'd had—especially from the last two days without contact—washed over me and I shuddered, tearing up. Again, I kissed the top of her head, then cleared my throat and turned to pull on my seatbelt and start the truck.

"Then let's get the hell out of here."

Once we were back on the road, I discovered that Tasha and her mom had gotten into a fight, during which her mom had thrown her phone at the wall and broken it. Tasha would have replaced it, but she hadn't been allowed to leave the house since the fight. I sensed there was more, but she just shook her head, a faraway look in her eyes when I probed her.

After she got out everything she was willing to share, she yawned, but asked about things on my end. I squeezed her into my side again.

"We can talk about it later. Go ahead and get some rest. I might need you to drive for a bit in a few hours. I haven't really slept in days."

She rested her head against my shoulder. "This is okay?" she asked sleepily, her body growing heavy as it leaned into me.

"Mm-hm," I murmured. It was more than okay. She could have climbed into my lap and I'd have figured out how to drive that way. The only thing that mattered to me was that she was there, and we were heading to start the next chapter of our lives—a chapter without the abuse we'd grown up with.

I sighed at the memory—one so fraught with anxiety and fear and pain, but also the beginning of a different future for us—then looked up at the clock in the hospital break room. *Damn it.* Only fifteen minutes had passed. I was going to lose my mind before it was time to leave for this trip.

Chapter Thirty

Drew

I'd been smiling at Tasha for the entire flight. I couldn't help it—her cheeks were pink with excitement, she was grinning, her eyes sparkling. Seeing her happy and excited made me feel the same way. Even my insistence that she use a wheelchair in the airport, despite her intense aversion to doing so, hadn't been enough to drag her spirits down.

"Drive faster, slowpoke," she said, looking out the window of our rental car. I could see her thumbs drumming her legs.

I chuckled, understanding her impatience. Not that we had any specific plans other than getting checked into the hotel and grabbing dinner somewhere. Then the next few days would be the book expo and all our exploration of the city would come after that.

"I will never understand how you've never gotten a speeding ticket," I replied. "I'm driving slightly over the speed limit already, and you'd be flying if you were behind the wheel."

She shrugged. "I'm just that good, I guess."

"It doesn't make any sense. *I* have gotten a speeding ticket before, and I drive much slower than you do."

"You're just not as cute as I am," she said, batting her eyelashes, then laughing.

I snorted—I couldn't argue with that.

When we stepped into our hotel room barely forty minutes later, I couldn't help but beam—it was actually as beautiful a room as it had looked online. It was a penthouse suite with a kitchenette, small table for eating, living room with a pull-out sofa bed, and separate bedroom. The exterior wall in the living room was nothing but glass with unobstructed views of Pittsburgh.

"Jesus Christ, Drew," Tasha said, her eyes scanning. "They didn't have anything more reasonable available?"

I stepped past her, wheeling the cart with our suitcases toward the bedroom. "What's unreasonable about this?"

In the bedroom, I quickly and methodically unpacked the suitcases, then tucked them into a corner of the closet and rolled the luggage cart back out. When I passed into the living room, Tasha was staring through the window, still standing where she had been, still wearing her coat, her hands with white-knuckled grips on her crutches.

"What's wrong, Nats?" I asked, pushing the cart near the door and stepping over to her. It was then I noticed her cheeks were damp. "Nats?" I asked, placing a hand on her back.

She startled, turning and looking up at me. There was a combination of fear and upset in her eyes and my heart felt constricted in my chest. I smoothed my hand slowly up around her back and waited. She turned back toward the window and let out a deep sigh.

"I like the view and thought you would, too. I didn't know it would bother you."

"There's a lot you don't know about me," she said softly, still staring toward the window.

She hadn't meant it to, but that comment felt like a knife to my chest. At one point, I'd known everything there was to know about her. For many years that was true. It wasn't until the last several years that things I knew nothing about because of the distance between us began to happen. I didn't like that there were things I didn't know, like why this window was so upsetting for her. And I wanted to know what all those things were.

"We can change rooms," I said.

She shook her head. "No. This room is beautiful."

"It doesn't matter, Tash. If you're not comfortable here, then I don't want to be here, either."

Tasha examined my face for a minute. "I don't *want* to be uncomfortable here, Drew. I want to have a different kind of memory." She looked like she was going to speak again, but then her eyes fell.

"Talk to me, Tasha. You know you can tell me anything. And you can ask me for anything. What do you need?"

She sighed again and moved toward the window on her crutches. When she stopped right in front of it, she shuddered. "Can I have a hug?"

I took her crutches and leaned them against the glass next us, then pulled her into my arms, tucking her head under my chin. It wasn't our normal hug—she was huddled against my chest, her arms tucked between us with her palms on my chest. I shifted my stance to be broader to help her feel even more surrounded. After several minutes this way, she told me that Duncan had insisted on fucking her to stake his claim over her when they arrived in Vegas, and it had been against a window like this one.

I remembered exactly what I was doing when that happened. I was sitting in therapy with Becka, arguing with her. I was worried something was going to happen to Tasha—I had been from the instant she'd told me she was going to Vegas with Duncan—and I couldn't have been more right. But instead of doing something about it—instead of telling Tasha about my shifting feelings for her or that I'd wanted to kiss her way more than I had at the airport, instead of flying to Vegas to be there for her or having gone back to Brinkley right away rather than trying to stay in Chandler—I'd tried to make it work with Becka even though I knew there wasn't anything worth the effort to save in our relationship. If I had done any of the myriad things I could have done that were more true to how I felt, so much would have been different for Tasha.

She wouldn't have been raped on display. She wouldn't have married Duncan. He wouldn't have hit her or pushed her into a coffee table or burned her or broken her leg. She wouldn't have been psychologically terrorized by the asshole.

I squeezed her tighter, apologizing silently over and over and over. Then I apologized out loud to her. She shuffled closer against me.

"It's not your fault," she said.

I ran a hand over her hair, then cradled the back of her head, placing a soft kiss on top. "I should have been there for you."

"It's not your job to keep me from making shitty decisions."

"No, I can't stop you or make your decisions for you, but I *can* be there for you, and I wasn't when it mattered most. If I had—"

"If I had just listened to my gut about Duncan instead of being so focused on not being alone, none of it would have happened. If I'd just picked up the phone and called you or even just texted you about a thousand times that I didn't, maybe none of it would have happened. It's my fault I got myself into the situation I did."

"No, Tasha—it's your fucking family's fault. Because they're the reason you didn't listen to your instincts, the reason—"

"We can play this blame game forever, Drew," she said, sounding weary. "But I don't want to anymore. I just want for things to be different—to not do the same stupid shit anymore. I want to move on. I want to be happy for once."

"How can I help you do that, Tasha? Because I want you to be happy, too, and I'll do anything for you."

"I know you would," she murmured. "And I'd do anything for you."

"So tell me what to do."

"This. You're doing it."

Her words sucked the air from my lungs in a shaky exhale and I kissed the top of her head again. As many mistakes as I'd made, at least I was getting things right now.

"You're like a damn kid in a candy store on Christmas," I laughed as I watched Tasha bouncing onto her toes in front of me as we waited in line to meet another author.

"Do you have any idea how cool these people are that you're meeting with me?"

I lifted my hand carting several very heavy tote bags full of books. "I know how much their books weigh."

She rolled her eyes. "You're cooler just because you've met them."

"Just meeting them makes you cooler?" I asked, quirking an amused brow.

She drew back. "No. It makes *you* cooler."

I chuckled and she smirked back at me. I'd been worried about her tiring out and had brought the wheelchair we rented from a medical supply store for the week—it was at the coat check—but she was still going strong. She could still overdo it, not noticing pain and fatigue in her leg because of her excitement, but I was making sure every thirty minutes or so we stopped to just to see how her leg was feeling.

"They do this every year, right?" I asked.

"Mm-hm."

"And you have a book coming out next year, right?"

"Yes," she replied, narrowing her eyes.

"So are you going to be sitting at one of these tables the following year?"

She shook her head. "God no. I'm a nobody."

"No, you're not."

She rolled her eyes, though she was smiling and her cheeks pinked slightly. "I mean in the book world. They'd never have a newbie author here unless they were a best seller, and that is like a one in many millions chance."

"I bet you'll have a table here for the first expo that happens after your book is released. You're a better writer than you even realize. Your books are going to be wildly successful, and you'll be at the top of all the best seller lists faster than any author in the history of authoring."

She laughed, blushing deeply now. "That is not going to happen, but it's sweet that you think so."

I grinned, content that she thought I was sweet. I wasn't trying to be—I just believed in her and wouldn't be at all surprised if everything I said came true—but I'd take it.

She tipped her head toward my right. "Do you see that couple near the front of the line for that table over there?"

The couple looked to be in their forties, maybe, two men. One had his arm around his partner's shoulders, the other around his partner's waist.

"Yeah."

"Watch them for a minute."

I did as instructed, though it felt weird. Tasha often sat and observed people, but I was nervous about it for some reason. The couple never noticed, however. They were deep in conversation, one of the men using his hands to gesture expressively, the other nodding, facial expressions changing as he listened, except for the love spilling from his eyes. From time to time, he leaned forward while his partner was talking and kissed his forehead or cheek or temple. I turned to Tasha, my eyebrows raised.

Her eyes flicked to mine then back to the couple. "Aren't they cute?" she asked quietly with a soft smile. "They're just so wrapped up in each other. And relaxed together—you can see that. There's no tension at all in the way they're standing or touching each other." She shot a fleeting glance at me, then looked away again. "I want to have a relationship like *that* one day. One that's survived a lot and left you stronger for it."

"How do you know they've survived a lot?" I asked, curious. She seemed like she knew, not like she was making up a backstory.

She tipped her head toward them again. "That author they're in line for? She exclusively writes novels with LGBTQ main characters."

"How the hell do you know that?" I asked, shaking my head in amazement.

She shrugged. "I've read a few."

"Are they any good?"

"Yeah, they are."

"Huh." I rubbed my jaw. "Are there any authors here you haven't read?"

Her eyes moved toward the ceiling. "I don't think so." She gave a small shake of her head. "Anyway, what I was saying. That author was the first to make a statement like that, and it's obviously huge for the LGBTQ community since they weren't, and still aren't, really, well-represented in literature. The fact that couple knows that—which they obviously do or they wouldn't be here to meet her—and are openly gay in a world that still isn't entirely accepting tells me they've been through a lot together."

I studied Tasha's face, so animated as she talked, and suddenly felt this sense of smallness in her presence. She was so funny, so smart, so observant, so compassionate and empathetic and caring... how could I *not* be in awe of her? It felt like my heart was groaning under a weight as it beat in my chest, pressing against my ribs as if it had grown too large for the space it occupied.

"I want to write a story about this couple. Would you mind jotting a few notes for me?" she asked, still focused on the two men.

I swallowed over the intense wave of emotion I felt. "Sure."

"Really? You'd mind?"

"What?"

She smirked. "I asked if you would mind and you said yes."

"Smart ass. You know what I meant."

She winked.

I pulled her notebook and pencil out of one of the tote bags and opened to the first clean page. I jotted down several notes that she dictated, and when she was finished, I added a few more. Who knew when she'd open to this page and read what was there—she said sometimes she didn't revisit notes for years—but one day she'd know exactly how I felt in this moment.

I hope you know and never forget how amazing
you are. The most amazing person I've ever met.
The biggest pain in the ass with the biggest heart.
You were worried about me carrying around all
your books today, but it's a very small price to pay
for spending the day near you. You were also

worried I'd be bored here, but I could never be bored when I'm with you—I can watch and listen to you for hours. You're my favorite person in the world and I love you.

207

worried I'd be bored here, but I could never be bored when I'm with you—I can watch and listen to you for hours. You're my favorite person in the world and I love you.

Chapter Thirty-One

Tasha

Drew had been talking for nearly an hour straight at dinner on our last night in Pittsburgh. We'd spent our last day visiting historical music sights and a musical history museum where they had guitars of apparently very famous guitarists who were from Pittsburgh. He'd been at least as excited as I had been about the expo, and now he couldn't stop talking about everything we saw, sprinkling in additional bits of musical history and trivia.

"You're laughing at me," he said suddenly, though he was also laughing as he said it.

I nodded. "Yup. You're so into this stuff. It's cute."

"More like boring."

I shrugged. "To-may-to, to-mah-to."

He snorted and I chuckled.

"What would you rather talk about?" he asked, taking a bite of his neglected dinner. It was rare he didn't finish well before I did, and yet tonight I was finished while he'd barely touched a single morsel on his plate.

"Not a thing," I said. "I was kidding about it being boring. I'm learning a lot from you. Some of these musicians' lives have even given me some ideas for stories."

He quirked an eyebrow. "Does that mean I get credit in your books when you write them? Like you'll actually put my name in there to thank me for not shutting up about music since it gave you the idea for your story?"

I shook my head, laughing. "Maybe."

He ate a bite of food, his eyes more blue this evening and glowing like they were lit from behind. It was the happiest and most carefree he'd ever looked, and my heart warmed to see it.

"You have to show me when it happens. It's now a life goal to see my name in print in my best friend's book."

I shrugged a shoulder. "I can show you that already."

He stopped with his fork halfway to his mouth. "What?"

"Yeah. You're in my acknowledgements already."

"Which book?"

"All of them. I'll show you when we get back if you want. Well, I'll show you two of them."

"Why only two?"

"I've only written three books."

"The third is the autofiction?"

"Yes," I replied, my face heating. I knew what was coming next.

"It's written? When can I read it?"

I looked down and watched my fingers twirl my wine glass by the stem. "I don't know."

I'd promised him he could read it, but that was before I wrote it. Now that it was written, I wasn't sure I ever wanted him to read it. There were things in there he didn't know about, and he'd know those things weren't fiction. And then the part that was fiction... I'd written in a romance, though it had a bittersweet ending for the characters. My protagonist's secrets come out and allow her to finally move on from what happened, but they also cause irreparable damage to her relationship with her best-friend-turned-lover, and their lives diverge for the first time since they were kids.

Permanently.

I didn't want that part to become nonfiction, too.

"How about when we get back?" he asked with a playful wiggle of his eyebrows. "I'm dying to read what you wrote about me."

"It's not that flattering, you know," I teased. "I'm just trying to spare your feelings and your self-esteem."

"I thought you told me if I was nice you wouldn't write me as... what was it you said? Without muscles and with a limp?"

I laughed. "Yeah. And *with* a mullet and pustules. A story of unrequited love for a rabid racoon."

"Yeah, that was it. But I was nice, so you couldn't have done that."

"Who said the truth is much better?"

"Ouch." He took his last bite and placed his fork on his plate. "That was delicious."

"Was probably better when it was hot." I winked. "They have brownies," I added, quirking an eyebrow in question.

"Obviously," he agreed.

※

The last morning in Pittsburgh, I packed, showered, dried my hair, and dressed first. While Drew was showering and getting ready, I stood at the large window in the living area and looked out over the city. Each day we'd been there, the window had been less and less unsettling to me, and this morning, for the first time, I barely thought about what had happened with Duncan. Instead, I was looking at the cityscape before me, trying to find all the places I'd been with Drew, thinking about the last week of exploration and laughter.

I heard Drew approaching before his hand touched my back.

"You okay?" he asked.

Turning my head, I smiled. "Yeah."

I leaned my head onto his shoulder, and he slid his hand over to give me a side hug. I sighed, closing my eyes briefly.

"You see that really tall, grayish building?" I asked, pointing out the window.

Drew followed where I was pointing. "Yeah."

"That short building to the right of it is where the expo was."

He squinted, leaning forward a few inches. "That means the museum is... right there, with the green roof, I think?"

"I think so."

We spent the next few minutes going through our week together by pointing out where in the city we'd been. Drew ran his hand up and down my arm, then kissed the top of my head.

"This was one of the best trips I've ever taken," he said.

"What's the best?" I asked, shifting to relieve the pressure from my crutches, genuinely curious. I knew definitively what my worst trip ever was, but I wasn't sure I could pick a best. I'd taken quite a few trips with Drew before, and there were things I loved about each of them. It would be hard to pick one.

Though it was easy to remember the most impactful one—the very first one. The one when I ran away from home a few months before my eighteenth birthday. My last week home, alone, while Drew was looking for housing and employment was the worst week I'd ever had, and not just because of his absence. My mom had been angrier than normal because Wayne, my stepfather, had been unemployed for weeks, and as usual she took that anger out on me. But even that wasn't the worst part. The worst was being stuck at home without school to escape to while Wayne was home all day. His abuse had escalated rapidly that week when he realized he had unfettered access to me because we were home alone. I didn't really have anywhere to go, but I'd have found a place to hide out during the day if I hadn't been grounded already because of sneaking off to say bye to Drew at graduation. I'd been forbidden to speak to him ever since he'd attacked Wayne.

In the days between hugging Drew in our graduation gowns and seeing him standing outside my window to take me away, I'd learned that Wayne could be worse than he'd ever been before.

Much, much worse.

When I'd tried to tell Drew in the truck as we put miles between us and our parents, I couldn't. I didn't know how to explain to begin with, let alone when he hadn't known how bad things with Wayne already were ever since he'd been in juvenile detention. Drew would have blamed himself, and I hadn't wanted to do that to him, so I'd kept it all to myself.

After sleeping for a while in the truck the night I ran away with Drew, I took over driving while *he* slept, grateful he'd insisted on teaching me to drive a stick shift when he got his truck. If he hadn't, I wouldn't have been able to help, and he was clearly well beyond exhausted. I didn't wake him until we made the final exit from the highway, and he gave me directions to our new temporary home. The building was rundown, the landscaping worse, but it looked like heaven to me because it wasn't the home I was fleeing. And it wasn't the motel I'd originally expected.

Once we'd carted my belongings inside, I looked around as Drew gave me a quick rundown. There were a handful of plates, cups, bowls, and utensils, one pan and two pots in the kitchen, some cheap toiletries, one queen size air mattress and a set of bedding, and Drew's guitar. We had no sofa, no television, no real bed, no table or chairs. But we had each other and freedom and I broke down crying in relief. Drew turned sharply toward me, then his feet ate up the space between us and he wrapped me in a bear hug. We stood like that for a very long time, both of us emotional with relief.

"I only have the one mattress right now," he said as we pulled apart. "I didn't want to spend any more money before we had some coming in."

"That's fine," I said. "I'm sure it's perfect."

"It's yours," he said. "I'll sleep on the floor if you let me have one of the blankets."

I yawned and stretched, ready to go to bed. It was barely dinnertime, but we'd been on the road all night and most of the day, and the release from fear after our escape left me feeling like I hadn't slept in years. He yawned just after I did.

"We can share," I said, kicking off my shoes and crawling onto the mattress, settling on my side still fully clothed. I was too tired to care about changing into pajamas. I patted the space behind me. "Lay down."

The mattress dipped and shifted under his weight as he climbed on behind me and pulled the blankets up over us. When he stopped moving, I scooted backward until my back was pressed against him.

Touching him helped me feel safe—the only person whose touch had ever been comforting. He slipped an arm around my waist and squeezed me in a hug.

"We're safe now. *You're* safe now." He spoke in a deep, grave voice and kissed the back of my head. "I was so scared when I couldn't reach you," he added, almost in a whisper, like he was thinking out loud to himself.

"I was so scared you weren't coming. I was sure you weren't. I almost unpacked my stuff."

I felt his body tense against me. "I wasn't late."

"No, but I just didn't believe you'd actually come back for me. That you'd risk seeing your parents again, risk getting arrested and going to jail for me. You got out—you did it. You were gone. Why would you come back and risk everything?"

He was crushing me against him so hard I could hardly breathe. "I told you I'd never leave you behind, Tasha. Never. *Never.*"

He had. He'd told me he'd never leave me behind. He'd told me I'd never have to go through what I had again once he got me out. He'd told me he would never let them hurt me again. But I'd already had enough experiences in my life to know that absolutes like never weren't real.

And now, so many years later as I stood in this hotel room with him, I wasn't sure if I believed in absolutes any more than I ever had. Except that now, with the way Drew was watching me without answering my question about the best trip he'd ever taken, I wanted to more than I ever had before.

Drew's gaze felt like a physical touch caressing my face, which heated under his scrutiny. Those feelings that had no place in a friendship raged inside my chest, my heart tripping over itself. The longer he looked at me, the harder it was to breathe, the hotter my skin became.

Then he leaned forward, almost leisurely, and held his mouth to the corner of mine like he had twice before, his hand cupping the back of my head. It felt like the world was moving under my feet, and I was sure I'd have fallen over if not for his arm around me. My breath jerked out of my body as violently as my heart was beating. He pulled back a little, quick bursts of his breath breaking across my face.

"It was never an accident," he said, his voice low, his eyes searching mine.

I swallowed—I couldn't speak. My mind was racing.

His hand pulled me toward him, and he kissed me again, but this time it wasn't just a corner of my lips he was touching; my entire mouth was molding to his. I felt so much at once, I couldn't process it all and my eyes filled. I wanted to cry, but I didn't understand why. He stepped back, his lips slow to leave mine, his fingers reluctantly lifting from my cheek. His eyes were darkened in color and stormy, but still with that light as if backlit, and focused intently on me.

I looked down, blushing and biting my lip. My whole body shivered as I felt that kiss all over again. When I chanced a peep, he was still watching me. I took a deep breath, trying to slow my exhale. Then Drew cleared his throat and stepped toward the door where our suitcases were already packed onto a luggage cart. It was checkout time.

Chapter Thirty-Two

Tasha

Things were decidedly awkward with Drew. They had been since we'd kissed in the hotel a few hours earlier. Neither of us were talking much, and every time I looked at him, his eyes were already resting on me, intense, as if he was trying to figure something out. I wanted him to kiss me again, and I also wished it had never happened. I wasn't sure what to say or how to act or where to look or anything, really. I wanted to reach over and hold his hand on the plane, and again when he was driving us from the airport, but I never did. I stared at my hand, willing myself to do it, but nothing happened. It was like the connection between my brain and my muscles had been severed. I couldn't remember ever, in my entire dating life, feeling as nervous around a guy as I now did. What did that mean?

We stopped on the way to get Watson from the pet daycare, and he lost his doggie mind, trying to figure out who he was most excited to see, hopping on his feet back and forth between us. It was sweet and left me feeling so loved. I melted into mush inside as I watched Drew interact with him, hugging and kissing him from his knees, letting Watson lick him and jump all over him. I felt a sharp pang of guilt that Watson didn't live with Drew anymore. It had to be so hard on Drew. I thought about suggesting Watson go home with him now, but I already knew Drew would refuse—he said he wouldn't consider it until I had gone two weeks without needing any kind of assistance to walk, not even the cane I used when I wasn't using my crutches.

With a very happy and excited Watson in the car, Drew drove us to my apartment and brought up my suitcase. I was exhausted and worked on unpacking while Drew took Watson for a long walk. I was in the kitchen, taking stock of what I had and making a grocery list, when they returned. Watson bounded in and nuzzled me on his way to his water dish. Drew walked over and leaned back against the counter next to where I was bent over it, working on my list.

"Groceries?" he asked.

I nodded, blushing. *Why the hell am I blushing? He asked me if I was making a grocery list.*

"I can run over to the store for you before I go home."

"That's okay," I replied, knowing he was tired from all the travel, too. "I can have them delivered."

"I can do it for you, Tash. I don't mind. Then you don't have to pay a delivery fee."

"I know, and I appreciate it, but I'm sure you're ready to get home after being gone for a week."

My breath stuttered when he tucked some hair behind my ear, and I got stuck in his gaze.

"The only place I want to be is wherever *you* are, Tasha. I'm only home when I'm with you."

Holy shit, I couldn't breathe. I straightened up and looked away, trying to find some air. Drew was my friend, but I was one hundred percent positive that was the most romantic thing anyone had ever said to me.

"Jesus Christ, Drew," I muttered. "How the hell am I supposed to respond to something like that?"

He stepped closer. We were now so close I could feel his body even though we weren't touching. So close we were breathing the same pocket of air.

"Say you feel the same way."

"I *do* feel the same way," I said, my voice barely above a whisper as I got lost in his eyes. "But we're friends—*best* friends."

"Yeah," he said, his voice deep and scratchy. "We are."

His hands snaked into my hair, cradling my head, and he stepped forward again. Our bodies made contact, his forehead against mine. I sighed and closed my eyes. All my awareness was where we were connected skin-to-skin or through our clothes, my nerves exploding with sensory messages.

"That doesn't change how badly I want to kiss you right now, though."

Oh my god. My head was spinning like a top. I wanted that, too, but I was also afraid of it. Afraid of what this would mean for our friendship. His mouth pressed against the corner of mine, and I decided right then that was my favorite place on my body, my favorite place to be kissed. He pulled back and hovered over my lips, waiting, and I shifted to touch my mouth to his in a soft kiss. He kissed me back with increasing pressure, and then his tongue, soft and warm, grazed the seam of my lips... then against my tongue. It was a long, slow kiss that left me dizzy and disoriented. I'd never in my three decades on the planet been kissed like that or felt this way while being kissed. It was... incredible.

The kiss ended and he gave one more soft, chaste kiss to my lips, then straightened back up, grinning, his thumbs moving over my cheeks.

I grinned back, my fingers resting over my lips, not sure what else to do—I couldn't even begin to put together a coherent thought. After a beat, he gently pulled my hand away and kissed me again, this time as if he was making up for lost time and couldn't get enough. I couldn't, either. His hands roamed down from my face, over my sides, then lifted me by my hips to the countertop.

Okay, that's hot.

He stepped between my legs, and we continued. We kissed for so long my lips were sore and my ass was numb. Over and over, we started to pull apart, but then one of us would go back for more. It wasn't until Watson began whining and insistently pushing his nose between us because he was hungry that we ended up stopping ourselves.

Drew helped me down from the counter, sounding as breathless as I felt, and fed Watson, then left to get my groceries. While he was gone, I laid back on my sofa, humming while I stared at the ceiling, replaying the last minutes before he'd left and giggling to myself. If I hadn't had a leg that wasn't fully functional yet, I'd have been dancing around my living room. It was the same breathtaking feeling in my stomach that I'd had after we kissed as teens. Back then, it was the first time I'd ever felt that, and it had scared the shit out of me, as had the thought of things changing between my best friend and me.

Had it been the same for Drew? All this time, had we been living our lives searching for the person that fit when we'd had it with each other all along? For all those years, should we have been together? I thought back on all the failed and messy and painful relationships I'd had over the years, not to mention the abusive one I'd had with Duncan. Could all of them have been avoided?

Or was I just jumping into the idea of a relationship with Drew because I didn't want to be alone? I'd done it enough times in the past—I easily became infatuated with whoever the guy was, committing to them with little to no hesitation. I just never realized what I was doing until things had ended. Was I doing that same thing now with Drew? This was the longest stretch I'd ever gone without a boyfriend... Was that why I felt the way I did? Was it nothing more than desperation out of fear of being alone?

I didn't think so, but I hated that I didn't know because I didn't trust myself. And I needed to know before I messed up the best thing ever to happen to me—my friendship with Drew. I needed to stop things with him before they had a chance to go any further and give myself more time. I needed to meet other people and see what happened... see if I felt a pull toward them, too, or if it was still Drew.

When he got back from the store, I couldn't meet his eye. We unpacked my groceries together as he hummed to himself, and I was intensely aware of the proximity of our bodies to one another, of every brush of our arms. My heartbeat felt like it was originating in my face, and my skin was on fire. And, again, I couldn't think of anything to say. I thanked him for going to the grocery store and said I was going to head to bed.

Drew stepped over and wrapped me in his arms. It felt so good to be there that I settled my cheek against his chest, inhaling the smell of his skin. He was the only person I'd ever known whose skin smelled that good. He kissed the top of my head, then rested his chin there.

"I had the best time with you," he said, his voice deep and quiet. "Thank you."

I nodded against him. "I did, too. Thank *you.*"

"I think we should do it more often."

"Well, that'll be hard since the expo is only once a year," I teased, smiling into his chest.

I felt his huff and short chuckle. "I meant we should go places together more often, brat. Go on trips together. I like traveling with you."

"I can't say no to an offer like that."

He pulled back, using a hand to gently lift my chin, and then he was kissing me again. By the time I remembered I wasn't supposed to be doing any more of that, it was too late, and I couldn't locate any willpower to stop kissing him back.

He rested his forehead against mine, our breathing heavy. "I'll be here in the morning by six thirty."

I nodded.

"Goodnight, Tasha." He pressed our lips together.

"Goodnight, Drew."

Chapter Thirty-Three

Tasha

I was awake well before Drew was supposed to arrive the next morning after having spent much of the night awake, replaying the previous week with him, including the amazing kissing from the night before. I'd never been just kissed like that before; it had always come with expectations of getting naked... and sex. But there'd been no expectations coming from Drew, and that had made it even better. I was torn, because I wanted to kiss him like that again—I wanted that so much it was hard to breathe when I thought about it, but I also knew I shouldn't because I needed to work on myself before I'd have a chance of not fucking up any good thing to happen to me.

Then again, I'd never felt this way before. The way I felt around Drew—even before things began shifting between us, even while I was dating Duncan and the guys who came before him—was unlike anything else... with *anyone* else. Didn't that count for something? Maybe. But if I was right, if it really was different with Drew, that wouldn't change over a few months of us keeping things the way they used to be between us. And if it did... well, I wouldn't have ruined my friendship with the most important person on the planet to me.

I started a pot of coffee and watched it brew after feeding Watson. My thumbs drummed incessantly against the countertop and I kept looking to the door, waiting for Drew to knock before letting himself in the way he always did in the mornings. At first, I didn't know what to expect when he arrived, but then I thought about how he'd kissed me goodnight as if it was the most natural thing in the world for him to do, and I knew what would happen when he walked through the doorway if I didn't do something to stop it first. I grabbed up my phone and typed out a text message.

No more kissing.

The instant I clicked send, however, Drew knocked and came through the door. My heart hammered into my throat, and I didn't know where to look. His eyes were intense, so I lowered my gaze to escape his. But his lips pulled into a grin and looked so damn kissable. Shit, this was going to be harder than I thought. I forced my eyes further down, but that was a mistake, too, because his body was made to fill out sweats perfectly. I raised my eyes again and Drew stepped in front of me, Watson jumping excitedly by his side. There wasn't even the tiniest hesitation before he kissed the corner of my mouth. My traitorous body leaned into him as if I hadn't just decided we couldn't do things like that anymore.

"Good morning," he murmured, his eyes glowing. He still had that joyful, happy look about him that I'd noticed in Pittsburgh, and damn if it didn't make my knees weak having it directed at me.

"Good morning," I replied breathily. I felt as if I'd just finished a set of sprints.

He whistled to Watson and walked over to where the leash hung by the door. I watched as he bent to put the leash on Watson, admiring the way his ass looked in his pants, then blushed and forced my eyes away when I realized what I was doing. But then I made yet another mistake by looking up and catching his eye. He was looking at me in a way that made my breath catch, as if his eyes couldn't get enough of seeing me. I very much so wanted him to kiss me again like he had the night before.

As if he'd read my mind, Drew dropped Watson's leash and closed the distance between us, taking me into his arms and kissing me with that same hunger I'd just been thinking about. I kissed him back, my arms circling his neck, my body molding to his as he squeezed me into him. The thought crossed my mind that I'd have been okay with nakedness following this one.

"I was thinking about that kiss all night," he said with a smile. Then he touched his lips to the corner of my mouth again before turning and finally heading out to walk Watson.

I slumped against the counter, my body weak and flushed. I felt awake and alive and giddy, like I'd somehow crossed over from reality into an alternate version of my life I'd never even dared to dream about. I closed my eyes briefly, reliving the last few minutes, until my phone vibrated on the counter. I lifted it to see a new message from Drew asking when I'd sent my last message to him.

I let out a controlled breath, my heart racing. How did I reply? Considering I'd sent it and then kissed him. It had flown out of my mind when he walked in the door, and now reality had returned. We couldn't do what we'd been doing anymore. I typed a quick reply.

Just before you walked in the door.

Is it a joke?

No.

The three little dots appeared, then disappeared without a message. I hobbled around restlessly, not sure how he would react, until he and Watson returned a while later. A tense silence thickened between us as I waited for him to speak first so I could get an idea of what he was thinking.

He stepped over to where I was leaning against the counter and leaned against the opposing counter, facing me with his arms crossed over his chest. He examined my face for a long, uncomfortable minute or two.

"Why?" he asked. It was obvious that word had taken effort to utter.

I thought about saying something snarky because he'd given no context to his question, but I realized as I opened my mouth that snark was my go-to when I wanted to deflect from what I was feeling, so I didn't do it this time. Instead, I used all my willpower to hold his gaze. He deserved for me to be serious and straightforward, and for me to look him in the eye. Just the way that one word had passed his lips betrayed that he was already upset.

"I need to be alone."

"Tash, you don't ever have to be alone again," he said, stepping forward to straddle my feet and rest his hands over mine. I shifted my weight and moved our clasped hands between us.

"That's not what I mean."

"Then what *do* you mean?"

I sighed. "I need to know that I *can* be alone. I've never really been alone before because I was too scared to be. Since all this"—I gestured vaguely down at my legs—"is the longest I've ever gone without a boyfriend since we were in college, Drew." I couldn't do it anymore and looked down. "It's pathetic. And—"

"Don't call yourself pathetic, Tasha."

"I don't know what else to call it," I muttered. "Regardless, I need to know that I can be alone." My eyes flicked to his, then away. "And I need to know that... this... what I'm feeling right now... is real."

I peeked up again and Drew's brow was deeply furrowed, his eyes gray and cloudy. "You don't think what's between us is real?"

He was hurt—I could hear it in his voice.

Damn it, Tasha.

"It's not that. It's just... every time I was single for more than a few days, I promptly fell for the first guy to pay attention to me at all. The first guy to ask me out, I said yes to. And kept saying yes to until he got sick of me or he cheated on me or something. And then we'd break up, and by the time I blinked, I was with the next guy."

I paused, taking and releasing a deep breath, then forcing my eyes back to his. "I'm afraid I'm doing that again. And I don't want to do that anymore. I want something real or nothing at all. And if we let this thing we've started develop into something and then I discover I *was* just doing that I-don't-want-to-be-alone thing again, our friendship would be destroyed. And no matter what else happens, I want to have your friendship. It's the most important thing in my life. I don't want to fuck it up."

Drew's jaw tightened, but it wasn't anger this time. His eyes were glassy. "Okay."

Even so, we found ourselves kissing in the elevator on the way down to the gym only minutes later. I couldn't even say who started it because one second we were two feet apart and staring at each other and the next we were kissing with our hands all over each other.

"You know," I said between kisses. "This is the opposite of not kissing."

Drew kissed me again, his tongue delving deep into my mouth and lighting my veins on fire with want. In fact, I'd never wanted so badly to sleep with someone as I did with him right then. His hand squeezed my hip as he pulled back and rested his forehead against mine. We were obscenely out of breath.

"It most certainly is," he panted out.

I let out a soft chuckle. "Maybe we start with the no-kissing thing now."

He nodded with his forehead against mine, and when he did, our lips brushed. Several minutes later, we came up for air again.

I bit my lip. "Okay, *now* we'll start."

He smirked, kissed my cheek, and at long last we walked in to start our workout, now twenty minutes late.

It was my first day using only a cane, including for my PT and workout, and I was definitely tiring out faster than I had been, though the adrenaline pumping through my body at being so close to Drew with memories of his mouth on mine masked the exhaustion.

"You're really strong today," Drew said as he racked the bar after my bench press, my last exercise for the day.

I sat up and turned to face him, taking time to catch my breath before we switched places for his last set. I grinned. "Does that mean I can ditch that cane soon?"

He tipped his head side to side. "Maybe. I know you don't want it, but you can do more harm than good if you stop using it too soon. Let's aim for two weeks to get you ready to walk without it for an entire day. By the end of the week, you can start going without it for short periods. How's that?"

I nodded; the next two weeks couldn't pass quickly enough as far as I was concerned. I was *so* ready to be back to normal physically. Of course, I also didn't want to do something to slow down my healing or re-injure my leg, so I'd follow what Drew told me to do. I looked down and smoothed my hand over my legs, looking at all the scars I now had on both. They were reminders of what I'd been through with Duncan, but also reminders of my childhood since I knew it had shaped me into the person who'd allowed myself to get into the situations that caused them.

"Nats?"

"I'm good," I said, standing carefully and avoiding eye contact. "Time for your last set."

We switched spots after Drew piled on more weights to the bar, then he pushed through his last bench press set, almost failing on the last rep. I was nervous for a minute when I thought he might because I wasn't sure I could hold that much weight without damaging my leg, but he managed to get the bar up and I helped him rack it.

He dropped his arms to his sides, breathing heavily, his bare chest heaving and sweaty. I watched the movement of the tattoo on his chest, wondering for about the ten thousandth time what the hell the tattoo was. He'd never told me, which made me think it had something to do with Becka and he hadn't wanted me to know because of how much I didn't like her. I knew he wasn't with her anymore, but a surge of jealousy pulsed through me at the thought of him having gotten a tattoo for her. That was *our* thing.

"So when are you getting that covered?" I snapped as I looked at him over the top of the bar. I hadn't meant to sound that snippy, but couldn't keep my aggravation out of my voice.

His eyebrows drew together as I watched his upside-down face. "Getting what covered?"

I tipped my chin down. "That tattoo on your chest."

His hand shot up to cover his tattoo in a protective gesture. "I'm never getting this covered. Why would I?"

I shrugged, feeling my face heat up, and headed toward our water bottles at the foot of the bench. "Just figured you wouldn't want anything from *Becky* since she left you."

Drew laughed and I shot him an irritated look. I didn't find it funny at all that he had the damn tattoo, let alone that he wanted to keep it. And I definitely didn't find it funny that it bothered me so much.

"Tasha," Drew said, sitting up.

"What?" I bit out, bending over and grabbing my water bottle without looking at him.

He snagged my hand and I turned, then he pulled until I sat facing him in a straddle on the bench, our knees touching.

"I have never seen you this jealous before," he mused, doing a shit job of holding back a grin.

I rolled my eyes. "Whatever," I muttered. "I'm not jealous."

"You are," he said, laughing. "I mean, you always were, especially of Becka, but this is a whole new level."

I rolled my eyes again and crossed my arms over my chest. He tugged my arms apart and took my hands in his. When I finally looked up and made eye contact, he spoke.

"I've never tattooed myself for anyone but you, Tasha."

I stared at him, his words rolling around in my mind. "Then... why won't you even tell me what that is?"

He raised my right hand and pressed my palm over his tattoo. I could feel his heart hammering into his chest harder than it should have been. He was nervous.

"Becka and I got into a huge fight—*huge* fight—when I told her I was going to fly out to go to your five-year checkup with you. We fought for weeks, and eventually I caved and ended up trying to save my relationship with her rather than just flying out anyway. When you told me you were clear still... god, Tasha." He stopped, his jaw trembling, and let out a tense breath. His eyes were flitting around restlessly. "I was so... I'd been so scared..." He looked away. I could see the moisture on the verge of spilling over his eyelids. "I got this tattoo for you. Because you were cancer-free after five years. Because

I wished I was there with you. Because I wanted a way to keep you with me always, no matter what, as close to inside my heart as I could get."

I remembered clearly how it had felt at that checkup, how momentous it was because the risk of recurrence was much lower after five years. Just the memory made me feel weak with relief all over again.

Drew moved my hand to expose his tattoo, then grasped my index finger and traced the tip over his skin. "N... A..."

Drew continued, but after the second letter, I understood what he'd done. It was Natasha. He'd actually tattooed my name on his body. I was mortified for having felt jealous, for having acted the way I did.

"I guess you can keep it," I muttered, my face in flames.

Drew smirked. "And Becka didn't leave me, Nats. *I* left *her*. When I got all your messages the morning after you married Duncan, it felt like my life had imploded, that it was over. I realized that day that I'd rather be alone than with Becka. That was also when I stopped denying to myself how I felt about you." He got a faraway look in his eyes. "I wish I'd done that even a day earlier so I could have stopped what happened with him."

"I've told you before, it's not your job to keep me from making stupid decisions."

With a shrug, he said, "Maybe not. But it *is* my job to be there for you, and I failed you that night." He shook his head, staring through the floor. "I failed you because I was so jealous and pissed off that you were in Vegas with him that I shut my phone off when you called. I figured you were drunk and calling to tell me how much fun you were having, and I was already losing my mind—that would have been too much." His eyes fell to my legs, his fingertips tracing the scars on my thighs. "But I wish I'd answered. Even if that had been the case, that would have been easier to handle than what happened to you because I was too busy feeling sorry for myself to pick up my phone. I'm so sorry, Tasha."

"There's nothing for you to be sorry for, Drew." I grabbed his hands and gave them a shake until he looked back up at me. "You're entitled to feel however you feel, and there's no contract that says you must answer your phone no matter what. I know I was mad—"

"You said you hated me," he interrupted, his voice thickening with emotion. "You'd never said those words to me before. That fucking hurt, god it hurt. Especially because I deserved it."

"I was mad—I never hated you. I overreacted. I was actually hating myself for not being able to do what I knew I should have without you. I'm sorry I said that."

I leaned forward and pulled Drew to me. He slid his arms around me, too, and held me tight. We hugged for a long time, letting things heal between us, before we decided to head back to my apartment.

Chapter Thirty-Four

Tasha

The no-kissing thing was a serious struggle for Drew and me. We'd ended up kissing in the kitchen in the middle of drinking water after working out. Drew had whispered into my ear that maybe we should just start on a new day, and I'd agreed, so we'd spent just about every second we had together that day with our mouths touching. The next morning, we managed not to touch each other when he first showed up to walk Watson, but then somehow started kissing when he got back with him. It was a coin toss every time we saw each other for a few days whether or not we'd be able to keep our mouths and hands to ourselves.

However, leading up to Christmas, I was walking without the cane and Drew didn't need to come to walk Watson for me anymore, and with some added distance between us, we'd finally figured out how to keep our relationship strictly in friendship territory again. I didn't want to—I didn't like things that way—but was resolute that it was necessary for me to spend some more time alone.

Two days before Christmas, I hummed as I returned from a midday walk with Watson. I'd just texted Drew to let him know that all had gone well with the walk sans cane and that I hadn't overdone anything the way he'd worried I would. I enjoyed my walks with Watson and savored them since he'd be moving back home with Drew in a week or two like we'd agreed. I walked in the door with Watson and noticed as I hung his leash that the poop bag dispenser was missing—it must have popped off. *Again.* Like it did nearly every time we walked.

"Be right back, boy," I called to him and stepped out. He'd pooped when we were almost back to the building, so I knew it had fallen sometime after that and was likely in the hallway or elevator. I scanned the area just outside the door, along the hall toward the stairwell, then my heart dropped and I froze just out of reach of my door.

Coming toward me down the corridor was Duncan.

I stared at him, unable to move. Drew had been worried he'd show up at some point, regardless of the protective order I had, but I'd begun to think it wasn't going to happen. He stared back at me as his feet ate up the distance between us, but I couldn't read him.

"What are you doing here?" I squeaked out, backing gradually toward my door.

"You served me with divorce papers without even talking to me, baby. I know we can work this out."

I shook my head. "There's nothing to work out, Duncan. We're getting a divorce."

He slowed but didn't stop until I'd backed into the wall; I'd meant to get to my door, but came up short. I could hear Watson's sniffing and light whining from inside, but I couldn't get to the door to let him out.

"You're pressing charges against me, too. It was an accident, Tasha. I didn't mean to hurt you. Sometimes I just... I made a mistake. I never meant for you to get hurt. I was so scared when you fell down the stairs."

"I didn't fall, Duncan—you pushed me."

"I was trying to grab you, baby. I'd never push you down the stairs like that."

I shook my head again. It wasn't true—I *knew* it wasn't true because I was there when he did it. But this was the same thing he'd told the police.

In a quick movement, he lifted his arms and leaned them against the wall on either side of me, caging me in and bringing him inches from my face. I turned my head to the side and tried to inch sideways toward my door as much as I could with his arm now in the way.

"I'm going to go to jail if you don't drop the charges, Tasha. Jail. They think I'm some abusive monster or something. You have to tell them the truth, that it isn't like that. That what happened was an accident. I know you're mad that I yelled at you and you got hurt, and I'm sorry, but, baby, you have to tell them the truth. And I promise I'll do better. I love you, Tasha, baby, you can't divorce me. We vowed for better or worse, but you're running at the first sign of worse."

He rubbed his cheek against mine and I nearly vomited. I smashed the side of my face against the wall as much as I could to minimize the contact.

"Get away from me," I said, my voice quiet and tremulous, though I wished it was loud and strong.

"I know you've been with him—that he's the reason I couldn't find you here and the reason I can't reach your cell phone. Did he change your number?"

I could hear the anger rising in his voice, and with it, the panic in my body grew stronger.

"I knew he was going to cause problems for us. I told you that before he ever came out here. That's why I told you no to him coming to see you, but you didn't listen to me. And now he's ruining our marriage."

"Our marriage is ruined because you abused me, Duncan."

Both of his hands slammed against the wall on either side of my face, and I jumped, my eyes closing tight and my breath stalling. I wasn't sure if that was all he was going to do. I leaned a little further and felt my doorknob with the very edges of my fingertips. Just another inch, then enough of my fingers were touching it for me to twist it open.

In an instant, Watson was there between us, growling, teeth bared at Duncan. Duncan jumped back, his hands up in the air, his eyes fixed on Watson.

"That's his fucking dog from the video—is he inside your apartment right now?" he yelled.

If he were, you'd be unconscious right now, you asshole, I thought to myself, not wanting to enrage him more by saying it out loud.

I closed my fingers around Watson's collar as he crept forward toward Duncan in response to the shouting, his growling growing in intensity. "It's okay, boy," I soothed. As much as I relished the thought of Duncan being hurt and getting a taste of the pain he'd inflicted on me, I also *didn't* want to hurt him—then I'd be no better than he was.

"We're getting divorced. The only thing you're doing by refusing to sign the papers is delaying the inevitable, because it's happening whether you like it or not. And I'm not dropping the charges, either. I believe you feel remorse, but that doesn't excuse the things you did to me."

"Tasha—" he started through clenched teeth, his hands now balled into fists as he moved toward me.

"I will let Watson go if you take one more step!" I shouted. Well, it wasn't quite that loud, but it was above the whispering volume I'd had so far, and my voice wasn't noticeably wavering anymore. "And he *will* bite you. He doesn't like people upsetting me."

Duncan's eyes flashed with rage as they narrowed at Watson. He was considering taking his chances. I felt sick and my hand shook where it grasped Watson's collar. I loosened my grip to make it easier to let go if I needed to, then inched my way to my apartment with Watson in front of me. Once I had backed inside the entryway, Duncan took a step forward.

"Don't fucking do it," I bit out.

I reached my hand around the back to lock the knob, then, with as much speed as I could muster, I pulled Watson inside with me and shut the door. Something slammed against it from the outside a split second after it latched closed, then again and again, as I scrabbled to get the deadbolt across and flip the security guard. Duncan was shouting, but my ears were ringing louder and I couldn't understand him. I rushed into my bedroom, Watson on my heels, and slammed the door, locking it behind me for good measure.

My fingers fumbled to unlock my phone, then I texted Drew to tell him Duncan was outside my apartment and that he was angry. I could hear Drew's voice in my head telling me to call the police, so I did that next before even waiting for him to text me back. Duncan must have been in a different kind of rage because he was still shouting and slamming against my front door when I heard sirens nearing. Or maybe it was the same kind of rage he always had, and he was just still going because he hadn't hurt me yet. Maybe he would have kept going the other times if I hadn't been bleeding or had broken bones.

Watson's ears perked up shortly after the sirens shut off outside the building and the shouting and banging had stopped, then he whined and pawed at my bedroom door insistently.

"Tasha!" Drew's faint, muffled voice carried into the bedroom, explaining Watson's behavior.

Shaking, I stood and, with a firm grip on Watson, headed to the front door. Drew's panicked face showed through a small open gap, unable to get in because I'd flipped the security guard. I pushed the door closed, flipped the security guard the other direction, then opened the door and was engulfed in Drew's arms.

I huddled there, trembling uncontrollably, and was still there when two police officers arrived to talk to me. I cleared my face of tears, took a deep breath, and went to the kitchen to sit on a stool at the island; my legs were not going to support me for much longer. I relayed everything to them as they took notes and asked questions here and there, feeling a bit disconnected from myself, almost as if I was watching someone else doing what I was doing.

Eventually the police left, and when they did, I got a good look at the outside of my door, which was covered in dents. Thank god for the metal door. If it had been made of the same cheap, hollow material as the doors inside the apartment, Duncan would have busted through it with just two or three hits. After closing the door, my feet shuffled me around until I was facing Drew.

"Jesus fuck," I muttered.

Drew ran his hands up and down my arms slowly. "What do you need right now?"

Eyes darting around restlessly, I said, "I don't even know." My mind was no better, flitting from thought to thought, playing out a million different ways things could have gone with Duncan. "Do you have to leave?" I asked, making eye contact at last.

"No. I got coverage for my patients at the hospital for the rest of the day."

"Okay." I swallowed. "I was so fucking scared, Drew."

"I know," he soothed. "But you're okay. He didn't hurt you."

I shook my head. "Because of Watson. He would have if it hadn't been for Watson. He was furious."

"And because you had the forethought and guts to let Watson out with you."

Watson, having heard his name several times, lifted his head from where he was leaned into my legs and nuzzled my elbow where my arms were crossed over my chest until I lowered a hand to scratch behind his ears.

"I want Watson to stay with you," Drew said, his voice resolute.

"He's *your* dog."

"I want him here, Tash. Duncan will hopefully be stuck in jail after today, but if he's let out for any reason... Watson should be here."

I sighed. "Let's see what happens with Duncan first. Deal?"

"Okay." His brow was deeply furrowed, his mouth drawn, his eyes as stormy as they could get. "Why don't I go with you to talk to the office about the door, then you and Watson come back home with me for the rest of the day? I can play guitar, we can watch a movie, I'll make you pancakes for dinner... What do you think?"

What I thought was that his idea sounded about perfect. Being in my apartment felt unsafe right then. I wanted to be somewhere far away from what had just transpired... somewhere I felt secure and could maybe rid myself of some of the lingering panic in my body.

Chapter Thirty-Five

Drew

It was a relief to bring Tasha home with me—I didn't want to let her out of my sight. And I was incredibly grateful that I was able to be there for her with so much support from my practice; I'd worked in a practice before with doctors who really only cared about themselves, and I felt lucky to have found this practice where everyone supported each other. In fact, I decided to send Courtney flowers as a thank you for covering my patients while I was making dinner for Tasha, though because of Christmas in two days, they wouldn't be delivered until the day after.

After an afternoon spent singing and playing guitar, and a dinner of pancakes, roasted potatoes, and eggs, Tasha and I settled on the sofa with a reality tv series about blown glass on Netflix that we'd discovered before she'd moved back into her apartment.

"I wonder if there's a way to take a glass-blowing class," Tasha mused with a yawn halfway through the second episode of the next season.

I shrugged with an answering yawn. Except that I *did* know, because I'd known from her reaction to the first episode we'd ever watched that she'd want to take a class if she could. So I'd searched until I found one I was going to surprise her with. "You ready to go home?" *I* wasn't ready for her to leave, but it wasn't up to me. And if she was yawning, she might be tired enough for bed.

"Mm-mm," she replied, shaking her head, then yawning again. She rested against my shoulder, and I slid an arm around her. She fit perfectly that way, as if my body had been created expressly for her. "Can I stay?"

My heart flipped, and I kissed the top of her head. "Of course. You can always stay."

Tasha shifted so more of her weight rested against me, and by the end of the episode, she was sound asleep. I was also exhausted after the adrenaline and anxiety of the day; I could only imagine how tired *she* must have been. I lowered the volume and let the show play in the background, though I wasn't paying attention to it anymore. I was gently combing my fingers through Tasha's hair and thinking about how quiet and lost in her thoughts she'd been all day. It reminded me of how she'd been the first few weeks after she'd left the hospital. And how she was for a long time after I met her when we were kids. Especially that first night.

I'd noiselessly slipped out of my bedroom window without checking outside first. I did it all the time and never saw anyone, which made sense since my bedroom was in the back corner of the house and my window was on the side. The bedroom of the girl who lived next door was twenty or thirty feet away facing mine, though I'd never talked to her before. I'd seen her in school, but she kept to herself and I did, too, really, aside from the "friends" my parents forced me to have.

My feet reached the ground, and I turned around and froze. Watching me was the girl from next door, the bright moonlight reflecting in her eyes, which were barely visible above the knees she was hugging into herself. I stared at her, trying to figure out if I should climb back inside, but realized she'd snuck out of her bedroom, too, so it wasn't likely she was going to say anything to either of our parents.

I headed for the backyard like I usually did, glancing back over my shoulder. The girl's face was now hidden, and I could see in the light from the moon that her shoulders were shaking—she was crying. I knew what that was like—I'd done it more nights than not since I could remember. I knew how lonely it was to have only yourself and couldn't leave her there that way. I turned around and crept toward her until she raised her head, her eyes wide in fear. I held my hands up to show her I wasn't going to do anything, then beckoned for her to follow me.

"Come on," I whispered.

She hesitated, undecided, so I whispered to her again to follow me, and she pushed to her feet and trailed behind me, her eyes darting over her shoulder every few seconds. We made our way silently through my backyard to the large, detached garage where my dad kept his restored antique cars and other stuff I wasn't allowed to touch. I opened the left door—the one I kept oiled with WD-40 so it wouldn't make any noise—and waited for the girl to follow me inside before closing it. I stepped around and closed the blinds in the windows, then turned on a dim lamp. I'd done it so many times I knew my way around in there even in complete darkness.

Once the lamp was on, I got a good look at the girl. She was standing hunched with her arms wrapped around herself as if she was trying to disappear... another feeling I was all too familiar with. Her hair was matted and in disarray, and I could now see that she had a handprint on her cheek. I narrowed my eyes toward her house as anger surged through me.

"I'm Drew," I said, holding my hand out.

She just stared at me, and I felt like an idiot. I didn't exactly have good social skills—maybe fourteen-year-olds didn't shake hands when they met. My arm started to fall back to my side, but she reached out to catch it.

"Natasha," the girl said, shaking my hand. "But everyone calls me Tasha."

I gestured toward her face. "Mom or Dad?"

She looked down, the other side of her face now turning red.

"I'm not judging. My parents hit me sometimes, too."

Her eyes rose back up. "I'm sorry," she said, in an almost delicately soft voice. She hesitated. "My mom. But I'm used to it. She usually does worse."

"And your dad just lets it happen?"

She huffed, her eyes flashing. "My dad doesn't give a shit about me. He hasn't since I was born. I don't even know him. The jerk my mom is married to is my stepdad—my third one. And the only thing he cares about is that I let him do what he wants."

My hair stood on end when she said her last few words, a dark sense of foreboding settling over me. "What do you mean?"

She shook her head. "I don't want to talk about it. What about your parents?"

I shrugged, turning and heading toward my dad's hidden liquor stash, pulling out a bottle of whiskey. "They don't hit me that often. Just when I *really* disappoint them. I mean, everything I do is a disappointment—nothing's ever good enough. I'm not smart enough, I'm not tall enough, or strong enough. I don't keep my room neat enough or help out around the house enough, and when I do, I don't do a good enough job of washing dishes or vacuuming or whatever the fuck it is that day. And, today, I'm not 'good-looking' enough, either," I added, using air quotes.

I took a swig of whiskey from the bottle, then held it out toward her. She shook her head and instead wandered around, looking at things.

"They're wrong, you know. You *are* cute. And we're still kids—we're not done growing yet. You'll get taller. I bet they're wrong about everything else, too. I bet you're good at all those things."

I took another swig of whiskey, watching her trail her hands along the shelves of tools and stored decorations and gardening supplies, my heart slamming repeatedly into my chest. "You think I'm cute?"

She glanced at me, then away. "Yes. But I don't want a boyfriend or anything. I'm just telling you because your parents are wrong." She turned to face me again. "And assholes."

"Hear, hear."

She stepped over and grabbed the bottle from me. "To the founding of the asshole parents club."

She tipped it up and poured a small amount into her mouth, then coughed and choked as it started down her throat. I patted her on the back, and she laughed between coughs once she got it all down.

"Fuck," she said with another small laugh.

"You get used to it."

She sipped again, still coughing but less violently, then gave a sharp shake of her head and resumed her exploration of the garage. I stayed where I was, just watching her. It was strange not to be alone, and I wasn't sure how I felt about it, though I was leaning toward liking it.

"So you do this a lot?" she asked.

"Do what?"

"Sneak into your dad's garage and drink his alcohol."

I shrugged. "They're assholes a lot."

She nodded somewhat absently. "Your dad plays guitar?" She pointed to a guitar tucked under a workbench.

"He used to."

"Is he any good?"

"I don't know. I've never heard him play."

She pulled the guitar out with care. "Do you play?"

I shook my head, bitter. "No."

She turned to me and tipped her head in question. "Why not?"

My eyes found my feet. "My parents said they didn't want to waste money on an instrument when I'd never be able to play it well enough to make up for it."

"Are you serious?"

For some reason, her incredulity struck me as funny, and I laughed. That was par for the course for my parents. She walked over with the guitar and shoved it toward me. I raised my hands and stepped away.

"No way. My dad would kill me."

She strummed it then held it back out to me. "If he doesn't know you drink his alcohol, he won't know if you touched his guitar. Take it."

I looked at the guitar, debating.

"I bet you'd play well if you wanted to."

"You have a lot of confidence in someone you don't even know."

This time, *she* shrugged. "I just have a feeling about you."

I stared at her, and she stared back at me. Not only was that the exact same way I felt about her, but it was also the most encouraging thing someone had ever said to me. I felt like I could become a rock star if I wanted to right then because this girl had a feeling about me... because she believed in me.

My tongue darted over my lips. I shoved down the fear of what my dad would do if he ever found out and accepted the guitar. It was weird to hold—I'd never held one before, let alone this one. I'd asked to hold it once and was told never to touch it if I knew what was good for me. Just like my dad's precious cars. And everything else he owned.

Tasha told me I was holding the instrument wrong, then showed me how to hold it properly and taught me the different parts of the guitar and two basic chords.

"How do you know so much about guitars?" I asked, gingerly strumming one of the chords.

"I don't actually know that much. What I told you is everything I know. I watched a guitar lesson for beginners on YouTube."

"You want to play, too?"

She lifted and dropped a shoulder. "I just like learning how to do new things."

I played around on the guitar for a while and Tasha was quiet, sometimes watching me, sometimes looking off into the distance. Eventually, I knew it was time for us to go to bed so we wouldn't be falling asleep in school the next day, a sure way to incur parental wrath—at least for me. I carefully replaced the guitar where Dad kept it before turning off the light and opening the blinds.

I made my way over to Tasha and grabbed her hand, trying to ignore that it felt like a firework exploding inside my body when I touched her, as I guided her to the exit and opened the door for her to walk out. I followed her, carefully closing the door back up, and we trailed across the dew-soaked grass of my backyard side by side.

"I go out there around ten pretty much every night. If, you know..." What the hell was I trying to say? And why did I feel nervous about inviting her to hang out in my dad's garage?

She frowned. "I don't know. I've never snuck out before—I just couldn't breathe if I didn't get outside tonight, you know? But I don't want to get caught."

I felt deflated. I *really* wanted her to keep coming, I realized. I liked being around her. "I've been doing it for two years, and I've never been caught." I looked up at the moon, then back to Tasha. "Just, like, do something to let me know if you want to come and I'll wait for you."

"Okay." She looked toward her window. "I'll see you around in school."

"See you around."

"And thank you." She gave me a small smile.

I smiled back but didn't say anything, and we both headed to our windows. I laid in bed for a while before falling asleep thinking about the girl from next door, wondering if she really would talk to me in school or not, but happy regardless that she'd come with me. Though I didn't like that her parents beat her—it made me feel a kind of anger that was almost out of control.

The next day, she'd waved and smiled at me in the halls at school, and that night, when I climbed out of my window, her bedroom curtains were open. I wondered if that was a sign that she wanted to come and decided to wait. I was about to give up and head to the shed when she slipped out with a small bag, smiling and giving me a wave like she had at school. When we got inside the shed, she emptied her bag. She'd brought brownies, a guitar instructional book she'd checked out from the library, and a worn copy of *The Complete Stories of Sherlock Holmes.*

Over the next few weeks, we became inseparable. We started eating together at lunch, walking to classes together, sitting together when we rode the bus, and walking home together when we didn't. Then at night, once our parents were asleep or passed out or otherwise occupied until morning, we sat together in my dad's shed. I practiced playing his guitar, and we took turns reading stories from her favorite book, often snacking on brownies one of us had made. Sometimes we talked about what was going on with our parents, over time learning everything there was to know about each other.

I'd known after that first night that Tasha was different from anyone I'd ever met. I'd known by the middle of the second night that she was my favorite person in the world and always would be. The night a little over a month later when she told me her stepfather made her do things in front of him naked while he watched her, I'd considered spending my life in jail because I wanted to go next door and kill him. I wanted to kill both of her parents for what they did to her. And a few months later when she used the money she was saving from her part-time job to buy me my own guitar so I could play whenever I wanted, I'd known I would never love someone the way I loved her. I'd known right then and there that there wasn't anything I wouldn't do for her, that I wouldn't hesitate to die for her. She was the kind of person the world overlooked and took for granted as if she wasn't worth the time to notice when, in reality, it was the world that would never be good enough for her.

Chapter Thirty-Six

Tasha

Christmas Eve, I was drained. I'd woken up twice with nightmares and just felt sapped of energy. Even so, Drew and I worked out like we usually did and walked Watson together. Drew was off work for a few days because of the holiday and decided to kick off his time off with us doing an online painting class together, so that's how we spent the afternoon after finding a craft store that was open where we could stock up on painting supplies.

He set down his paintbrush like he'd done at least a dozen times in the last two hours and lifted his phone, snapping a picture of me while I was focused on trying to make realistic looking leaves on a tree.

"Why the hell do you keep doing that?" I asked with a chuckle without looking up.

"You're adorable when you're concentrating. You scrunch your mouth to the side and your eyes narrow."

"And you glare when you're concentrating," I said.

"No, I don't," he laughed, setting his phone down and picking his paintbrush back up. As I watched, his glare set in when his brush touched his paper.

"Yes, you do." I gave him a lopsided smile. "It's cute."

He rolled his eyes. "Cute? Watson's cute."

I looked down at Watson lying near my feet, his left ear lifted after hearing his name. "No, Watson's handsome, aren't you, boy?"

"So I'm cute and my dog is handsome?"

"Sometimes," I clarified. "You're cute *sometimes*."

"Only sometimes?" Drew chuckled, now facing me. When I looked up, his eyes were sparkling with good humor.

"Yeah. Obviously not when you do obnoxious shit like leave me without toothpaste in the tube."

He laughed. "You're just pissed that I won this round."

I bit my tongue. "The war's not over yet, Drewy Baby."

He let out a cross between a groan and a growl. "I hate that shit," he muttered.

"I know." I smirked, then winked. "That's why it's so much fun."

"Brat."

No one on the planet would think being called a brat was a good thing, but my chest warmed. It was something Drew had called me for years, and only when I was both annoying and amusing him, because as much as he wanted to be aggravated with me, he couldn't be. I liked the familiarity of it after how much had been changing since his visit eight months earlier.

I grinned at him, and he shook his head with his eyes narrowed playfully, but then his expression changed. His gray-blue eyes darkened and the playfulness in his features faded. My heart sped up and the sound of the painting instructor in the background faded into static; all I could hear was my own heartbeat and breath. My eyes fell, resting on his lips. They were slightly parted, but then they pressed together as he swallowed. The motion pulled the breath right from my lungs.

He reached over, unhurried, and slipped my paintbrush from my fingers, resting it down on the paper towel situated next to my paper. I watched as his hand traveled from my paintbrush through the air toward me until his palm slid against my cheek. As his hand moved further into my hair, his face grew closer to mine until we were sharing the same small pocket of air.

"I know we're not supposed to kiss anymore, but goddamn I..."

Drew's voice, which was soft and deep, trailed off. But he didn't need to say anything else because I could see his unspoken words in the depths of his eyes. It was all he could think about—he wanted to kiss me more than he wanted anything else right then. And I felt the exact same way. My reasons for reinforcing a friendship boundary suddenly were hazy and unimportant. I leaned in closer, halving the remaining inches between us, then halved them again as I lifted a hand to his wrist.

Our kissing was still so new and yet familiar, and it felt as if we'd been kissing our whole lives but like it had been a lifetime since the last kiss all at once. His lips and tongue were soft, taking their time getting to know mine again, and that unhurried gentleness was making something inside me unravel. I'd never felt so cherished or vulnerable kissing someone before. There were tears pushing their way to the edges of my eyelids, and it was hard to breathe in an entirely different way. It was like my insides were lying there in the open for inspection, and I had no idea who was going to show up or what they would do. It was such an intense fear and excitement all mixed together that I considered pulling away just to take a break from it; it was nearly overwhelming. Instead, I kept waiting for the kiss to turn more desperate and wanting—a type of desire I was familiar with—but it didn't. And the longer it didn't, the more exposed I felt.

I reached a point where I wanted to say no more. I wanted to pull away and tell him we couldn't do that again, ask him to take me home, and lock myself up in my apartment. I couldn't even define the way I felt right then, but it was too much of it. And yet... I couldn't make myself do any of that. I wanted to stop it... but I wanted more to find out what would happen if I didn't. As much as the sensations felt like too much for my body and my heart, I was also intensely curious and intrigued by them because I'd never in my life felt that way before. Every time we'd kissed, I'd tasted these complex, nebulous emotions, but now I was swimming in them—they were everywhere at once.

There was a slam somewhere nearby, and I jumped and yelped, traveling for an instant back to Duncan trying to bust his way through my front door. A flood of mental images followed—it took only fractions of a second for it to begin—of every moment Duncan had been angry, every moment he'd scared me, every moment he had hurt me.

"Nats," Drew said, his hands grasping my upper arms and keeping me from falling from my stool because of how violently I'd jumped. "What's wrong?"

I shook my head as Drew's face became blurry. "The slam," I whispered, now realizing it must have been a neighboring apartment inhabitant that shut their door a little too hard. Even so, my eyes raced around as if Duncan could appear out of thin air.

Drew slid to the edge of his stool and pulled me into his chest. I could feel his heart beating wildly under my cheek as he held me snug against him and I huddled inside his arms, wanting to be surrounded by him, so no part of me would feel exposed to danger. His hands smoothed up and down my back, then one moved from the crown of my head down the length of my hair, over and over and over.

"You're safe, Tasha," he murmured. "He'll never hurt you again."

I nodded against his chest, but how could he be so certain? Never was a long time.

"*Never*," he repeated with emphasis and another kiss to my crown. "I promise."

Later, after we finished the painting class, I suggested I head back home. I'd already showered and put on fresh clothes after we worked out, but after being so upset, I wanted to wash all the remnants of anxiety and upset down the drain and watch cheesy Christmas movies in sweats until I fell asleep like I normally did on Christmas Eve, hopefully snuggled with Watson. When we arrived at my apartment, however, I hesitated before crossing the threshold inside.

Seeing the dents in my door made me nauseous. I shuddered, then forced myself to step inside.

Drew followed me, closing the door quietly behind him, then grabbed my hand in his. He gave it a squeeze. "Why don't you pack a bag and just stay with me for a few days?"

I shook my head, staring absently at the ostensibly innocuous strip of wall to the left of my tv.

"Why not?" Drew asked, releasing my hand to slide his arm across my shoulders and pull me into his side.

Instantly, I could breathe a little easier.

"You'd be coming over in the morning anyway. And otherwise we'd both just be sitting at home alone. It's the holidays—you spend those with family. And we're family, right?"

I nodded, looking up at him with a soft smile. "Yeah, we are."

The only family we recognized. The only family we really needed.

He kissed the side of my head. "So pack a bag. Consider it visiting family for the holidays."

I took some time to debate his suggestion, but there was no point—I didn't want to be in my apartment right then. Unlike being in Drew's apartment with him, it didn't feel safe or comforting to be in mine again yet.

With a bag packed, we grabbed more of Watson's food and headed back to Drew's. Once there, I took the shower I'd been wanting, but in lieu of tossing on the sweats I'd packed—sweats that belonged to Drew before I'd swiped them for myself—I raided his drawers until I found his scrubs and tossed them on with one of his soft concert t-shirts from college. Why did he have the most comfortable clothes?

He laughed and shook his head when I emerged into the living room. "I need a padlock on my dresser when you come over."

I lifted my eyebrows. "Wouldn't stop me."

"You're giving those back. I need those pants for work, and I love that shirt."

I scanned the clothes I was wearing and smirked. "I'll think about it."

We settled on the sofa, Drew's Christmas tree in the corner with a few small gifts under it. One gift each for each other—that had always been our rule—and several for Watson, who was spoiled. Though I was cheating this year and had *two* gifts for Drew inside the package. With a lasagna in the oven, we kicked off our Christmas movie marathon with *White Christmas*.

Chapter Thirty-Seven

Drew

Tasha and I had fallen asleep on the sofa together during *A Christmas Story* after lasagna, brownies, and rye whiskey, so I woke on Christmas morning with her in my arms, still asleep. My back protested severely, but I'd stretch it out later—no way I was getting up until she was awake and ready to start the day. While it hadn't involved a sofa, I'd dreamed about falling asleep and waking with her in my arms many times over the years. I'd never taken it for granted when I was able to during those short few months when we were first living together and shared a single air mattress, and yet I appreciated it even more now.

Watson shoved his nose under my hand with a small whine. "Easy boy," I whispered, scratching behind his ears. "Don't wake Tasha." He marched his feet in place and whined again. "Okay, okay," I acquiesced, giving him a final scratch. "I'm getting up."

I leaned down to kiss Tasha's cheek before moving and waking her; she was so peaceful and beautiful in her sleep. But I stopped just before making contact. I didn't want it to wake her up and startle her in a bad way. She'd said a few times there were things I didn't know about—maybe one of her exes had done something to her in her sleep. I didn't want to discover that because I did something to trigger her. Instead, I carefully shifted myself out from under her.

She smiled at me after blinking herself awake. "Good morning," she murmured, her eyes resting on me in a way that felt almost like a caress.

She seemed different, though I couldn't quite put my finger on what it was. Less guarded? More present? Something. She was looking at me in a way that allowed me to see into her, though, and it took my breath away.

I smiled back, tucking her hair behind her ear. "Good morning." *Now* I kissed her cheek. "Merry Christmas."

Watson whined loudly and we both laughed.

Tasha sat up, yawning. "I'll come with you—just give me a minute to throw on some sweats so I don't freeze."

After walking Watson, we pulled our coats off, hanging them in the coat closet, and I unhooked Watson from his leash. When I looked back up, my heart literally skipped a beat. Tasha was watching me, her expression warm, her mouth curved up into a small smile, her cheeks and nose rosy from the cold. In that split second, I could see it:

Our future.

I could see us living in a house with a big yard for Watson and a deck and a cute wooden fence. I could see us laughing as our children tackled Watson and he licked their faces. I could see Tasha reading bedtime stories as I brushed our daughter's hair, our eyes meeting every so often, accompanied by the same expression she was wearing now.

That flash of a future together felt as real as if it were actually a memory, and I slid my palm against Tasha's as I straightened back up, then slipped my fingers between hers. A wave of intense feeling washed over me—something like love, but more—and I filled with longing. Her eyes were on our hands, and she was breathing into her shoulders suddenly—shallow and short breaths. Leaning forward, I pressed my lips to hers, slowly, gently. The flush on her cheeks deepened.

"Presents?" she asked in a breathy voice that made my stomach feel like there were bubbles inside it.

I kissed the back of her hand. "Okay. I'll make some coffee."

With another quick touch of my lips to her hand, I turned toward the kitchen, reluctant to separate from her. I heard her take and release a noisy breath as we headed in opposite directions and couldn't keep myself from grinning. I felt happy in a way I'd never thought was real—similar to the kind of happiness I'd always felt with Tasha, but somehow deeper and more settled. Things with her right then just felt... right. It was the most right anything had ever felt. As if everything in our lives had been leading us here, to this moment, all along. To this point in time when we could finally be together.

With fresh coffee in hand, I joined Tasha and Watson in the living room. Though we had only a handful of gifts under the tree, Tasha sat on the floor to hand them out, Watson draped over one of her legs, his eyes watching her every move. That dog had worshipped Tasha since the day I'd rescued him. As much as I loved him and he loved me, he and Tasha had some sort of bond I wasn't privy to. Much like how, in the world of people, Tasha and I had always been connected in a way we'd never been with anyone else and that no one else could understand.

Tasha accepted her coffee with a smile, and I couldn't resist bending to place another chaste kiss on her lips. Her cheeks were pink when I pulled away and I was grinning uncontrollably again.

As usual, we began with Watson. He got a bag of enormous Greenies chews—his favorite—a new rawhide, several new toys, and a replacement bag dispenser for his leash that shouldn't fall off all the time. After excited exploration of everything, he settled next to Tasha with a Greenie.

"This dog and Greenies," Tasha said, shaking her head as she rubbed a hand over the top of his head. His eyes shifted to her, but he didn't slow with his chewing. "Okay, your turn."

I accepted the gift she held out, turning it over in my hands before deciding it was a book. My heart jumped—maybe it was a copy of her autofiction so I could finally read it. Curious, I unwrapped it. With the wrapping paper off, however, there were two surprises.

"Tash," I began with my brows drawn, holding up a book in one hand and a small envelope in the other. "What...?"

She grinned with a twinkle in her eye. "I cheated this year. I couldn't help myself."

I chuckled. "I did, too."

Her eyes grew wide, and we both laughed. I moved to her side, shifting Watson so I could take his place next to her, our backs leaning against the wall. I gave a shimmy as I settled in with our hips, shoulders, and thighs touching and she giggled. I looked back down at my hands, deciding to start with the book.

It had a black cover with the words *Searching for Never* in white above Tasha's name, also in white. The back and thick spine had no words at all. I looked up, curious.

Tasha was tapping her thumb against her leg. "It's the autofiction. A draft I had specially printed for you—it's messy, I'm warning you. And not that much ended up fiction. But I promised you I'd let you read it once I had a completed draft. Though I'm not sure I want you to."

I stared at her, taking in what was happening. She was exceptionally nervous right then about me holding her book. And yet she'd given it to me. Despite what she was saying, I believed she actually *did* want me to read it—at least some part of her did. I flipped through the pages, wanting to read it right that instant.

"Do you think you'd mind actually waiting to read it? Just a while longer?"

I watched as her eyes clouded over, then lifted her hand and kissed the back of it. "I won't read it until you tell me it's okay for me to. Thank you for giving it to me and trusting me."

"I trust you more than anyone," she said, her gaze falling. "It's just that..." She let out a controlled sigh. "There are things you don't know about me."

Those words again. "And they're in the book?" I asked gently.

She paused. "Yeah."

"Well, I won't read even a page of it until you tell me I can." It would be a struggle, but I wouldn't. It already felt like torture not to start reading it to find out everything I could. I wanted to know *everything* about her.

She looked up, relieved. "Thank you. I know it's a weird thing to give it to you and then ask you not to read it."

I snorted. "Not the weirdest thing you've ever done."

She chuckled. "No. That would probably be when I asked you to get a pedicure with me."

"Not even close. It was when you texted me out of the blue and asked me if I had anything against wool."

Her chuckle deepened. "I forgot about that."

"I had no idea what I was getting myself into when I said I didn't." She'd signed us up to help shear sheep for a day on a farm local to our college, and then had brought part of a dirty fleece back with us, which she'd insisted I help her clean. She spun it using a drop spindle we created with a stick and an old CD before she crocheted her handmade yarn into something that loosely resembled a scarf. She'd become interested in following the production of textiles from source to finish, and that had been her way of exploring it more deeply.

"I don't think that was any weirder than you asking me if I was going to see anyone for a few days before finals our senior year of undergrad."

Now it was my turn to start laughing. I knew exactly what she was referring to; I had freaked out about a final I needed to ace to get into grad school and asked her if I could use a marker to mark and label her body: bones, muscles, tissues, joints... everything. The final involved doing something similar, and it was the best way I could come up with to study. But the only markers I could find with a fine enough point were permanent. She'd worn a bikini—a white one we bought so I could label that, too—and the skin under the cloth was the only untouched skin on her body. She'd looked like she had really crappy, fading tattoos over just about every inch of her skin for *days*.

"Okay, we're both weird," I acquiesced. "But at least you're my kind of weird and I'm your kind of weird."

"A bit presumptuous with the second part of that sentence, aren't you?" she asked with a straight face.

I knocked my leg into hers. "Hmph."

"Okay, open the other thing. That one I'm not going to be weird about, I promise," she said with a laugh.

I opened the envelope, and inside was a single folded piece of paper. I unfolded it and read the page, printed from the website of a local rock-climbing gym. Tasha had purchased a climbing course for two that would cover basics both inside and outside the gym. I'd been interested in rock climbing ever since we saw a special documentary about it our senior year in college, but there was nowhere to learn where we lived then, and after Tasha moved away, I stopped trying out new things anyway. My heartrate kicked up with excitement.

"So you're doing this with me, right?" I asked, looking up from the paper.

She tipped her head sideways. "Maybe. It was a package deal for two, but you can do it with anyone you want."

"Then you're doing it with me—you're who I want to take."

"Maybe one of the other doctors in your practice would be interested," she suggested.

"Don't care," I replied, leaning over to kiss her cheek. I knew she was scared of heights. Because of that, climbing was one of the few things she'd ever encountered that she hadn't been so sure she wanted to try. "You're who I choose." I looked down at the tickets again and had an urge to jump up and get dressed. I wasn't sure how I was going to wait until classes restarted in the spring. "Thank you," I added, turning toward her.

She turned, too, so our faces were only inches apart. "You're welcome."

I leaned partway across the narrow space between us. I wanted to kiss her again, but needed to leave it up to her; there'd been quite a bit of kissing since the day before, even though she'd been reinforcing the no-kissing rule before that. She leaned across the remaining distance, and so we kissed, no more than a gentle brushing of our mouths. I let out a sigh as we pulled apart. I could get used to kissing her like that. Used to kissing her whenever I had the urge. Used to this new kind of closeness it was already bringing. It was the kind of closeness I'd been searching for with Becka for years, and the whole time, I'd already had it.

Right here.

With Tasha.

Chapter Thirty-Eight

Tasha

My breath was still stuttering out from the soft kiss we'd just shared when Drew leaned across in front of me to lift the remaining gift under the tree and hand it to me. It was a manila envelope with a red ribbon tied in a bow on it. If I wasn't already eager to find out what was inside, I would have been now; his eyes were dancing with excitement, the grin he'd already been wearing even broader.

"Open it," he said.

His impatience was adorable. And I couldn't resist messing with him. "Don't rush me," I admonished with a faux glare. "Maybe I want to take my time and savor it. Christmas lasts all day, you know—maybe I want to save it for later."

He narrowed his eyes back at me, quiet for a beat before speaking. "Bullshit. I give you five minutes—*tops*—before you rip that thing open."

Ha, I thought. *Two* minutes would have been pushing it. I just wanted him to think I'd wait, but he knew me too well. I could out-stubborn him with just about anything, except when it came to gifts from him. They were always the best and I spent all year waiting to see what he'd come up with for Christmas. And he'd said he had broken the one gift rule, which meant there was more than one gift inside that envelope. I was practically twitching with eagerness to open it.

"Whatever," I laughed, rolling my eyes.

I used my fingertips to unwrap the thread and lift the flap of the envelope before reaching in and sliding out a few sheets of paper. My eyes scanned down the first page, and I was grinning so hard my cheeks hurt—it was plane tickets for both of us. We were flying to California in October. I moved the page so quickly I gave myself a papercut and sucked at the sore spot on my finger while my eyes scanned the second page. Hotel reservations, at a hotel on the beach.

"Oh my god," I said, my eyes widening and my heart beating faster in excitement.

California was another state I hadn't been to yet, and I'd never stayed in a hotel on a beach before. Hell, I'd never even been to a beach at all before. I pulled up the first page again, checking the dates on the tickets to see how long we'd be gone for. Just over two weeks. I squealed and thought I might pass out. I couldn't believe it.

"Thank you, thank you, thank you!" I shouted, flinging my arms around him, the papers still clutched in my hands.

His chest rumbled with laughter as he hugged me back. "As much as I could keep you here like this all day, there's more in there."

I pulled back, then flipped to the next page. I had to read more carefully to understand what I was looking at: a five-day glass-blowing course for beginners.

"No. Fucking. Way." I turned to him. "How the hell did you find this? How did you even *know* I wanted to do this? I've been trying for weeks to find something around here."

He winked and smirked. "I'm just that good, Tash." He chuckled. "There isn't anything around here. It was hard to find something. There was that one and one in like Iowa or something, in the middle of nowhere. I thought you'd like California more and figured if we stayed a bit longer we could check out Hollywood, the redwoods, and some of wine country."

"You definitely overdid the presents this year," I said, feeling a stab of guilt as I realized how much money this all must have cost him. I knew he could afford it, but it was a lot to spend on me.

"Not even close," he replied, sliding his arm around me and pulling me in. "And this was only the first gift."

"Oh, shit, Drew," I said with an awkward laugh. "Whatever it is, return it. You've already spent too much."

He pressed his lips into my forehead, lingering. "There's no such thing as too much when it comes to you, Tasha. You're more than worth anything and everything. And it's *my* money, anyway—I can spend it however I want, right?"

"Well, yeah, but—"

"Okay, then. So if I choose to spend it on you, I can." Another kiss to my forehead. "Besides, I didn't spend it on *you*—I spent it on *us* because I'm doing all of it with you."

I sighed, wanting to argue, but not sure how to. And he wouldn't listen anyway. He pushed to his feet, telling me to stay where I was, and grabbed his guitar. I stared out the window at the snow falling while absently petting Watson, who was still happily gnawing on a greenie next to me.

Drew resettled on my other side, scooting a little this way and that until he could comfortably play with us still so close we were touching. I closed my eyes and settled in, figuring he was going to play some Christmas songs, as was our tradition. He surprised me by playing a collection of Sam Tinnesz songs, starting with the two that inspired our tattoos, followed by "Overcome" and "Feels Like Home." With every passing verse, every chord, my body relaxed against his and tears slipped from the corners of my closed eyes, but I didn't wipe them away. They weren't tears of sadness—they were tears of *feeling*. I felt so much I couldn't hold it all in, and that's how it came out.

I could have sat there all day with Drew playing and singing, but I felt him shifting and knew he was setting his guitar down. I sniffled, but otherwise didn't move, wanting to stretch out as long as possible the way I felt: complete. His body shifted again, and I lifted my head as he cupped my cheeks, wiping away my tears with his thumbs. He'd done the same thing more times than I could count in the past, and it always felt intimate, but nothing like him doing it right now. With the way things had been shifting between us into this nebulous not-just-friends-but-technically-not-more-than-friends space—which I didn't know how to even think about let alone define, especially the last few days—it was like the barrier between my feelings and my ability to really *feel* them was now missing.

It was on the tip of my tongue to tell him that I loved him. I'd known I was in love with him for quite some time now, but I'd thought if I didn't want to long enough, it would go away. It hadn't. And suddenly the words didn't want to stay in my mouth—they wanted to come bursting out. I choked them down, trying to force them to stay inside. We were seriously crossing the friendship line with all the kissing we were doing, all the kissing I was sure we were *going* to still do since it was about all I could think about, but what would happen if we officially changed what kind of relationship we had? I'd never had a relationship that worked out, and I'd been left at least as many times as I'd done the leaving. It would happen with Drew, too, if we made this something more. He would tire of me and find someone else, or I'd do something to sabotage us like I'd done so many times with other men. And I couldn't bear the thought of making Drew hate me. Being mad at me was one thing. As was us sometimes going long periods without talking. But hatred was something I couldn't stomach.

That was as far as my thoughts made it before they scattered as if they'd never been when Drew's breath broke across my face. I sucked it in greedily, and we kissed again like we had the day before. That same gentle, unhurried exploration, and like the day before, it unraveled me at the seams and left me wide open.

We kissed until my ass was so uncomfortably numb it was distracting, then got up and had a late breakfast. After we'd eaten and cleaned up, it was nearly midday and still snowing outside. We bundled up and took Watson out for a long walk, complete with a stop at the dog park where Watson tore around with other dogs, excited by the snow. Drew and I sat together on one of the benches, his arm behind me, and it dawned on me that was what it would be like if we were a couple and lived together. We'd walk Watson together and sit on that same bench together all the time. Maybe not that much would really change; maybe I didn't need to be as worried as I was.

I turned, taking in Drew's profile as he watched Watson gallivanting in the snow. His expression was softened, a gentle curve to the corner of his mouth betraying his amusement at his dog's antics. Drew was the best man I'd ever met, and I had a hunch that would be true until the day I died, even if I lived for thousands of years. His eyes shifted and found me looking at him. I could feel my cheeks beginning to heat at being caught, and then he kissed me. With a grin and a squeeze to my shoulders that held me even closer to him, he looked back out toward Watson.

I had an urge to giggle. There was nothing funny, but I just felt so happy. It all felt so natural, so easy with him. Things always had, but it still did as we shifted into whatever this thing was between us. On impulse, I leaned over and kissed his cheek. His eyes crinkled at the corners as his grin pulled wider.

We never even spoke while we were at the dog park, but it felt like so much had passed between us. Things had always been that way—we didn't necessarily need to use our voices to communicate with each other. We knew each other so well and were so attuned to one another that we could often read each other's thoughts just based on body language and facial expression. When we were in college and dated other people, they always found it strange at first, then threatening. But that had never mattered to us.

Back at the apartment, I huddled under a blanket on the sofa alone and started the next movie in our Christmas movie marathon. Despite my repeated shouts for Drew to hurry up with whatever he was doing, he kept saying he'd be there soon and not to wait for him. What the hell was he doing? When he emerged a little over halfway through the movie, I could tell something was bothering him, so I paused it.

"What's wrong?"

His eyes flicked to mine as he lowered himself down next to me and shook his head. "Something's just taking a lot longer than I thought it would."

I leaned into him. "What is it? Maybe I can help."

He shook his head again. "No. This isn't something you can help with."

"What is it?" I asked again, lifting my brows at him.

For the third time, he shook his head, then tipped it toward the television. "Play the movie."

Drew spent the rest of Christmas distracted and still was the next morning, his focus on his phone even while we were walking Watson. The closest I'd ever seen him to the way he was had been during college when he was nearing an exam, but he wasn't taking any classes that I was aware of.

"Are you taking a class or something?" I asked as we walked back into his apartment.

"What?" he asked, his eyes coming up only briefly. "No."

"You sure?"

"Yeah, why?" he looked up again.

I inclined my head toward his hands. "You're glued to your phone and really distracted."

He let out a frustrated sigh and locked his phone, then set it down on the counter and ran a hand through his hair, his leg bouncing. I reached out and rested my hand on his arm.

"If you can wait a while longer to eat, I'll go ahead and make the mac-n-cheese and we can have it for brunch instead of having breakfast. That way, you can deal with whatever's going on while I'm cooking."

He looked away and pulled a hand down his face. "Okay. Thank you." With a peck to my cheek, he left the kitchen for the den, where his computer was.

I moved around, humming Christmas songs to myself, preparing mac-n-cheese. Drew's phone dinged and vibrated on the counter; he'd forgotten to take it with him. I rinsed my hands from mixing the pasta and cheeses by hand, dried them, then grabbed up his phone to take it to him. As I lifted it from the counter, however, another message came in, illuminating his screen.

My feet stopped moving and I stared at the two notifications, trying to make sense of what I was seeing. One was a photo of a bouquet of flowers and the other a message that read, "I got the flowers. They're beautiful!" Both messages were from a Courtney.

Sluggishly, my eyes lifted from his phone to stare in the direction of the den, pain spreading throughout my body, originating in my chest. Drew had a girlfriend. He'd been kissing me and touching me—he'd even slept in the same place as me two nights in a row—and he had a girlfriend. And his distraction and irritation must have been because the flowers he sent her were late—why else would flowers arrive the day *after* Christmas? As hard as I tried to find one, there was no other explanation. I'd never have guessed he'd do something like that—I'd have staked my life that he wouldn't.

And I'd have been wrong.

I blinked hard, my jaw set, willing away the tears. I wasn't going to cry over him—at least not while I was still in his apartment. And what right did I have to be upset anyway? We were friends and nothing more. I'd thought that was changing, but I'd been wrong. He was probably just horny or something—who knew. That's what all my exes who cheated on me told me. That they were horny, often drunk though not always, and that the woman they cheated on me with meant nothing to them.

Oh god. I'm the other woman right now. I'm the one Drew will be telling his girlfriend means nothing to him if she ever finds out we were kissing.

"You sure you're okay?" Drew asked for at least the tenth time as he drove toward my apartment, his leg bouncing.

After preparing the mac-n-cheese, we'd eaten brunch together, if you could call what we did eating together. He'd finished his bowl, but was distracted the entire time. I'd pushed my food around my bowl without taking a single bite. I'd felt sick and couldn't begin to contemplate eating anything. Drew hadn't even noticed.

I gazed unseeing out my passenger window. "Yeah."

"You seem off, Nats."

"It's been a long few days."

"Even considering that. It's something else."

"I just need rest and to be back home and get back into a routine, that's all."

Generally speaking, I didn't like lies by omission, but I also didn't feel equal to having a conversation with him about what I'd discovered. When I looked at him, I felt more hurt and angry than I ever had when my exes had cheated on me, and I didn't know how to articulate it to him.

Back at my apartment, the discomfort between us grew tenfold. Drew had come up with me like he normally would, but this time I didn't want him there. I'd never not wanted him there before and I didn't know how to tell him that. Even so, he could sense it, and there was hurt in his eyes when I stole glances in his direction.

"I think I'm just going to take a bath, read, and go to bed early," I said after a monumentally awkward silence, petting Watson absently. "Thank you for the gift and for letting me stay with you for a few days."

"You can stay again, you know. You can stay as long as you like."

I could feel his eyes on me but kept mine trained on the floor between us.

"Thank you, but I want to be here."

"Tash..."

He reached out, but it felt like something was burning off my skin where his fingertips touched my arm, and I stepped away to freshen up Watson's water dish for the second time since we'd arrived. Drew was still standing in the same spot, considering me with his brow deeply furrowed, when I finished with the water dish and walked past him to my door, opening it. I was basically kicking him out. I'd never done something like that before, and I felt guilty even before I saw the deepening of the hurt in his face.

"I'll see you in the morning?" It was usually a statement, but not this time.

"Of course," I replied automatically, but as soon as I did, I realized he probably wouldn't. I needed to be away from him for a while until I could see him without feeling all the painful emotions I now had and didn't want.

When Drew was finally out of the apartment, I sagged back against the closed door, Watson whining and pushing his head under my hand. Everything felt so confusing and upsetting. Maybe in another day or two, everything would make more sense. Right then, though, *nothing* made sense.

Chapter Thirty-Nine

Tasha

A week later, nothing made any more sense than it had. I'd cancelled working out with Drew all week. I'd still worked out, I'd just done it alone. Same for my PT exercises. Which meant I hadn't seen him in a week. He'd invited me to dinner every day, but I'd declined every time. I was nervous about seeing him again as I waited for him to arrive to pick up Watson.

Duncan had been arrested and was being held without bail until his trial, which meant I no longer needed Watson for protection. And as much as he felt like *my* dog and I was going to miss him like crazy, he wasn't *actually* my dog, and it was time for Drew to have him back.

My thumbs tapped my thighs as I leaned against the counter, waiting. Drew would be at the door any minute. And sure enough, only seconds later, he knocked. Watson rushed him like he always did, and Drew gave him plenty of love in return before straightening back up.

"You sure about this?" he asked. Worry was etched into his features. And exhaustion. He looked like he'd aged a lot more than a week since I'd last seen him.

"Yeah, I'm sure. It's time for Watson to go home. This was only temporary."

Watson had ambled to my side like always, and I used both hands to scratch behind his ears before kissing the top of his head. I had Watson's bed and toys all gathered already, and Drew ferried everything down to his SUV, then returned for Watson.

With leash in hand, Drew walked toward me, where Watson was smushed against my legs. He stopped in front of me, but instead of bending to hook Watson into his leash, he was fiddling with the hook. He looked up, catching me off guard, and I couldn't look away. His eyes were intense and swirling and pained.

"What did I do, Tasha?"

My gaze slid away. "I don't know what you mean."

"Yes, you do."

"You didn't do anything," I replied, though my voice trailed off at the end, not even remotely convincing.

"Please tell me. I've spent all week trying to figure it out and I can't. I don't know why you're mad at me."

"I'm not mad at you." Though I realized as soon as I said it that I actually was. I had no reason to be, but I was. I was angry because he'd hurt me. But it wasn't from doing anything wrong, because he hadn't actually done anything wrong... at least not to me. It was so goddamn confusing. "This is why we never should have kissed," I muttered.

"What is?"

"This!" I shouted, gesturing between us. How could he not see it? "We've never been like this before, Drew, but now? We started kissing and it fucked everything up!"

"Nothing is fucked up, Tasha."

"Our friendship is. It..." I inhaled sharply just as my voice broke and stared at the ceiling.

"Our relationship is different since then, but it's not fucked up."

"That's *why* it is," I said tearily. "Because it's different. I want to have what we had back again. I don't want this."

"Tasha—"

"Just go," I interrupted, feeling weary. "I don't want to do this and make things worse. Please just leave."

He bent and hooked Watson's leash on him. Watson whined, unsure whether he should be excited for a walk or worried about how upset I was. Some of my anger melted away. I was really going to miss this dog. I kissed the top of his head again.

"I'm going to come for your PT tomorrow," Drew said, his voice resolute. He shifted the leash to his other hand.

"No." I glanced up at him. "I don't want you to do that."

"It's already been a week off from PT, Tasha. You can't just stop yet—your leg isn't fully healed."

My eyes scanned the floor between us. "Just send me any new exercises and I'll do them myself."

"You need to see a therapist—there are things you can't do on your own for this. You know that." He sighed, pulling his hand down his face. "If you won't let *me* do it, I can transfer you to someone else in the practice. I think Courtney has a few openings—I'll have her reach out to you on Monday."

I laughed coldly, narrowing my eyes at Drew. Of all people on the planet, I'd never have guessed he'd stoop that low. "I can't believe you. You aren't the person I thought you were."

He appeared to be genuinely baffled and upset. "What do you mean?"

"You really think I want to work with your girlfriend?"

He stared at me, then blinked. "What?"

"That *is* the same Courtney you sent flowers to, isn't it? Or is there another Courtney?"

I hated myself as I said those words, as I listened to the jealousy in my voice. I hated that I felt that way when I knew I had no right to because Drew and I were only friends. At least we had been... I wasn't sure our friendship could come back from this.

"Is that what this is about?" Drew asked, drawing back. "Because I sent Courtney flowers?"

I looked away and tried to swallow, but my tongue was stuck to the roof of my mouth.

"Tash," Drew said, his voice much lighter than it had been—he almost sounded amused, which just infuriated me. "Look at me."

"I saw the text messages when I picked your phone up to bring it to you when I was making mac-n-cheese," I said, still not looking at him.

He sighed. "I sent Courtney flowers as a thank you for covering me on such short notice the day Duncan showed up here. I wanted to show her that I appreciated her help so I could be there for you."

"You were distracted and irritable and constantly on your phone—it was because the flowers were late."

"No, that's because... it's something else but has nothing to do with that."

My eyes flicked to his. Was he telling the truth? Drew had never lied to me before—at least I didn't think he had—but that sounded like a tale one of my exes would have given me. And I'd always been stupid—and desperate—enough to believe their stories until I stumbled upon evidence they couldn't deny. I didn't want to be that stupid or desperate anymore.

Drew leaned down and unhooked Watson, giving him a scratch behind his ears.

"What are you doing?"

"We're talking and I didn't want to make Watson sit on a leash for however long that takes."

My arms were already crossed over my chest, but I tightened them. "We're *not* talking—you were leaving."

Drew ignored me. "You really thought something was going on with Courtney?"

My face was in flames as I tipped toward believing him. "Yes."

"And that's why you've been shutting me out all week?"

The flames got hotter. "Yes."

He stepped closer and gently grasped the back of my arms, dipping his head. "Courtney is another therapist in the practice who has covered for me a lot recently. I wanted to show her appreciation for that. That's all there is." He squeezed my arms lightly, then ran his thumbs back and forth. "The only person I want is you, Tasha."

"Drew—"

"Let me get this out, please," he said, his voice low.

"Drew," I said again, louder. "Please don't. I don't want... I want our friendship back. I want back what we had before. When we weren't awkward around each other, when I didn't get jealous."

He raised his eyebrows.

I smirked. "Okay, when I didn't get *this* jealous." My expression fell and I looked past him toward the door. "I miss us the way we used to be." And I did. Because I missed joking and having fun without the tension of not knowing what to expect or what to say or do. I missed the ease between us before there was this maybe-not-friends thing officially happening. Yeah, maybe we'd flirted with that friendship line in the past if I was being completely honest, but we'd never crossed it. And if we kept heading in this direction, everything would end between us one day in catastrophic ruin, just like every other relationship in my life ever had, and I couldn't bear to lose him that way.

"I love you, Tasha."

"I love you, too," I responded hastily.

"No, Tasha. I *love*-love you. For me, there's no going back. There hasn't been for a long time. I've loved you for years, I just didn't want to see it. That's why I never fully committed to Becka, why I decided to leave her, why I came to Brinkley. I *love* you."

My mind was racing in a thousand directions at once and I couldn't speak. I could barely breathe. Drew bent and pressed a kiss to the corner of my mouth, slow and soft. My heart did somersaults.

"I need to think," I eked out.

"Okay," Drew said after a brief silence. Then he re-leashed Watson. "Can I come in the morning?"

"I..." My eyes were still scanning the ground unseeing. "I don't know. I need... I don't know." I couldn't put together a coherent thought... because my best friend had just told me he love-loved me. The same best friend I was in love with, but desperately didn't want to be.

Drew left, and I was still struggling to put together coherent thoughts later that day when I got a text message from him. It had a link and said: Finally have your second gift—this is what was taking my attention.

When I clicked on the link, it opened YouTube and the video that played back was of Drew and me on Christmas morning when he was playing his guitar and singing. I'd had no idea he was recording us, though I hadn't been paying any attention to what he was doing right before he sat and started playing. He had, though, and he'd uploaded each song as a separate video. He had a channel I was apparently already subscribed to.

I cried as I watched the videos, my chest splitting apart, and felt even more conflicted about my insistence that there could be nothing but friendship between us. In the video, the way I felt about him, and the way he felt about me, was so apparent, so obvious. I felt like an idiot for having thought he was hiding a girlfriend from me; men who looked at women the way he looked at me in that video didn't do things like that.

But it didn't matter, because it didn't change that one day things would burn and crumble between us, and then we wouldn't even have our friendship left. It didn't change that we would one day have hatred between us if we tried to date, and I couldn't stand the thought.

I texted him and told him he could only come if we were strictly friends—that there would be no more telling me he loved me and no more kissing. That we couldn't see each other at all anymore unless he agreed.

It was a long time before he responded, and when he did, it wasn't what I expected. Rather than agreeing because our friendship was as important to him as it was to me, he told me again that he couldn't go back to the way things were, that he wasn't able or willing to act like he didn't have feelings that he did, and that he'd have someone from his practice call me on Monday.

Chapter Forty

Tasha

My stomach was in knots as I approached the courthouse to testify in the trial against Duncan. I'd prepared with my lawyer, and with Drew before we'd stopped seeing each other right after Christmas, but no amount of preparation could have made me feel settled about seeing Duncan again. I wanted with every cell in my body to turn around and hide in my room at home. I could easily understand why so many people didn't press charges; doing so was terrifying.

Not for the first time by far since Drew and I had all but ended our friendship, I wished he was there. We'd only texted a few times over the last six weeks, and I missed him all the time—missed hearing his voice and seeing his face and feeling him nearby—but I felt his absence even more deeply now. I'd never gone through something this significant without him before. I slipped my phone from my jacket pocket and navigated to my text messages with him, my thumbs hovering over the screen.

What would I say? *I know I shut you out for the last almost two months, but do you think you could forget about that for a day and come support me in the trial where I'm testifying about my ex-husband beating me? You remember—the one you warned me about and I married anyway. Thanks!* Ugh. I couldn't do it. I needed to figure out how to get through this alone.

Just as I was figuring out how to do *everything* alone since I didn't have friends and wasn't touching the dating pool with a thousand-foot pole. I had recently looked up a local meetup group for single people looking to make friends, but hadn't actually gone to any of the events yet. I looked at the schedule every day, but felt paralyzed and couldn't make myself do any more than that. I had no idea how to make friends—I had precisely zero past experience to refer to. Walking into the courthouse right then, though, brought to the forefront exactly how alone I really was, and if I wanted to do anything about that, I needed to take that first step and put myself out there. Yes, people might reject me, but I survived rejection growing up, and I could survive it again, I supposed. At least that's what I was going to tell myself. As soon as the trial was over, I'd pick an event and commit to going and meeting some new people.

With a deep breath that didn't really help at all to calm the nerves in my stomach, I pulled the courthouse door open and walked inside. It took a bit for my eyes to adjust after the bright sunshine outside before I could read the overhead signs to figure out which direction I needed to go. But even after reading them, I wasn't entirely sure. There was a sign for a clerk to my left, so I turned in that direction, my step faltering when I heard my name from somewhere behind me.

I spun around, then came to a complete standstill. In my focus on the signs, I hadn't taken time to look around me, so I'd missed Drew sitting on a bench along the wall to the right of the entrance. He rose to his feet with a tentative smile and headed toward me.

"What are you doing here?" I blurted out in surprise.

"Same thing you are," he replied.

"But... you're not testifying. Dr. Macklin is." Dr. Macklin was the surgeon who'd repaired my leg.

"I'm here for *you*, Tasha," he said quietly. "And to see that bastard finally get locked up the way he should." He ran a hand through his hair, started to reach toward me, then apparently thought better of it and shoved his hands into his pockets. "The clerk's down that way—you check in there and then we're in courtroom six, on the third floor."

We made our way silently down the hall to the clerk, where I checked in, and then the silence—along with my anxiety—grew as we made our way toward the designated courtroom. When we reached our destination, I didn't want to walk inside. Drew stepped ahead and opened the door, holding it ajar for me to pass inside, but instead of walking in, I panicked and backed away.

"I can't. Not yet. I just need a minute," I said, turning and rushing toward the end of the hall where there was a window looking out on a small courtyard area.

Drew was behind me; I could feel him there without needing to look. His presence felt solid and steadfast and allowed me the space to breathe out some of my fear and find my courage as I focused my eyes on a barren tree below. I imagined what the courtyard must look like in the spring and summer when the grass was green rather than brown, and the trees had leaves on their branches, and the mulch beds had flowers blooming. There'd be birds chirping and flitting from tree to tree, squirrels running up the trunks and over branches, bees buzzing around the flowers. The image was calming, and I took a deep slow breath, closing my eyes to hold onto it and allow Drew's strength to flow across the space separating us and into me.

At last, I was ready—at least as ready as I was going to be—and turned. Drew's eyes were questioning, and I nodded. We headed back to the courtroom entrance side by side. This time when Drew pulled the door open, I walked inside ahead of him with only a slight hesitation. While my legs quaked, they didn't give out as we found seats. I thought I'd pass out as my eyes scanned frantically for anyone I might know, but I didn't. With each passing second that felt like I might die before it was over but found me continuing to breathe, I began to realize I would be okay. I would make it through whatever ended up happening.

Suddenly, I heard Drew's voice in my mind, something he'd said to me at one of my lowest points when I was suicidal the year I turned seventeen. *You're stronger than you'll ever know. As tough as it gets, Tasha. You shouldn't have to be, but you are. You can make it through anything—you just have to survive one minute at a time.* He'd been more right than I'd understood before this moment.

Reaching over, I slid my fingers between his and squeezed, our semicolon tattoos touching. His fingers curled over my hand and squeezed back. I knew what he was saying: that he was there and that he understood. No matter what was happening with our relationship, regardless of the distance I'd put between us, I'd be eternally grateful for everything he'd been to me since that night he climbed out of his window to find me crying outside mine when we were only fourteen. I wouldn't have still been alive to sit there with him in that courtroom if it hadn't been for him. I wouldn't have ever believed I was worth more than what Duncan was doing to me—that the way he treated me was even wrong—if it hadn't been for Drew and everything his presence in my life gave to me over the years.

Four hours later, I wasn't sure I could take much more waiting for our case to be called. Every second that passed made the anxiety spiral higher, and there was only so much my body could take. My head was pounding and my ears ringing, my eyes burned, and I had trouble focusing. Luckily, a recess was called for the lunch hour, and Drew and I made our way from the room. We both let out loud sighs and powered our phones back on, having shut them off as instructed when we entered. The first thing I was going to do was talk to my lawyer to find out where he was and why our case hadn't been called yet.

As soon as my phone was on, it buzzed with multiple notifications: text messages and missed calls, all from my lawyer. My eyes flew over the texts, then I listened to the voicemail he'd left in disbelief, shaking my head as I stared unseeing ahead of me, my eyes flitting around restlessly.

"What is it?" Drew asked when I lowered my phone after listening to the voicemail for the second time in a row.

I shook my head again. "I think..." I looked up at Drew, my eyes beginning to flood, and smiled, though there was nothing funny or happy about the situation. It was more a smile of relief. "If I understand correctly, there's no trial anymore. Duncan—he decided to take a plea bargain or something. So I don't have to testify." I handed my phone to Drew. "Here—listen."

I watched Drew's face carefully while he listened to the voicemail, his expression shifting from concentration to relief. He handed my phone back, the same odd smile on his face that I had on mine.

"That means it's done, right?" I asked, searching his eyes for confirmation. "He's going to prison and... and... and that's it? It's finally over?" I desperately hoped he had the same understanding of what my lawyer had said.

He moved his head in a slow nod, his eyes full of emotion. "It's over Tash. He's behind bars and can't hurt you or anyone else."

I barreled into his torso and squeezed my arms around his waist as he wrapped me in his, while I cried tears of fear and relief and myriad other emotions I couldn't identify yet. As Drew had said, Duncan was behind bars where he couldn't hurt anyone anymore. It would take some time, but his investments were going to pay for my medical bills, too. And now I never had to worry about him again.

Except...

I pulled back, wiping my face. "It's not over yet—not quite. I'm still married to the asshole."

"Not for much longer," Drew said soothingly, his hands smoothing up and down my back.

I pulled my phone out and immediately called my divorce lawyer. Drew kept a hand running up and down my back as we made our way back to the building entrance. By the time we'd made it to the main sidewalk that led to the parking lot, I'd been assured by Roger that, with Duncan's guilty plea, my divorce would be finalized within a month; our state granted immediate divorces in cases of incarceration. Not only that, but in those cases, the fact that Duncan was contesting the divorce would no longer be cause for delays in the process. I now had an end in sight for the marriage I never should have entered.

I shared the news with Drew, speaking rapid-fire like it was one long run-on sentence. I was elated, though that elation was accompanied by some amount of shame that I'd gotten myself into the situation to begin with, an emotion Drew realized I was experiencing without me saying a word about it.

"Stop blaming yourself for Duncan," he said, sliding his hand down my arm, prodding me to pull my hand from my pocket.

When he laced our fingers, his were already cold from the bitter air around us. I pushed our hands into his coat pocket to keep the back of his hand from getting any colder and didn't say anything. I wasn't sure how to respond.

"You know what he did wasn't your fault, right?" Drew persisted.

I sighed, something occurring to me for the first time. "You know, what set him off every time he got angry enough to hurt me was you. My relationship with you. As many times as I told him we were just friends, he didn't believe me. And while he shouldn't have hurt me the way he did... I think... I mean, he wasn't actually wrong."

"Yes, he was," Drew said resolutely. "We were only friends then."

"Were we?" I murmured. "I mean... you kissed me at the airport. And if you had kissed me a second time then, I think I would have kissed you back."

"But I didn't, and you didn't. While kissing you the way I did was borderline, we were only friends then."

His words rolled around in my mind. They were true, but they also weren't. We'd been determined we were only friends—and we hadn't made out or slept together—but emotionally, it really hadn't been any different than it was right now.

"What if I had a male friend—not *you*—who I cuddled on the sofa with while he was singing to me? A friend whose clothes I kept and wore, a friend I did those fitness challenges with, and did normal date-like things with. A friend who kissed my head and my cheek regularly, a friend I held hands with and got matching tattoos with. Imagine us, except the guy is someone else. I mean, hell, Drew—we never had sex or made out or anything like that, but my relationship with you has always been way more intimate than my relationship with anyone I've ever dated before, even though I *did* have sex with those guys."

Drew flinched at my last words and my face heated. Of course—I didn't want to think about him having sex with other women, either. I'd just been trying to demonstrate a point: that maybe Duncan hadn't been as wrong as I'd thought. Maybe he'd had a legitimate reason to be jealous after all.

"I get your point," Drew said after a while. "I'd go fucking crazy. I almost did already because of you dating, but I lied to myself." He let out a soft chuckle. "I told myself—very convincingly—that you didn't have sex with anyone you dated. Or make out. Or laugh the way you did with me. It was the only way I could keep myself from doing something monumentally stupid and dickheadish to make sure you guys broke up on the spot. When I told you at the airport that I wished you didn't have a boyfriend? That was the first time I said that to you, Tash, but it wasn't the first time I'd thought it. Not by a long shot."

"Duncan saw that. I mean, not what you just said, obviously, but how things were between us. He said he saw it in the way we looked at each other. It really wasn't fair to him. And maybe he wouldn't have done the things he did to me if you and I actually *were* only friends the way friends should be."

Drew stopped and stepped in front of me, his eyes stormy and his jaw square and tightened. "Listen to me, Tasha. Duncan would have hurt you eventually no matter what, because he *hurts people*. You just asked me how I would feel if I was in his shoes, and I can tell you right now I love you more than he ever did. I said I'd go fucking crazy—and I would. I'd lose my damn mind if you had this kind of closeness and intimacy with someone else. But you know what I'd never, never, *never* do? Hit you. Put a hot coffee pot on your leg. Push you off a chair or down the stairs or hold you against a wall by your throat. Or hurt you in any other way. *Never*, Tasha. I might yell—in fact, I probably would. I know for damn sure I'd cry because my heart would be broken. I likely wouldn't bathe for a while and might forget to walk or feed Watson. I'd try to talk to you, and I'd want to hold you. But I. Would. Not. Hurt. You."

I nodded; I knew he wouldn't. He was possibly the only person on the planet I believed with every fiber of my being would never lay a hand on me for any reason. And in theory, I knew that's how it should be with anyone in your life, but it was easy to feel at fault for what Duncan had done—especially now that I was no longer in denial about how Drew and I felt about each other.

"What you do or don't do doesn't matter, Tash—you don't deserve to be hurt for it. It could never justify someone hitting you. *Never*. And someone who does something like that is going to do it no matter what. You are in no way at fault for what he did to you. And you are in no way at fault for not knowing sooner that he'd do it. Your expectation *should* be that people aren't going to hurt you—there's nothing wrong with you for that."

I continued to nod vaguely as I listened and let his words sink in. I knew these things already, logically, but emotionally, I often lost sight of them. It helped to hear them. Maybe if I heard them enough times, I might believe and remember them.

We slowed to a stop by Drew's SUV. "Lunch?" he asked, his eyes hopeful.

I began to shake my head no, but then changed my mind. It was so wonderful to be near him again, and I wasn't ready to go back to the distance between us, back to being so utterly alone. "Sure."

Chapter Forty-One

Drew

In spite of the occasion that brought Tasha and me together for the first time in six long weeks, and the ways we'd already grown apart in that time, it wasn't difficult to fall back into a more normal dynamic by the time we arrived at a restaurant. It was so good to see her again that my chest hurt; even though I was sitting across from her, I still missed her as much as I had been every minute of every damn day since I'd last seen her.

I'd even recorded myself playing and singing a Sam Tinnesz song called "I Don't Miss You" that summed up perfectly what the last weeks had felt like without her. It was one of several I'd recorded, and I was planning to upload them all to the YouTube channel I'd created but hadn't done it yet. I wasn't sure of the best way to approach the distance between us; I didn't want to push her further away when I was trying to get her to see that I was never going anywhere. That I'd be there for her until my body turned to dust one day. And I didn't know how to navigate through all the feelings I couldn't act on.

For the time being, though, things felt like us again. And maybe this time she'd be willing to take a chance on me. It had been six weeks—was that enough time for her? As I laughed at her snarky, scathing summary of a book she'd read recently, I felt hopeful. And happy. I loved watching her so animated about something; it didn't matter what it was. The only thing that mattered was that she enjoyed talking about it. Since I'd met her, there was nothing I loved more than listening to her chattering away unafraid, hearing her laughter and seeing her smile and shining eyes. I sat back in my chair, twisting my rocks glass with a few more mouthfuls of whiskey instead of drinking it—I wanted to stretch this meal out as long as I possibly could.

As she used a hand to tuck some hair behind her ear, I had a flash of watching her do that another time, far in the past. We were both sixteen and her parents had gone away for the weekend. I told my parents I was staying with a friend but actually stayed at Tasha's with her. We pretended for the weekend that we had no parents, that it was just us living together in a life free of the abuse we dealt with every day. I made us pancakes and she made us mac-n-cheese and we baked brownies together. We watched movies and I played my guitar and she read her favorite passages from her favorite books aloud to me. It was a perfect weekend. The first perfect weekend I'd ever had.

We'd pretended we were married on Saturday afternoon. It began when I handed her a can of unopened soda. She stared at it for a minute, obviously somewhere else. Then her eyes focused on me, and she grinned.

"Why thank you, my darling, how kind of you," she said. "I so appreciate that you brought me something to drink."

I laughed.

Her smile faltered a bit. "I think I'd die of a heart attack if my mom ever said something like that to me or Wayne after we handed her an unopened can. I did that once and she threw it at my face, calling me a lazy, ungrateful bitch." She was staring into the past again, her hand absently rubbing the side of her face; where the can had hit, I guessed.

"Well, you're very welcome, love of my life. Is there anything else I could possibly do for you?" I asked with a silly flourish, wanting to distract her from her painful memories.

She grinned, refocusing on me again. "And that's nothing like Wayne, that's for sure. I don't think any of those words have ever come out of his mouth."

And so, it became a game for the afternoon; everything we said to each other was with exaggerated politeness and care and affection as we pretended to be a happily married couple—an embellished version of what we thought a happy marriage would look like.

That night was the one time in our childhood that we kissed. We'd continued our game all the way through the evening until we were yawning and ready for bed, goofy grins plastered on our faces. With our pajamas on, just before she climbed into her bed and I climbed into her sleeping bag on the floor next to her bed, we turned to each other.

"Well, my darling," she said in that same affected voice, with a tiny giggle, "I wish you a good night."

"And you as well, my dear," I replied with another stupid flourish. "May you have only the sweetest of dreams and awaken refreshed."

Tasha giggled again, and I suddenly wanted to kiss her. I'd wondered about it before, had small urges to, even, but it was nothing compared to right then. Every nerve ending I had was screaming for me to take her in my arms and kiss the hell out of her.

I held my hand up and whispered beside it as if I was trying to keep someone from hearing me. "I'm pretty sure happy couples kiss goodnight."

She sucked in a breath and her cheeks turned pink, her teeth sinking into her lip before she nodded, then tucked her hair behind her ear. "I think you're right," she whispered back.

I wanted to touch her as I leaned in for the kiss, but wasn't sure if that would be okay with her, so I didn't. Our lips brushed, just barely, then I leaned further until they were molded together. Fireworks detonated inside my veins, my chest—everywhere in my body. I didn't move until I thought I'd pass out from needing to breathe, and even then I only pulled back just enough to suck some air in at the same time Tasha did, and we went back for another kiss. This time, our mouths still weren't open, but they weren't exactly closed either. Her top lip was settled between mine, my lower between hers.

I was sure she could hear my heart hammering into my throat in the silence while we kissed. Then it was over, and she pulled away, tittering nervously, her eyes cast downward. She crossed her arms over her chest. I wanted to uncross them and wrap them around me instead. But I didn't. Instead, I watched as her lips rolled under.

"Well, good night," she breathed.

"Good night," I replied.

I laid awake staring at the ceiling for most of the night, wanting to know if she was also awake. She'd dozed off with me enough times that I could usually tell from her breathing, but I couldn't hear anything over my own cacophonous heartbeat. I wanted to talk about the kiss. I wanted to do it again. I wanted to know if it had felt as electric to her as it had to me.

The next morning was the first time we'd ever been awkward around each other, and I decided to bring up the kiss during breakfast. I was hoping to do it again, though perhaps even more, I didn't want her nervous around me. I liked being the person she was always comfortable around—her person, as she'd called me.

"So, last night..." I started. I tried to swallow but my mouth felt like I'd been in a desert for a few weeks without access to water.

She made a sound that wasn't quite a laugh, but didn't say anything.

"That kiss," I said, trying again. "It was...w—"

"Weird, I know," she interrupted.

My mouth closed. I'd been about to say "wow" but now wasn't sure I should since she'd called it weird. "Yeah, definitely," I replied, my voice trailing off and my heart sinking.

"I mean, we're best friends," she said after an uncomfortable few seconds. "Like brother and sister."

Oof. That hurt—that wasn't at all how I thought of us, I realized. Best friends, yes, but brother and sister? No. "Yeah," I agreed anyway.

"So it was like kissing a sibling," she said, her voice trailing off at the end.

"Yeah, like kissing a sibling," I echoed.

And that's what I told myself for years. I said it in my mind so many times, tried so hard to change my memory from one of ecstatic feeling to awkward weirdness, that I mostly believed it for a long time. I told myself the feelings I had were because it was wrong for us to kiss, not because it was right.

But sitting in the restaurant, watching her tuck her hair behind her ear like she had that night so many years earlier, there were flutters in my gut again—flutters I'd only ever felt with her.

"Do you remember the weekend I stayed with you while your parents were away?" I asked as I drove her home. "We were sixteen."

She nodded, looking thoughtfully out the window. "Yes."

"Do you remember us kissing that night?"

Her cheeks were red when I caught a glimpse. "Yes. I wasn't going to forget my first kiss."

"That was your first kiss?" I asked, incredulous. I'd had no idea. I'd always assumed she fooled around and just hadn't told me since I was a little overprotective even back then.

"Yes."

I'd intended to ask her if it had really been like kissing a sibling for her, but now I wasn't so sure. What if it had been? And that was her first kiss? If I had known, I would have... I didn't know. I was thinking I would have made sure it was good for her, but it wasn't like I had all that much experience back then—she was only the second girl *I'd* kissed. I'd hit a growth spurt at last and shot up in height, though I was only beginning to fill out my lanky frame; girls had just begun to notice I even existed.

"Why do you ask?" she asked.

I cleared my throat. "I was just thinking about it. It…" I sighed and decided to just tell her how I'd really felt back then. "The next morning was the only time I've ever lied to you."

"You lied to me?"

"Yeah. I did."

"About what?"

I looked over at her, and she was watching me intently. One side of my mouth curved up. "That kiss was nothing like kissing a sibling, Nats."

She chuckled to herself, though the red on her cheeks deepened. She waited to respond until I'd pulled into a parking space.

"That was the first lie I ever told you, too," she said. "I was sure you were about to tell me it was weird, so I said it first so I wouldn't have to hear you say it, and then I couldn't make myself shut up."

I was relieved I wasn't the only one who'd felt something, but was distracted by the first few words she'd said.

"First lie?" I asked.

Her entire demeanor fell, and she turned to face out her side window. "I told you there are things you don't know."

"But… I guess I didn't realize that meant you'd lied to me."

Her head shifted up and down. "I'm sorry."

I reached over and squeezed her hand. "I'm sure you had a reason, Tasha. Don't apologize." I paused. "I want you to know, though, that I've never lied to you since then and I won't lie to you ever again. Not even about something small."

She let out a heavy sigh, remaining otherwise silent for a minute or two. Finally, she turned to me and gave me a small, genuine smile.

"Thank you for today. For coming to support me and for lunch. It was a really great day with you. After we left the courthouse, anyway."

"I had a great day, too." I inhaled deeply, searching for my courage. "Let's do it again."

"Maybe," she said noncommittally. I knew it meant she was already planning to turn me down.

"How about tomorrow?" I persisted. The next evening was the monthly practice dinner, and significant others were always welcome. There was no reason Tasha couldn't be my date for it. "Dinner at Brighton's at six thirty."

"I... don't know," she replied, her thumbs rapidly tapping on her legs.

"Just think about it. I'll be there, and I'd really love for you to come."

Chapter Forty-Two

Tasha

My phone buzzed in my hand as I headed to my writing desk with a steaming cup of coffee the morning after lunch with Drew. I hoped it wasn't him asking me if I was coming to dinner because I still hadn't decided. I was torn about what to do. Seeing him again had severely weakened my resolve to enforce my friendship boundary, but it hadn't completely broken it. Every time I thought back to how I felt when I saw that he'd sent flowers to Courtney, I remembered why I didn't want to go down this road—I never wanted to feel that way again. Even though he'd told me why he'd sent the flowers, and I believed him, I hadn't been able to make myself work with her for physical therapy. As a substitute, I was working with another doctor in the practice until I was done in a few weeks.

I scanned my screen. There was a notification from YouTube. Odd. I opened the notification and my heart tripped. Drew had uploaded more videos to his channel. I clicked the link in the notification and heard Drew's voice.

"This song sums up how I feel every day without you, Tasha."

He took a deep breath, his eyes closed, his features tight with emotion, then began to play and sing "I Don't Miss You" by Sam Tinnesz. As soon as it was over, I clicked on the next one, "We're Gonna Make It," which had a similar dedication at the beginning. Lastly, I listened to the third one, "Changes."

"Goddamn it, Drew," I muttered, sniffling and wiping the tears from my cheeks with the heels of my hands. I ran my fingers gently over his image on the screen.

I vacillated between going and not going to dinner with Drew after watching the videos. I wanted to—*fuck*, I wanted to. Just as I wanted to try a relationship with him. Do things differently than I ever had before, see if I could get things right this time. But if I didn't... the consequences would be so severe. I wouldn't have him in my life at all. And wasn't this distant relationship better than nothing? If it hurt to watch him sing to me already when things weren't exactly bad between us, how much worse would it be if we hated each other?

I texted Drew and told him I wouldn't make it for dinner, then turned my focus to cleaning up my autofiction manuscript so I could submit it to my editor and see if the publishing house wanted to take on another book from me. I hoped so—I didn't want to start from scratch submitting query letters to a mile-long list of publishing houses again.

Despite the resolve I had when I texted Drew that I wasn't going, I couldn't stop thinking I should go, and the closer it got to dinnertime, the stronger the urge became. *Fuck it*, I thought, standing abruptly. *I'm going.*

An hour and a half later, I was finally ready and pacing in my living room. Was my dress appropriate? I didn't have much to choose from, and I'd never been to this restaurant before. I'd looked it up online to get a feel for it, and it reminded me of the restaurant I'd gone to with Duncan the night before he pushed me down the stairs; this was also the dress I'd worn then. I didn't like that it was the same dress, but I didn't have the budget for buying anything new—especially after how much the lawyer was costing me. I'd be getting reimbursed as part of the plea bargain, but it could apparently take months—even years—before I saw any of that money. Until then, I was on payment plans with everyone I owed money to. Drew had tried to pay—for my medical bills as well as the lawyers' fees—but I'd refused. It was *my* problem to figure out—not *his*. But in the meantime, I didn't have much money and couldn't afford a new dress.

I left a little early because I couldn't stay in my apartment for even a minute longer, and forced myself to dismiss any concern over the dress the best I could since there wasn't a damn thing I could do about it. Once I'd made the decision to go, the time hadn't passed swiftly enough. The more I thought about it, the more excited I was about surprising Drew. I'd get to see his genuine reaction to seeing me because it would be unexpected. And maybe that would help me figure out what to do about us.

Because I was so early, I got out of the cab several blocks away so I could walk the rest of the distance. I forced my feet to move slower than they wanted to, and with each step closer, I became more excited. I was going to do it, I decided right then—I was going to tell Drew that I was ready to give us a chance as a couple and see what happened. I was nervous as hell, but also couldn't wait to see his reaction now that I'd made up my mind.

A block away from the restaurant, a permanent grin stretched across my face. I probably looked like an idiot walking down the street that way, but I didn't care—I didn't care about anything right then except getting there and seeing Drew so I could tell him what I'd decided. At long last, I approached my destination. I pulled the door open, stepped inside, and stopped short. Everything inside me stopped for a beat. It was the same feeling I'd had when I saw Drew's text from Courtney, except worse because I should have known better. After how many times I'd been cheated on and lied to, I should have known how to spot a coverup.

Drew was standing there off to the side of the hostess stand with a blonde woman wearing a black cocktail dress. He had her arm in his hands, his fingers moving toward her elbow. Both of them were watching his fingertips advance along her forearm. The first I could move was to shake my head as if that would make what I was seeing any less real. I stepped backward toward the door, but I couldn't tear my eyes from Drew and the stunningly beautiful woman he was with. Then he looked up. It was a quick glance that didn't even register me before his eyes fell. I turned and fled before he did.

I was near the next intersection when Drew appeared in front of me, stepping directly into my path and grasping my upper arms. I yanked my arms away and put some space between us.

"Don't touch me," I said through a clenched jaw, moving to go around him.

"Where are you going, Tasha?" he sidestepped to stay in front of me. "I thought you weren't coming, then you did, but now you're running away as soon as I realized you were there?"

"Leave me alone," I bit out, trying desperately to keep from crying right there on the street in front of him. I felt so monumentally stupid. Why *wouldn't* he have someone else? Compared to me... who *wasn't* a better option? "Go back to your girlfriend."

"Whoa." He stepped closer and gently touched my arms again.

This time I didn't have the wherewithal to jerk away. The anger had faded to hurt, and that hurt made it hard to move.

"What girlfriend? I don't *have* a girlfriend."

"I saw you with blondie back there," I snapped.

"Her name is Sandra, and she's Paul's wife. Her elbow locked up and I was helping her get it released so she could move her arm."

I shook my head. I wanted to believe him, but I remembered every time I'd believed someone when I shouldn't have.

Drew gestured toward the restaurant. "Come on. Come with me and you'll see. You'll get to meet her. I think you'll like her."

Regardless of what he said, the pain was still swirling inside my chest from thinking he was with someone else.

Drew lifted a hand and traced my hairline before cradling my jaw. "If you believed you're as amazing as you are, you wouldn't be so worried about other women. And you *are* amazing, Tash. And the only woman I want. And I know you've been lied to by a lot of men, but I'm not one of them, and I never will be. You've known me since we were kids, Tash. You *know* you can trust me."

My jaw trembled. He was right. I *did* know I could trust him, that he was nothing like the men who'd cheated on me and never would be. Just as he was right that I didn't believe I was all that worthwhile; I left a path of mess and destruction and was always just moments from another bad decision.

He kissed my forehead as tenderly as his hand was resting on my face. "Come to dinner with me." He kissed my forehead again. "Please. Be my date."

I was a ball of emotion, though foremost was possibly mortification at my mistake followed by such childish behavior. "You had to chase me down the fucking street," I muttered.

He pulled me into his chest. "It was less than a block. I'd have followed you a lot further than that." His chin rested on the top of my head. "I'd follow you to the far corners of the universe," he murmured so softly I barely heard him.

I sighed and some of the tension left me with my outbreath. Stepping back, I touched the corners of my eyes where tears were attempting to escape but hadn't fallen yet. When I was done, Drew intertwined our fingers and led us back toward the restaurant.

"I didn't say yes yet," I muttered, though I was going to.

"Oh?" he replied in faux surprise. "My mistake."

I rolled my eyes, but I was also starting to smile again.

"You look incredible, by the way," he added. "I like the dress even better when you aren't wearing makeup."

"What?" I almost stopped walking in my surprise, glancing down to where there was a glimpse of my dress between the open sides of my coat. "When else have you seen me wear this?"

"I saw you in a restaurant with it. It was actually the night before your leg was broken. I was there with the practice that night."

I did stop now and stared at him. "Your table was in the back room, diagonal from the bathrooms."

He nodded. "How did you know that?"

"I saw you, too. I was waiting in line to use the bathroom and I saw you. Duncan and I went out to celebrate my editor accepting my edits on my manuscript. I wanted to share it with you, but I couldn't because of Duncan. I wanted to talk to you that night, but I was terrified of what might happen if I did and Duncan saw. I had no idea you knew I was there."

"I saw you when you left the bathroom. I jumped up from the table and set off after you, but when I saw Duncan in the next room, I stopped. I didn't want to cause problems. I knew he was hurting you—I'd seen the bruises on your face when you were in the hospital to have your cyst removed, and I knew the story you told me wasn't true. I didn't want to set him off and make things worse for you." We started walking again. "Anyway, you were wearing a ton of makeup that night. You were still beautiful, but nothing like you are now, like this."

I perused the ground with a huff. "Right. No makeup—which I think you're the only man who prefers that—and then this." I gestured vaguely down at my legs, which were bared from mid-thigh down, leaving all my scars on display. While I generally wasn't super self-conscious about them, they weren't exactly attractive, either.

With my hand still in his, Drew wrapped his arm around my lower back and squeezed my hip. "You're fucking gorgeous, Tasha." I watched his eyes travel down my body, then back up, returning to mine with a heat in them. "Gorgeous. All of you."

He opened the front door to the restaurant and waited for me to walk in ahead of him, dropping my hand and pressing his fingertips lightly into the small of my back as he followed me. We were shown to a large table bustling with chatter and laughter, the blonde woman from earlier seated between another woman and a man. As we sat, Drew introduced me to everyone—all the other doctors from his practice and several significant others—avoiding using a label for me. Everyone was friendly and welcoming before turning back to their conversations.

The evening was fleeting, and I enjoyed watching Drew in his element, interacting with other professionals he worked with. It was a side of him I hadn't seen before, and it was satisfying to see how happy he was with his work and where he was doing it. I was also proud of him—he'd worked exceptionally hard to get where he was. And he was so damn smart—he'd never really believed it, but he was.

It was obvious everyone at the table held an enormous amount of respect for him, though he appeared to be oblivious.

Whenever he wasn't eating, Drew was holding my hand or had an arm around me or a hand resting on my knee. It was all so intimate and casually familiar, and I felt that exposing thing happening again—the same baring of my insides that had happened when we kissed around Christmas. I had that same urge to tell him—to shout it at the top of my lungs—that I loved him. Every time he glanced at me while he was talking or listening, his eyes smiling, that urge grew stronger. In lieu of saying it, though, I squeezed his hand harder and found my eyes having trouble leaving him as the evening wore on.

I wasn't the only one, though. Drew's eyes lingered on me longer and longer each time he looked at me, too. Then, while the waiter was setting down everyone's desserts, Drew's eyes found mine and he grinned. I grinned back, feeling giddy, and he leaned over and kissed me right there at the table. It was like living in a dream of a beautiful alternate reality.

"Do you wanna come back to my place for a while?" Drew asked as we walked toward his car. "We can watch a movie or something. Watson would love to see you, too."

My heart ached to see Watson again. It had been a long time that felt even longer after getting used to seeing him every day. But, how well the evening had ended notwithstanding, there had been a rollercoaster of emotions, and I was drained and needed to sort out my thoughts. I couldn't stop hearing Drew's voice telling me I wouldn't be so worried about other women if I knew how amazing I was. I wasn't sure about amazing, but surely I should have some amount of self-confidence, and I knew I had none.

"Not tonight," I said, climbing into the car and buckling my seatbelt. "Give Watson a kiss for me, though, please."

Drew gave a nod of agreement, and I turned to look out my window. It was now dark, and the streetlights sparkling far into the distance looked like stars when I softened my gaze. It was one of the things I liked about living in a city—how magical it seemed once the sun set.

"The city is so beautiful at night," I thought aloud, still gazing out my window as Drew navigated from the parking lot.

"Yeah, it is," he agreed. His hand pulled mine apart; I hadn't even realized I was clasping them tightly together in my lap until he did that. "What's on your mind, Nats?"

What was on my mind? Where to begin? I had so many conflicting emotions, so much excitement and fear swirling together. Part of me felt ready to take the risk on a relationship with Drew, like I'd decided earlier, but part of me was sure that I would do something to fuck it up beyond repair. Again, his words echoed in my mind; it was *that* reason I'd fuck things up. Because I had no self-worth... no self-love at all. I'd pretended I did for as long as I could remember, but it was long past time to stop lying to myself.

"Despite starting with a chase down the street, I really enjoyed tonight," I said.

He kissed the back of my hand. "I did, too."

My heart was pitter-pattering in my chest. "I want more of that."

His hand tightened around mine. "Me, too, Nats. God, me, too."

"But without fucking everything up."

He turned to me before returning to the road. His hand was now squeezing the life out of mine, his leg bouncing. "What are you talking about?"

"You said I wouldn't be so worried about other women if I had any confidence, basically. And you're right, Drew. I don't have any. You also told me almost a year ago I had no self-respect, and you were right then, too. And it's still true today."

"Tasha—"

"It's true. *You* know it is. *I* know it is. And until it *isn't* true anymore, I'm going to fuck up any good thing in my life. The thing is, though, I don't want to fuck *us* up, Drew. I *can't* fuck us up. You're too important to me."

"Tasha—we can get through this together. We've gotten through everything else in our lives together, and we can get through this, too."

I studied his profile as he drove. His face was tense, the corners of his mouth turned down. It did nothing to take away from how good-looking he was, though. I'd watched his profile change as he went through puberty into adulthood, and as the years since then had passed, but his profile, whatever it was at the time, had always been my favorite. I pulled my hand from his and touched the side of his face. His eyes moved to me, then away as he focused on pulling into a parking space in front of my apartment building. He shifted into park, then turned to me, moving my hand over to kiss my palm.

"Everything we've gotten through before was as friends," I said, breaking the silence. "Things are different between us now. We couldn't go back to being just friends the way we were even if we wanted to, and I don't think either of us really wants that."

He shook his head.

"I need to fix myself, Drew."

"You're not broken, Tasha."

"I *am*, in—"

"You're not!" he almost shouted, his voice impassioned. "Everyone has things to work on, but that doesn't mean you're broken."

"I *feel* broken, Drew," I said as calmly as I could. "I feel like I'm in thousands of pieces and scattered around, and that those pieces are morphing and shifting shape and will never fit back together again, if I could even find them all."

"I can help you. We can figure it out together."

He blurred as my eyes filled. I loved him even more for wanting to walk through this darkness with me, but I knew he couldn't. Not this time. This was something I needed to do myself.

"I have to do this alone."

He shook his head, slowly at first, then more vehemently. "No," he said, resolute. "You don't. I promised you years ago that you would never have to do things alone anymore, and I meant it. Stop trying to punish yourself."

"I'm not this time, I swear. But I do need to do this alone, Drew. I've leaned on you for most of my life."

"And you can lean on me for the rest of it."

"I…" I sighed, staring up at the ceiling over my head. "I know. I need to know how to rely on myself first, though. I need to figure out how to love myself."

"If you could see yourself through my eyes… you would love yourself more than anyone in the universe until the end of time."

"Jesus, Drew," I said, some of my tears spilling over. I swiped at them and stared wide-eyed ahead of me to dry up the remainder.

"I mean it, Tasha. You have no fucking idea how much I love you." He slipped a hand behind my head and pulled me toward him as he leaned in and held our foreheads together. "You are the reason this life is worth living, Tasha." He swallowed loudly. "Please don't do this."

I sniffled, Drew's vetiver and orange scent making it past the stuffiness from crying. I loved that smell. "I have to."

"So what does that mean for us?"

"Well," I chuckled. "We've already proven we can't be just friends anymore."

His head moved side to side against me and I heard a soft chuckle in return.

I sobered, my body feeling heavy. "I have to do this alone. I can't… risk… what might happen between us if…" I shook my head. "I can't do that to you, can't hurt you like that."

"Tash—"

"I know you don't agree, but I can't."

He sniffled loudly then pressed his lips to mine. I kissed him back, trying not to cry—not yet. And then he began to sing "Even if it Hurts" by Sam Tinnesz. I lost my battle against the tears and they soaked both of our faces.

"I'd die for you," he said when he finished the song. "It doesn't matter to me if you hurt me, Tash. The pain is nothing as long as I have you."

"I know." *And I love you for that.* "But it matters to *me*."

He nodded against me, his cheeks damp. "Okay. But I'm never going anywhere, okay? I'll be here when you're ready."

We kissed for a long time the same way we had on Christmas Eve, and I knew every second that passed was going make it harder to walk away.

I kept kissing him anyway.

But then it was time for me to go inside.

Time for Drew to go home.

Time for our paths to diverge, not knowing if they'd ever come back together.

Chapter Forty-Three

Tasha

I made a lot of changes in my life after I walked away from Drew; I'd hurt us both tremendously already by doing that, and I needed to make sure it was worth it, that I hadn't done it for nothing. To start, I bought and devoured just about every book I could find on trauma and healing and domestic abuse. There was a lot I learned about the things I'd been through in my life, as well as about the links between the past and the present and how to begin to unravel those links. That was what I needed most... what I needed to work on the most. If I could do that, then maybe one day I would have a real chance at a healthy, fulfilling relationship in my life.

While working through all the books I bought, I decided to overhaul my autofiction novel and submitted it to my editor. It was now a waiting game to find out if it would be accepted or not. In the meantime, I began another autofiction about my relationship with Duncan—the words just came pouring out of me. I wanted to tell the story of living in an abusive relationship and maybe help other people find a way to escape before something like what happened to me happened to them.

I also started journaling based on a recommendation in several of my trauma books. At first, I was afraid I'd spiral into depression like I did in my teen years and become suicidal again, but this time without Drew to keep me from making an attempt on my life. Little by little, though, getting everything out was helping me rather than making things worse. There was a rush of shit—about my parents, about my lack of friends, about my clinging to guys, about my failures with Drew—when I first began, and *that* was overwhelming, but then things slowed to a pace I could manage. And as I continued to journal, I found that was helping me to feel less and less desperate about not ending up alone. I was learning about myself and how to be comfortable in my own company for the first time in my life.

As good as all that was, however, I knew it wasn't enough; I needed to have friendships in my life. I needed to be able to meet and connect with people—not for the purpose of distracting me from feeling lonely, either. I needed to learn how to truly connect with another person who wasn't Drew. I needed to put myself out there.

For the first time in weeks, I pulled up the calendar of events for the meet-up group I'd found. In the next week, there were two events: a group photography class and the grand opening of a local whiskey distillery. My heart ached—I wanted desperately to go to the distillery with Drew, but I couldn't invite him. It was too soon. I wasn't ready yet.

I glanced over at my phone, smiling. Just that morning, I'd received a link to another song performed by Drew. He was now sending songs to me every few days. They were in no particular order, and I suspected he chose them based on how he was feeling. That it was his way of respecting my request to not text while still letting me know he was there and thinking of me. I'd begun to count on those links as reassurance that he was still willing to wait for me.

But for now, I needed to pick an event. I didn't have a camera aside from the one on my phone, so the photography class was out. Which left the distillery. And my desire to take Drew there notwithstanding, that seemed to be the better option anyway; nothing like a little alcohol to make the awkward feel a bit less intense. My eyes scanned through the events over the next several weeks and lingered on a running group that met weekly. That I'd start doing as well in a few weeks when it was a little warmer outside. I missed working out with someone—even though I didn't care that much for running, maybe I could find a new fitness partner in that group. I created reminders for both in my calendar, then returned to my new manuscript.

I did at least six circles in the parking lot at the distillery, nearing the entrance, then turning and beelining back toward the bus stop, before I overcame my nerves enough to walk in the front door. I had to do it—I knew I did—but fuck if I wanted to. It was about the last thing I wanted to do. Meeting people as me—the real me—was something I'd never done before. I wasn't even sure I *could*. And what if I did it and everyone hated me? What if the real me was just the kind of person other people couldn't care about? What if the real reason I had no friends wasn't because I'd never tried, but because I wasn't the kind of person anyone wanted to be friends with? Was that something I really wanted to find out? I didn't think it was—I kind of preferred living in ignorance in this case. But what made me keep heading back toward the entrance was thinking about what was on the other side if I could just push through: Drew. And there wasn't a thing on the planet I wouldn't do for that man.

My eyes darted around nonstop, trying to determine for each person I saw if they were there because they needed to make friends like I did, or if they were more normal and there with someone already. There was a part of me that wanted to hide my head in a paper bag—being there for a meetup like this was like screaming to the world that I was so pathetic I couldn't even make friends in the way a normal person would. My breath stuttered out as I proceeded further inside until I saw through the crowd a group of people standing around, some talking, and most looking as awkward as I felt; there was no doubt that was the group I was looking for.

There was a mix of men and women, and it struck me how normal they all looked. None of them looked pathetic in the way I felt by being there. They just looked like your average people trying to get to know others. Maybe this wouldn't be quite as bad as I'd been afraid it would be—at least I found some comfort in knowing I wasn't the only one who felt awkward being there. With an attempt at a deep breath that didn't really work, I forced myself to smile and stepped up to the group.

A few minutes later, I'd met the other twelve people there, my head spinning with all the new names. As I listened to the bits of conversation that started and stopped, I ran through their names over and over again, desperately not wanting to forget them. Wouldn't that be a great first impression if I had to say "hey you" to someone? Before long, we and another ten or so people were ushered to start a tour of the distillery. At the end of the tour, we'd have a table with snacks and a tasting. I slipped my small notebook and pen out of my back pocket as the woman leading the tour kicked things off. I furiously scribbled down the names I'd heard with an identifying characteristic to go with each, a trick I'd researched online to help you remember people's names. Turning to a fresh page, I began taking notes on what we were learning about the distillery and the process of making whiskey—maybe it would come in handy in a book one day.

By the end of the tour, my hand was a bit cramped from the copious notes I'd taken, but I had pages with information on how the distillery functioned. It was fascinating and I had an urge to call Drew just to tell him all about it. *Maybe one day I can bring him here.*

"Hi. Tasha, right?" The woman speaking had made her way to my side as we filed into a large tasting room. She was a few inches taller than me, had short dark hair, green eyes that sparkled, and a mischievous grin.

I smiled back. "Yup. And you're Betsy?" I mentally crossed my fingers.

"The one and only," she replied with a wink.

I liked her already, I decided. She seemed like she had a sense of humor.

"I noticed you writing in a notebook during the tour."

I nodded. "It was interesting and you never know when knowledge like that might come in handy."

"Do you always keep a notebook and pen on you?"

I nodded again, a little embarrassed now.

Betsy's grin widened. "Same," she whispered conspiratorially as she slid a notebook a few inches out of her purse to show me before dropping it back inside. "You a writer, too?"

Now *I* grinned. "I am. A novelist. What about you?"

"Oh, I write a little of everything, but I've been on a short story kick recently. What kinds of novels?"

I blew a breath out. "Um, most recently, autobiographical fiction."

Betsy's eyes widened and she bit her lip in excitement. "You have a fucked-up life, too?"

I burst out laughing. I couldn't help it. I'd never met someone who'd throw out a line like that so easily. "Damn near as fucked up as it gets."

She linked her arm through mine, chuckling. "We have so much to talk about."

I liked Betsy more the longer the afternoon wore on. She was friendly, blunt, and had a very dark sense of humor that had me in stitches the entire time we were out. After the meetup was officially over, we went out to a bar and got some food and more drinks.

Aside from Drew, I'd never found it so easy to laugh with and talk to someone before—especially another female. And talk I did— we both did. She told me about finding her husband and best friend in bed together and deciding she needed a completely fresh start. She'd picked up and moved to Brinkley a few weeks earlier. Before that, she'd been raised by alcoholic parents who sounded like a cross between my parents and Drew's. I told her about my family life as a child and my marriage to Duncan. I talked a lot about Drew and how he'd saved my life when we were growing up, and how we'd fallen for each other but I'd put some distance between us before I fucked things up. She'd listened sympathetically and told me, her eyes misty and faraway, about the one man she'd known who was good in the way Drew was and how she'd destroyed that relationship with her extreme jealousy and determination he wasn't faithful because she was so afraid of losing him. It was exactly what I was sure I'd do with Drew if I didn't learn how to love myself first and I told her that. She told me it was going to suck to do it, but it was worth it, and that she'd tell me what she learned along the way to help make it easier.

By the time we parted ways nearly eight hours after we'd met, I felt much like we'd known each other our whole lives. We exchanged numbers and already had plans to get drinks together again in a few days' time. Betsy had also told me about a writing group she'd just joined and insisted I give it a try with her. High on having found someone I had so much in common with, I agreed and would be attending my first weekly writer's group four days later.

All in all, it couldn't have been more successful. As I laid in bed that night, thinking back over the day and battling an urge to call Drew and tell him all about it, I remembered the trepidation I'd felt when I arrived at the distillery. How I'd nearly decided to give up on trying. Even if Betsy and I didn't end up friends in the long term, I had a confidence I'd never felt before that I could find a way to connect with other people; a confidence I'd nearly sabotaged myself out of. That realization strengthened my determination to push through my self-doubt and keep putting myself out there, to keep doing the things that were uncomfortable, because this new feeling toward myself was something I wouldn't trade for the world.

Chapter Forty-Four

Tasha

How long you been running?"

The question came from a man named Jimmy who'd fallen into step with me as we jogged through the streets downtown the first time I joined the running group. I hadn't known what path we would be taking, and I was rather anxious to discover that we'd be running past Drew's apartment, the dog park where he often took Watson, and the hospital. It would be weird if I saw him for the first time in months while I was doing—*without* him—something I used to do *with* him.

"Depends on what you mean," I replied with a short laugh. "I've been running since I was a teen, but I don't usually run long distances like this."

"Five miles isn't that far."

"It is when you don't usually run more than a mile at once," I retorted with another laugh. "I'm more accustomed to running as a warm-up before lifting, then doing sprints for strength and cardio."

I also wasn't used to carrying on a conversation while I was running, and I was now embarrassingly out of breath. I focused on my breathing as Jimmy talked so I wouldn't have to stop to get it under control. He told me about how he used to be an ultra-marathon runner and do iron man competitions until he damaged just about every structure in his knee, and now he only ran two or three half-marathons a year and most of the time didn't run over eight miles at a time. I could hear in his tone that he really missed it.

"You don't think you'll be able to run a marathon again?"

"I might be able to. But my surgeon said if I tore up my knee again, I could count on not running again at all. I decided not to take the risk. I'd rather run some than not at all, you know?"

I looked over and gave a nod. "So what do you do, Jimmy?"

"I'm an electrical-mechanical engineer."

"So what do you do, Jimmy?" I repeated with a chuckle.

He laughed. "I work on prosthetics for a medical device company."

"Oh, that's cool," I said. I'd never met someone who worked a job like that. "So, like, you make robotic arms and legs and stuff?"

"Kind of. I'm more in the research and development side. We work with other specialists to try to find ways to improve prosthetic function so it better mimics an actual human limb."

"Okay, that's not just cool. That's *really* cool."

"What about you? What do you do?"

I shook my head, feeling embarrassed again. "Nothing like that. I'm not making the world better like you are."

"Let me guess... are you a personal trainer?"

I laughed. "You think I'm a personal trainer? I'm flattered."

He grinned. "You said you lift weights, and you're tolerating this run better than I would have expected of someone who doesn't run much—we're about three miles in."

"No. I'm not a personal trainer. I'm a writer."

"What kind of writer?"

"I write books."

"What are some of your titles? Maybe I've read some. Though most of my reading relates to my job."

"You haven't. I haven't been published yet. My first book will be out later this year—in September."

"Can I pre-order it?"

"Yes, but I'm not sure if it's the kind of thing you'd like to read."

"What genre is it?"

"Literary fiction. And I'm warning you—it's a little dark."

He asked me question after question, and we chatted and laughed, and before I knew it, the run was over. I was sweaty and tired and hungry... and really impressed I'd made it the full loop without having to take a break to walk. My leg was exhausted, but felt good—I wouldn't have even attempted the run without medical approval.

Before leaving, I took some time to properly stretch out the leg I'd broken as I'd been advised; it was tight after that run. It would probably be sore the next day, too, but nothing I couldn't handle.

"Your leg okay?" Jimmy asked with a nod as he stretched his side. "You're favoring it with your stretches."

"Yeah," I said, keeping my eyes averted. "I broke my leg in the fall and my PT said if I was going to do this, I needed to do some extra stretching."

"You're still in PT almost a year later?"

I kicked my leg a few times after my quad stretch. "No—I just checked with my therapist first."

"What did you break?"

"Snapped my femur in half."

He sucked in a loud breath. "How'd you do that?"

I squinted at him, then back down at the ground. How was I supposed to answer that question? It wasn't any of his business what actually happened, but it was an innocent question born of natural curiosity. On the one hand, I didn't want to talk about personal things with strangers, but on the other, I didn't want to hide what happened—hiding the past was how people ended up broken the way I was. How long did you need to know someone before you told them something like what happened to me, though?

Fuck it. If I'm going to be friends with someone, they have to be able to handle my lack of filter as well as my history. Betsy handled it. The writing group handles it. If we're going to be friends, this guy will have to handle it as well.

"My ex-husband pushed me down a flight of stairs."

That wasn't the first time I'd said the words "ex-husband" for Duncan, who I'd been officially divorced from for a while now, but a wave of nausea passed over me anyway.

Jimmy started to laugh then looked at me and his laughter faded, his brows knitting together. "You're not joking."

I gave a solemn headshake. "No." I wished I was—this man couldn't ever understand how much I wished I was. I stuffed my hands in my pockets and opened my mouth to fill the awkward silence and say I'd see him in a week, but he spoke first.

"I'm sorry." He meant it—I could tell he did.

"Me, too."

He rested his hands on his hips. "I'm starving."

"So am I."

"Wanna grab lunch?"

I almost said no—this had already been a lot, even though he'd been pretty easy to talk to—but I reminded myself that I had to push through that desire to run away when things got tough if I was going to make friends. "Sure."

"There's a create-your-own place with great food just a few blocks from here." He'd said it as a statement, but looked at me, an eyebrow quirked in question.

I smiled. "Sounds good."

We talked as we meandered down the street toward the restaurant through the increasing late-summer heat and all through lunch. Conversation flowed easily between us, and I decided I really liked his company.

I discovered he was nine years older than me, a widower, and that his wife had died almost five years earlier from breast cancer. My heart ached for what he and his late wife had been through. I'd been lucky with my cancer story, and even so it had been the hardest, most terrifying period in both mine and Drew's lives. Seeing what Drew went through was in some ways the worst part of the whole ordeal. I shivered while Jimmy was talking, grateful again that my latest checkup had been clear.

The results of that recent visit constituted the only time I'd texted Drew since the night I'd gone to his practice dinner with him. And while he hadn't texted me other than in response to that message, as I'd requested, he continued to send me YouTube song links. I'd considered, again, texting him and inviting him to meet me for the running group, but hadn't. I still hadn't worked on myself enough to feel confident I wouldn't fuck things up with him.

"You alright?" Jimmy asked, bringing me out of my thoughts. His brow was lowered.

"Yeah," I said with a head nod, realizing I had a few escaped tears. I swiped them away and gave him a small smile.

"Have you lost someone to cancer, too?" he asked.

I shook my head, my eyes focusing on my nearly-gone lunch in front of me. "No. *I* had cancer." I looked over and Jimmy had paled. "I don't anymore," I rushed out. "I've been in remission for years."

He studied me for a moment before taking another bite of his lunch. "You've been through a lot."

For some reason, his words made me feel teary. I laughed softly at myself and blinked the moisture away. "So have you."

He nodded and asked my thoughts on lunch, and conversation remained on lighter topics as we finished. After walking together back to the lot where we were both parked, we parted ways with a wave, and I was smiling as I climbed into my car.

I'd made another friend.

Chapter Forty-Five

Tasha

The writer's group rotated where we met, and after putting it off for months, I'd been nervous about hosting the first time. Thankfully, having everyone over had gone well, even if it was a bit cozy in my tiny apartment. We'd chatted through where we all were and provided feedback on Carly's manuscript. I liked my writer's group, but I was closest with Betsy, who was staying after everyone else left for dinner and a movie.

I breathed a sigh of relief as I shut the door behind the last person, my apartment much quieter without a group of chatty, half-tipsy people.

"So that was fun," Betsy said, pouring us each a fresh glass of wine.

I laughed. "It wasn't so bad."

"I told you it'd be fine for you to host here."

"I was thinking about the manuscript critique." It was the first one I'd participated in since I'd joined the group, and I'd worried about hurting Carly's feelings with my constructive criticism.

Betsy took a sip of her wine. "I told you no one would be an asshole about it."

I tipped my glass to her in acknowledgement. "You did."

"I mean, what would be the point? The purpose of a group like this is to help each other grow, and no one's going to grow if they're getting shit on."

I laughed. "As always, you have a way with words."

She winked. "Speaking of words... have you exchanged any with your Greek God?"

My laughter faded and I stared down into my wine glass as I twirled it leisurely by the stem. Six months after I told Drew I needed space to work on myself, I felt like I might be ready to try things with him without fucking everything up, but it looked as if he'd moved on. It had been two months since he'd sent me a song. "No."

"Text him, Tasha," she said. She'd been saying that to me for weeks.

I shook my head. I couldn't do that. I was the reason for our separation, and if he'd moved on, how would it be fair of me to mess things up for him by texting him?

"Text. Him," she repeated, raising her brows at me.

"I can't do that," I said. "He's... he's probably found someone and that's why he stopped sending me videos. How selfish would it be for me to be like, hey, I know you're happy now, but let me screw that up for you because I'm finally ready after making you wait for half a year."

"You don't know why he stopped. You're making an assumption. From what you've told me about you guys, there's no way he's just suddenly moved on and you texting him would be unwelcome. Just text him."

I stared into my glass again, my heart hammering in my chest at the thought of doing what Betsy suggested. What if I texted him and he didn't respond to me? Or what if he responded and said I was too late? What if he'd had enough time to think about all the ways I'd made his life harder over the years and now wanted nothing to do with me ever again? At least this way, when we'd parted, it had been on good terms. I wasn't sure how I'd cope with having my last memory of Drew being him basically telling me he hated me. I couldn't risk it. Besides, he'd been sending those videos as his way of letting me know he was thinking about me and was waiting. How much clearer a message could he send by stopping?

I downed the contents in my glass. "So what're we watching?" I asked, changing the subject. I didn't want to talk or even think about Drew anymore.

As much as I hadn't wanted to think about Drew, it was all I could do after Betsy left when the movie was over. I cycled between grabbing my phone to text him and putting it down, determined that was the worst possible decision I could make. I wished I could make up my damn mind about what to do.

But hadn't that really been the point of all the distance between us? For me to learn how to live and find happiness *without* Drew? And here I was, again, with my happiness hinging on his presence in my life. Except... this was different. I had other things in my life that made me happy, other people in my life who mattered to me. Like Betsy and Jimmy and the writer's group.

Did I want Drew in my life?

Yes.

But did I need him?

No.

I didn't need him.

I just had to remember that and let him go.

Chapter Forty-Six

Drew

I was at one of the dog parks near my apartment the first time I saw Tasha since she'd walked away to work on herself. She was jogging side by side with a guy. I'd almost missed her—there was a group of runners that passed by every Saturday morning, and I never paid much attention—but something had made me look up that morning. Was she part of the running group now? Was that a new friend? Or was he her boyfriend?

These were the thoughts I had every Saturday morning as I watched them when I walked Watson before rushing in to work at the hospital. I grimaced at the last thought, though after seeing her running with this same guy for weeks—months, really—I was beginning to think it might be. But, at the same time, it couldn't be a new boyfriend. It *couldn't* be. Tasha and I were made to be together. Knowing it was going to happen if I could just be patient was the only way I'd made it through the last seven months without her.

I sighed. I needed to send her songs on YouTube again. I was doing it regularly for a long time, the only way I could think to communicate with her while respecting her boundaries, to make sure she knew my feelings for her were only growing stronger, but I hadn't been able to for quite a while. One of the other partners in my practice had been recovering from a sudden heart attack and open-heart surgery, and while we'd all split up his patients, I'd taken the most, as well as all his hours at the hospital. I'd been working around the clock for the last several months without time to even take a breath. But Jack would be back soon and I'd have time to do more than work and sleep again.

I watched them running down the street until they turned and I could no longer see them, resting my hand over my chest. I missed her. I missed her *a lot*. I missed seeing her eyes glow when she was talking about writing or seeing something new. I missed hearing her laugh when one of us said something stupid or funny. I missed being able to look at her a certain way and her understanding what I was thinking without me having to speak, and being able to read her thoughts in her eyes. I missed the way I felt when I was around her—like the world was a beautiful place to be, and like I was understood and cared about. Like I could always be me, and no matter what, that was okay and enough.

Except maybe it wasn't... maybe that was why she was with this other guy instead of me.

But I wasn't ready to give up yet. I'd been following Tasha's book release online, and her release party and book signing was in two weeks. I was absolutely going to be there—I would have been no matter what—and hoped she'd be ready for us to talk.

With Jack back to work, I had a lot more time on my hands. I started re-recording songs for Tasha with new dedications, and once I was satisfied, I planned to upload one per day so she'd know I was always thinking about her. As I worked on recording new videos, however, my eyes kept landing on the copy of Tasha's book she'd given me for Christmas. I'd told her I wouldn't read it until she told me it was okay to, but she couldn't exactly do that when we weren't talking. And she'd only asked that I wait a little while. It had been nine months since then.

It wasn't the first time I'd gone through the same mental debate, though every time it ended with me leaving her book sitting where it was, remaining unread.

Until today.

I picked it up and opened it to the dedication.

For Drew—together kept me alive

Tasha had called her book autofiction, but after an hour of reading, I hadn't read a single word of fiction yet. There were things I hadn't known, like that she had a crush on me starting that first night we met and some of the horribly shitty things her mother said to her, but I knew those things were true. I also learned that she heard more of what happened with *my* parents than I'd ever realized and discovered just how angry and protective she'd felt over me. I couldn't help but smile as I read it because I'd felt the same way about *her*.

As the sky darkened, I found myself engrossed in Tasha's novel, often forgetting to read as I got lost in memories brought up by the words on the page. There was also something uniquely gratifying about finally understanding what had gone on in her mind during some of our teenage interactions. I took a break to feed Watson and myself and to take Watson for a nice long walk as I did every evening now that I had more time. When I got back inside, I sat down and continued reading, itching to text Tasha that she was a talented writer. And she was—the way she could describe what happened in such a way to communicate not only what happened, but also how it was impacting her, so clearly and succinctly, was impressive. I was also awed by her honesty and bravery. The things she lived through back then weren't easy things to talk about, and she wasn't shying away from any of it.

I flew through pages where I remembered everything that happened and slowed down, not wanting to miss anything, when there was something new. Then I reached something I'd always wondered about, but she'd never been willing to talk about: what exactly happened the day I attacked her stepdad on their front porch and in the following weeks until I was released from juvenile detention.

I saw the anger in Drew's eyes when he looked at my stepdad and I shook my head. But when Wayne touched me inappropriately low on my back, Drew snapped. In the blink of an eye, he was there hitting Wayne. There was screaming in the air, and I realized afterwards that it was mine. It took a minute or two, but then Wayne had Drew down and was hitting him. I saw the rage in Wayne's eyes and knew what it meant—he wasn't going to stop until he felt he'd done enough to teach him a lesson, and that might be enough to kill Drew. I threw myself over Drew to protect him. I'd rather Wayne kill me.

Wayne lifted me as I screamed and clung to Drew and tossed me across the porch. I hit my head, landing over a porch chair, and it felt like my ribs snapped. For a second, I couldn't move or breathe, but I could see Wayne hitting Drew again and forced myself up—I had to protect him. Again, I got myself between them. Drew was unconscious and I locked my arms and legs around him, and this time Wayne couldn't get me off before we had an audience gathered in front of our house. Sirens grew louder—someone had called the police. Wayne eventually stopped trying to get me off Drew, deciding he'd rather kick at us.

At the hospital, my left eye swelled closed and I had a concussion and two cracked ribs. I didn't care about any of it, and they ended up giving me a tranquilizer because I was screaming for them to let me go to Drew. I was afraid he was dead, and no one would tell me anything—my parents had told them not to. A nurse ultimately took pity on me and whispered to me when we were alone. She told me he was stable. He had seven broken ribs, a broken nose and cheekbone, twenty-three stitches, and bruised kidneys and lung. He'd be in the hospital for a while, but he'd be okay.

It wasn't until I snuck next door to ask his parents about him two weeks later that I found out he'd been taken straight from the hospital to juvenile detention and that Wayne was pressing charges. His parents said they weren't surprised, that Drew was always trying to figure out how to disappoint them, and I lost it. I screamed at them and told them they didn't deserve a son as wonderful as Drew. I told them they weren't capable of love and the only disappointment was them.

They called my parents. My mom used one of Wayne's belts on me until I was bleeding for being disrespectful. Wayne was quiet, but that rage was there in his eyes. I knew something was coming from him, too—I just didn't know what or when. When my mom was done and left to buy liquor, he followed me into my bathroom and locked the door.

"Take off your clothes."

I hated him more than I'd ever hated him before after what he'd done to Drew. So, though I knew better, I glared at him and refused.

"You can take them off or I will."

I contemplated trying to stab him with my nail file until he reached for me, and I jerked away and started removing my clothes myself. I left on my bra and panties.

"All of them."

My stomach lurched, but I did as he said. When I was fully naked, my arms crossed tight over my chest and my legs pressed together, he told me to turn around, then ran his fingers around the bloody cuts on my back. Without a word, he pulled out peroxide and bandages and cleaned and covered every cut. The way he was taking care of me, but after making me get naked, was nauseating in a whole different way than before when he just watched me do normal things, like brushing my teeth, naked.

When he was done, he turned me around and looked at me. I couldn't tell what he was thinking and had no idea what he was going to do next.

I froze on those last words, not sure if I could read any more. My stomach roiled with what might be coming next. I wanted to close the book, but had to continue reading. I read about how he'd looked at her and grabbed her wrists. How she'd threatened to call the police if he didn't let her go, that she'd show them the bruises and the cuts and tell them they all came from him. How he'd told her they'd never believe her, and when she said that I would corroborate what she divulged, he'd laughed and said he was pressing charges and making sure I was locked up for years.

I read about how she begged him not to do that, not to ruin my life like that, and how Wayne asked what she'd give to him in return. How he'd told her he would only do it if she gave him a blow job whenever he asked for one, that it was her choice whether or not I was locked up and would lose my future or whether he'd drop the charges against me. How she'd done what he told her to in order to give me my freedom and protect me from the consequences of what I'd done trying to protect her.

I gagged, then threw up all over my hallway when I didn't make it to the bathroom. I couldn't catch my breath; the thought of what that bastard did to Tasha because of me was too much. And we were just kids. Teenagers. I'd lost my temper and she'd paid for it. For a year before I turned eighteen and got us out of there. Everything I had was because of what happened to her. I felt disgusting, and I wanted to give it all back—my money, my job, my degree. None of it was worth what happened to Tasha. Nothing could ever be worth what happened to Tasha.

I remembered sitting in the hospital, every breath excruciatingly painful, wanting to live so I could protect her. I'd had no idea she'd have been safer if I'd died. If I *had* known, I would have found a way to die for her. I'd have done anything to keep her safe. But I hadn't known and now it was too late. And it was all because I'd let my anger override logic and attacked Wayne. If I hadn't done that...

I broke down, not sure I could ever forgive myself for that moment of weakness... and not sure I could ever even look at Tasha again without seeing how I'd failed her and what had happened to her as a result. I was also furious. She'd been so worried about hurting me when this was what she'd been through? Why the hell had she done that? Didn't she know I wouldn't have wanted that? I squeezed handfuls of my hair, wanting to rage about what she'd done for me. Wanting to find Wayne and kill the bastard.

I picked up my phone and opened my messages with Tasha, but I couldn't figure out what to say. I wanted to tell her that I loved her and was furious with her, I wanted to yell at her, and I wanted to cry. I did nothing, however, except go back and stare at those pages I'd just read, trying to accept what I'd learned.

The next morning, bleary-eyed, before a pot of coffee had even finished brewing, when all I'd done was take Watson outside long enough to go to the bathroom, I picked Tasha's book back up and continued reading. There may have been more in there that I didn't know about, and I *needed* to know it all. Every word, every single thing that had happened to her.

I wondered as the hours passed if I'd *really* needed to know it all. When I was reading about everything going through her mind the times she'd become suicidal, when I read about Wayne progressing to raping her the night she ran away with me, as I learned about the horrible things her boyfriends since college had said and done to her, I wasn't sure I'd be able to breathe again. Until I remembered that she'd lived it... If she could make it, then so would I when all I was doing was reading about it.

While she omitted certain things—like her battle with cancer and her relationship with Duncan—nothing I'd read was fiction until closer to the end of the book. Rather than taking time to work on healing herself as she did in real life, she wrote about us dating until one day she told me all her secrets. And in the book, her secrets broke me. I loved her, but I couldn't move past the things that had happened to her on my account, and we parted ways for good. It was then she found herself, after *I'd* walked away from *her*.

It was what she'd been afraid of the whole time, I realized—that we'd never have any kind of relationship again once I knew the things she'd kept from me. As I closed her book, the last page read, it dawned on me that she hadn't been too far from the truth. I'd been thinking as I read that I could never talk to her again—that I didn't *deserve* to talk to her again after everything she'd been through because of me. The things that Wayne had done to her because I attacked him... the things he'd done to her because I'd left her behind for a week before I got her out of her parents' house... the things her boyfriends had done because I was too scared to admit my feelings for her back then.

I'd already thought I would never be able to forgive myself, and if I couldn't—if I couldn't look at her without seeing what had happened to her—there would never be a future for us. I wasn't sure how the hell I was going to move past what I'd learned, but I would find a way because the only thing worse than facing it all would be losing Tasha for good.

Chapter Forty-Seven

Tasha

artlett's?" Jimmy asked as we moved through our post-run stretching routine together. Having lunch together was now just what we did after running; the only thing in question was *where* we went.

"Sounds good," I replied with a groan.

My hamstring was tight. We'd picked up the pace that day and tacked on an extra couple of miles since Jimmy was preparing to run a half-marathon. I was exhausted and would be sore the next day, but it was a good kind of exhaustion and soreness—it was because of exertion rather than an injury.

"Still feeling okay after that?" Jimmy asked. He was watching me with growing concern.

I deepened my hamstring stretch. "Feeling great," I replied with another groan. "Just a little tight."

"Your leg's alright?" He was looking at the leg I'd broken.

"Totally fine," I laughed. "Don't worry so much."

He gave me a friendly smile. "We pushed it really hard today— I'm just making sure it wasn't too much."

I let out a huff, straightening up. "I can handle it. I can handle a lot more than you might think."

His face sobered. "I know."

He was thinking of the bits and pieces I'd shared with him about my past, but I'd actually just been thinking about fitness.

"I didn't mean that stuff," I said. "I was just talking about working out. I used to work out all the time with my best friend. It was kind of a point of pride for me to keep up with him. He's six feet tall and really strong, for reference."

We headed toward the restaurant. "Used to? I thought you said you still worked out."

"I do," I replied, my heart tripping a little to be talking about Drew. "But not with Drew anymore. We aren't..." I trailed off, not sure how to explain. "We haven't talked in a long time."

A sideways glance revealed that Jimmy was watching me with curiosity. He wanted me to elaborate, I could tell, but he wouldn't push me to. He never pushed me to tell him things. It was part of why I opened up so much—the lack of pressure created space for me to want to share. Not this, though—the situation with Drew was different. I'd accepted that he'd moved on, that I'd taken too long, but accepting it didn't mean it wasn't still painful.

"I'm sorry," Jimmy said.

My eyes refocused on him and I gave him a sad smile. "I am, too."

I let out a sigh, trying to figure out how to change the topic, but now my thoughts were lingering on Drew.

"So," Jimmy started, changing the topic for me. "Your book is live in three days. How are you feeling?"

I let out a nervous titter and rapped my thumbs against my leg as we walked. "Excited. Terrified. What if no one reads it? What if no one likes it? What if my publisher regrets publishing my book and spending all this money for a launch party because they can't even make that up in sales?"

"Well," Jimmy said after a thoughtful pause, "your publisher has been around for a while. I looked them up, and they have a lot of bestsellers. I'd bet they know something you don't about how successful you're going to be. They're not going to take a chance on a book that has a high probability of failing." He shrugged. "They're gonna have an entire department that does nothing but market research that feeds into their decisions on who and what to publish. They wouldn't have given you a contract—let alone an advance—if there wasn't a very good chance your book is going to be popular."

I'd never thought about it that way and it was helpful. I smiled and told him so. He smiled back, this softening thing happening around his eyes. It had begun happening with some frequency when we were together, which was rather often now that we were meeting three to five times a week to run together and almost always ate together afterwards.

We talked a little more about the launch party, which Jimmy insisted he wanted to come to, though I was sure he'd be bored, then I asked him how things were going with his latest research on how to mimic human pinching between two fingers well enough to pull petals from a flower without damaging them. Whenever he talked about his career, I got a little lost, but I'd gotten comfortable enough to stop him and ask him to reword or to define terms so I could follow what he was saying, which he was always more than happy to do.

"You have any plans today?" he asked as we stood from the table after paying our bill for lunch.

"Just a shower," I laughed. My skin was sticky with dried sweat, and I knew I didn't smell so great.

"Wanna grab a matinee and maybe some dinner after?"

"Like…"

His lips softened the same way his eyes did. "Like a date. I like you, Tasha, and I'm asking you on a date."

My breath caught, though I tried to hide it. I hadn't expected that. I'd joined the running group to make friends, and I liked being friends with Jimmy. He watched me, waiting patiently for me to respond. The only thing to betray anything other than calm in his demeanor was a slight shifting in his weight from foot to foot, a minor increase in the intensity of his gaze. I blew out my long-held breath, looking away. It had been almost a year since I'd dated someone, unless I was counting the dinner with Drew the last time I talked to him, and I'd had it in my mind for months that the next person I'd date would be Drew.

But Drew had moved on—it wasn't going to happen, I reminded myself. I examined Jimmy's face—a face so different from Drew's, with his clean-shaven jaw and short salt-and-pepper hair. He was different from Drew in so many ways, from his shorter and narrower frame to his more logical and practical way of thinking. He didn't have a love for the unknown, though he didn't seem averse to it, either. But one thing he *did* have in common with Drew was that he truly listened to me when I talked, no matter what it was about. He didn't laugh at things most people would and gave me the impression that he understood on some level how hard parts of my life had been. Maybe if I gave this a chance, I could grow to care about him the way I cared about Drew.

"A movie and dinner?" I asked, though I didn't know why—that was what he'd asked me to do.

"Or dinner and a movie." His eyebrows lifted.

I laughed. "Okay. Which one?"

He smiled. "You choose."

"Let's do dinner first, then a movie."

It would give me time to not only shower, but to figure out what the hell to wear and try to come to terms with the fact that I was going on a date.

My first actual date since Duncan.

And it wasn't with Drew.

Dinner with Jimmy passed much like our lunches did, filled with easy conversation and the occasional light laughter, then we went to the theater. I didn't watch traditional television and never went to the theater, so I'd been unaware there was a movie out about a writer who discovers that as she pens her story, that story begins to unfold in her real life. The movie was at times touching and romantic, and at others hilariously funny. We were both still chuckling and talking about it when he pulled up outside my apartment building.

"I had fun," I said, turning to face him, still grinning from talking about the movie. "Thank you."

"I did, too," Jimmy replied.

He reached over and rested his hand over mine, and I sucked in a breath, my grin fading. It was the first time someone had touched my hand in that way since Drew. I wasn't sure if the intense feelings coursing through me were from Jimmy's touch or memories of Drew's.

"Maybe we can do it again," he said.

After a short delay, I responded. "Okay."

He smiled. "I'm looking forward to it."

He reached up with his other hand and his fingertips touched my jawline. I knew we would kiss if I didn't do something to indicate I didn't want to. But I didn't know if I wanted to or not. I was nervous, but I wasn't sure what I was more nervous about—that it wouldn't live up to kissing Drew? Or that it would?

The kiss started off gentle, growing to a moderate intensity before Jimmy pulled back first. I left my eyes closed for a minute, still feeling his lips on mine. He was a good kisser—a *really* good kisser—and I almost leaned forward to kiss him again. Instead, I blinked my eyes open and bit my lip to temper my grin.

I laid in bed awake for hours thinking about that kiss with Jimmy, comparing everything about it, every nuance, to kissing Drew. There was no question that kissing Jimmy was unlike any other man I'd ever kissed—there was simply no comparison—except for Drew. I felt giddy and excited to see Jimmy again, and I even looked forward to kissing him again. But when I thought of kissing Drew, the excitement for what I felt for Jimmy waned. Because as much as I'd liked the way I felt with Jimmy, it still couldn't compare to how I felt with Drew.

But it was early, I reminded myself. I hadn't known Jimmy that long, and I'd known Drew for sixteen years. I simply needed to give myself time and keep from making mental comparisons. It wasn't fair to Jimmy, or a potential future with him if things worked out.

As much as I told myself to stop comparing Drew and Jimmy, I couldn't. The guilt I felt for doing so wasn't enough to make it stop. It felt like the difference between black and white and color when I compared them; even if the black and white was exceptionally good for having no color, it was still black and white. I kept telling myself to give it time, because I really did like Jimmy, but I wasn't sure I could.

My launch party was starting in a little over an hour, and Jimmy would be there at some point. I'd pay really close attention to how I felt when I saw him, how I felt around him, and use that to help me decide how to move forward. We were supposed to go out after the party for dinner, drinks, and live music, though I wasn't sure I should have agreed yet. I couldn't decide.

I wore a new dress that I'd treated myself to, courtesy of the advance I'd received for *Searching for Never*, and pulled my hair back into a messy updo. I'd purchased new makeup for the event, but decided after staring at it for a while not to wear it. I was on a quest to be only myself at all times and makeup just wasn't me. Much like I had over a year earlier when Drew came to visit, I tossed all of it into the garbage, promising myself not to buy any again.

And then it was time to go, and as I neared the venue, thoughts of Drew and Jimmy faded into the background, excitement for my debut novel taking their place. I'd dreamed of a day like this from the moment I discovered how much I loved wielding a pencil as a young girl. And now, somehow, that dream was coming true.

Chapter Forty-Eight

Drew

I'd never had so much trouble getting dressed. Then again, I'd never cared as much as I did right then about how I looked. Eventually, I narrowed it down to two options, though I couldn't seem to decide between them. Any other day in my life, it would have been easy to decide, but a lot was riding on how the evening ahead unfolded, and looking my best could only help me.

"What do you think, Watson?" I asked, looking down. Watson was lying on the bedroom floor near the entrance to the closet watching me with his head on his paws. I held up a black button down and charcoal gray pants in front of me. "Black? Or...." I swapped the clothes for a gray-blue shirt and black pants. "Blue?"

Watson stared at me, one of his ears giving a small twitch. I sighed.

"Blue," I said to Watson a few minutes later, after holding both outfits up in front of the bathroom mirror. "It makes my eyes more blue, and Tasha has always liked that. But maybe with the gray pants rather than black. Yeah?"

Watson lifted his head with a whine, then sat up and looked around. He missed Tasha as much as I did.

"She's not here, boy."

I set the clothes on the bathroom counter and squatted down to scratch behind his ears the way he liked. He propped his nose on my shoulder and gave me a look that was clearly asking me to rectify the situation.

"I'm trying, buddy. I'm trying."

With another sigh, I stood and dressed, then headed to the living room. Once there, I looked down at several objects I hoped would help me out, assuming I found a chance to talk to Tasha alone. The first was a printout from the local climbing gym where Tasha had purchased the introductory climbing course for me for Christmas. I hadn't done it yet—I wanted to do it with *her*—and they only had one more course before winter. So I'd signed us up for it and printed the confirmation page with both of our names on it.

The second item was a list of preparatory material for the glass-blowing class that was coming up soon. I'd purchased the tickets and the class for the two of us and was hoping that reminding her of that—as well as making sure she knew how much I still wanted to do it with her—would help her to see that nothing had changed for me.

The third object was the most important: her book. The autofiction. I'd read through the book again over the last two weeks, but this time I'd slowed down and made notes in the margins. The notes told her what I was doing or thinking at the time she was writing about, or about my thoughts now—sometimes both. I wanted her to understand my side of her story, both then and now, so she'd know without a doubt in her mind how I felt about her. How I would *always* feel about her. She'd titled her book *Searching for Never*, but she didn't need to keep searching. It was here, waiting for her. She'd already found it—she just needed to believe it.

The final item was something I hoped she still wanted. She'd told me years earlier that a piece of jewelry she really wanted was a necklace to commemorate the books she published, a reminder that her dreams of being a writer had come true. I'd picked out a chain with a small ring stamped with the title of her novel that was releasing, *Behind The Stares*, along with the publication date on the back of it, and already had the ring for her second book that was releasing in another five months, which I'd give to her then. She'd had tons of jewelry—cheap, thoughtless, common jewelry—from Duncan when she left him, and I hoped that experience hadn't destroyed the desire she'd once had for this necklace. It was a risk, but one I found worth taking. I'd been planning what this necklace would look like and researching custom jewelers for years.

The papers I folded and slid into my pockets along with my wallet, keys, and the small wrapped jewelry box. The book was also wrapped, but didn't fit in my pocket, so remained in my hand. I took a slow breath in, reaching back with a hand to massage the back of my neck, which was tense and sore. Every day closer to seeing Tasha and trying to get her to see how much I loved her still had brought with it an ocean of nerves. There were so many ways this could go— and most of them weren't in my favor.

Watson whined and nudged my hand, and I scratched behind his ears, then bent and kissed the top of his head.

"How do I look?" I asked, turning in a circle.

Watson cocked his head at me.

I laughed, then rubbed over his head before taking his face in my palms, looking at him gravely. "Cross your paws, Watson. I need this to go well. You do, too. Because if it goes well for *me*, you'll also get to start seeing Tasha again."

Watson whined and thumped his tail at Tasha's name. I smiled and kissed his nose. "I know. Exactly."

The launch party and book signing was being held in a large local bookstore, and it was bustling as I approached. I hoped the bustle was all in honor of Tasha and her new book. She deserved to have a fuss made over her. I was nearly to the front door when I spotted her through the row of windows across the front of the building, and I stopped to watch her for a minute.

She was seated at a table with copies of her book set up, a number of people standing and chatting behind her, all holding champagne flutes, and there were six people in line, holding copies of her book, waiting to have her sign them. A grin stretched across my face as I watched her look up and smile, taking time to chat with each person. She was glowing as if there was a powerful light source inside her, her large brown eyes sparkling with life and excitement. Her hair was down and soft around her shoulders, and I had a flash of memory from the day I'd dried her hair for her. It had looked much like it did now when I was finished. I could feel the silky strands in my fingers again and my chest throbbed.

The line of people waiting for her to sign her book eventually ended and she stood, taking a few steps to join the people behind her, one of which handed her a drink. She engaged in animated conversation with them, and I realized they must all be friends of hers. Now I was no longer smiling and even more nervous knowing I might be meeting her new friends; I hadn't thought about that because I wasn't used to her really having any friends aside from me. I was happy for her, but also anxious; I needed to be sure I made a good impression on them.

The woman standing immediately to Tasha's right looked directly at me, then leaned in toward Tasha and said something to her. Tasha laughed and rolled her eyes, then looked toward the window. Her laughter faded, her lips falling into a straight line as our eyes locked. I could see from as far away as I was that her cheeks were turning red, just as I could see her mouth start moving—saying something to the woman next to her, I assumed. Her lips twitched, began to pull back into a smile, then fell before trying again. She couldn't decide. That's when I smiled again, for some reason feeling relieved by her reaction. Then—with a deep breath—I left my spot near the window and headed through the entrance.

Tasha's eyes followed me as my feet carried me closer to her, and I fantasized about taking her into my arms and kissing the hell out of her when I reached her, but I knew that was just a fantasy—I couldn't actually do that. We hadn't seen each other or even spoken in the better part of a year, not to mention she might have a boyfriend.

I hoped not. I hoped I was wrong.

"Hi," I said, when I reached her.

"Hi," she breathed back.

For a heartbeat or two, it was only the two of us. No one around us existed, none of the space between us had happened. It was just us, as we'd always been.

"Congratulations, Nats," I said, tearing up. "You fucking did it. I'm so proud of you."

She nodded, her eyes visibly misty as well. "Yeah. I fucking did it. Thanks to you."

"I had nothing to do with it. This is all you."

She shook her head. "No. You gave me a reason to keep going."

I lifted a hand to swipe at my eyes. At the same time, someone cleared their throat, and Tasha looked as startled as I felt to have a reminder that we weren't actually alone.

"Are you going to introduce us to the Greek God?" asked the woman to Tasha's right.

Tasha's eyes shot fire at the woman, who just laughed. I already could see why they were friends and chuckled.

"Everyone, this is Drew."

I inclined my head, curious about the looks of recognition in almost every set of eyes of the half a dozen or so people standing there.

"And Drew, this is Betsy," Tasha said, indicating the woman to her right with a laugh.

I shook Betsy's hand, followed by the hand of each person there, trying to keep track of all their names. I learned almost everyone standing there was part of a writer's group Tasha had joined and they had become friends, the exception her editor, Clara.

Another group of people walked up to the table to have their books signed before we had a chance to talk at all, and Tasha sat, greeting them.

"You're *Drew*-Drew, right?" Clara asked.

I tried not to laugh. "I'm not sure what that means."

"You grew up with Tasha?"

"Oh," I replied, nodding. "Yes. Tasha and I grew up together since we were fourteen."

"I'm curious, and maybe you can help me out. Tasha submitted a book to us recently that she said was autofiction."

"She did?" I couldn't help grinning.

Clara shook her head slightly. "She didn't tell you? We're publishing that one, too."

Of course they were. I beamed.

"Anyway," Clara continued as Betsy elbowed me lightly and handed me a flute of champagne. I tipped my head in thanks. "I'm trying to figure out how much of the book is real life and how much is fiction."

"You'll have to ask Tasha," I replied. If she didn't want to share that information, I wasn't going to do it, either. It was *her* life and *her* story to tell—not mine.

"I did. She told me most of it was true."

"Okay."

"Is it really?" she asked, leaning in. Before I responded, she shook her head and let out a short laugh. "Of course you haven't read it, though. Or have you?"

I'd heard Tasha rave about Clara for years, and if it wasn't for that, I wouldn't have been able to speak as calmly as I was about to. I was trying to give Clara the benefit of the doubt, but it bothered me that she didn't believe Tasha and that she was trying to get me to tell her if Tasha was telling her the truth or not. And none of it even mattered when it came down to whether or not they were publishing her book.

"Imagine for a minute that you've been through the hell Tasha writes about in that book. Imagine all those things happened to you." I paused, taking a slow, deep breath to calm down. "Imagine the impact those things would have on you, and how much courage it would take to tell people about them." Another pause. "Now imagine not being believed."

Betsy and a couple of the writing group folks grinned after I stopped speaking, Betsy nodding. The others in the group looked bewildered, and Clara's eyes were narrowed in thought.

"There's more darkness in this world than many people know, but not knowing about it doesn't mean it doesn't exist. If someone tells you some horrible thing happened to them, you believe them.

You admire them for having the courage to tell you. You should feel humbled that they trusted you enough to tell you. You don't question if they're telling you the truth."

I could see Clara chewing on my words and took a sip of my champagne, looking down at where Tasha was chatting with another person whose book she was signing. I was glad she hadn't heard Clara.

"I'm sorry," Clara said a minute later. "My job makes me curious, but I never thought about how that might come across in certain circumstances."

I gave a small nod, then Clara was drawn into conversation with one of the other writers.

"I like you," Betsy said, still grinning. "You're feisty."

I snorted. "Only when it comes to Tasha."

Betsy and I chatted through the end of the event, and I learned more about how she and Tasha had met, what Tasha had been up to the last few months, and based on the questions Betsy asked, it was obvious Tasha had talked quite a bit about me and our history together. I enjoyed talking to her and found myself laughing on several occasions—there were quite a few ways in which Betsy reminded me of Tasha, and her snarky humor was one of them. Betsy was sharp-witted and funny.

Tasha, meanwhile, was never able to get up from her signing table. I knew she'd be exhausted, but I was thrilled for her nonetheless. I'd done research and knew these things didn't always go so well, especially for a new author. But it would definitely give Tasha a confidence boost that so many people were buying her book and wanting her to sign it and talk to them about it—a confidence boost she more than deserved.

Chapter Forty-Nine

Tasha

Drew's appearance caught me by surprise, and between that and being so busy with people wanting me to sign my book for them and talk to them about it, I completely forgot about Jimmy. Forgot he was supposed to be at the event, forgot that I was supposed to go out with him afterwards... forgot he even existed, honestly.

After the last person walked away from the table, I stood and stretched, a bit self-conscious about how short my dress rode up my legs when I did. Of course, Drew was watching me when I looked over, and I blushed, just like I had when he'd arrived. He'd been there for hours, but I hadn't talked to him at all aside from the few words we exchanged right after he came inside. Betsy raised and lowered her brows at me, her eyes moving to Drew and back, clearly wanting to know what was going on. I had told her he'd moved on and never expected him to show up. I rolled my lips under and gave her a small shrug in response.

"This was amazing," Drew said, gesturing around us.

I couldn't wipe the grin off my rapidly heating face. "Yeah. It kinda was." I looked over at Clara. "I have Clara to thank for that.

And Yolanda—she's the publicist who planned this whole thing, but she had a family emergency and couldn't come."

She winked at me. "You keep writing great books, and we'll keep throwing you parties."

"So, where do you wanna start for cleanup?" I asked her, taking in everything around us that would need to be done.

Clara waved her hand at me. "You? Nowhere." Her eyes widened. "I almost forgot, though. I have something for you. Stay here for a minute." She stepped away toward the bookstore's office.

"I have something for you, too," Drew said, his voice quiet and deep.

My bare arms broke into goosebumps. It was so good to hear his voice again. I looked down at the wrapped item in his hands that looked like a book, but instead, he reached into his pocket and pulled out something smaller that was wrapped in the same paper. I accepted it and looked up. Drew's eyes were radiant blue, his shirt intensifying the color. God, I loved when he wore blue. Especially button downs when he had the top two buttons opened. I sucked in a breath and shifted my focus from his chest to the gift in my hands.

People were starting to leave, however, so I paused to say good-byes to everyone. All except Betsy, Drew, and Clara, who hadn't returned yet, headed out of the bookstore, then I again looked down at the wrapped item in my hands. I knew when the paper was halfway off that it must be jewelry and my stomach lurched. Drew had never bought me jewelry before, and I wasn't sure how I felt about it. Duncan had loved buying me jewelry, and I'd thought it was a sign he cared about me, even though jewelry wasn't something I had ever really liked all that much. Now I realized it had been nothing of the sort; it had been a way for him to make sure I felt indebted to him, and a way to distract me from the things he did to me.

My fingers trembled, and Drew rested a hand on my back. That only made things worse, because now my heart was racing from the contact. I flipped the case open and found inside a delicate chain with an equally delicate ring on it. Lifting everything closer to my face, I could see there were words on it... the title of the book I'd just released. My mind jumped back to telling Drew when we were teens that I wanted something like that one day if I ever got published.

"I can't believe you remembered what I said," I murmured, lifting the charm in my fingertips.

"I remember everything you say," Drew replied just as quietly. "I hope you still... after what happened with Duncan—"

"It's perfect," I rushed out, because it was. Of course it was. Drew had never given me a gift that *wasn't* perfect. And this was nothing like the popular, overpriced jewelry Duncan had always given me, and I knew it didn't come with expectations of any sort. "Will you clasp it for me?" I lifted the necklace and held it out to him, trying to hide that I was sniffling and about to cry.

As Drew clasped the necklace around my neck, Betsy asked what it was and leaned over to get a closer look at it.

"It has the book title on it," I said, fingering the disk again. I wasn't sure I'd be able to *stop* touching it.

"I'll give her a charm for each book she publishes," Drew added.

"Ooooh, that's perfect."

I nodded, still sniffling, still battling tears. Though I lost that battle when Clara reappeared with a basket containing a mug, small chocolates wrapped in famous quotes, and custom pencils and bookmarks branded for my book.

"Congratulations, Tasha," she said, giving me a small hug.

I excused myself to the bathroom—I had to pee after hours of sipping champagne, and I needed to splash some cold water on my face so I could get back in control of my emotions and quit crying in public. Once I was calm and confident that I could keep from tearing up again, I headed back out, intending to help clean up regardless of what Clara had said.

The first thing I noticed was that Drew, sleeves now rolled up nearly to his elbows, was helping Clara with the cleanup efforts, which didn't surprise me in the least. Drew could never just stand around when someone was doing something he could help with. He simply wasn't wired that way.

The second thing I noticed was Jimmy, holding a copy of my book and reading one of the signs Drew and Clara hadn't packed up yet. My eyes darted to Drew, then back to Jimmy a few times before Jimmy looked up. He gave me a broad smile and stepped toward where I'd stalled after seeing him.

"Congratulations, Tasha!" He leaned in and kissed my cheek, a hand curling lightly around my forearm.

I froze—I couldn't even reply, my heart hammering into my throat.

"I'm so sorry I'm late and missed it all," he continued. "We had an emergency in the lab. I left as soon as I could."

"Th-that's okay," I stuttered, mentally berating myself for having forgotten he was coming. I peeked over at Drew, hoping he hadn't noticed, but he was standing still, a box in his hands and staring at us, his entire body rigid. *Shit, shit, shit.* Now I couldn't look away from him.

"You ready?" Jimmy asked.

My eyes still refused to shift away from Drew, as hard as I was trying to make them. My lips parted to speak, but I had no idea what to say. The event was over, so it was time for Jimmy and me to go out as planned, but no, I was *not* ready to go. And I knew right then I never would be... not with him. "I..." *I can't even remember how to speak, apparently.*

Drew set down the box he'd been holding and headed in our direction, Betsy following, her eyes widened in mock horror. I narrowed mine at her, and she grinned. She found the situation entertaining. I did not. But I *did* find *her* funny, so I almost laughed when she waggled her eyebrows and gave me an exaggerated wink. Finally, I looked at Jimmy, consumed with guilt. He was watching Drew and Betsy approach with a pleasant, curious expression.

Betsy spoke first. "Hi, I'm Betsy," she said, glancing at me with laughter in her eyes as she held out her hand.

I shook my head to break myself out of my stupor. "I'm sorry. Yes, Jimmy, this is my friend, Betsy. Betsy, this is Jimmy." They shook hands and exchanged quick pleasantries, vaguely familiar with each other from things I'd told them. Then Jimmy turned to Drew. I swallowed—or tried to over what felt like a handful of cotton balls that had suddenly appeared in my throat. "And this is my... this is..." For some reason, I couldn't get the words out. I wasn't even sure which ones to use. My ex-best friend who I fell in love with? The man I was *still* in love with? The reason I was about to cancel my plans for the evening and wouldn't be rescheduling?

"Drew," Drew finished for me, holding his hand out toward Jimmy.

"Jimmy," Jimmy said, taking his hand. "Nice to meet you."

Drew inclined his head politely and they shook, then Drew's eyes returned to me. When I peeked over, Jimmy was glancing back and forth between Drew and me, obviously deep in thought. I tried to swallow again, though my mouth was somehow becoming drier by the second. I had no idea what to do or what to say. No matter what, someone was going to end up hurt. All I knew for sure was that being there with Drew right then, one thing had become undeniably clear: if I had a thousand years, and he was completely perfect in every way, I still wouldn't ever feel about Jimmy the way I felt about Drew. I'd thought maybe I could with enough time, but being in Drew's presence again had dispelled that erroneous belief.

Jimmy nodded as if he was figuring something out, his eyes softened, then he gave me the first fake smile I'd ever seen from him. I gestured outside, knowing I owed him some sort of explanation, but needing space from Drew first.

"About tonight," I started once we'd reached the sidewalk.

Jimmy held up a hand. "No need," he said.

"I'm sorry," I rushed out, wringing my hands. "I didn't know he was coming—we haven't even talked in so long—"

"Tasha," Jimmy interrupted gently, his hand brushing mine. "It's okay."

"I really do like you—I swear I wasn't leading you on."

"I don't think you would," he replied, glancing through the windows to where we'd left everyone else. "I *do* think you and Drew have something unfinished between you, though."

"I'm sorry," I said again.

The corners of his mouth curved up a tad. "Life's short, Tasha. You know that better than most. Don't spend it sorry for what makes you happy in the time you have." He turned and looked down the street with a sigh. "See you Saturday?"

I gave him a weak smile. "See you Saturday."

He kissed my cheek with his customary gentleness, then nodded toward the inside of the building. "I hope it works out for you," he said, then turned to walk down the street.

I looked back inside for the first time since I'd walked out with Jimmy and saw Drew helping Clara again, though his eyes were nearly constantly on me. I couldn't figure out if that was a good thing or not, but decided there was really only one way to find out and, with a deep breath, headed back in the front doors. Betsy raised her brows at me as I neared, and I gave her a small shrug.

"He's a helper," she said, tipping her head toward Drew.

I looked over at him and smiled, my chest warming. "Yeah. He is. He always has been."

"And he's hotter in person," she added, watching Drew.

I smacked her arm. "Stop that, Betsy," I hissed, laughing.

"He's got a nice ass," she said, shrugging at me as Drew bent to fold up the table legs.

I snorted. He did, but I didn't say anything.

"Don't tell me you haven't noticed?"

I rolled my eyes. "Oh my god, Betsy. Of course I have. But stop staring at him."

She leaned into my shoulder. "So what happened with Jimmy?"

I looked toward the front of the store. "Over before it really started."

"How mad was he?"

I shook my head. "Not at all, actually. He said Drew and I have something unfinished between us and told me he hopes it works out for me."

"Hm. You seem to be a nice guy magnet."

"Ha!" I practically shouted. "I'm more like a creep magnet, and those two are the anomalies."

She looked behind me and smirked. "Your first anomaly is headed this way." She leaned forward and we hugged. "Good luck," she whispered into my ear, then pulled back. "Drew, it was nice to meet you," she said over my shoulder.

Trying to hide my stuttering breath, I stepped to the side before turning to face Drew, too.

"It was nice meeting you, too, Betsy," Drew replied, reaching out to shake her hand again.

Less than twenty minutes later, Drew had finished helping Clara load her car—they'd both refused to let me help—and we'd bid her goodbye. Which meant it was now just Drew and me standing in the darkening bookstore parking lot. And neither of us could figure out what to say for several minutes, instead scrutinizing each other from head to toe and—for my part, at least—blushing furiously and squeezing the life from my fingers.

"Dinner?" Drew asked, breaking the silence between us, his hand scrubbing his jaw.

My heart raced. "Sure." Though I wasn't even remotely hungry.

"Do you mind running back to my place to let Watson out first?"

I grinned. "Not at all. I'd love to see Watson."

Drew grinned back. "He'd love to see you, too."

Chapter Fifty

Drew

Watson lost his mind when I opened the door with Tasha, taking both of us down in a tumble of limbs outside my apartment. He was whining and licking her and climbing all over her as if she'd come back from the dead, which I understood because it had felt much the same for me when I first spied her in the bookstore, but Tasha's leg was still healing.

"Watson, no, boy!" I shouted. "Tasha—are you okay?"

"I'm fine," she giggled as Watson's tongue swiped over her face. "But I might need a shower after this."

"You sure your leg's okay?"

"It's great—I'm fine, worry wart."

Relieved, I sat up around Watson's frantic body. I looked down at them, but then almost instantly looked away. Tasha's dress had ridden all the way up her thighs, leaving her black lace panties exposed. Heat rushed to my face, and I resisted the urge to look down again. I stood and held Watson back long enough for Tasha to get to her feet before anyone else appeared in the hallway, then we set off to walk Watson.

The walk didn't go much differently than the greeting in the hallway had, with Watson constantly circling Tasha, vying for her undivided attention, and nearly tripping her in the process every few seconds. Each and every time that happened, my heart skipped out of fear of her breaking her leg again, despite knowing it was nearly impossible because of the metal rod the surgeon had inserted. Regardless, I was relieved when we made it back to my apartment without incident.

"Do you mind if I wash my face real quick?" Tasha asked as we stepped inside.

I shook my head. "Not at all. Where would you like to go? I can call ahead while you're cleaning up."

She sighed, giving me a tired smile. "Honestly? I'd be content not to go anywhere. While awesome, today was a *lot*. I'm not even hungry because of all the excitement. I'm worn out more than anything."

I nodded and she headed for my bathroom. Taking her home when she came back out—before we'd had a chance to talk or connect at all—was about the last thing I wanted to do. She was likely to go back to keeping distance between us. I ran a hand over my face, then rested it over the wrapped book sitting on the counter. I'd give that to her when I took her home. Maybe—just maybe—it would be enough to keep her from shutting me out again.

"Ready? I can take you home," I said when she returned from the bathroom.

Her face fell. Her mouth opened, but she didn't say anything.

"You said you didn't want to go anywhere."

"I meant..." She looked down at the floor as she petted Watson absently. "It doesn't matter. I can go home."

"Is that what you want? Or not? I'm happy to do whatever you want to do, you just have to tell me. I can't *always* read your mind, you know," I added with a smirk.

Her mouth curved into a smile. "I'd like to stay, actually. I meant that I didn't want to go out somewhere, not that I wanted to go home yet."

I watched her carefully for her reaction to what I was about to ask. "Are you sure your boyfriend would be okay with you hanging out in another man's apartment?"

Her face paled and it looked like she didn't breathe at all for a moment. Neither did I, waiting for her reaction.

"You guys run past Watson and me at the dog park every Saturday morning. And I saw him kiss you tonight."

I watched as her thoughts bounced around inside her head, but she didn't speak any of them. I wanted her to say something—*anything*—but she didn't. Her eyes filled with tears that she then blinked away, but nothing aside from silence sat between us. And the longer that silence stretched, the more something inside my chest ripped violently apart. What I'd been afraid of was true; she'd found someone else to spend her future with.

"What is it?" I asked.

"What is what?" she asked, her brows drawing in further than they already were.

"What isn't good enough, Tasha?"

"Good enough for what?"

"For you."

"What are you talking about?"

"What..." I stopped, my voice cracking. I took a few controlled breaths, staring at the ceiling, then tried again. "What about me isn't good enough? What's lacking? What..." I swallowed, my jaw trembling, looking for answers in her eyes. "What would make me... good enough... for you?"

"Oh, Drew," she said softly. "Why do you think you're not good enough?"

"Because you don't want me, Tasha. Because I told you I love you and you chose a stranger over me."

"I didn't," she replied, her voice barely audible now.

I waited and the silence stretched out between us again. I was so angry and hurt that I couldn't even put together words to form a sentence. "Damn it," I hissed, swiping at the few tears that had slipped out and stepping toward the door. "You should go," I said, thinking, *Because this hurts too damn much.* I cleared my throat as I held the door open, waiting. "I'll drive you home."

She nodded and stepped into the hallway ahead of me, her feet moving sluggishly now. Then she stopped walking altogether before we'd reached the elevator. I halted and she turned to face me.

"Can we go back inside and talk?" she asked after a beat. "Please?"

"There's nothing for us to talk about, Tasha," I replied. It would only make things hurt worse than they already did.

"Yes, there is," she replied, resolute. "And it's important. Please, Drew."

My jaw clenched but I turned around. Tasha let out a rush of breath and followed me back to my apartment. We didn't go any further than the kitchen where we leaned against counters opposite each other. I waited, silent, for her to say what she wanted to say.

"There's a meetup group thing I joined a while ago that I can find out about activities or whatever where there are others looking for people to do things with. It's not for dating, just for making friends. I've done a photography course, a gardening course, stuff like that. It's how I met Betsy." She paused, glancing at me before looking back down at her feet. "And it's where I learned about this running group on Saturday mornings. Jimmy was already part of the group and we hit it off on the first day. *As friends.* That's why I was there—to make friends."

She glanced up at me and I watched her, expressionless. I was trying to stay separated from any feelings until I was alone. After a brief hesitation, she continued, telling me about how she and Jimmy began to run together more often, then eat meals together, then how one day Jimmy told her he liked her and asked her on a date. She'd realized she liked him, too, so she'd said yes.

"Why are you telling me this, Tasha?" I bit out, my leg bouncing violently in place.

"We *just* started dating, Drew."

"I don't care how long you've been dating him, Tasha—you chose him over me! What does he have that I don't?"

"I didn't choose him over you."

"I *told* you, Tasha—I *told* you I'd be waiting for you. I *told* you I loved you and that I'd be here when you were ready. And for months

I've been waiting for that day—and I'd have waited years for you. But then you decided to date someone else!"

"You'd moved on, Drew!" she shouted at me.

"I never moved on, Tasha!" I shouted back.

"Yes, you did," she said, her jaw tight. "I knew what you were doing by sending me songs all the time via YouTube—you were telling me you were thinking about me. That you were waiting. That you would be there. But then you stopped—for *months*. What the hell was I supposed to think? After four months of sending me things almost daily, tell me what I was supposed to think!"

I pushed off the counter and paced through the kitchen in front of her. "I told you I would wait for you," I said again. "I *told* you that. I promised you."

"Tell me what I was supposed to think, Drew!" she shouted again, her eyes flashing angrily. "I wanted to call you and tell you I thought I might be ready, but after everything I've put you through, how the hell was I going to do that to you if you'd moved on? And it looked a hell of a lot like you'd moved on to me."

My feet stopped in front of her. "I was *busy*, Tasha! I was barely sleeping. Jack had a heart attack and was out for months, and we had to pick up the slack—most of that ended up on my plate. I didn't have time to think, let alone record songs and screw with YouTube—I even had to hire a dog walker for Watson." I leaned back against the countertop again, my hands hanging over the back of my neck. "What do you want from me, Tash?" I scrutinized her face, which was closed off—the only thing I could tell was that she was unhappy. "I've done everything I could think of to *show* you how I feel about you. I've *told* you how I feel about you. I don't know what else to do."

Her jaw trembled ever so slightly. "I thought you'd moved on," she said again, her voice quiet and tense with pain.

Most of my anger faded when I realized how upset she was, too. We were both hurting. "And because of that, now *you've* moved on," I muttered under my breath.

I tipped my head up to study the ceiling and tried to figure out what it was I really wanted. I knew I wanted Tasha, there was no question, but did I want her enough to ruin her new relationship? I'd met the guy—and as much as I'd never like someone who was dating

Tasha, I didn't get the sense he was some asshole, either. He seemed like a decent guy. Maybe he'd make her happy. Was I willing to ruin that because I wanted the person making her happy to be me?

The answer was no. As much as I wanted it to be yes, it wasn't. My wants would never come before Tasha's.

"It's okay," I eventually said, still staring at the ceiling. I couldn't look at her right then—I'd fall apart if I did. "It sucks—it really fucking sucks—but it's okay. All that matters is that you're happy, Tasha. That's what I really want for you. All I've ever really wanted for you." I fought the urge to look down when I heard the sounds of her crying.

"Drew—"

"It's fine, Tasha—I mean that. But you have to go. I can't do this right now."

Chapter Fifty-One

Tasha

I could see even through the tears spilling from the corners of my eyes that Drew's jaw was trembling. Not to mention that I'd known him long enough—been through enough with him—to hear in his voice that he was about to cry, too. I felt panicked, unsure what to do. I'd been wrong about him moving on, and now I'd hurt him—*again*. How the hell could I fix things this time?

I stepped away from the counter and reached up to grasp his wrists and tug. He didn't budge at first, his muscles tensed, but then grudgingly allowed me to pull his hands down, finally tipping his head from his examination of the ceiling. The pain in his eyes sucked the breath from my lungs, and I couldn't speak at first. Then, when I could, I wondered if I should just leave instead. If it wouldn't be better for him if I did, so I wouldn't hurt him more than I already had.

As I spiraled, sudden clarity hit. I realized that old habits and a lifetime of self-doubt were responsible for that thought. I knew what I wanted, and I should allow myself to voice that. Besides, Drew was worth fighting for, and this might be my only chance to do it.

"Before I leave, I want to say something to you."

He nodded and swiped quickly at his dampening face.

"I never would have gone on a date with Jimmy if I hadn't been so certain you'd moved on. And I realized tonight that, even though I thought you had, I couldn't continue to date him. He's nice and smart and thoughtful and nothing like anyone else I've ever dated, and I like him, but what I feel with him is nothing compared to what I feel with you. Seeing you tonight was a reminder of how much I can feel for someone, and staying with someone who makes me feel less would be shortchanging myself, something I promised myself I wouldn't do anymore." I blinked rapidly, trying not to get any more emotional than I already was. "I decided I'd rather be alone than settle. But the thing is... I don't want to be alone, either, Drew. I want to be with *you*."

There was a moment of suspended time when I could almost see Drew processing what I'd said, and then he engulfed me in his arms. He squeezed me so hard I couldn't really breathe, but it was barely enough. I squeezed him back with every ounce of strength I had, my heart tripping over itself at feeling his arms around me again. His kisses poured over my face, every inch, over and over, before pulling me into his arms again.

"I love you so much, Tasha." His voice wavered with emotion.

There wasn't even a hint of hesitation this time. "I love you, too, Drew."

A puff of air passed my ear as if my words had pushed the breath from his lungs.

"But there's something I need to tell you," I said, pulling back. Blood rushed through my ears. I'd never wanted him to know, but he had to because I couldn't keep it from him anymore. Not if we were going to try a relationship. "You have to know so you can make a decision about whether or not this—*us*—is something you can do."

"There is nothing you can say that would make me walk away from you. Ever. Nothing I couldn't forgive or find a way to understand. Nothing I couldn't learn to live with."

"You say that because you don't know."

He took my face in his hands, his thumbs smoothing over my cheeks. "I say that because it's true. I don't know what you're going to tell me, but I *do* know it won't make me love you any less. It won't make me want you any less. Nothing could do that."

His eyes were cloudy and swirling and intense, and the longer I looked into them, the more I believed that maybe what he was saying was true. Though he could be wrong—he'd never been hurt the way this would hurt him.

My thoughts scattered as Drew leaned forward and kissed me. My chest hurt and felt like it might implode, and I didn't care—I didn't want it to end. If it hadn't been already, it was definitely now confirmed that the way I felt kissing Drew was because it was Drew. It was nothing like the kiss with Jimmy and was as amazing as it had ever been.

Drew's arm circled my waist, his fingertips gently caressing my face as he kissed me in that same caring way that left me feeling undone and deeply exposed. It was just as unnerving as it had been before, but rather than feeling tempted to end it, I embraced it. If there was ever someone I could trust to handle all of me with care, it was Drew. What we were doing and all the things it made me feel were all I could think about until Watson nudged us with his nose and whined before stamping impatiently around us.

Drew, with an arm still around me, pulled back and reached out to pet Watson. "I know you're hungry—I'll get you some dinner soon."

Watson let out a half-whine-half-howl and I laughed.

"He said, 'Right now, Daddy,'" I said, my face leaping into flames.

"Yeah," Drew replied with a soft chuckle, stepping back and running a hand through his hair. His cheeks looked as flushed as mine felt.

I watched as he pulled out Watson's food and fed him, then returned to me, standing so his feet straddled mine and slipping both of his arms around my waist.

"Tell me," he said soberly.

I inhaled deeply. "I'm afraid to," I whispered, looking down toward the floor.

He lifted my chin so I was looking at him again. "It's not going to change anything between us. You'll see. You told me the things

Duncan did to you, Tasha. You told me about him raping you against a window in Vegas in detail. Whatever it is you *haven't* told me... I can handle it. If you've lived through it, I can live with hearing about it."

"Those things were... this is different."

"Is it what's in your book?" he asked. "Is that what you're scared of telling me?"

I gave a short nod, watching the swirling in the depths of his eyes, so much more blue than gray because of his shirt. He leaned forward and kissed the corner of my mouth, lingering before straightening up.

It was still my favorite place to be kissed.

He pointed down the counter toward the wrapped item he'd had with him all evening. "That?"

"Yeah?"

"It's your book."

"You're giving it back to me?" I asked, bewildered. I hadn't expected that. And it hurt—it had taken a lot for me to print it and give it to him.

He stepped over and grabbed the book, pulling off the paper as he returned to his spot in front of me, then handed it to me.

"I read it already. I know you didn't tell me to yet, but I did. Then I read it a second time and wrote in some things I thought you'd want to know in the margins."

Everything froze. "Y-you read it?"

"Yes." He lightly grasped my upper arms, his thumbs smoothing over them.

"And... and..." My eyes flitted around, seeing nothing. I wasn't sure why I felt so panicked that he already knew. "You still want me?" I blurted out.

"Fuck yes, I do," he replied, his voice deep and strong. "It changes nothing about how I feel about you."

I gaped at him.

"I admit, I was furious and devastated at first—I can't tell you how badly I wish none of it had happened—but it doesn't change anything for me."

He lifted my hand from the counter, and I looked up at him. His eyes had lost none of their intensity—there may have been even more—and I couldn't look away. He held my gaze as he brought my hand close to his face, then kissed my palm. Now I was dizzy, and my body was tingling with awareness. He flattened my hand over his heart and held it there, his thumb running over the back of it.

Then he began to sing the songs from which we had lyrics tattooed on our legs. When the tears started down my cheeks, he cradled my face and wiped them away with his thumbs, then kissed the skin they'd touched, his own gathering just below his lids. He touched our foreheads and noses together and sang through the final words as I pressed both hands into his chest.

As his voice faded from the last word, we both took in a ragged inhale, and then his lips rested against mine, soft. He pulled back just millimeters, and I tilted my head forward to bring our mouths together again. His arms circled my waist and he hugged me tight, lifting me from my feet. I wrapped my arms and legs around him and hugged him back with everything I had. I wasn't sure I'd ever let him go.

Kissing again, our tongues explored deeply this time. I was compressed so tightly against him that I could feel his heart beating against mine, and for some reason that made me want him even more. I wanted to be somehow closer, so I could feel his every breath, his every thought.

Drew locked his arms under me and set off through his apartment without breaking our kiss, bumping into the counter, and the wall, and every corner and piece of furniture along the way. By the time we knocked into the doorframe at the entrance to his bedroom, I couldn't stop giggling.

"I don't think you could possibly have walked into anything else."

His chest rumbled with laughter. "I've never tried to walk through here basically blind."

My body slid leisurely down the front of Drew's until my feet reached the floor. He gently tucked my hair behind my ear, then his fingertips whispered over my cheek and jaw, his eyes touching every inch of my face. He bent and we started kissing again, unhurried.

Want built within my veins, spreading out to the very tips of my fingers and toes and every hair follicle on my head.

My skin buzzed as his fingers skimmed down my arms, leaving goosebumps in their wake. I raised my hands from his hips to wrap them one at a time around his neck. He lifted me and laid me on his bed, lying on his side right next to me. His hand flattened against my cheek as he continued to kiss me in that way that made me feel so vulnerable. The longer we kissed like that, the more vulnerable I felt, and the more vulnerable I felt, the more I wanted him. I reached down and pulled his shirt tails from his pants, inch by inch.

His breath caught, then his hand found the hem of my dress and crawled up my torso, taking the material with it while I unbuckled his belt. I pulled away from kissing and undressing him to try to breathe, though it seemed my lungs just didn't know how to do that anymore. Drew watched me, his palm against my belly, before gradually pulling my dress over my head, off my arms, and tossing it aside. He watched his hand as it explored, flattening between my breasts.

Everything I felt right then was new. *Different.* From the way every cell vibrated with awareness to the way I felt sexy at being on display for Drew, his eyes taking in everything about me. I'd never felt anything but disgust when someone looked at me even close to naked, and I could feel that self-disgust wanting to take over, but it didn't. Not with Drew. Not with the way he was looking at me as if I was something rare and precious and sacred. Not with the way his eyes were filled with love and not just lust when they rested on mine.

When he leaned over me to kiss me again, I unbuttoned his shirt and pushed it off over his shoulders. Moments later, we were both naked, and he grasped the inside of my thighs one at a time, moving them to the side before shifting his weight over me. I lifted my hips, and he met my movement, his hardness sliding against me. He kissed me, a palm smoothing over my cheek, then pulled back to search my eyes, his heart pounding against my chest.

He didn't say anything—he didn't have to. I understood. He was asking for permission, making sure I *wanted* what was happening. No one had ever done that before.

No one.

A wave of emotion crashed over me, and my eyes welled with tears, my heart constricting painfully. I wanted what was happening more than I'd ever wanted sexual intimacy before. The only time someone had ever asked was the first time I had no doubts or reservations about what was happening.

I swallowed. "Yes." I could have nodded, answering as silently as he'd asked, but I wanted to use my voice—it felt good to use my voice.

His lips were against mine again as he shifted and rolled his hips, using a hand to guide himself, and then he pushed inside me. My gasp was loud in the quiet.

So was his.

My senses were filled with Drew—the feel of him against and inside me, the sound of his panted breaths breaking over my face, the sight of his eyes, dark and swirling and intense, focused so intently on me, the musky vetiver and orange smell of his skin strong in my nostrils.

It was almost overwhelming. Almost too much as he moved in and out of me unhurried, his lips exploring every inch of my face, every inch of my neck, my collarbones. His touch, his movements, were somehow both strong and gentle, and I felt cherished as we made love. Even when the gentle began to fade to be replaced by stronger and more powerful motions, I felt nothing but safe and loved.

Drew was lying half on top of me, his face tucked against mine, his lips dropping kisses to my cheek every few breaths. My body was relaxed under his, except the butterflies that kept appearing every few seconds when I thought about the fact I was lying there with him. He slid a hand from my shoulder up to frame my face and pressed another, harder kiss to my cheek.

"I can't believe what you did, you know," he said, his voice low.

I knew he was talking about what he'd learned from reading my book. "You'd have done the same."

He lifted up to an elbow so he was looking down at me. "I would have, but I never wanted that for you." He kissed me. "I hate what happened to you." He touched our foreheads together for a minute, then pulled back to look into my eyes again. "But it changes nothing for me. *Nothing*." He kissed me again. "I love you and I want you, Tash. I always will." He crushed me into his chest, and I buried my face in the crook of his neck, now crying. "I swear to god, there'll never be a day, no matter what happens, that I don't. Every muscle, every bone, every organ—every fucking cell in my body loves every cell in yours."

"I love you, too, Drew. I have for years. Maybe even from the very beginning. I'm scared of messing things up and losing you, but I'm more scared of never taking a chance on something real, and loving you is as real as it gets."

"I'm so sorry," he said with gentleness that bordered on tender. "I wish I could undo the past and not have gone after Wayne."

"You were trying to protect me, Drew. No one had ever tried to protect me before. I couldn't believe you'd done that for me."

"But what he did to you because of it... Jesus, Tasha. I don't know how you survived it, and you kept it all inside. I can't even imagine. I wish I could take it away from you, make it have happened to me instead."

"I'm glad it didn't," I replied.

"I wasn't worth what you went through. I wish you hadn't done that."

"That's not true." I hesitated, then said something I'd been thinking about a lot since I'd relived what had happened while writing about it. "And the thing is... Wayne was already escalating in what he was doing. He'd started touching me sometimes while I was naked—not just watching me. It was only a matter of time before he'd have forced me to do those things anyway. At least this way, you still had your future."

"None of that makes what he did to you okay. Not then, not before I attacked him, and not the night I got you out of there."

I shook my head. "No, it doesn't. But I can't change it, either." I sighed. "At least I've got you."

He kissed the corner of my mouth. "You do. You'll always have me, no matter what. I'll never let anything like what Wayne or Duncan or your mom did to you happen again. *Never*. I will never leave you, I will never hurt you the way they did or let anyone else do it, either, and I will never, *never* stop loving you."

My fingers moved lazily through his hair. "That's a lot of nevers. Never is a really long time."

His thumb slid over my cheek, and he kissed the corner of my mouth again, lingering. "When it comes to loving you, never is nowhere near long enough."

Chapter Fifty-Two

Tasha

As Drew and I settled on the floor leaning against the sofa next to each other, the Christmas tree sparkling in front of us and Watson sniffing at the presents underneath, it was hard to believe how much had happened since we'd sat there only a year earlier. Hard to believe how different things now were between us.

We'd decided to put off the rock-climbing class until the spring because of a cold front coming in that would make climbing outside unpleasant, but we still took our trip to California and it was the most amazing trip of our lives. We watched the sun set every evening, walking on the beach hand-in-hand, an experience I fell in love with in a way I never expected, and explored everything California had to offer around the glass-blowing course. We bickered again much like we always had, laughed often, and learned a lot about glassblowing, the redwoods, making wine, and more. When we got back home after over two weeks together around the clock, it was an adjustment to not see each other during the day. We discovered we valued more than ever our time together in the evenings and didn't spend a single night apart. By Thanksgiving, we decided there was no reason to keep two apartments, and I cancelled my lease and moved in with Drew.

It was the best decision we could have made. Living together had always come easily to us, and it was no different this time. We just meshed well; it felt more natural than being apart. And a month later, it was hard to remember life before we were a couple and living together. Our lives fit together as if they'd been designed to do exactly that. I'd even introduced Drew to the running group, and he and Jimmy were friendly to each other. I wasn't sure they'd ever be *friends* exactly, because of me, but they were chatty when we were all running together and never spoke ill of one another. It was more than I'd dared to ever hope for.

I peeped under the tree, taking a sip of my coffee before setting it aside to hand out gifts. We'd thrown our one-gift rule out the window entirely, and there were quite a few under the tree in addition to the customary large pile for Watson. I handed them out one at a time, though Drew had pointed to one and told me that gift was for last. I had one I was saving to give him until the end, too, so I was curious what he had up his sleeve.

That curiosity only grew after I opened tickets for another trip, this one to the Caribbean, including a stay on the beach. Of course, he'd thought he was funny and also packaged up my favorite sweats and t-shirt to swipe from him.

Soon, though, we were down to the last two gifts.

"You have to open yours last," I said.

He shook his head. "Nope, you open yours last."

"No can do, Drewy Drew."

He chuckled and leaned forward to give me a quick kiss. "We'll open them at the same time, then."

I narrowed my eyes.

"That's the best I can agree to. Take it or leave it, brat."

"Fine."

I grabbed the two presents, handing one to him. Mine I could already tell was a book—a heavy, hardcover book. What the hell could it be? I looked over at him, bewildered, then burst out laughing. His face was at least as perplexed as mine, holding the small gift that was the size of an index card.

"On three?" I asked, shimmying my hips in place.

Drew reached over and cupped the back of my head and kissed me soundly. "I love you, you know."

I still blushed almost every time he told me that—which was more times than I could count each and every day.

"I love you, too."

I leaned in to give him another quick kiss and somehow ended up straddling his lap with his hands gripping my hips, then skimming up my sides under my shirt. I dropped the gift I was holding onto the floor to wrap my arms around his neck, but the loud *thump* pulled him from the moment. He leaned his head back against the arm of the sofa and studied me, running his hands along my thighs.

"Gifts first," he said, reaching over to grab my gift from the floor and hand it back to me.

"Okay," I agreed, though my heart was hammering right out of my chest. My gift was something rather unconventional, and I hoped it was well-received.

We opened our gifts at the same time while I was still sitting on his lap, our hands bumping as we removed the wrapping paper, making us both chuckle and keep pausing to give each other quick pecks on the lips and noses. Even so, my heart had made it to my throat by the time he got the rest of the paper off his gift. The only thing that kept me from passing out from not breathing was being thrown completely off-kilter by the fact that Drew had wrapped my old, severely worn copy of Sherlock Holmes collected stories. And not only that, but it looked like he'd fixed the binding and somehow repaired some of the missing lettering on the spine and front cover.

I looked at him in confusion at the same time he quirked a questioning brow at me, and we laughed again, though both laughs sounded a bit thin and nervous.

"Turn it over," I said, eyeing the tribal-looking bar of interlocking Celtic hearts printed onto an index card.

Drew turned it over, then shook his head, puzzled. My heart sank. He turned it back over, holding it up for me to see the back—it was blank.

"What?" I took the card from him and flipped it back and forth a few times. Nothing changed. But I knew I'd written on the back of it. Then I rubbed the card between my thumb and forefinger and it separated into two cards. I'd had a stack of them when I'd put the card together, and I must have accidentally picked up a second one when I went to wrap it. I laughed. "Sorry—that wasn't supposed to be there. Here." I handed the correct card to him with the writing side up. He read out loud.

"Since you've tattooed yourself for me three times already, I wondered how you'd feel about doing it again? This time on your left ring finger." His eyes shot up to mine, filled with both moisture and laughter. "Is this a proposal?"

My face felt like I was holding it in coals. "Yes."

"You're asking me to marry you?"

I looked away, mortified now. What the hell had I been thinking? "Yes."

He laughed. Not the nervous titter we'd both done a moment earlier, but a full-on laugh that rumbled from somewhere deep in his chest.

I wanted to smile, but I was also confused. "Does laughter mean yes?"

He didn't answer my question. "Open your book."

"In a minute. Is that a yes?"

"Tash—open your book. Trust me."

With a small huff—and feeling almost nauseous at being left in limbo after proposing to him—I did what Drew requested and opened the cover of the book. There, in Drew's handwriting, was a small arrow and a page number. I flipped through, and when I reached the designated page, there was a word underlined and another page number scrawled into the margin. I bit my lip, oddly excited by this wordy treasure hunt, as I flipped back and forth through the book until I had his message: *I will never love you less today than I did yesterday or more than I will tomorrow. Believe in never with me?*

On the last page, he had taped a ring using painter's tape that left the pages undamaged when I pulled it off. I lifted the ring, laughing and giddy, and slipped it onto my finger. "Yes, of fucking course, yes," I said, throwing my arms around him.

He held me tight to him, his chest still shaking with his own laughter. "Same. If I could, I'd tattoo myself right now," he said into my hair.

"You know, a tattoo is permanent. It'll never come off," I said.

He cradled my head and moved me back until his eyes were gazing into mine. "I know. I'm ready for never with you."

And I was ready, too, because after so many years of searching for it in all the wrong places, I now believed it existed.

Acknowledgements

It is that time again and every time I'm facing this specific page, I think it'll be easier than before, but writing this for my eighth book isn't really any less difficult than it was for the first.

A huge—no, enormous—thank you to my family for supporting me and being patient with me when I'm lost in my fictional worlds. And especially to my husband for loving me the way you do and providing me with fodder for these stories. You're both my best friend and my love and you always will be.

Kayli, you are the bomb diggity and then some. Whatever I send to you, you magic into the most beautiful version possible of what I envisioned, in the most caring and empathetic way. You have apparently limitless patience with my manuscripts, my wild ideas, and the rabbit holes I sometimes (okay, often) fall into. Every time I send you something, I'm filled with excitement because I know over the course of working with you on that project, my skills as a writer are improving. Thanks for being an amazing editor and the best human. Love you to pieces.

Thank you to everyone out there who encourages me to continue, whether it's a friend asking me whenever we chat about what I'm working on and how my books are going or a reader messaging me with a note about how much they loved a book or a passage they read or how they connected with it. This means more to me than you'll ever know.

A special thank you to Robin, who's been there from the very beginning, reading and providing feedback on many of my manuscripts. Your support and encouragement have been invaluable in getting me to where I am today. You're the best.

As always, I have so much gratitude for my production staff: Jo for my ebook formatting and Murphy for my *beautiful* cover. No matter how vague or specific I am, you come up with something stunning and better than I could have imagined. I absolutely adore the way this cover looks and hope you never, ever stop doing what you do.

About the Author

Katherine Turner is a multi-award-winning author of realistic contemporary romantic fiction that explores the depth and range of human emotion and compassion, the resilience of the human spirit, and the roles love, family, and friendship play when healing from past trauma and abuse. She is passionate about using words to foster compassion, understanding and healing, whether that's through her fiction or sharing her own personal experiences and healing journey via her blog and as a speaker.

Katherine lives in Northern Virginia with her husband and two daughters, and when she's not reading or writing, she can be found outside exploring nature.

Playlist

All songs are by artist Sam Tinnesz

Sound Off the Sirens
Darkside
No Escape
Be Here for You
Ready Set Let's Go
Man or a Monster
Never Leave Your Side
Even if it Hurts
Play with Fire
I Don't Miss You
Feels Like Home
Hold on For Your Life
Heart of the Darkness
Changes
We're Gonna Make It
Overcome